WITHOUT AUTHORITY

WITHOUT AUTHORITY

Book Two in the Jane Smith Trilogy

CHARLOTTE TAFT

Cover Art & Design by 100 Covers

EMPRESS
PUBLICATIONS

WWW.EMPRESSPUBLICATIONS.COM

Dedicated to my mother, Sylvia, and my father, Harry.
Thank you for being the first ones to listen to my stories.
I hope you would be proud.

CONTENTS

"Choice is a dialogue with the being who may come to life through our body. We can do no more than to bring our awareness to this sacred conversation.

Something is learned from every life and every death. Choice gives us freedom, and choice asks us to accept what we have done."

~Melody Ermachild Chavis

PROLOGUE

Milagro, New Mexico, February 2016
Eight months before Jane's death
Nine months before Trump's first victory

Abbie and I were eating scrambled eggs. They tasted delicious, but I pushed the food around on my plate so she wouldn't worry that I didn't have much of an appetite. I sat on the red walker I had named Ruby. It turned into a seat when I got tired. What a great invention. I was still reeling from a sleepless night.

"Oh, Abbie. I had the most terrible nightmare."

"What was it about?" she asked. She put her coffee down and tucked a strand of long red hair behind her ear. I was struck once again by how much she looked like her grandmother. My dear Lucie.

"I dreamed they declared abortion illegal in the United States. Women were wailing in the streets—dying on the steps of the Supreme Court. They took buses to Mexico. They begged for money to travel to places where abortion was legal. It was awful. Do you think it could happen?"

"I don't see how," Abbie answered. "They've been trying to overturn Roe v. Wade ever since 1973."

"Nonetheless, legal abortion is always under attack. We need to get this book out soon if it's to make any difference." I stopped and took a halting breath. I felt a tinge of fear and grief from my nightmare. "I realize I won't live long enough to see this project to completion. My old friend Brigitte told me a rabbinical quote that was something like, 'You are not expected to finish the work. Still, you must do your part.' I hope I have done my part. Will you promise me that you will finish the books?" At 102, I wasn't afraid of dying, but I was afraid of dying without completing the most important work of my life—sharing the stories of more than 75 years of abortion care.

Abbie put her hand on my shoulder. "Jane, we have all your journals, so everything I need is there. I will make sure your stories are published and distributed, even if I have to sell them out of the back of my car. I was raised to believe abortion was wrong. There was so much I didn't know. Your stories changed my mind. You took me to the heart of women's decisions about abortion—to a dimension I never imagined. People need to read about your work."

In the 1970s, I was in my fifties living in France, when the modern Women's Movement, the Civil Rights Movement, and the Gay Rights Movement began to gather strength in America and spread around the world. Before that, women couldn't get credit or buy property. Rape and physical brutality were considered par for the course in marriage. After a divorce, women were often left penniless. They couldn't choose to have a tubal ligation without their husband's permission. And they had no choices when they became pregnant. In my lifetime, people like me were arrested or institutionalized for being gay. Anyone who didn't fit the white heterosexual norm could be discriminated against in any way. All over the world, people were treated as second-class citizens because of race. Little by little, our voices were heard, and our lives and stories began to matter. What happened in the United States spread across the globe. But the backlash spread, too. We must be vigilant to keep the rights and freedoms for which we have fought so hard.

I wonder if it is too much to ask Abbie to document the tales of my life—stories that are so foreign to the world in which she grew up. As a child, Abbie spent only a few weeks with her grandmother, Lucie. She never knew the brilliant, impetuous seven-year-old Lucie I met when I was her teacher in Paris in 1939.

The truth is that Lucie was not cut out to be a mother, so her daughter Tildy suffered. Today, they would call it 'failure to bond.' In turn, Tildy's daughter, Abbie, suffered. Tildy feared and distrusted women, so Abbie learned that women's lives are not to be taken seriously. Can she tell my stories faithfully? Stories of women's courage—stories of women who broke the rules to save themselves? I am so different from her mother—can she truly understand me? If Abbie doesn't tell these stories, they will never be told—will never be heard. It will be up to me to share effectively enough to reach across the vast misogyny of her upbringing into her heart and mind.

We began our publishing project nearly a year ago by gathering up my scrapbooks, letters, and journals. Abbie and I spent hours together in my bedroom with a tape recorder, me talking into the night until my voice was hoarse or I was overcome with emotion. Outside my room, women bustled with the work of providing abortion care in the New Mexico convent. Does it surprise you that in 2016, I preferred to do abortions in a convent instead of a clinic? I'm old. I like to do things the way I'm used to doing them.

I told Abbie about Paris in 1939, about her grandmother Lucie, Dr. Levy, and all the women whose lives intersected with mine over these many years. Sharing these stories has made all those wonderful women present again. But the frightening times and the terror are present, too. Sometimes it is too much and I have to rest.

The book still isn't finished, but Abbie says we have too much for one volume. During one of our very rare disagreements, I said, "I don't care how long the book is. I am 102. It is a long life, so it is a long story."

"Jane, you don't understand. I've been researching this. No one will publish it. We need to divide it into three books."

"I just listened to an audiobook that must have been longer than mine. Something by Elizabeth Gilbert. It was enormous and the main character traveled all over the world, just like my story."

"Elizabeth Gilbert is a famous writer. Her books have even been made into movies. I'm sorry, but no one knows who you are."

"You don't imagine that a 102-year-old woman who can still think is enough of a phenomenon to publish the whole thing in one volume?"

Abbie laughed softly.

"I'm sorry," I said. "I don't mean to be grouchy. That last section about your grandmother nearly dying of an illegal abortion in 1950 when she was 18 was distressing. I still can't forgive myself for being thousands of miles away doing abortions in Japan with the Navy when Lucie had no one to turn to. I didn't get much sleep last night."

"I know. I didn't either," she said.

"Is this project going to be the death of us?"

"If it is, let's make it count. Now about this trilogy we are writing…"

"You are telling me there is a certain number of pages we are allowed to have in each book?" I asked.

"Not the pages—they do it by the number of words. We need somewhere around a hundred thousand words in each of the three books."

"You are going to *count* the words?" I exclaimed. "You'd better start right now or I'll be dead before you're finished!"

"The computer counts the words," she said.

"As I live and breathe. In 1931, when I took the typing class my father insisted upon, I could never have imagined this."

"And I'm afraid each book has to stand on its own," she said in that careful way one speaks to a woman who is one-hundred-and-two.

"Wouldn't it be easier just to tell people to read the books in order?"

"Yes. But the people who know about publishing say we can't do it that way. We can indicate which is Book One, Two, and Three. But people will read the books in whatever order they want."

I was flummoxed. "That is crazy. So, you make a list of all the things someone would miss by starting with the wrong book, and you sprinkle them in so the reader is not totally confused and lost?"

"Yes, I think that is exactly what we do," Abbie said.

"Well, if you are determined to do it that way, then *you* do the sprinkling. I can't recall details even when I read books in order. I hate not remembering which child had the cat, who had the rat, and who went to the dance with Harry Potter."

"Okay. I'll be in charge of sprinkling."

I am doing my best to keep my promise to Jane. **Without Permission** *and* **Without Authority**, *the first two books of the trilogy, are now available on Amazon or wherever you buy your books.* **Without Apology** *follows soon. The stories of Jane's remarkable life transformed me—opened doors to a world I had never imagined. I hope she would be as proud of these books as I am.*

Abbie Wilder

CHAPTER 1

HELL NO

Connecticut, May 1950

We were all on edge. Just a few days earlier, we had been sitting vigil over a very sick Lucie. After she regained consciousness, she still slept most of the day, but the doctors assured us she would recover. Lucie was almost eighteen. I had first known her as my favorite student when I taught seven-year-olds at my Aunt Mathilde's boarding school in Paris. Both her parents were dead. Bernard Levy and I rescued her from Occupied Paris when she was eight. I loved her like my own, but I couldn't keep her. Sadie and Hymie Goldfarb adopted her. Then I left to join the Navy. I hadn't seen Lucie since she was twelve, but I still recognized the mischievous little girl. Her long red hair had turned darker—almost auburn. Her face was thinner. She had grown up.

Against nurses' orders, we crowded into the small hospital room. Sadie rubbed Lucie's feet with lotion. Such tenderness. She had chewed off her usually bright red lipstick—the evidence of fear. Hymie, a chemist, opened and closed the blinds depending on Lucie's preference, and made her laugh at his terrible jokes.

"Why doesn't carbon ever make the honor roll? It always gets a 'C' in chemistry." Hearing Lucie giggle made me want to cry with happiness.

Dr. Levy paced incessantly in the small hospital room, as if he'd heal Lucie by clocking in enough miles. He gave her ice chips, read to her, and urged her to eat the bland food and Jell-O that appeared in front of her three times a day. Though Hymie was her adoptive father, Levy would always be her Papa.

At sixty, my mother, Sylvia, had grown weary of waiting for a grandchild, so Lucie called her Nana. Not prone to emotional displays, Mother showed her devotion by interrupting her knitting long enough to change the water in the vase of Lucie's favorite daisies.

We took turns spending the night on the uncomfortable lounger and I hovered as if Lucie were a porcelain doll. I hovered as much from guilt as from love. I was not there when Lucie needed me.

On one of those busy mornings, I needed a break. When I went into the bathroom, the mirror reflected a very tall, exhausted middle-aged woman. I compared my thirty-six-year-old self to the earnest twenty-five-year-old girl who sailed to Paris before the war, embarking on unimaginable adventures. I'd left my hair the same as it had been then—mousy brown, painfully straight, shoulder-length, and parted on the left. I saw the same plain face, but at that moment, strained with hope and confusion. A non-threatening face. A face you'd never guess had broken so many rules—had helped smuggle dozens of girls out of Occupied France. A face that bore the effects of betrayal and despair and too much drinking. I also saw a wiser face—one tested by tragedy—a face like a palimpsest, a piece of papyrus that has been written on and erased over and over but still bears traces of the original.

I heard shouting and rushed back into the room.

"Hell no! Over my dead body will Lucie be involved with that... that... that person."

My jaw dropped. My mother was never loud. She knew how to land a criticism without raising her voice. She glared at us.

"What he did is immoral, illegal, disgraceful, and a scandal. He nearly killed her. Jane Smith, you ought to be ashamed. Have you forgotten that Lucie is only seventeen years old? You are all mollycoddling her!"

Sadie, Hymie, and Levy were as stunned as I was.

Mother ranted on. "This... this boy—this man, whoever he is—took advantage of her. Now she says she loves him? I won't stand for it." She threw her knitting into a carpetbag and stomped out. If we hadn't been in the Intensive Care Unit, she would have slammed the door.

"*Sacré bleu*!" Levy said. "I have never known your mother to swear."

"It's my fault," Sadie said, her eyes wide. "I said I guessed we'd have to meet the boy who did this. Who Lucie says she loves. Your mother just exploded."

"Jane, has she said anything like this to you?" Levy asked.

"No. In fact, she hasn't said much at all. But it sounds like *her* mother. Granny was a strict Catholic, so Mother was brought up with that as a child. I'll never forget the terrible things she told me about abortion. Not easy to let go of."

"Does she blame us? Because she sneaked around with this boy behind our backs?" Sadie asked.

"Does she want us to send Lucie to military school?" Hymie said.

"To juvenile detention?" Levy added.

"To a convent?" I sputtered. We all laughed, but I needed to be sure my secret was safe.

I beckoned Levy to follow me out into the hall, hardly registering the harsh smell of antiseptic.

"Have you told my mother what we did in Paris?"

"No. Of course not. I kept my promise."

I was shaking. "She can never know."

Levy nodded.

I gestured down the hall. "I'm going after her."

CHAPTER 2

SHE IS RUINED

I had a hunch I would find her in the chapel. As I made my way down the corridor, the word 'Paris' resounded in my mind. At one time in my life, Paris meant freedom. The beginning of my real life. A place where I had risked everything for justice. The longer I stayed in Connecticut, where I grew up, the more invisible I would feel.

The chapel was empty except for my mother, sitting up very straight in the front pew. The walls were pale blue, and a plush carpet muffled my footsteps. There was a faint smell of smoke from the candles burning on the altar. She startled when I slid in next to her.

"Darling, I don't want to talk right now. Can you give me some time?"

"Of course."

"What must you think of me? I made a fool of myself losing my temper like that."

I didn't say anything.

"I'm trying to pull myself together. But you don't understand what is at stake for Lucie after this... after what she did. She is ruined. No decent man will marry her. She will never have children. She'll spend her whole life trying to forget about this stain... this..." she balled up her fists. "I can't even say that word. I am so upset. We must never speak of this."

That last comment reminded me of something her mother, my Granny, once said to me about abortion. As I listened to my mother's diatribe, any hopes I had that she might accept the work I was born to do, the work that defined me, vanished like stars at dawn. I longed for her approval, but the space between us was filled with lies and secrets. What was I going to do? I couldn't leave Lucie again. Or my mother. But how could I abandon Dr. Nick and my work in Japan? The work of my heart? If I stayed, I'd be at loose ends, as my father used to say. I'd probably be alone for the rest of my life. My head was swimming.

"Mother, you have my word."

"And this man? This dangerous boy? This alleged medical student. Will you forgive him?"

"It's not about forgiveness. Lucie loves him. You know how much she means to me. I want her to be happy."

Mother turned toward me, her hackles up. "And you think *I* don't want her to be happy? She is like a granddaughter to me."

I raised my palms to deflect the anger. "Of course you do."

I took a risk and put my arm around her shoulder. She let me. We sat like that until she gave a great sigh and said, "I just can't believe that Lucie would do something so vile." She leaned over and put her head in her hands. Then she stood up.

"I'm all right now," she said. "Let's see what we must do to get our girl home."

We walked back to Lucie's room, my thoughts in turmoil.

CHAPTER 3

I'M GOING TO KILL THAT BOY!

Until the frantic call from Dr. Levy telling me Lucie was in a coma as a result of an improperly done abortion, I worked for the Navy in Kyoto, Japan. I was a mess after a disastrous breakup. At the medical clinic, I did just enough to get by until I could go home and drink enough to numb the pain. I was not exactly *in* the Navy, but that is another part of the humiliating story I'm not going to tell right now. I had already planned to spend June in Connecticut to attend Lucie's high school graduation. I had a lovely, restful trip scheduled over several days. Instead, because of Levy's call, I flew directly to New York on a long, miserable flight on a plane designed for freight, not people. When we landed, my mother drove me directly to the hospital. I sat by Lucie's bed, so sure I would lose her that I had a terrible nightmare that she died and I oversaw her funeral. Days later, even after getting some rest at my mother's house, the nightmare rattled me. And now that we knew Lucie would survive, I was determined to make sure that whoever did such shoddy work could not harm another girl.

Lucie dozed off and on, only occasionally fully awake. We knew she was feeling better when she complained she was bored. Soon she was going to the bathroom on her own and wanted the television on. She was telling all the nurses that she had to get ready for her high school graduation. In four days, she was so improved the doctor told us he would discharge her.

The following morning, we made quite a procession with an aide wheeling Lucie down the hall in a wheelchair. We took the elevator, and the enormous front doors opened to a splendid day. I wanted to sing as we transferred Lucie into the Goldfarb's blue Dodge. Less than a week before, we were not sure that Lucie would make it. That there were secrets to keep and to tell was the least of my worries.

After the short drive, Hymie helped Lucie into the house. The cocker spaniel, Ellie, named after Eleanor Roosevelt, nearly knocked Lucie over, but Sadie picked up the wriggling pup and deposited her next to Lucie on the bed. That little dog brought a smile to Lucie's eyes that I had been waiting to see.

Lucie looked at her parents. "I am sorry I lied to you. Oliver is a little bit older than I am, and I didn't think you would allow me to see him."

Sadie perched on the edge of the bed. "How old is he?"

I interrupted. "I think Lucie needs to rest. We have plenty of time to get into all that later."

I thought I had given her a reprieve, but Lucie was determined to charge into the fray.

"He is only twenty-four. We met at the Cloisters when my school was on a field trip."

"Twenty-four!" My mother's voice was sharp.

"Why didn't you say anything?" Hymie asked.

Lucie held Ellie in front of her.

"You wouldn't have let me see him if you had known, would you?"

Hymie shook his head. "No. He is much too old for you."

"I'm almost eighteen. Anyway, that's why I didn't tell you."

"And just what is this young man's *last* name?" my mother demanded.

"His name is Oliver Butterfield Hanover III," Lucie said proudly, as if she had named him herself.

Levy looked surprised. "Is he related to the Hanovers who founded the Women's Hospital?"

"Yes. His father and grandfather. That's why they can't know about his mistake. He is following in their footsteps to become a brilliant doctor. I know he will be. And I will be a doctor's wife."

Hymie mumbled under his breath, "I'm going to kill that boy."

I put my hand on his arm. "No one is getting killed today." I turned to face Lucie. "And no one is getting married today, either. Lucie, you can understand why we are worried. You are underage. He is older than you are. None of us has even met this young man. How can we give our blessing when… well…" My mother glared at me. "When you have been so sick. Now, no more secrets!"

Mother reverted to her usual sunny self, perhaps relieved I had avoided the forbidden word *abortion*. "There is nothing to worry about right now but getting you well enough for your graduation. That's going to take plenty of rest, young lady. No overdoing it."

"Yes, Nana Sylvia. I mean, no. I won't. But…"

"Don't even start, young lady. Just don't."

My mother's tone was unequivocal, and Lucie gave up. We each gave her a kiss with the admonition to sleep before lunch, then began to file out of her room.

"Would… Mam'selle, would you sit beside me while I go to sleep?" Lucie asked, with sugar in her voice. Nearly dying can let you get away with almost anything.

I glanced at the others, and they nodded their approval. Looking forward to some alone time with Lucie, I pulled the comfy chair away from the window, moved it next to the bed, and sat down. I should have known that Lucie had her own agenda.

CHAPTER 4

LIES, SECRETS, AND SILENCE

"Mam'selle?"

Her voice sounded a bit hoarse, so I leaned over to hear her, touched that she used the nickname she gave me when I was her teacher.

"I'm sorry Mam'selle. I was sure you would come home from Japan if I needed you. I wanted to wait until you got here, but he said we couldn't delay any longer."

"I understand. I can't even imagine how frightening this was."

She cleared her throat. "Mam'selle, I heard you."

"What, Chérie? What do you imagine you heard?" My stomach did flip-flops. I wanted to put my fingers in my ears.

"You thought I was still unconscious, but I heard you." Lucie sat up, pushing the pillows behind her. "I heard everything you said."

I blushed. "People will say all kinds of things in a crisis. I was afraid you were going to die." I knew what she meant. I had promised to tell her the truth about myself if only she would wake up. I would have done anything. Promised anything.

"You said you never should have gone so far away. You said you had loved a woman."

The too-recent memory of being so deceived, failing at love—nearly made me swoon. "May I?" I asked, pointing at the head of the bed.

Lucie moved one of the pillows over against the headboard. I climbed up beside her.

I said nothing.

Lucie began again. "I am not shocked. Jane, I'm not a baby. Remember how I got in trouble for writing that term paper about *The Children's Hour*? Apparently, my school considered a play about love between women a forbidden subject. But I don't."

My face flushed and my heart beat like a hummingbird.

I put my hand on her arm. "You don't understand how serious this is. It's not like writing a school paper. Sexual deviance is a crime. I got kicked out of the Navy because of it. Moral Turpitude. It's just… it is a failure… unnatural. I certainly can't tell my mother. Anyway, that relationship is over."

"Someone in Japan? In the Navy?"

"In the Navy, yes. An admiral's daughter. We lived together for four years, but it didn't work out."

"And you never told me?"

"Hmph. Just like you never wrote to me about this boy in your life."

"Not so fast. I'm talking about you." This nearly grown Lucie was no pushover.

"You also said you are doing abortions. After what I went through, don't I have a right to understand what you meant?"

I faced her. I had experienced the Nazi occupation, rape, and traveling thousands of miles to do the work I loved, but this was taking courage I didn't think I had. Finally, I found my voice. "For many years, our dear Dr. Levy and his wife Rachel helped Parisian women who needed abortions. When the Nazis killed Rachel, there was no one to help him, so he asked me."

"If only I had known!"

"He and I have lamented that you didn't. But it was a long time ago, and it wouldn't have been appropriate to tell you."

"But you said *you* wanted to teach Oliver."

"Even though Dr. Levy no longer does abortions, *I* do. In nursing school, I worked with a doctor who wanted to give our pregnant patients a choice about what to do. We found a way to provide them with safe abortion care, which was, of course, quite illegal. I learned to do abortions. And now I do them in Japan."

"Is abortion legal there?"

"Not exactly. After the war, the United States became a sort of guardian of Japan, helping to rebuild the country that had been decimated by the war. When they recognized the threat of widespread starvation, they decided to permit abortion."

"And you do them? You actually do them yourself?"

"Yes."

"Does everyone else know?"

"Only Dr. Levy. *Please* don't tell anyone. Especially my mother." My conversation with her in the chapel still burned. "I'm ashamed to ask you to keep my secrets. I can't tell her." I sounded like a child. It was strange to reveal things I had never told anyone. I had no choice but to trust Lucie. "When I was a child, I was told always to tell the truth. But living in Occupied Paris taught me a different lesson. Lies and secrets meant survival. My work in abortion has required secrecy no matter where I lived because of the misguided laws of men. And when it comes to loving a woman, telling the truth can cost you everything. Everything you love or value. Now, when it is safe, I tell the truth. If I must, I tell a lie. If I can, I stay silent."

"Are you going to go away again?"

"I am not sure. I missed you so much. And my mother and Levy. But I can't explain how much my work means to me. Even my disastrous love affair—as painfully as it ended—taught me I don't want to be with a man. If I stay, I can't have either love *or* work."

"But…"

"That's how it is. I can't be true to myself here, even in secret. And I have kept more than my share of secrets."

"I understand. If I hadn't gotten pregnant and ended up in the hospital, my relationship with Oliver would still be a secret. If we are speaking of secrets, can I assume you will be keeping the secret of my abortion? I still want to go to graduation, and this little personal detail wouldn't sit very well with Miss May's College Preparatory School, would it?"

The very idea made us laugh.

Lucie continued, "I am wondering, what is the difference between a secret and a lie? Is it a lie if you don't tell anyone?"

I shrugged my shoulders. Because I couldn't come up with an answer. Despite wanting to be a good model for Lucie, I was hardly one to talk about honesty. I gave it a shot, anyway. "Do you remember asking me that same question when you were little?"

"No."

"We were tangled up in so many lies and secrets. We obtained forged identity papers for Jewish girls who needed to get out of Paris; we hid the girls by dressing them in Mathilde's school uniforms. So many secrets we asked you children to keep—lies we asked you to tell."

"You did that for little Jewish girls like me?"

"Exactly. But we didn't simply want to get you to a *safer* place. Levy and I wanted to bring you to America. Where the Goldfarbs could give you a good life. Where your religion wouldn't matter."

"It's just that… I sort of told Oliver a lie."

"You mean something in addition to the fantasy that you are twenty-one?"

"Yes." She stopped for a moment. "I didn't tell him my real name. I told him my name is Lucie Fortier."

"*Lucie!*" I was shocked.

"It's not exactly a lie. It *is* my father's name. I just didn't… I didn't want to tell him I am Jewish."

"Oh, Lucie. I can't believe it. You were always so proud of your heritage. I remember the pictures you sent me of your Bat Mitzva. What happened?"

"Then you should also remember how I was teased and criticized by the girls in my class. Remember that girl who said the Jews killed Jesus?"

"Yes. I remember. They should not have said that to you."

"But they did. Things like that happened over and over. I just got so tired of having to defend myself. I wanted a little break."

"How are your parents going to feel about that?"

"How is *Oliver* going to feel about that? And *his* parents? I wanted it to be easy for once. I thought we'd go on a couple of dates. I didn't plan to fall in love with him."

I put my hand in hers. "Little girl, this is going to be a hard one to sort out."

"That's just it. I don't know how to sort it out."

"Oh, yes you do. You just don't want to accept it."

She burst into tears.

"I suggest you dry those tears. Being sweet little Lucie is not going to work this time. This is a knot for a grown-up to untie."

I drew my knees to my chest and put my arms around them to signal a change in tone. "This has been quite the conversation. Thank you for keeping my secrets, and I will keep yours. We'll pretend you have had a lovely nap. And now, do you want some lunch?"

"I thought you would never ask."

We took our seats around the Formica kitchen table. Lunch was a quiet affair. It seemed that we had tacitly agreed not to talk about any of it, which suited me fine.

In the kitchen, I pulled Levy aside to tell him Lucie was aware of the work we did in Paris, and admonished him to keep the secret from everyone else. That's one of the problems with secrets—the more people who know, the less secret they are.

CHAPTER 5

OLIVER BUTTERFIELD HANOVER III

After lunch, as my mother and I said our goodbyes, Lucie drew me aside.

"Jane, I need you to back me up. You'll like Oliver. He is tall and smart—just like you. He is a doctor, just like Doctor Levy and Papa Hymie. He would do anything for me. He feels so awful about how everything turned out. He understands how you worried about me. And he wants to apologize to all of you. And when we are married, my last name will be Hanover—a lot easier to live with in this world than Goldfarb, you must admit!"

I did have to admit that, although I thought it a bit cowardly. Not like the brave Lucie I had known as a child. But having the last name 'Smith' meant I would never experience the taunts and discrimination she'd experienced in school, so I could hardly pretend to understand what she had gone through.

I still had my judgments, but I said I would do my best to support her.

In my childhood, there was one time my mother could not be disturbed—when she was in the bath with a drink. Her long soaks were her antidote to life's problems, large and small.

That night, I poured myself a glass of wine and had a hot bath.

I would like to tell you that I looked forward to meeting Oliver Butterfield Hanover III, the so-called 'love of Lucie's life,' but I don't like to lie—unless it's unavoidable.

A few evenings later, my mother, Levy, the Goldfarbs, and I met to make a plan. We sat on my mother's porch. The sun had just set, and the sound of the peepers in her garden filled the air. Because our first meeting with Oliver was to include his apology for nearly killing Lucie, we agreed not to hold it in a public place. The five people who had sat vigil in that hospital room were in no mood to forgive or forget. I feared that we'd need to hold Hymie down to prevent him from committing Oliver-cide.

Hymie and Sadie agreed to host the event in their parlor. At first, my mother refused to meet him. "I am of a mind to say that we simply should not permit her to continue to see this boy, let alone invite him into your home."

My mother had not been the strict one in my childhood, but she took on a bit of my father's stern spine after he died.

"If only that were possible, Sylvia," Levy said. I still loved hearing how he pronounced my mother's name—Seelviah. "You haven't ever lived with Lucie, but I can tell you that throwing down the gauntlet, or drawing a line in the sand, or whatever you are contemplating, will not work. Lucie isn't a child any longer. She won't stand for it. Wouldn't it be worse if she *s'enfuie avec lui?* What is it… If she went with him?"

I put my hand on his arm. "Eloped. That's the word in English. And yes, that would be terrible. But you are both being a bit dramatic. She is not even 18. She is not going to elope." I looked at my dear mother. "Levy is right. We can't simply issue commands. I am afraid we must meet him."

Hymie Goldfarb looked pained. "I agree with Jane. We tried laying down the law a few times, didn't we, Sadie?" Sadie nodded in agreement.

He continued. "And it didn't get us anywhere, did it?" Sadie shook her head again, this time somewhat more vigorously.

With a pained look on her face, Sadie added, "All we have ever been able to do is to reason with her. Even at eight, it was like negotiating with a foreign power." We all laughed knowingly.

I chimed in. "Well, first of all, she's not getting married at the age of 18 to someone *she* hardly knows, and we have not even met. She has to wait at least a year. But we are going to have to meet him."

We agreed. My mother reluctantly acquiesced, since Lucie was the closest to a granddaughter she'd ever get. Though she said she wouldn't promise to be civil.

Lucie brooded over how to tell Oliver she was Jewish. The untying of this particular Gordian knot was not a pretty thing to watch. She finally blurted it out, and he didn't much care, except to acknowledge that his parents *would* care. I insisted that she confess to the Goldfarbs. They were devastated. My mother and Dr. Levy were very disappointed. And I… I had to appear disapproving, but sadly I understood all too well the wish to hide something about yourself that you recognized would not be accepted by people you loved.

On the appointed evening, Oliver arrived at the Goldfarbs right on time. Lucie ran to the door the second we heard the bell chime.

She opened it wide. "It's him!" she exclaimed.

Oliver Butterfield Hanover III stood on the landing holding a bouquet of pale pink tea roses, Sadie's favorite by coincidence. His aqua blue sport coat, pink Oxford shirt, pea green slacks, and loafers with no socks made him look a bit like an Easter basket. I hated those naked ankles. He wasn't bad looking, but he was the kind of young man born already looking stuffy. I imagined I saw his father and grandfather in him, and I expected he'd lose his light brown hair early. Could Lucie be as certain as she claimed that this was the man she wanted to wake up to for the rest of her days? The idea made me shudder.

Sadie welcomed Oliver and accepted the roses gracefully. She took them into the kitchen to find a vase. Lucie ushered Oliver into the living room. Their next stop was my mother. Oliver proffered a box of chocolate-covered cherries, her favorite. My mother blushed as she said hello and accepted the gift. Hymie offered a firm handshake and said, "Hymie Goldfarb." Levy pulled himself up to his full 5 feet 8 inches and said, with his outstretched hand, "Lucie has told us a lot about you." So far, it seemed like the Oliver Hanover fan club. I was the last to say hello. He had been coached by Lucie because he gave me a slender volume of the poetry of Edna St. Vincent Millay. It was a lovely gift, and I tried to smile as I thanked him. I'm sure it irritated Lucie that I didn't appear as gracious as the others.

I noted with some pleasure that I was taller than Oliver. I spent so much of my young life being self-conscious about being too tall for a girl. At the high school Cotillion dances my mother made me attend, I was a head taller than all the boys, so I had a habit of noticing men's height.

Sadie and Hymie's informal parlor had pale cream wallpaper and standing lamps. There were two small couches and a game table surrounded by four chairs. Hymie pulled two of the gaming chairs next to the sofa to make enough seats for all of us. Sadie put a plate of salty pretzels and sweet Fig Newtons on the coffee table with a pitcher of tart lemonade. Once we sat with lemonade in our glasses and snacks on little plates, Oliver began.

"It is wonderful to meet all of you who are so important to Lucie, who is so important to me." He put his hand on his heart. "I can only hope you will forgive me for harming Lucie. I took advantage of her when I only meant to love her. I am ashamed." He lowered his head. My mother responded first. "You *should* be ashamed, young man. Regardless of what she told you, Lucie is only seventeen years old. You had no business…"

"You're right. I have no excuse except that I love her with all my heart," he said, looking at Lucie with a pained expression. This was unexpected. None of us knew what to add to that. After an awkward silence, he continued. "Please tell me what I can do to earn your trust."

The Oliver we met that evening was not at all what I had anticipated. The Oliver that Lucie presented to us was humble, considerate, deferential, and so deeply apologetic that he won my mother's sympathy. It was, incidentally, an Oliver I never saw again. I should not underestimate Lucie's ability to coach his behavior. She could turn Mussolini into the tooth fairy if it served her purposes.

Sadie and my mother seemed impressed, but were still skeptical. Hymie and Levy grudgingly gave him points the way men slap each other on the back when they have been outplayed in rugby. I remained hostile, but tried to keep a smile on my face. Lucie looked as though she had won the sweepstakes.

After some comments so banal, I thought I would scream, I asked Oliver if he would help me bring some sodas in from the garage. I could easily reach them myself, but I needed to get him alone.

Once out of earshot, I turned to him with a stony expression.

He said, "I deeply regret what happened to Lucie. But my parents—you understand, I had no choice."

Self-serving, I thought. So self-serving.

"Tell me what Lucie has said about me. About my work," I said.

"Naturally, Lucie has told me all about your involvement with… with that. We tell each other everything."

I knew that wasn't true. Even though she had finally told him she was Jewish, Lucie still kept some secrets to herself.

"If she told you, then you know how important it is to keep it a secret. Only Dr. Levy knows."

I pointed to the cans of ginger ale on the top shelf. He spoke as he reached for the box. "Just as you know how important it is that my parents don't find out about… about what happened to Lucie," he said, setting the soda on top of the washing machine.

He couldn't even say the word. Much less accept responsibility in the matter.

We sized each other up. We shared a mutual distrust—what Cold War politicians would later call 'mutually assured destruction.' I'd have to be wary around him. I put my shoulders back and stood at my full 6 feet. It wasn't usually my way to intimidate someone with my height, but for Oliver, I'd make an exception.

I asked, "How did your parents handle the fact that Lucie is Jewish?"

Oliver looked down. Then he looked away. Then he cleared his throat.

"You haven't told them, have you?"

"It was Lucie's idea. We just told them her name was Lucie Fortier and that her father was a scientist who died during the war."

"Oliver, you *have* to tell them. This is a secret you can't keep."

"I know. My mother has already set a date for the engagement party at their club, which doesn't allow Jews. But I have a plan. I am an only child. I'm going to tell them that they have to agree to our marriage if they want a grandson to continue the illustrious name of Hanover. They will have to capitulate. And they'll just have to find another place to hold the party."

I didn't trust this young man. Not because he had ruined Lucie—as my mother would put it. But because he had the power to ruin *me*. Like two countries whose armies send spies to determine which has superior firepower, Oliver and I were entangled by the potency of our respective secrets. Our respective lies. We each recognized the dynamite that had the capacity to blow our lives to proverbial bits.

I shook hands with Oliver and waved him back into the house, saying I'd be right in. I stayed in the garage for a minute, deep in thought, assessing the danger. I was dismayed that my darling Lucie thought she was in love with Oliver. But I reassured myself it wouldn't last. This was a first love. Lucie was too good for him. Surely she would see through him. Lucie was still enough of a teenager that I thought she might double down on her devotion to Oliver if she sensed opposition. So, for the time being, no one would witness anything but cordiality from me towards Oliver Butterfield Hanover III.

As I came back inside, I saw Lucie and Oliver standing in the pantry.

"How am I doing?" He grinned.

She stood on her tiptoes and kissed him on the cheek.

"Perfect. Just remember what is needed for apologies. Be humble and contrite."

It was like being backstage at a performance. If Lucie was the puppet master, she was doing a great job.

CHAPTER 6

WHY EVER NOT?

By 10 p.m., we'd said our goodbyes to Oliver, and Lucie went to her bedroom, thanking us all for giving him a chance. My mother, Sadie, and Hymie laughed as they washed the dishes. I cornered Levy.

"What did you think of him?"

"He seemed like a very polite young man."

"Yes, but…"

"Jane, I know you too well for 'yes, but.' What do you want to say about him?"

"He was too good to be true. I don't think of my mother as shallow, but she seemed completely won over by his courtly manners. He convinced her he was some kind of Prince Charming, with roses, and chocolate-covered cherries, and poetry that Lucie obviously told him to bring. The Goldfarbs seemed to love him. And you think he is a very polite young man. But this is also the guy who bungled an abortion on Lucie—almost killed her—to save himself from his family's disapproval."

Levy interrupted. "To save Lucie, too. Surely you don't think she wanted to have a baby."

I had to agree. "I just hope he is a passing phase. Many first loves don't last."

"Don't be too sure. Lucie seems pretty determined, and when she sets her mind to something…"

He was right.

I made several attempts to warn Lucie I worried about her future with Oliver.

"It's just that he is so, I don't want to say *stuffy*—but more—well, more *formal* than you are. I am afraid he will want to rein you in—that your natural energy and exuberance won't fit well with his rules."

"He doesn't have *rules*, Jane. And he loves my exuberance. He loves my unpredictability and spontaneity."

"Perhaps. Perhaps he loves it now, but what attracts us to someone can become stale. When he is a fancy doctor, won't he want a fancy doctor's wife?"

"You worry too much, Jane. I don't need you to rescue me. I'm happy, and this is what I want."

That settled that.

Lucie and Oliver had shared several dinners with his parents. According to Lucie, they adored her. She admitted she might have hinted at being distantly related to Belgian royalty.

"I only said it was possible. It *is* possible, isn't it? I just want them to like me. They have to like me enough to still like me when Oliver tells them I'm Jewish."

Apparently, he finally did. Oliver and Lucie were sitting at the kitchen table, unaware that Sadie and I were in the adjacent library, sorting through Lucie's old textbooks to decide which were in good enough condition to donate.

Oliver's voice was serious. "I want you to trust that it's going to be all right."

"I'll try. But what did you tell them? *How* did you tell them?" Lucie asked.

"I planned it for Saturday dinner at the yacht club. I knew they wouldn't raise their voices there. I started by saying I had something to tell them about you. My mother interrupted to say how much they like you—and how delightful it is that you're related to the Belgian royal family."

Lucie made a little yelping sound. Sadie raised her eyebrows. She had intervened in a few of those "Belgian royalty" stories when Lucie was younger. Even when trying to tell the truth, Lucie managed to spin another web of half-truths.

"Mother said she hoped I was about to announce our engagement."

"Oh," Lucie said. "They want you to propose?"

"They did. I think they still do."

"What happened next?" Lucie asked, her voice tight.

"I wanted them to feel some sympathy, so I reminded them that you'd endured serious hardships during the war."

"That was smart."

"I told them your mother died when you were an infant and your father when you were in elementary school. My mother interrupted again, wanting to know if it was your father's side that was connected to royalty. I dodged the question. Then I came right out with it and told them you'd learned your parents were Jewish."

"As if I just recently found out?" Lucie asked.

"Well... I might have given that impression."

"What about the Goldfarbs?"

"I didn't mention them at first."

Sadie's look of concern had turned to anger. But we both stayed quiet—we wanted to hear the rest.

"Then what happened?" Lucie asked anxiously.

"My father said something like, 'Surely not. There must be some mistake.' I said the Goldfarbs adopted you after Dr. Levy rescued you from Occupied Paris. That's when they started insisting that's where the 'misunderstanding' must have come from."

"Misunderstanding?" Lucie asked sharply.

"I'm not sure what they meant. Something about Jews sticking together—so the Goldfarbs 'had' to say you were Jewish."

"Oh. Oliver, is this going to get better or worse?"

"A little worse at first. But it ends better."

"Well, just tell me. You're making my stomach hurt."

"I kept insisting it wasn't a mistake. That you 'are' Jewish. I told them I don't care—I love you."

I had to press a finger to my lips and hold Sadie's arm to keep her from storming into the kitchen.

"My mother said something about your red hair, that you don't 'look Jewish.' My father worried it would affect my career to marry someone society wouldn't accept. Then he made a horrible comment about there being women you date and women you marry."

This time, Sadie had to hold *me* back.

"Oliver, that's awful. I'm so sorry," Lucie said.

There was a brief silence I took to be a kissing interlude.

Then the conversation resumed.

"It was hard. But I told them you're the one I want to marry, and that we're planning a wedding in Paris. After a lot of questions I couldn't answer, we agreed to continue the conversation the next morning. I wasn't in the room, but I know they stayed up late talking. When I woke to the smell of bacon, I knew it was going to be okay. My dad only cooks breakfast on Sundays when he's in a good mood. He made scrambled eggs, bacon, toast, coffee, orange juice—the full spread. I complimented the food and waited."

Oliver paused, then continued with a hint of pride.

"My father cleared his throat and said they understood I was set on marrying you."

"You *are*, aren't you?" Lucie asked.

"I am, dear one. I wouldn't have gone through all of this if I didn't love you."

Another kissing interlude.

"I told them we hoped for their blessing. I had a card in my back pocket—the fact that if they wanted to know their future grandson, they'd have to accept you—but I didn't even need to use it. My mother burst into tears and said how much they love their Ollie."

I could just picture his smug little grin. Their Ollie, I suspected, was as stubborn and unyielding as my Lucie.

"She said they'd do anything for me. My father said their friends didn't have to know *everything*, and they'd find a way to make it work."

"Does that mean they won't tell their friends?" Lucie asked.

"I don't know. But they love the idea of a Paris wedding."

Sadie and I exchanged a look—realizing, perhaps at the same time, that the Hanovers welcomed a wedding abroad because it spared them the awkwardness of explaining a Jewish bride to their yacht club friends.

Then I heard the scrape of a chair.

"Lucie Fortier Goldfarb," Oliver said. "Will you do me the honor of becoming my wife?"

I could picture him on one knee, velvet ring box in hand.

Lucie squealed. "Yes, yes, yes!"

Another kissing interlude.

Then Lucie called out, "Mama! Jane! Come see my ring!"

Did she know we'd been listening all along?

When we entered the kitchen, Lucie and Oliver were both beaming. She held out her left hand, and we admired the impressive diamond solitaire.

The question was officially popped.

A couple of weeks later, the Goldfarbs invited the Hanovers to join them, my mother, Levy, and me at their favorite Italian restaurant. We had polite, even cordial conversation about the weather, the tulips starting to grow in our gardens, the relative qualities of the Chevrolet Bel Air compared to the Buick Super Riviera, batting averages, and a few moments devoted to the exact shade of yellow of the new appliances recently installed in the Hanovers' kitchen. Over dessert we listened to Oliver and Lucie plead their case, and agreed to a wedding the following year. Almost immediately, Lucie started talking about her plans for getting married in Paris. And so, *alea iacta est*, the die is cast. Little did I know how the decision to go to France would impact our lives and the lives of hundreds of women.

The Hanovers did everything they could to avoid the social fallout of Lucie's unfortunate heritage. Hymie and Sadie agreed, against their better judgment, that the wedding announcement in the *New York Times* would say

Lucie Fortier was engaged to be married to Oliver Butterfield Hanover III on Wednesday, July 4, 1951 in Paris, France.

Lucie tried to justify the sleight of hand by explaining that Oliver told her they wouldn't get any gifts from his parents' wealthy friends if they realized she was Jewish.

"Is that so important to you, Lucie? Fancy presents?" I asked.

"Not to me, but it is very important to Oliver."

The Hanovers hosted a lovely engagement dinner, where everyone minded their manners and mercifully refrained from conversations about politics or religion. The only hiccup was that Maisie Hanover complained that she had to change the dinner venue twice in order to find a place that permitted Jewish guests. A detail she could have kept to herself.

The trouble didn't end there. The evening of the event, I arrived at the restaurant early to deliver a centerpiece, only to learn that Maisie had ordered a dinner of baked ham. I cornered her as she flitted about inspecting napkin colors and other essential details.

"Maisie. You can't serve ham tonight. Most Jewish people don't eat pork."

"They don't? Why ever not?" She was distracted, moving a fork an inch to the left.

"That is beside the point. You have got to change the menu."

Maisie stopped and looked at me for a moment. "Miss, ah, Smith... you're not...?"

An ugly silence hung between us.

"Jewish? Am I Jewish? Well, let's see. I'm not sure. I'll have to ask my mother. I might be. After all, my late father was a banker." I sneered as I said it. She turned on her heel and huffed off to find the manager.

We ate fish that night, but I felt sick to my stomach all evening. I wondered what in the world Lucie was getting herself into.

CHAPTER 7

WE ALL KEEP SECRETS

It was graduation day—June 8, 1950. My mother, Levy, the Goldfarbs, and I sat in the front row on folding chairs on the large side lawn of Lucie's school. I forbade Lucie from inviting Oliver to the ceremony. The twenty-four girls in the senior class wore long white dresses and carried bouquets of long-stemmed red roses. The graduates sat on a raised platform in front of rows of teachers decked out in black robes with cowls of various college colors.

My mother whispered to me, "Are you sure no one knows about... the unpleasantness?"

"Positive. As far as they are concerned, Lucie had appendicitis. It was Levy's idea. Fortunately, he has friends at the hospital, which is the *only* reason they didn't involve the police. That and the fortunate choice of the ambulance driver not to take Lucie to the Catholic hospital. Otherwise, this might have been a public disaster involving the authorities."

My mother gave a dark look at the mention of the word hospital. I was treading too close to the unspeakable reality.

"Oh, darling. This could have been so terrible," my mother said.

My nightmare about Lucie's death still haunted me.

"I hate it that she has to carry this secret all her life," I said.

My mother drew back and looked at me. "Jane, we all keep secrets," she said, raising one eyebrow. "Surely you are keeping some yourself."

Since my many secrets weighed heavily on me, I just nodded. In my shame, it was impossible to imagine that my good-as-gold mother had any secrets.

The headmistress gave a welcome. She introduced the graduation speaker, the author of several well-loved young-adult books. The address was inspiring and brief. I couldn't take my eyes off Lucie, who looked like an innocent angel. After the author sat down to a polite round of applause, the girls walked up, one by one, for their diplomas. Anderson, Chase, Ehrhardt, Goldfarb— and there she was, walking gracefully and giving a slight curtsey as she accepted her diploma. She turned and smiled at me. Lucie got the most applause of all the girls.

The headmistress once again stood at the podium to announce the special prizes. I smiled to myself as I recalled how proud I was to be chosen for one of them nearly twenty years before.

"This year, the Schuler Mathematics prize goes to Elizabeth Martin."

Polite applause as an attractive girl with brunette hair in a pixie cut went to the podium to accept her prize.

"The prize in the Sciences goes to Annalise Gunnarson."

More polite applause and a girl with almost white-blonde hair made her way up. My mother told me in a whisper that she was an exchange student from Sweden.

And a few more prizes that I didn't care about.

And finally—*finally,* the one I was waiting for.

"And it gives me great pleasure to announce the Headmistress Award for the year nineteen hundred and fifty. This award is given to the senior who, through her loyalty, integrity, and friendliness, has contributed most to our school's high standards of character—to the girl who, in her maturity and character, shows the greatest promise of an adult sense of responsibility for her school and her community. I am delighted to present this year's Headmistress Award to—"

Amid the clapping and pandemonium, I wasn't entirely sure I'd heard her name—but there, going up to the podium with a huge smile on her face, was my darling Lucie. It was disquieting to realize that they would never have given her the award if they had known about the abortion. And they would never have given it to me—nearly two decades earlier—if they had known I'd one day find myself in bed with an admiral's daughter. I thought about life, how human beings are much more complicated than we appear. Secrets have their benefits, except that they leave us thinking we are frauds.

After the graduation, I had to face the fact that I didn't want to go back to Japan. Almost losing Lucie made me realize that I had been away for far too long. And I didn't want to go back to all the things that reminded me of the sad, jilted Jane I had left behind. I stowed the memories associated with Betty away in one of the locked drawers where I kept the unpleasant aspects of my life. I felt happier than I had in a long time. Except… except that I dreaded calling Dr. Nick, my dearest friend and my boss, in Kyoto. I thought about putting it all in a letter, but that wasn't fair. He always said how much he depended on me, and not just because of my skill as a nurse. It was much easier now that he had a boyfriend, Bai, in his life. The nurses he'd added to the surgical team allowed me to think that I was no longer essential. I decided it would be best to call him at home. Nick was a night owl, so he wouldn't mind if I called late. I planned to call him at nine the next morning, which would be 11:00 p.m. in Japan, but at lunchtime the phone rang, and my mother picked it up.

"Yes, she is here. May I say who is calling? Why, yes. This is her mother, Sylvia Smith. Jane has said so many wonderful things about you. Hold on, she is right here." She handed the phone to me with a look of concern on her face. She didn't even have to say who it was. I had told her about my decision to stay, and about how much I dreaded telling Nick.

I took the receiver, reluctantly, and put sunshine in my voice.

"Nick, I was going to call you tomorrow. My goodness—what time is it there? One in the morning?"

"It's two, Janie." Nick is the only person I allowed to call me Janie. "I couldn't wait to call you. How are you? Is everything... I mean, how is it all turning out?" Nick asked in his kindest voice. I had told him that Lucie sur-vived the abortion, but there was so much going on that I hadn't called him again.

"I am so sorry I didn't call. Lucie got out of the hospital and has been doing so well that she attended her graduation yesterday. It was just perfect. So everything is great," I said.

"And you... how are you doing?" he asked. I knew he was afraid that Lucie's crisis would send me back to the bottle. If she had died, I'm sure it would have.

"I am good—really good, Nick. I didn't realize how much I missed every-one until I got here." I sighed.

"Oh Janie, I am so relieved," he said. "I have been worried about you. When you left you were so..."

I carried the phone with its extra-long cord around the corner into the other room. I hadn't told my mother everything.

I lowered my voice. "I know. I was a disaster. But I got through Lucie being in the hospital without a drink, and I haven't had one since. Thank you for taking such good care of me and thank you for worrying about me."

"Janie, you know I love you. Bai and I both do. The whole catastrophe with Betty was partly my fault. I had been told bad things about her—but then when we were all together you seemed so happy I hoped it was just mean gossip about the admiral's daughter."

"Nick, I assure you that I am completely responsible for my time with Betty. I had my suspicions long before her other girlfriend, Sandi, with an 'i,' turned up—but I disregarded them because I didn't want them to be true. Hey, this call is going to cost you a fortune. Do you want to talk tomorrow from the office?"

"I am not worried about the cost, Janie. I just couldn't wait any longer to talk to you. You know me, I have been pacing the floor. There is no point in trying to put this off any longer." He sighed a deep sigh. "You're not coming back, are you?"

"No, Nick. I'm not. I feel so bad about leaving you in the lurch. Is your mother still pressuring you for grandchildren?"

"That's never going to stop. I can't thank you enough for shielding me from the matchmakers. You were the best pretend girlfriend I could have asked for. I'll just tell her our engagement is off and that will give me more time. Japan is so far away that there is no one to check up on me. For the first time in my life, I can be myself."

I was well aware of the relief of being far enough away that you can be yourself.

"I'm glad to hear that. Anyway, I was honored to be your imaginary fiancée. Will you be okay at the clinic since you've trained such a great staff?"

"None of them is you. No one is. But I understand, and I thought this might happen. We'll be just fine. I will never be able to thank you enough for your friendship. I have learned a lot from you."

"And I from you. I'll send back the diamond ring from our make-believe engagement."

"NO! No way. I want you to keep it. I will always be your friend, Janie, and that is just a way for you to remember me."

"I will always remember you, Nick. Always."

CHAPTER 8

SCHOOL DAYS

My decision not to return to Japan paled in importance with Lucie's decision not to go to college. She was adamant. After nearly losing her, we all found it difficult to argue.

"But what are you going to do with yourself if you don't go to college?" I asked, trying to sound concerned instead of frantic.

"You don't need to worry about me. I'll find a way to get the education I need when the time is right. Oliver and I have been talking. We don't just want to get married in France—we want to live there. At least for a while. His French is quite good, and he can finish his medical training in Paris. Jane, would you... would you consider staying too?"

The seed of an idea was planted.

Oliver Butterfield Hanover III was twenty-four. Six years' difference meant nothing between adults, but it seemed like a great deal to me. I continued to worry whether Oliver was the right choice for Lucie, but she seemed to adore him, and he seemed to adore her, too.

I had promised Lucie that I would teach her inept abortionist how to do an abortion procedure correctly, and teach him I did. His attitude toward our studies did nothing to assuage my concerns. Lucie insisted on being included.

"You must admit that I should know these things," she said petulantly. "I almost died because I didn't." She was clever enough to recognize the power of this argument, and she used it liberally to get whatever she wanted that hot summer.

Oliver had two weeks off before his last year of classes started, and we made the most of the time. Like so many other things, we kept our mini-medical school a secret from my mother. We set up an impromptu schoolroom in Dr. Levy's apartment, over our neighbor's garage. It was a warm morning, and the sun streamed through the windows. I placed a blackboard on an easel, and I had several of the textbooks Levy gave me in Paris all those years ago.

"Isn't Dr. Levy going to be here?" Lucie asked cheekily.

I refused to rise to the bait. "As you are aware, he is busy right now. A boatload of people has just arrived from Italy. His job with the Unitarian Service Committee makes him responsible for finding housing and work for them. Besides, I know more about this subject than he does. I'm sure he will be happy to sit in with us later if Oliver needs the perspective of a physician."

Lucie was all school-girl, sitting up straight in a wooden chair. Her hair was tied back, and she wore a skirt and patterned blouse. Oliver sprawled on Levy's couch wearing khakis with a pink Izod polo shirt. Those terrible pale, naked ankles were on full display.

"Before we start, I want to be sure our agreements are clear. Oliver, I will not tell your parents that you performed an abortion on Lucie, and you both agree not to whisper a word of my involvement in abortion to anyone. Especially my mother." They both nodded vigorously, and Oliver sat up a bit.

"Okay. I'll begin. As you can surmise, abortion, or its equivalent, has been part of human life from time immemorial. There are many reasons an abortion might be procured, the chief of which is the scarcity of the basic essentials to sustain new life, including food, shelter, and safety." I stopped. While Lucie scribbled furiously in a notebook, Oliver sat idly in his chair, fiddling with his keychain.

"Oliver, are you going to take notes?" I asked, not kindly.

"I have an eidetic memory, Ja... Miss Smith. I am able to retain anything I read or hear. That's why I graduated from college so early."

"Well, that is lovely for you. And given the circumstances that have brought us to this point, I hope, for your sake, that you are right. I promise that you will have ample opportunity to display your extraordinary mental powers."

"I am willing to listen, but I have already decided to specialize in dermatology so I will never be awakened in the middle of the night for an emergency. And I am quite sure I shall never use this training," Oliver said, rather pompously. "I am never going to do another one of... of these."

He was too sanctimonious to use the word abortion. "That is entirely up to you," I said. "But I think we can all agree that in the absence of training, you have already done one too many."

Oliver had the good grace to look sheepish.

Lucie looked up from her notebook. "*I'm* taking notes, Jane!" I marveled at how she was sometimes seventeen going on thirty, and sometimes seventeen going on seven.

"To continue—because of recent events, I have decided to begin by describing complications of abortion and how to diagnose and treat them."

Lucie raised her hand.

"I don't think we need to be quite that formal in a class of two, Lucie. What do you want to ask?"

"What did you mean by 'abortion or its equivalent?' See, Oliver, I have an excellent memory as well."

"Lucie, if you are going to treat this as some kind of competition, we will never get to the content!" I said, already exasperated. "What I meant was that in some cultures, infanticide is used to achieve the same result as abortion." Lucie gasped. "Many people, perhaps including you, consider abortion a more moral choice because it ends life before birth. Others, the Catholic Church included, assert that there is no distinction between the fertilized egg, or embryo, and a baby. Perhaps it is because they need to collect as many souls as they can, so they assign a soul to a fetus."

"Hold on," Oliver interrupted, "I am here for a lesson in medical care, not for a diatribe against the Church." Oliver was Episcopalian, like my father, which was as close as many New Englanders came to being Catholic.

"Sorry," I said. "I am just tired of old men telling women what is moral and what isn't. Let me continue. Abortion in trained hands, and especially when done early in pregnancy, is extremely safe. In fact, it is far safer than childbirth. Abortion done by unskilled and uneducated practitioners, with disregard for cleanliness and lack of follow-up, makes abortion dangerous. The terrible scourge of unsafe abortion is entirely caused by the laws of men."

I looked pointedly at Oliver, who was frowning. Then I continued with the distinctions of abortion by method: using herb or toxin; insertion of a foreign object; curettage; and finally, by Dr. Nick's siphon, the newest and, in my opinion, safest approach. I explained various possible complications of each technique—and discussed which signs, such as cramping, passing blood clots, fever, and elevated blood pressure, might accompany each complication. As I spoke about septic infection, I found it hard to talk. I tried not to cry—unintentionally reliving the all-too-recent ordeal of fearing for Lucie's life.

"It's all right, Mam'selle," Lucie said as she put her arm around me. "I'm all right."

I took a moment to compose myself.

"One of the most obvious ways to avoid infection is to use a proper autoclave for the sterilization of instruments."

"I swear my roommate told me boiling the instruments would be enough," Oliver said. He was squirming a bit, which didn't bother me at all.

"Let's hope your uninformed roommate doesn't attempt to teach bacteriology," I said.

I launched into treatment—when something could reverse or cure the complication. I threw in ectopic pregnancy as a potentially fatal complication of early pregnancy, even though it technically has nothing to do with abortion, and then called it a day. It was an intense few hours. I realized that I had started with the complications in part because I needed to put them behind me. As always, when I thought about things that could go wrong, I could picture my patient Mimi's pale face and lank hair. Even with my nurse's training—even with a safe method of abortion in our clinic—even with physicians backing me up, I had never fully shaken off the dread of that terrible night in Paris when that young woman died in my arms as a result of a massive infection from an abortion that someone else had performed improperly.

Within a week, we completed our training using a papaya to simulate a uterus, which allowed Lucie and Oliver to practice inserting the tube and using the curette. By the time we were done, I was convinced that both of them could do a creditable job of performing an abortion. Then I turned to the emotional work—a discussion of how to talk with patients about their feelings and how to give them support.

Oliver had no interest at all in that component of abortion. I didn't see any benefit in forcing him to stay. The last thing I wanted to encourage was a callous abortion provider. So for him, class was dismissed. But Lucie was an avid student. I told her stories of the women I had worked with in Paris, California, and Japan—the women who were so very clear about not wanting a baby and the ones who were in turmoil. That gave me the opportunity to ask about her own abortion.

"How did you feel about it? Did you want to have an abortion, or did Oliver pressure you? Did you even know what an abortion was?"

"To tell you the truth, I was mostly in shock. I didn't want to have a baby—I don't know if I ever want children. But I recognized that being pregnant was a disaster. So when Oliver suggested an alternative, I jumped at the chance. I didn't really know what an abortion was, but if it meant I wouldn't be pregnant anymore, that was what I wanted."

"Do you have any regrets? Any bad dreams?"

"No. No regrets. Now that I have recovered, I am just relieved."

"I am so glad." I gave her a hug.

"But after you left Paris, how did you end up still doing abortions?" she asked.

I told her about the special clinic that my friend Dr. Nick and I set up in Alameda as part of the Navy Nurse Corps, where we gave medical care to Mexican migrant workers and also provided abortion care. I explained that we took the risk of doing abortions because Nick had leverage. Because he was homosexual, he was privy to the sexual peccadillos of some of the top naval administrators. I told her about the secret post-war naval program to provide abortion care in Kyoto to stave off mass starvation. I told her what I had learned about the range of feelings women had, from clarity and relief to worry and guilt. I told her about helping women look deep into their own hearts—about the fears and hopes they had for the children they already had. About their fears of being selfish. About bringing the Virgin Mary into the room when Catholic women needed forgiveness.

Then we alternated playing the roles of patient and clinician so that Lucie could practice. Telling their stories after all these years was like inviting those women to be with us. Remembering them, their courage and their trust in me, was so powerful. When we were done, I had the sense that something more needed to be said.

"Lucie, would you think it odd if I say a prayer for all of them? For us?"

"I have never seen you pray, Mam'selle, but it feels like the right thing to do."

I closed my eyes and summoned the litany from so many years ago that I'd invented for my first patient, Françoise.

"Hail, holy Queen

Mother of Mercy—

Our Lady of Perpetual Grace—Honor our love and courage—

Remember our goodness.

Show unto us

Thy forgiveness

And thy mercy."

Invoking these stories and these women was an initiation for Lucie into the hidden inner lives of women. The young Lucie of my memory was forever gone, turned into a woman who had moments of such depth that I was brought to tears.

CHAPTER 9

SUCH A NICE BOY

One evening after dinner my mother decided it was time to make plans for me. "Sweetheart, it is so good to have you back. Since your father died, it has been lonely in this big house. I was thinking… do you remember my friend Mrs. Miller? Her son is divorced and has just moved back from the Midwest. He is such a nice boy, and very tall. Shall I invite them for dinner one night soon? I don't mean to put any pressure on you, darling. I just want you to be happy. Are you thinking about getting a job? I have a good friend who works at the hospital. I'm happy to help you get settled."

I'm afraid my consternation must have shown on my face. Settled? Oh, no. Just what I didn't want to be. Settled and set up with a very tall divorced guy. Perfect. What was I going to do? I needed my life to mean something. I needed a bit of risk. It is not a coincidence that I was so committed to the work we did during the war years. Adrenalin fed me. And my mother wanted to create a safe, ordinary life for me.

"Thanks, Mom. I'm not looking for a nice boy. Lucie and I are going to do some volunteer work." Not wanting to say more, I kissed her on the cheek and went to bed.

That summer we celebrated Lucie's eighteenth birthday. She told me earnestly that all she wanted for her birthday was a promise that she and Oliver could get married in Paris the following year.

"I want to get married at the convent, Jane. It would be so perfect." I became 'Jane' when she wanted to sound grown up.

The convent. I could almost smell the lemony scent of Dr. Levy's Paris apartment where a patient's father made me a gift of an abandoned convent next to his dairy farm in the countryside outside of Paris. He thought I was a nun because of my teacher's uniform and he was adamant that I had saved his daughter Françoise's soul by helping with her abortion. I still had the heavy black wrought-iron keys he gave me that opened the gate and the old building, and the deed I signed that day.

"Lucie, I have no idea where this idea of getting married in the convent has come from. We don't have any idea if the building is still standing—or if my deed will be honored. You were so young when we went there. I'm sure you can't remember, but it was already ancient."

"I want Oliver to see the city where I lived when I was a child. Don't worry, Jane—I just know we are going to get married at the convent," Lucie said, smiling broadly.

After several such discussions, the Goldfarbs and I capitulated to the idea of a wedding in Paris. Oliver's parents insisted on paying for passage on the five-day voyage to France.

"All right," I said. "I can see there is no use trying to talk any sense into you. We can sail to Paris and you and Oliver can get married at a hotel. The families will fly over for the wedding. It will be fun. I miss Paris, too, and I'll be glad to see what it has become since the war."

"Have you thought more about what I asked you? If you would want to live in France again?" Lucie asked.

"I'm thinking about it. But please don't tell my mother. If I decide to stay there, I want to tell her myself."

We planned to sail almost exactly a year after Lucie's graduation. It had been a busy twelve months. Levy had spent weeks searching for his replacement as head of the Unitarian's International Refugee program. He finally found an ambitious young lawyer to take the job.

"Jane, I'm going to stay in France," Levy announced. "It's my home. It is where I belong. Lucie told me she has asked you to stay, too. Are you going to? We could find places to live near each other."

"I'm thinking about it." Thinking about it made me smile.

During that year, Lucie and I had thrown ourselves into working as a team for the Red Cross. The war had been over for five years, but some families were still in trouble.

One of our clients was a woman named Colleen O'Malley, whose husband Charlie returned from Europe physically intact but emotionally damaged. They had five children, ages one, two, four, twelve, and thirteen. The family was surviving on her salary as a laundress.

She told us about the painful reality of her life. "The older ones help out when they can, but I want them to finish school. Charlie just sits in one place all day, brooding. There is never enough money. When one of his army buddies comes over, what little money we have goes to cigarettes and whiskey. Then he gets angry and I have to protect the children. The priest asks me what I have done wrong to make my husband violent. Was the dinner late? Did I scorch his shirt? The Church says we must welcome as many children as God sends us. We can't afford to have any more, but how can I say no to him?"

I wasn't clear whether she wanted to say no to her husband or to the priest.

To give her a break, Lucie and I took turns playing with the younger children, wiping dirt from their faces, playing pat-a-cake, and changing diapers. We had no answer to her question.

We gave her iron pills for her exhaustion and I suggested she ask her husband to use prophylactics. Birth control was illegal in Connecticut, even for married women, but condoms had somehow slipped through the cracks as prevention of venereal disease. To get around the law, the American military stamped the condoms they gave out with the words "For the protection of sexually transmitted diseases only."

"He won't wear them. He says he is not visiting a prostitute."

By the time we got home from visiting them, Lucie was crying. She held the urine sample that we'd drop off at the lab.

"It's not fair! That woman is in an impossible situation. It is obvious she'll get pregnant again. Maybe she already is. With every new baby her nerves will be stretched thinner and they will have a harder time affording food for the others."

"You are right. And if birth control is so controversial, the government will never permit abortion."

"But you know how to do it. Couldn't you help a woman like that if she got pregnant again?" Lucie asked.

"Maybe. But even if I were willing to, she's Catholic. From her earliest years, she has been indoctrinated into the belief that abortion is murder—a belief that benefits the church but not its members. It's difficult to do something your church has taught you is wrong, even if you are in an impossible situation."

"Doesn't the church care about the children?"

"I'm afraid religion is as much about economics, politics, and power as it is about caring. Maybe more."

"With all that brainwashing, how can she even know *what* she believes?"

"Religion is most powerful when people, especially women, remain obedient. It is only when beliefs are challenged and we look deeper that our most elemental beliefs are discovered. That's my dream."

"What is?"

"To go beyond what women have been taught to do, to think, to feel. To help them find their own deepest beliefs—to help them find the courage to live according to what they *value*. To help women decide about pregnancy without interference. This is what I know how to do. But there is no chance of doing that work here. At least not now. I am a conductor without an orchestra. You saw how my mother reacted to your abortion. Even if it were legal, she'd never accept me doing that work. I'm just going to have to compromise. Perhaps this Red Cross work is the closest I will get."

Lucie was quiet for a moment. "I was just wondering. What if...?" she said.

"What if what?"

She seemed lost in her thoughts. "Nothing."

A very consequential nothing.

Four days later, we had Colleen's lab report.

"I can hardly bear to tell her she is pregnant again, although I suspect she already knows. Most women know their bodies, especially after all those pregnancies. She already looks like she is stretched to her limit."

"Is she the kind of woman you would have been able to help in Japan?"

"Exactly. And here we are in the supposed 'land of the free' and she can't do a thing about this. I can't do a thing."

Lucie suddenly had that seven-year-old 'I have a plan' look. "You did abortions for women in Paris when it was against the law. Why not here?"

My imagination flashed to a newspaper headline declaring my arrest for doing an abortion. My mother would disown me. I would be utterly alone. I turned and barked, "Lucie. Grow up. Get real. It is illegal. I'm not going to jail because a woman couldn't tell her husband no. Just forget it."

She backed away a few steps.

"Yikes. You don't have to act like that. I was just asking." We spent the rest of the day in silence.

I felt bad for yelling at her. I didn't usually do that. But even the threat of losing my mother's approval brought me to my knees. Lucie stayed in the car when I went in to tell Mrs. O'Malley she was pregnant. As I suspected, she already knew. I tried to be kind when I told her, but she didn't seem to have any reaction. Her affect was flat, like the comfort woman I had once treated in Japan. Like so many sailors I had seen, who came back from war, but never really came back. There are many ways to be at war.

CHAPTER 10

SUR LE CHEMIN DU RETOUR (ON THE ROAD BACK)

Spring, 1951

At breakfast, my mother and I discussed my plans.

"Jane, I'll miss you so much. Of course, I'll see you soon at the wedding, but that will just be a visit. It seems you just came home and now you are leaving. Are you ever going to come back?"

It had been so hard to tell her I was going to stay in France. I put my arm around her shoulder. I wasn't used to my mother sounding like a little girl.

"Mom, I honestly don't know how long I'll stay. I have loved being with you this past year. But I also loved living in France."

"It's going to be different, you know. It's not wartime. France still has a lot of rebuilding to do. And the excitement of saving all those little girls... well, nothing will be like that."

"You're right. I may not like it at all. Then I'll come back. I don't mean to be selfish. Will you be all right?"

"Of course, darling. And I'll write as I always do. Go and enjoy yourself."

We didn't talk about it again. Her loneliness weighed on me, but I needed to get away—to have the freedom to succeed or fail on my own terms.

My mother, the Goldfarbs, and the Hanovers planned to fly to France for the wedding. That gave Lucie and Oliver the chance to experience the five-day voyage aboard the SS America with Levy and me as chaperones. We loaded our luggage, presented our papers, and boarded the ship. After much confetti and champagne, the loudspeaker roared, "All ashore, that's going ashore." The parents bustled down the gangway. Lucie, Oliver, Levy, and I crowded the railing, flanked by our fellow travelers. As we waved our good-byes, my mother stood alone, looking melancholy. She would write as she always did. And I would see her soon at Lucie's wedding. But just then, she looked so forlorn. I was ashamed.

My mother had kept herself busy since my father died. She was always doing things for other people, as if she had to accumulate goodness points. Was writing to her almost every week for years and years like that? An obligation, like a bread-and-butter thank-you note? In my letters, I was chatty, but I always left so much out. My fears. Longings. Things that were out of bounds. It occurred to me that *she* might be leaving things out, too. That each letter we exchanged was like the carapace of a cicada—something left as a symbol of a life. Proof you were there, without revealing too much.

In my suitcase, I carried the little wind-up alarm clock she gave me when I sailed to Paris in 1939. On the red leather case embossed in what used to be gold were the words '*I Love You to the Moon and Back*.' On that first lonely trip to France, I was twenty-five, but I felt like a child. I read that inscription over and over again, searching for a hidden meaning. I even wondered if it came standard with the clock. It was not something my mother had ever said to me.

I pulled myself back into the present. Our vessel was called 'Queen of the Seas' for good reason. It had undergone a multi-million dollar restoration after it returned to the civilian passenger business after WWII. The ship *looked* like that million dollars! There was no smell of diesel this time.

"Well, this is certainly different from the crossing we made together from Lisbon on the last ship out of Europe," I said with a wry laugh.

"This time I only have to share a room with one man instead of bunking in the ballroom with hundreds," Levy agreed.

"I can hardly remember that trip," Lucie said. "Isn't that funny?" She turned to me. "But I remember that I made lots of friends and we played all over the boat. It seemed as though the voyage took a month."

We sailed passed the Statue of Liberty, everyone out on deck, waving to her as if to a family member being left behind. Lucie said, "I remember the first time I saw the Statue of Liberty."

Oliver smiled. "All of you are trans-Atlantic veterans," he said.

Lucie pushed his shoulder playfully. "You have been to a hundred more places than I have ever been," she said.

"But I've never sailed on an ocean liner," Oliver protested. "This is a very civilized way to travel." He gestured at the elegantly set table with a single white rose in a cut-glass vase and a bottle of chilled wine waiting for us.

If I didn't like Oliver's naked ankles, Oliver in Bermuda shorts was almost too much for me to bear. So much white skin. I stayed out of his way as much as I could.

It had seemed like an ironic symmetry to travel back to France by ship, the same way we had come a decade before. This time, Lucie and I shared an elegant stateroom with a balcony, and Oliver and Levy shared one across the hall. It was a bit awkward for Oliver and Levy to be in the same quarters. Levy hadn't forgiven Oliver for the shoddy abortion technique that nearly killed his beloved Lucie. And it was a bit strange for me to share a stateroom with Lucie, though I hardly saw her during the sail.

I was uncomfortable that Oliver's parents underwrote our trip as an engagement present. It had taken weeks for Lucie to convince me to accept their largesse—and weeks more to convince Levy to be part of the entourage, although I knew he wanted to go back to France.

"Jane," Lucie had said, in her most persuasive voice, "Oliver's parents are aware of what it means to me to have you and Dr. Levy with us. I promise not to be extravagant. You will not regret it. Please, Jane, Please!"

Oliver's parents insisted that this was what the 'young people' wanted. And they were relieved to have their Episcopalian son sailing thousands of miles away for his wedding to a Jewish girl. We did keep one secret from them. They were blissfully unaware of Lucie's abortion and their son's part in it—we all thought that was best, to say the least.

During our voyage, I woke very early. I dressed quietly in our tiny bathroom so as not to wake Lucie. She usually came to bed in the wee hours of the morning—sometimes just shortly before I got up. I'd go out and sit on a deck chair to watch the sunrise—wrapping myself in a thick plaid blanket, welcoming the salt spray on my face, often joined by an equally quiet and meditative Levy. I'd muse about the past and dream about the future—dozing off and on. A friendly steward brought us steaming cups of tea and replaced them when they got cold. At thirty-seven, I envied the twenty-five-year-old Jane setting sail into her future with nothing and no one to lose. My mind turned, as it often did, to my lost love, Betty. "*If they asked me, I could write a book…*" I couldn't get that danged song she sang for me out of my mind. All this time after leaving Kyoto, no matter how hard I tried to hate her, she was still my first thought in the morning and she crowded my dreams at night.

CHAPTER 11

ANNE-MARIE

France, 1951

Once we were settled at a hotel on the Left Bank, Lucie insisted we drive out to the convent. Levy and Oliver were reluctant to take the Peugeot Levy had just purchased on what they described as a 'wild expedition into the country.'

"Jane, you haven't been there in more than a decade. It must have disintegrated by now. It won't even be safe. You are being ridiculous," Levy argued. "After all, that's why we have booked Maxim's restaurant for the wedding on July 4."

"Don't tell me, tell Lucie," I answered. "She has it in her head that it is a sort of fairyland that will be the perfect place for her wedding."

"That is crazy!" he said. I realized he was afraid I was letting Lucie manipulate me after coming so close to losing her. And he was right.

"Look," I said. "The hotel manager is going to let us take his car. If it is too terrible even to camp on the floor, we will turn around and come back. Okay?"

Levy laughed. "Okay. But be careful. Don't let Lucie go poking around in the rubble, or you might lose her again!"

Lucie chimed in, "If we don't come right back, you'll know it's fit to stay in. Then will you drive out with more food and supplies in the Peugeot?"

"All right," Oliver said. "Who knows, Levy? Perhaps it won't be as bad as you think."

Was it possible that he winked?

Lucie nodded her head in agreement, and said to me, "Why does everyone assume it is going to be a wreck? Mam'selle, I remember the first time we saw it—it was so *beautiful!*" She was almost jumping up and down with excitement.

And so, Lucie I and started out in a battered yellow Citroen on the route to the cloister.

"It doesn't look the same," she said, tugging absently on her long red hair, her face pressed against the window.

"Hmm. What do you think looks different?"

"I'm not sure… maybe it's because we're not on that crazy bus. Or not with all those girls singing *Frére Jacques*. I don't know. It's just different."

"Maybe *you* are different. You were a little girl when we were last here—and now you are nearly a woman."

Lucie frowned at the nearly part.

"Nearly a *married* woman," she said. "Jane, I'm almost 19. You must get used to the fact that I am grown!"

My Lucie—seven, going on nineteen, going on thirty.

The countryside was lush green, with scattered fields of the last scarlet poppies of the season. It took me back to a different time. To a different me. An innocent young woman, earnestly wanting to save the world. Had I lost that vision because it was too hard? Too many roadblocks? Instead of maneuvering a rickety bus full of little girls, it was only me and Lucie. From the back seat came the scent of the fresh baguette, salami, and cheese we'd brought for supper, and croissants for the morning. In the trunk we had some bedding, the medical bag I always carried, and changes of clothes. And the bottle of Cabernet I had seen Dr. Levy sneak into the trunk. Were we planning a celebration? Lucie made me stop so she could pick a handful of poppies—my favorite flowers. *Coquelicots* in French.

The drive was shorter than it had seemed when I was driving a behemoth filled with children singing. Before long, we approached the formidable black wrought-iron gates covered in vines. I smiled to see that the brass sign I had affixed so many years before was still there: *Couvent Notre Dame de la Grâce Perpétuelle.*

"Why did you choose that name?" Lucie asked.

"Well, as you are aware, it used to be a convent, and that word fascinated me. It is from the Latin, *con venire*—come together. I guess I longed for a time when women would come together and take care of each other. It also intrigued me that the word 'coven' is from the same root."

"But why 'Our Lady?' Is she the High Priestess of the coven?"

I laughed. "In a way, yes. When I helped Dr. Levy with abortions, he asked me to wear my teacher's uniform, which resembled a habit. He recognized that forgiveness from a nun—a representative of the Church—would help heal women's shame, the unjustified shame they carried for doing the best they could for themselves and their families. The original name of the convent was 'Our Lady of Sorrows,' but I thought we all had too many sorrows. Do you remember the prayer I said when we were practicing? I made up that prayer to Our Lady of Perpetual Grace to comfort the women during their abortions. What the women needed—perhaps what all of us need—is to experience everlasting grace, forgiveness, kindness, things that only come when we open our hearts to each other. So that's what I named the convent."

Lucie kissed me on the cheek. "I wish you had been with me when I had my abortion. I would have loved a bit of that kindness."

"I wish that, too, beloved."

"Anyway, I want to be part of any coven you are leading," she said.

When I stopped the car, I handed the heavy key ring to Lucie. She hopped out and pushed the coarse iron key into the lock. When the massive gates swung forward, I was surprised not to hear the terrible screech of metal on metal that was the hallmark of our visits so many years ago.

As we drove down the entryway, we could see that someone had trimmed the hedges. Tulips and daffodils bloomed. I had a terrible thought that the French government had appropriated the property as a museum or sold it to some wealthy family. We parked in front of the building and again I was surprised. The fountain that I had only seen covered in dried algae now gurgled and splashed, and the dark wood of the massive door was polished and the doorknob gleaming.

"Lucie, my darling, I wish we could stay, but I'm afraid the house must now belong to someone else. I failed in my efforts to contact the French government about this property before we left America. I understand you are disappointed—I am too—but it is obvious that someone has been taking care of the convent."

"But Jane... can't we just knock on the door?"

"Okay." I lifted the heavy metal cross and knocked three very loud times, and waited. No answer.

"No one is here. I feel like we are trespassing. I hate getting into trouble. Let's leave before someone sees us. I still have the deed Françoise's father gave me, so perhaps a bureaucrat in Paris will help us find out who has taken ownership of the building."

Just then, I heard the crunch of gravel behind us. Two women approached in a small wagon drawn by a pony. The woman holding the reins was in her thirties, attractive in an earthy French way, with honey blonde hair under a white kerchief. The younger woman might have been in her twenties, though it was hard to be sure because her face was drawn tight with pain. She was smaller, with short-cropped black hair. She was pale and leaned against the blonde woman's shoulder, looking on the verge of collapse. They drove the pony under the *porte cochère* and the older woman hopped out and propped her friend against the seat. Deftly, she unhooked the pony from the wagon and tied him to a metal ring on one of the columns that framed the front door, throwing him a pile of hay from the wagon.

I could see they needed help.

"Quick, bring her here," I said. I motioned to a wooden bench at the side of the front door. Even as a trespasser, I automatically reverted to nursing mode. "She needs to lie down."

The blonde woman put the straps of a huge bag over her shoulder, and with her arm around the suffering woman's waist, brought her to the steps.

"I am Jane, and this is Lucie."

"I know who you are, but there's no time for talking. This is my husband's niece, Anne-Marie. She is pregnant, but I am afraid she is losing the baby. She has been bleeding, and it is coming out in—I don't know how to say it. Like jelly."

"Clots?" I asked.

"Oui. *Exactement*. Clots."

Anne-Marie moaned, and the three of us helped her up the stairs. The woman pulled a key from her apron pocket just as a dark cloud covered the sky.

"Let's get her inside before it rains. Then we need find a doctor," I said.

The front door opened smoothly and without a whimper, just as the gates had. I had a hundred questions, but obviously they had to wait. We got her into the house, and I was again astonished—the stone floor was swept clean and every surface was gleaming. There was a table in the kitchen, which had been devoid of furniture when I had last seen it. "Is there a bed?" I asked.

"Yes—a *droite*—to the right. But I think it will be too low."

"Too low for what?" I asked—trying to steer Anne-Marie to the right, while the woman tried to keep her in the kitchen.

"Too low to do what you have to do."

"We'll need to take her into the village to see the doctor," I said.

"The only doctor is delivering a baby in the next town. He has already been gone for a day, so perhaps the delivery is complicated—or he can't get back through the storm that is coming this way."

I stopped pushing Anne-Marie into the bedroom and instead helped get her into the kitchen. Lucie, the blonde woman, and I hoisted her onto the massive table as I thought about what to do.

"Is this your house?" I asked.

"No, Mam'selle, it is yours. *Mon ange*, do you not recognize me?"

Only one person had ever referred to me as her angel. I gasped.

"Françoise?" Could this woman be the girl whose abortion I helped with so many years before?

"*Oui!* I have waited many years for your return. Dr. Levy wrote to me that you were coming. When they told me in the village that a car had come by, I hoped it would be you and Dr. Levy to help me once again." We embraced. She turned the lights on in the kitchen and lowered her large satchel to the floor. "Where is Dr. Levy?"

"Levy is in Paris. Françoise, I can't help her. I'm not a doctor," I said. "We need to call someone."

"There is no telephone here yet. They tell me there is a long list and we must wait until the new lines are brought so far out."

"There is nothing I can do."

"But you are our Lady of Perpetual Grace… please… you have to help her. You are all we have."

Lucie looked panicked, but she calmed down a bit when she saw my composed expression. I realized what I had to do. By then, the rain pelted down—it was almost hailing—more than it was wise to attempt to drive through. I sighed.

CHAPTER 12

GO WITH LOVE

As I had done many times, I rolled up my sleeves and faced the task ahead of me. "Lucie, I'll need you to run outside and get my medical bag from the car. I have a sterilized pack of instruments in it." To this day, I can't explain why I always traveled with a pack of instruments the way other people carry a rabbit's foot.

"Will do," Lucie said, running out the door.

"Françoise…" Françoise had already unfolded a large piece of oilcloth that she tucked under Anne-Marie on the table.

Francoise said, "I expected we would need this. She has had so many of those clots. And her bleeding—so strange. Both bright red and dark."

I froze. I had seen those symptoms before. We nearly lost the patient, and we had a doctor and were in a hospital.

"I can't do this," I said, as much to myself as to Françoise.

I turned to her. "Anne-Marie is in real danger." I shook my head. "I don't know if I can save her."

"You are our only hope."

I had to recognize the truth of that statement. Pull yourself together, Jane!

I found my inner nurse and turned my attention back to where it needed to be. On the patient. Anne-Marie was in a lot of pain.

I reached out and held the young woman's hand. "*Ma chérie. Desolé de te faire du mal. Je veux seulement t'aider*." Anne-Marie was so groggy that I had no idea if she understood my apology for hurting her.

"I don't suppose you have any morphine in your magic bag?" I asked Françoise. "I'm going to need to palpate her abdomen, and that is going to be painful."

Françoise grimaced, "Oh, if only I did. She has been like this for a few days now and all I have is willow bark," she said, reaching into her apron pocket and pulling out some dried pieces of wood. I remembered that aspirin was derived from willow bark.

Lucie came running back, dripping wet, with my medical bag. She had the handful of poppies she'd picked. Françoise handed her a towel to dry her hair and also somehow a glass jar for the poppies. I opened the bag and rifled around until I found my instruments. There was an iron stove with a kettle on it and a stack of wood. "Françoise, can you light the stove so that we can boil some water? We can make a tea from the willow and that will help. Oh, if only we had a hot water bottle."

Françoise smiled at me and pulled a red rubber hot water bottle out of her amazing hamper.

With a crack of lightning, the lights flashed off.

I cried out in fear. Even though in the middle of the day, it was very dark. "Oh, no. Do you have a flashlight? A torch?"

"Better than that," Françoise answered. She turned and struck a piece of flint to light the tapers on the wall sconces, giving the kitchen an eerie flickering light. "Will that be enough?"

"It will have to do. Can you still light the stove?"

She put pieces of wood into the stove and lit them with the flint. The sound of the wood catching fire reassured me, and the warmth it gave off was an immediate antidote to the storm raging outside and to the fear I tried to push away from inside. By a miracle, there was water in the enormous kettle, so Françoise put it on the burner.

"I am not even going to ask you if there is a cup."

Françoise's eyes twinkled, and she went to one of the cupboards, extracted a blue ceramic mug, and placed it on the counter. By now, the storm was raging so hard that daylight had turned to night. Anne-Marie moaned and writhed on the table. We had no time to lose. I wanted to sit down and put my head in my hands and cry, but I realized that Lucie and Françoise—not to mention Anne-Marie—were counting on me to stay calm. So I did.

"Françoise, hold her hand and hold it tight. We'll give her some willow tea as soon as the water boils, but I need to see what we are dealing with." I spoke directly to the nearly unconscious woman whose life was in my hands. I didn't think she was able to hear me, so I didn't bother attempting a translation.

"Anne-Marie, I realize this is terribly painful. You have been very brave. We are going to do everything we can to take care of you and make you comfortable."

I decided to stay calm by going into teacher mode.

"This is a good opportunity to practice," I said to Lucie. "What do we need to know to start?"

Lucie looked toward the ceiling as if the answer were hiding there. "Um. We'd want to determine how far she is in the pregnancy."

"Brilliant," I said, and Lucie beamed.

Anne-Marie couldn't speak, so I turned to Françoise. "How long has it been since *les règles*? Her period," I added for Lucie's benefit.

"About three and a half months," Françoise volunteered.

"All right. So we'd expect a pregnancy of about 12-13 weeks. I'm going to palpate her abdomen. What am I feeling for?" As I had hoped, playing the role of professor was helping me stay in control.

Lucie looked very serious. She remembered our lessons well. "The fundus of the uterus. The rise of the uterus allows you to estimate the length of the pregnancy."

"Exactly," I said. "But let's give her some willow bark tea. Lucie, will you put those pieces of wood into the cup and pour the boiling water over it—careful not to burn your hands. And then will you pour the rest into the hot water bottle so that we can put it on her abdomen while the bark is steeping?"

Lucie nodded and did as I had asked.

I laid the water bottle on Anne-Marie's stomach, and her face relaxed. After a few minutes, she seemed more awake. I helped her sit up to sip the minty-smelling willow tea. With a deep breath, I closed my eyes and summoned the skill of my teachers. Then I held her hand and looked into her teary eyes and said, "*Anne-Marie, n'ayer pas peur. Je suis ici pour vous aider.* I am here to help you."

She whispered, "*Merci.*"

I called on courage to pass through my hands as I put on a glove and slid two fingers into her vagina and placed the other hand on her abdomen to feel the rise of her uterus. As I feared, the pressure made Anne-Marie groan again. When I pressed harder, she cried out. I did my best to ignore her pain. I turned to Lucie and directed her to place her fingers where mine had been.

"What do you feel?" I asked.

"This doesn't seem like twelve weeks, does it? More like eight or nine," Lucie said tentatively.

"Excellent again," I said. "And what does it suggest to you when a woman's uterus is smaller than you expect, considering the date of her last period?"

Lucie bit her top lip. "I remember that when it is larger than it should be according to the date of the last period, that might mean diabetes or hydrocephalus…"

"Correct… and smaller?"

Françoise interrupted. "I don't mean to hurry this class or whatever it is, along, but Anne-Marie is in terrible pain. Can't you just help her and talk about it later?"

That chastened me. Too much time working with patients under anesthesia.

"I apologize, Anne-Marie. Small for the dates might indicate a fetal demise." I explained the medical terms for Françoise in English so as not to frighten Anne-Marie. "This is a dangerous situation in which the fetus has died, but not been expelled from the uterus."

"Oh, I remember," said Lucie. "It is dangerous because the tissue can become necrotic. The woman's body senses the pregnancy as foreign tissue." She looked at me gravely. "In the worst situation, the woman's blood loses its ability to clot," she finished softly.

Françoise looked aghast.

"There is a risk, but I am confident that we can help her. You have gotten her to us quickly."

Two lies—the first was that I was at all confident, and the second was that there was any kind of 'us' to help. I agonized that Dr. Nick and Dr. Levy were not in the next room. There was only me, and I would have to be enough. The fear was unfamiliar—I was usually calm in an emergency—but the memory of another woman with these symptoms flashed in my brain.

Dr. Nick taught me to say the steps out loud. I began, my heart hammering in my chest. "The most important thing is to empty her uterus right away. Then I will massage it to help it return to its normal size." I tried to give Anne-Marie a reassuring smile. "Lucie, will you bring that small table over and open my instrument pack?" Did my voice crack, or was it just the seismic fault in my confidence?

In the background, the rain beat against the windowpanes and struck the ground, releasing the heady scent of earth into the air. I smelled it, even indoors.

I summoned my angels—those ten little girls from my aunt Mathilde's school in Paris who had watched over me all these years. And then, my face calm, my heart pounding, and my brain flashing images of blood transfusions, I turned back to Anne-Marie to save her life.

"Anne-Marie, can you hear me?"

Her response was weak, but she was present.

"*Je suis desolé de vous announcer que votre bébé est mort.*" There was no easy way to tell a woman that her pregnancy was no longer viable and that I had to empty her uterus. "*Je dois vider ton uterus pour te garder en sécurite.*" She closed her eyes and nodded feebly.

I worked hard not to let my fear show, but Lucie knew me well enough to sense it. Lucie became the calm one and helped me as I'd always helped her before. She began persuading me with her voice, as gentle as if she were guiding a scared horse.

"Jane—she is likely just having a bit of retained tissue. She isn't running a fever. Look and see if she is dilated—you can probably do a sharp curettage without even using another instrument. With the willow and this hot water bottle, she will be fine."

It shocked me to realize how thoroughly Lucie had absorbed my lessons. She shamed me out of my reluctance. I went to the kitchen, poured some of the hot water into the sink, and scrubbed my hands with a bar of what appeared to be homemade lye soap—not the perfect choice, but the best I had. Lucie brought iodine and sterile gloves. She opened the wrapping, and I slid my hands into the gloves. I had to admit, she was an excellent assistant. She carried a milking stool she found in another room and placed it in front of the table where Anne-Marie lay, crying softly. Françoise lit an oil lantern that she'd pulled out of the cabinet and set it on the floor next to me. Then she and Lucie moved Anne-Marie toward the end of the table and held her legs open. Lucie had put the iodine and instruments on a small table next to the stool so that I could easily reach everything I needed. She placed an enamel bowl on the floor. A tiny part of my brain was busy wondering where all the kitchenware had come from!

As I cleaned Anne-Marie with iodine and cotton balls, I made a mental note of the things that would have made it easier—an actual exam table, stirrups to hold the patient's legs, a better lighting system, antiseptic, and pain relief medicine. These thoughts calmed me and helped me go through the familiar motions. Anne-Marie had passed large clots, and the os of her cervix was partially open. I could see that she was well into the process of miscarrying. Just as Lucie had suggested, I was able to insert a narrow curette, an instrument with an edge that allowed me to remove tissue from the uterine wall. There was so much blood. Even in the dim light, I could see that the scarlet of the blood matched the scarlet of Lucie's poppies that Françoise had placed on the counter. As crazy as it seems, there was something comforting about the beautiful flowers being the same color as the frightening blood. With the next cramp, she passed another clot and grayish embryonic tissue, which was developed to about eight weeks. When I finished, I nodded, and Lucie and Françoise scooted Anne-Marie back on the table. Lucie put a cotton pad between her legs. I massaged her uterus firmly, but as gently as I could. She moaned again, but I knew the massage helped with the cramping as the low sound faded to a whimper. Françoise refilled the hot water bottle and put it on her stomach. And we were done.

My knees nearly gave way. I almost wept with relief to see that her uterus was contracting. And more important, her blood was clotting, so she hadn't developed the disorder that could have killed her. I picked up the enamel bowl to examine the tissue—everything was there. I placed the embryo in a small glass bowl with a bit of water so that Anne-Marie could see it later if she wanted. Its dark gray color confirmed my suspicion that the pregnancy had already died inside her. The embryo was a little less than an inch long. There was a visible skull and tiny limb buds that would have become arms and legs. As Lucie looked over my shoulder, I wondered what she was thinking. I hadn't asked how far her aborted pregnancy was, and I knew she might be having some feelings about seeing this embryo. A conversation for later.

"Go with love, little spirit," I said under my breath. "Go with love."

CHAPTER 13

C'EST FINI

The three of us helped Anne-Marie get off the table and shuffle into the bedroom. Françoise carried the lantern and spread the oilcloth on the bed before we helped Anne-Marie lie down. Lucie covered her with a blanket that she'd found folded in the chest of drawers.

Françoise bent over her niece. *"C'est fini, ma chère*. It is all done. And," here she glanced at me and I nodded in reassurance, "everything is good. Now you must rest."

The woman cried softly. "It is gone?"

"It is gone. I am so sorry," Françoise said.

Anne-Marie wailed as if everything lovely had been stripped from the world. I was completely taken off guard. The depth of her anguish frightened me. I wasn't used to working with women who wanted to keep their babies.

"You will try again, my dear. There will be another chance." Françoise stroked Anne-Marie's arm, and the tears abated. "Sleep now, *Chérie*," she said.

Lucie, Françoise, and I tidied up quietly. Lightning flashed. Thunder cracked. So we drew the curtains closed to preserve the somber quiet. Through it, Anne-Marie slept. We went into the kitchen and closed the door.

"Jane, je vous remercie," Françoise said, hugging me. "Anne-Marie has been married for only one year. She had a devastating miscarriage a few months ago. She was excited to realize that she might be pregnant again—she told me that she felt her body changing. This time, when the terrible clots began, she came to me. The village doctor had traveled to another town, so I had no idea what to do. Then I remembered that Claude said a car had entered the main gate, and I hoped that Dr. Levy would be here. But you didn't need him! You did it all yourself!"

"I am a nurse. Since the war, I have worked for the Navy in Japan, helping women who needed abortions." I turned to Lucie. "Françoise and I met many years ago. In fact, her parents gave me this convent."

"Jane, I must tell her the story," Françoise said. "The wonderful Dr. Levy freed me from a pregnancy at a most difficult and dangerous time, and Jane helped me enormously. For this reason, my parents gave her this convent as a gift. Our dairy farm is next door, and Anne-Marie and her husband live in a small house on the farm. And Jane, I was able to marry my Claude—the man I loved so many years ago. The German soldier who wanted to marry me was killed in Russia. I stayed unmarried until after the war, when Claude returned. We didn't have any children because Claude was hurt in the camp." There was pain in her eyes. "But it is all right. Our nieces and nephews visit us, and we are very happy." Françoise sighed deeply and turned to Lucie. "For all these years, I have thought of Jane as my guardian angel. And now I learn that she is serving as guardian angel for women—where did you say?"

"Japan," I said.

"Japan? It is legal in Japan?"

"Well, not exactly. But since the war, the Americans have been in charge. They decided to help women, and that's what I have been doing."

"I know they were a most terrible enemy, so it must be with great kindness and forgiveness that you help them. The women there are most fortunate to have you," she said. She turned and looked at Lucie. "*Chérie*, would you go to check how is Anne-Marie?"

"Of course. Shall I wake her just long enough to check her bleeding? And re-heat the hot water bottle?"

"Yes. Good girl," I said.

As Lucie left the room carrying the kettle, Françoise put her hand on my arm.

"Please forgive me, Jane, for bringing Anne-Marie to you. I saw your face. I remember that fear. I just hoped this was different—I believed with all my heart that this was not so bad as Mimi."

"Françoise—no need to apologize. I cannot allow something terrible that happened more than a decade ago to control me—something none of us could have done anything about. And you were right to bring Anne-Marie. She is lucky you are her aunt—and I am lucky you are my friend."

Françoise leaned over and hugged me again.

I laughed. "I am so glad to know what has become of you, Françoise. I think of you often. I am so grateful to have this inviting place to come home to. Is it you who has made the old convent so lovely?"

Françoise smiled. "Me and Claude. He never had a chance to thank you, but it is because of you and Dr. Levy that we are together. And it is because of your mother and the wonderful doctor that it has been so beautifully renovated. After your father died, your mother began to send money with instructions to make the repairs and order the furnishings. She wanted it to be a surprise. Dr. Levy coordinated everything. He hoped you would one day come back to France and make this your home, so when he told us you were coming, we redoubled our efforts to make it perfect."

"Ah, Levy. That rascal! And all the time he was telling me the cloisters had probably fallen to the ground. And, tell me, did Lucie know?"

"*Bien Sûr!* She is the one who told me how to furnish and what colors you would like."

"Ah, now everything makes sense."

"Now that you see how welcoming it is, will you stay, Jane?"

"Of course." I said, giving her a big hug. "And your parents?" I asked, a bit afraid to hear the answer.

"Ah, they died years ago. My father just couldn't bear to see what had become of our country. He served under Pétain in the Great War, so he nearly worshipped him as many people did. It broke his heart to see the French collaborate. And you met my mother, so you can imagine that she was not suited to take care of herself. By early 1944, they were both gone. I wish my father had lived to see the liberation. The day they tore down the swastikas was worth living for."

"Francoise," I said, "I am so sorry. And so sorry that you and Claude weren't able to—"

"Shh. Some things are not meant to be. I turned over that sorrow to Our Lady. You remember—*Notre Dame de la Grâce Perpétuelle*? I have never forgotten your voice as you guided me through the abortion that day," Françoise said, musing on the past. "I was so frightened. Your words calmed me and assured me God would not punish me. But tell me again, where is our dear Dr. Levy?"

"Levy is in Paris with Lucie's fiancé, Oliver. We agreed that they would come if it turned out that the convent was habitable—but that is the joke, isn't it?" I said, laughing.

Françoise smiled. "*Ah, oui.*"

"I guess they will arrive tomorrow or the next day, depending on the storm. Where are Claude and Anne-Marie's husband?"

"Claude and Thomas took the big wagon to sell cheese at a fair about a day's drive from here. Anne-Marie seemed fine when they left. They will be back in two days' time. So for now, it is just us women. Thank goodness the cows are in the barn and our young helper will do the milking tomorrow morning. The pony is safe under the *porte cochére*, and we are cozy inside, so all is well."

Lucie came back into the kitchen. She had heard the tail end of our conversation.

"Lucie—how is Anne-Marie?" I asked.

"She's good. Just spotty bleeding, and she said her cramps are better. She was back asleep before I left the room."

"That is a big relief!" I said with a deep, deep sigh. "I am going to look for the bottle of Cabernet Levy packed in the trunk. This is a night for a glass of wine for each of us—yes, Lucie, even for you. Françoise tells me that you were part of fixing up the convent, so thank you." I wrapped my arms around her. "No wonder you were so certain that you would be able to have the wedding here. How did you and Levy keep this a secret for so long?"

Lucie shrugged. "I wanted to make you happy after all you have done for me."

"I am very happy. And now we will plan your wedding!"

Françoise gave us a tour of the convent, beaming with pride at the four comfortable bedrooms she had outfitted with furniture and linens. I was still shaking my head at how the crumbling, abandoned convent I saw a decade ago had been transformed into such an elegant home. And that my mother had been thinking about me all this time. I was so happy she'd be seeing the results of her generous investment. When we came to one closed door, Françoise paused. I could have sworn I saw a look pass between her and Lucie, but before I could ask a question, Lucie said, "Claude is still finishing the plumbing in here."

We didn't have to brave the storm to get our food from the car because Françoise had everything we could want in her bottomless basket. It was late when we sat down for a glass of wine, with bread and pungent cheese. Anne-Marie was sleeping. Lucie looked as dazed as I felt, so I was not surprised when she kissed me on the cheek and excused herself to go to bed.

Sitting alone with Françoise, I finally let down. My shoulders ached with stress. I kneaded my neck and slowed my breathing. I had not imagined I would ever encounter Françoise again. We were the same women we had been a decade before when I helped Dr. Levy perform an abortion for a nineteen-year-old in a blue pinafore; and we were also completely different. The war had intervened. Time had intervened. The world itself was different. We had both grown up.

"Jane, you saved Anne-Marie's life," Françoise said, once again, this time a little shyly. "I have no right to ask anything more, and yet…"

"What is it?"

"Anne-Marie wanted this baby so badly. After her first miscarriage, she asked me over and over what she did to anger God so much that He would take her child. Like so many others in our community, she is Catholic and, just as I did, has learned her fill of lies about how bad and dirty women are. There is a part of her that believes she is being punished for loving her husband—for sex. You understand?"

"Of course." I understood all too well. The language of shame was universal among women, whether they whispered it in English, French, Spanish, or Japanese.

"How can I help?" I asked gently.

"I want Anne-Marie to have what you gave me—*Notre Dame de la Grâce Perpétuelle*."

I started to protest.

"Really, Jane," Françoise insisted. "*Notre Dame* has been with me all these years—the words you said to me in her name. You changed everything for me. You allowed me to heal. I forgave myself for all of it. That's what I want for Anne-Marie."

"I can talk with her," I said. "But it won't be quite the same. You were an impressionable young girl…"

"Anne-Marie is an impressionable young girl," Françoise said.

"But you thought I was a nun," I countered.

"*Exactement*," Françoise said, looking smug. "That is exactly what I want for her. You may think I am a silly fool," she continued, "But when we were emptying the convent, I found a cabinet full of old nun's habits. I couldn't bear to throw them away. I cleaned them as well as I could and put them back." She opened a cupboard in the kitchen and took out a folded garment that was all too familiar.

"Françoise, no. Put that thing away. It's been years since we have seen each other, and I have learned a lot. Women must forgive *themselves*. I will not put on a costume to trick Anne-Marie into thinking I'm a nun—an emissary from God saying she is absolved for the mythical sin of being a woman."

"Don't be angry, Jane. It's not that simple. From her earliest years, Anne-Marie has been told her sin is being a woman. That belief was etched into her heart and her mind. That's what happened to me, too. When I met you, I thought my life was over. Nineteen. Pregnant. Promised in marriage to a German commandant. Never to see my beloved Claude again. The only way I even had a *chance* of healing was to receive grace from a sister. Somehow, Dr. Levy understood that. And somehow you spoke in the voice of Our Lady. *Notre Dame* meant everything to me." Her gaze deepened. She reached out and took my hand. "Before my abortion, I tried to take my own life."

I pressed her hand to my heart. "Oh, Françoise."

"It was hearing the words you said to me—hearing that I was forgiven—that there was grace, that called me back. That allowed me to imagine I had value. And I could never have heard it if it hadn't come from a sister."

"But…"

"Anne-Marie is lost. There will be a time to teach her, but won't you give her the grace she can't yet give herself?"

I stroked the ancient black serge of the robes and smelled the familiar starch in the collar and headpiece. I sat up straighter as I remembered standing tall in my uniform, a flying buttress to protect ten little girls—girls who walked in two straight lines behind me as we passed the Eiffel Tower. *Was this so different? Another lost little girl who needed protection. Could I release my righteousness and give what was needed?*

"All right. I will do it just this once because I love you and I know you love her. But if you laugh at me..."

CHAPTER 14

BACK IN THE HABIT

By the following morning, the storm had passed, and the electricity came back on. I found myself in a slightly scratchy, musty, exceedingly short, black habit with a white wimple—my hair tucked in a cap. Sitting by the bed on a kitchen stool, I tried to describe the ceremony to Lucie. She asked, "Won't Anne-Marie realize it is you wearing those robes?"

"I can't explain it. The habit has a power of its own. While I am wearing these robes, she won't see *me* at all. She'll see a sister—someone she trusts."

Françoise perched at the end of the bed and Lucie sat on a chair across the room. I gently woke Anne-Marie, and when she looked at me with such hope, I realized Françoise was right—she needed Our Lady.

"Ma chére — tu es bonne — tu es pardonée completement, tu es aimée par le seigneur, Il a choisi de te guérir," you are good, you are forgiven, God loves you, and he has chosen to heal you.

Next, I spoke the words I said to Françoise during her abortion.

"Hail, holy Queen
Mother of Mercy—
Our Lady of Perpetual Grace—
Honor our love and courage—
Remember our goodness.
Show unto us
Thy forgiveness
And thy mercy."

Anne-Marie smiled at me. "Sister—you are here—you are giving me grace?"

I smiled back. "I don't need to give you something you already have. You *are* grace. I am here to remind you that you are good and worthy. This loss is not a punishment, it is simply the way of life. I hope that someday you will have a child to care for with your whole heart. The angels have taken this one back into their loving arms."

Although I was self-conscious about impersonating a religious figure, I wondered if Anne-Marie would ever have gotten what she needed without hearing it from a priest or nun. She would never hear it from them. I loved being part of something sacred—giving a woman a sense of her own goodness until she was able to give it to herself.

The following morning I woke early and dressed in my civilian clothes. We ate a light breakfast, supplemented by the cheese and salami Lucie and I had in the car. Anne-Marie was sad, but relieved to know that the baby had already died and we'd only removed it from her body. We wrapped the embryo in an embroidered handkerchief that Françoise found in her basket and took it to the churchyard. Anne-Marie insisted on digging the tiny grave herself. The three of us witnessed the burial. She kneeled on the moist ground and used the only tool we had—a large spoon—to dig into the dirt softened by the heavy rain. She placed the handkerchief and its precious contents into the hole so reverently that I sensed the power of an ancient, sacred ritual. Françoise sang a French lullaby, though the only words I understood were, "Good night dear treasure…," the tenderness in her voice made me cry. We left Anne-Marie to commune with the dream of a baby that was not to be.

I hadn't slept well, and I felt exhausted. I leaned back in the chair. As I fell in and out of sleep, I heard Françoise and Lucie talking. When Lucie described Oliver, I chastised myself for being so negative about him. In her eyes, he was a prince—the smartest, kindest man ever. Lucie said that Oliver took good care of her and made her feel safe. In return, Françoise shared that she met Claude and fell in love with him when she was also just a teenager. Françoise explained her family had promised she would marry a German commandant to protect them. She became pregnant with Claude, so needed an abortion to keep her and her family safe from Nazi retribution. I smiled to know that she and Claude found a way to be together after the war. I slept through the rest of the conversation, awaking in time for a light dinner. Anne-Marie joined us. Her reticence set the tone for a quiet meal. We retired early.

The next morning, Claude and Thomas appeared at the convent. Thomas and Anne-Marie went outside to sit together in the garden. Through the window, I saw them crying. He put his arms around her.

Claude brought in eggs and salty bacon that they purchased at the fair. While Françoise cooked breakfast, he and I talked. I was so happy to thank him for his wonderful work on the convent. Claude was a mason as well as a master plumber, an engineer, and an electrician. From what Françoise said, he could build or fix just about anything. After breakfast, as we washed dishes and listened to Claude's tales of a bridge he was helping to construct, Oliver and Levy drove up. I saw by their smiles that they were very pleased with their surprise. Everyone knew except me!

Anne-Marie and Thomas came inside. They both looked at peace. We made introductions, and Thomas took my hand and thanked me profusely for saving his wife. Françoise told them to take the small wagon—that she would come home later with Claude—and they bade us farewell.

After Anne-Marie and Thomas left, I took Levy aside to tell him about Anne-Marie's miscarriage. He looked frightened, and then relieved.

"Jane, how did you do it? How did you take care of her?"

"I quickly realized the situation. I have never handled this myself—let alone without a hospital and transfusion available—but I did what I learned to do. And thankfully it was all right."

Levy pulled me to him in an unusually spontaneous embrace. "I am so sorry I wasn't here. It was my idea that you and Lucie should come first to be surprised."

"It's all right. You couldn't have known there would be an emergency. And I was certainly surprised. The convent is exquisite."

"I'm sure Françoise told you that your mother paid for all of it. When your father died, he left more than enough for her to live on. Your mother asked me how she might share the funds with you. By then you were in nursing school in the Navy and it didn't seem as though you needed money for your day-to-day expenses. You had spoken so often about the convent that she was delighted when I suggested we have it restored. Françoise sent me photographs of the progress of the restoration, and I shared them with your mother. Sylvia will be so thrilled to see it all when she comes for the wedding," he added. "Don't worry. I didn't tell her it was going to be a clinic. I said it was going to be a school."

"What? What do you mean, it is going to be a clinic?"

"I thought that's what you wanted. Lucie said so."

My face flushed. "Well, that comes as a surprise." For a moment, I wasn't able to speak. A clinic. A clinic? Right here? I *had* told Lucie how much I wanted to be able to do my work. I couldn't help but think about it. Not just an abortion practice—a clinic of my own. Where I would be in charge of making the policies. Where I would take the risks. A frisson of excitement coursed through me. But abortion was as illegal in France as in Connecticut. I shook my head. "We'll have to talk about that later. I can't believe you managed to keep this secret from me. And you berated Lucie for her *fairy tale*. I'll bet she was bursting to tell me the news. Françoise bringing Anne-Marie was a complete surprise. I didn't know if I'd be able to manage it without you. Thank goodness I trained Lucie to help. She was wonderful."

"Sounds as though you handled it perfectly," Levy said.

"I was scared. And I couldn't help but think of Mimi."

"I think of her often. And I am often scared," he said, putting his arm around me. "What we have chosen to do involves great responsibility. You can't save every patient, but you saved Anne-Marie."

CHAPTER 15

UNDER THE CHUPPAH

Once I saw how the convent looked, I began to be excited about the wedding. We drove back to Paris, gathered our belongings, and moved everything into the convent.

Oliver's dermatology residency training was in Paris. He made a daily commute, walking to the train station, traveling to Paris, and reversing his travels on the way home. Lucie complained that he returned too tired to pay attention to her. That was not her only complaint. Unfortunately, they conducted many of their heated arguments in the garden where Levy and I could not block out the sound. A bone of contention was the guest list—the only thing we asked them to handle. One evening after dinner, they argued about Oliver's plan to invite his parents' friends.

"I am certain they won't come," he said. "Well, they probably won't—but they will give us great gifts, and it will benefit my career to stay in their good graces."

"I hate it that you are inviting them simply to get something out of it. That is so mercenary," Lucie said.

"My dear, that's life," Oliver replied. Yet another conversation that added to my misgivings about the suitability of their union. But that, as Lucie made abundantly clear, was none of my business. The stubbornness they had in common made their arguments miserable. For Lucie, every aspect of life was a competition between them. For Oliver, every conversation was a test of his manhood. It was maddening.

Françoise and I volunteered to handle the accommodations and food. We had nine empty bedrooms at the cloister, and Françoise and Claude had three more bedrooms at their farmhouse if we needed them. We only requested that Lucie give us a firm number of required rooms by June twentieth so that we could get the requisite furniture by loan or rental. My mother, and the Goldfarbs, and Oliver's parents and uncle, another prominent physician, were coming. I was delighted to learn that Socorro would be coming from Peru, and Paulette from Italy—the only two of the original ten girls with whom Lucie had stayed in touch. I considered asking whether I might invite Dr. Nick, but I decided against it. This was their day, and they had never even met Nick. He asked about the wedding in his letters, but I resolved to make do with sending him photographs.

Lucie insisted that a rabbi be part of the proceedings. "I am not going to turn my back on my heritage after so many people died for it during the war," she declared.

"But what about all the things you said about not wanting your name to sound Jewish?" I asked.

"I am a bride, so I don't have to be consistent," was her nonsensical reply.

So Claude and Levy set about building a chuppah. Lucie remained as delighted as Oliver was uninterested.

"The chuppah is important, Oliver," she said. "It symbolizes God's presence at the wedding and in our home. It is very important to me to get married in the garden under the chuppah." He acquiesced.

Oliver only went to church on Christmas and Easter, but he still had no interest in changing his allegiances. In those days, inter-faith marriages were very rare. Lucie's insistence on having a rabbi, and Oliver's insistence on having an Episcopal priest, made quite a challenge. With a bit of difficulty, Oliver's parents located an Episcopalian cleric who lived in Toulouse, who reluctantly agreed to be part of a mixed ceremony. Levy found a French rabbi willing to 'share' as we jokingly put it.

Françoise took Lucie to visit the cloistered nuns at Alençon who make world-renowned lace, and they returned with a carpetbag full of fabric. Every morning Lucie appeared at breakfast with a different piece draped over her shoulders as she made the impossible decision of which piece to take to the seamstress for the bodice of her wedding gown. If only she had chosen her husband as carefully as she chose the lace.

CHAPTER 16

GERTRUDE

Our Lady, June 1951

Françoise seemed to be dearest friends with everyone—not only everyone in the village, but everyone! A few days after we had moved into the convent, she told me that she had a friend who needed my help.

"I'm sorry to ask—I realize the wedding is only a few days away—but this woman needs you. Her name is Gertrude. I have known her for years. She is a good woman, but she already has four children and she and her husband are just scraping by to feed those. She can't afford another baby, and she doesn't want one. Will you help her?"

"We are not equipped to help her. Besides, abortion is against the law. We're about to host a wedding! I'm not going to threaten my safety, as well as Levy's and Lucie's. Can't she find someone in Paris?"

Lucie came into the room, overhearing the last part. "What are you protecting me from?"

"Oh, nothing. Just a figure of speech," I said.

She turned to Françoise and said, "It seems that my old teacher, who spoke often of the importance of honesty, has lost her way."

Obviously in distress, Françoise opened her mouth and then closed it again.

"Now I am sure it is something important. What were you two talking about?" Lucie asked.

"Françoise has a friend who needs help. She mistakenly imagined I could help her," I said.

Lucie looked at Françoise. "Your friend needs an abortion?"

Françoise took a deep breath and said, "Yes. But I didn't mean to cause trouble. Jane, you told me this was your work in Japan, so I just thought you would continue it."

"Isn't this just what you wanted?" Lucie asked. "Why do you suppose I was so persistent about getting married in France? You told me about your dream of helping women 'without interference'—isn't that how you said it? I was certain the convent would be perfect. Did you change your mind?"

By then, Levy and Oliver had wandered into the kitchen looking for lunch. Levy launched into the conversation.

"Why not, Jane? We can do this for the woman's safety. Heaven knows what she would find in Paris." He sliced sausage to eat on a baguette with Françoise's aromatic homemade mayonnaise and some grainy mustard.

Oliver put a piece of leftover chicken on a plate. He poured a small glass of white wine. "I, for one, am glad to see that you have come to your senses. Lucie told me about the guillotine. Levy, would you put us all in danger? I want *nothing* to do with this." He huffed as he took his food outdoors to eat in the garden.

"But no one would be looking way out here," Françoise insisted. "This is a whole new nation since the war—a new constitution. Surely it is just a matter of time before women will be free again. We'd just be ahead of the game."

"It is still illegal, and, to repeat myself, we are not equipped," I said.

Lucie gave a mischievous look. "Perhaps it is time to show her."

"Show me what?"

"I did what you wanted. I found the orchestra so you can be a conductor again!"

Lucie took my hand and drew me down the hallway to the last bedroom. She opened the door to reveal a fully equipped procedure room adjacent to a laboratory. Next to the examining table on the floor sat the Uterine Suction Apparatus, nicknamed USA, that my colleague Dr. Nick invented to make abortion easier, quicker, and safer. The mysterious room Lucie had said was still being worked on.

"But how?"

Lucie smiled. "I found Dr. Nick's phone number in your book. He was thrilled you would be working again when I explained we had a safe place. It took weeks for the machine to come from Japan. He sent it before we even boarded the ship."

"I ordered the examining table from Paris. It has everything, even storage," Levy said with a grin.

"They delivered the table the day I asked you to go to the market with me," Françoise added. They were all in on Lucie's plan.

I wanted to explode in frustration, but they had such hopeful faces.

"This is wonderful. Perfect. But we can't use it here," I said.

Lucie's mouth hung open. "But why not? You said that in Japan it was illegal but they let you. Couldn't it be that way here?"

"It was illegal according to the country's laws. But the United States military was in charge, and I told you they made a different rule out of necessity because people would starve if the birth rate had stayed at the pre-war level."

Levy broke in. "But you know as well as I do that abortion is always out of necessity. Have you forgotten the women? Their stories? This is the perfect place to provide care. This is why we got so excited about renovating it for you."

"You are all in on this scheme, too? Just like the renovations?"

"It's my fault, Jane. I told Nick it's what you wanted. I'm sorry," Lucie said, near tears.

"And Levy, you are saying this is what my *mother* wanted?" I asked.

"Uh. Well, no. When we started, we didn't realize your mother was so against abortion."

"Now you do realize that. And she is the one paying the bills. Do you think that is fair to her?"

"Must we tell her?" Lucie asked, wincing and shrugging her shoulders.

An uncomfortable silence ensued. One more secret from my mother. And this time it was using her money to bankroll something she abhors. How could that be all right? It was a bold new idea to me—this plan they had been hatching for a year. Why had I ever told Lucie I wanted a place to do abortions?

I took a breath and said, "Thank you so much for wanting to make my dream come true." I took Lucie's hand. "But we can't do it. We are out in the country, but not in Outer Mongolia. The police have cars, and unlike us, they have telephones. A bunch of strangers moving into the old convent would immediately be suspected. No. I am afraid there is nowhere on God's green earth that I can do the work of my heart without authority—without the interference of men's laws."

"Maybe you could help this one woman, Jane." Françoise looked nervous. "I shouldn't have, but I gave my friend Gertrude the idea you would help. Her sister wants to come with her. I am sorry I didn't ask you."

Against my better judgement—or more honestly, because I wanted to do it just one time—I acquiesced. When the others were in the kitchen, I sat in the procedure room and thought about all the women I had worked with and the complications of their lives. I wondered about Françoise's friend Gertrude and her story. I can't imagine what I would have missed if I had said no.

Even though we were immersed in plans for the wedding, we put Gertrude and her sister in one of the twin bedrooms.

Levy had an appointment in Paris he couldn't miss, so he left in the morning and wished us well. We had no procedure for keeping records, so I took Gertrude's medical history without making notes. I still relied on what I had learned from Levy so many years ago. The first thing was to appraise the patient with a critical eye. Gertrude was twenty-eight. She was thin and haggard with a dull, hollowed-out expression. It was an expression I had seen on the faces of men returning from prison camps. As Françoise told me, Gertrude had borne four children with no complications and had no medical problems except for being an exhausted mother. According to her last period, she was about seven weeks pregnant. Gertrude answered my questions in a flat, listless voice. This was the kind of patient I taught Dr. Nick to be wary of because their emotions were so hard to read. I had no idea what to do about my misgivings.

As I talked with Gertrude, my attention kept wandering to her sister. Sophie was about thirty—tall and elegant with fine bones. She had light blonde hair. I couldn't tear myself away from her electric blue eyes. The feeling I had in my stomach every time I heard Sophie's voice made me determined to stay far away from her.

Our plan was to have them be at the convent for three days—the first day to make preparations, the second day for the abortion, and the third day for recovery time. As far as Gertrude's husband was aware, she was on a much-needed religious retreat. His parents had come from Marseille to take care of the children. We completed the interview. Gertrude answered every question clearly and concisely. In spite of my concerns, I could find no reason not to go ahead with the abortion. I recognized that sleep would go a long way to improving Gertrude's state of mind, so I sent her to bed when we were finished talking.

Regardless of my determination to be aloof, Sophie seemed to be everywhere I looked. She was very cordial, and I am sure I seemed horribly ill-mannered.

"I am so glad to finally meet you," she said. "Francoise has been talking about the angel in her life for years."

"Well, I am no angel," I said tersely. "Sorry, I need to attend to… to something in the garden," I said, turning my back and going out the door.

Later that evening, Sophie insisted on helping Lucie with the dishes. I sat in the next room where I could overhear, but not be seen.

While she dried, Sophie talked about her life. I was fascinated.

"I was a professor of English literature at the Sorbonne. When our mother got sick, I left my job. It only made sense for me to care for her—after all, Gertrude has four children she loves but never really wanted."

"Whoa. That's quite a thing to say," Lucie commented.

"It's the truth. A truth she may not even have told herself. I have learned about telling the truth the hard way. When our mother first got sick, she and I were so uncomfortable together. We had never been honest with each other. We walked around on eggshells. Finally, it was too hard to keep secrets. Little by little, we shared our real lives. And we started to tell the truth—big truths and small truths. She told me that she wasn't afraid to die, but she was scared to leave me and Gertrude. I told her that I didn't like the rhubarb pie I had complimented her on all my life." Sophie gave a hollow laugh. "Mother told me that when she was in severe pain, she needed to be alone. I told her I was afraid of who I would be without her. Big truths and little truths. It transformed me. I can't lie anymore. I don't want to."

Overhearing Sophie made my stomach turn over. After all, some lies are inevitable.

"Mother died about two months ago, and I have been unsure of my next step ever since."

"Oh, Sophie, I am so sorry." Lucie said.

"Thank you. That is why this pregnancy has been so complicated for Gertrude. She confided in me that she felt guilty ending a life so soon after our mother lost hers."

"Goodness, she didn't tell Jane that."

"I know. Gertrude wants to make it seem that everything is very simple. But it's not. Maybe she was hoping that Jane really was an angel, and that she would wave a magic wand and make everything all right. I am so sad when I think about what Gertie was like when we were kids. She was a delightful, independent girl. She used to sing all the time. She hasn't sung for years. I'm afraid she sees her children as burdens, although she'd never complain about them. And she can never tell her husband about this. Jean-Jacques is a very pious Catholic. She adores him, so keeping a secret from him is weighing on her."

"Sophie, this is important. We need to tell Jane."

"Will you tell her?" Sophie implored. "I don't think Jane likes me very much. I don't want to intrude, but this has been troubling Gertrude. She is very private, so I'm not sure she will talk about it. You know the Catholic Church. Our priest used to say, 'We care for their souls from birth so that they will not stray.'" Sophie rolled her eyes. "The problem is that living real life and not straying are often in conflict."

"I'm Jewish—at least by heritage—so fortunately I have a different kind of guilt," Lucie said.

"You are lucky in that," Sophie said, "Although it is a bit strange to say that a Jewish woman is lucky after all your people have been through."

Lucie sounded serious. "You are so right. I was just a child when the Nazis occupied Paris. Jane and Dr. Levy rescued me, so I was safe in America with my adoptive parents, Sadie and Hymie Goldfarb, for the rest of the war. And I was also a bit oblivious. Sometimes I forget what it was like here."

"I didn't know your story. I am fascinated by all of this—and the convent. How did Jane and her husband come to be here?" Sophie asked.

"Her husband?" Lucie asked, looking surprised. "Oh, you mean Dr. Levy. No, they are not married. They are good friends and they work together."

"I noticed her diamond ring. Is Jane engaged?" Sophie asked nonchalantly.

"Um... no. That ring was a gift from an old friend."

"And the cloisters?" Sophie continued.

"It is all a long story, and it is Jane's story. I'm sure she would be happy to tell you," Lucie said.

"I don't want to bother her. I don't think she likes me," Sophie repeated softly. "I must be terribly in the way."

I cringed when Sophie repeated herself.

"Oh, I am sure she likes you," Lucie said. "And you are not in the way at all. You have been very helpful. And Jane... well, Jane is a bit... well, she is complicated. Anyway, *I* like you," Lucie said. I could hear her wiping her hands on her apron and embracing the older woman.

"I hope our being here isn't too much of an imposition just before your wedding," Sophie said. "I've been thinking about how I might thank you. There's a poem by Yeats I think you'd love. I've written it down for you."

"Thank you so much." There was silence as Lucie read the poem. "Oh, Sophie. This is so beautiful. I might even have it read aloud during the wedding."

The water swished in the sink as Lucie and Sophie finished washing in silence. I heard the clatter as they placed dishes on the shelves. Sophie said, "I am going to tiptoe into our room so that I won't wake Gertrude. This is the first real rest she has had in a long time."

CHAPTER 17

I WAS *NOT* EAVESDROPPING

Lucie puttered around for a moment and then called out, "Jaa-aane. I know you are in there. Are you eavesdropping? Come in and drink a glass of wine with me."

I was embarrassed to have been caught. I went into the kitchen carrying a sheaf of papers. I plunked them on the table and Lucie poured me a glass of wine.

"I was *not* eavesdropping," I said, trying to convince myself. "I was working on some… well, I was working…" I ended there.

Lucie sipped her wine. "Oh good. Working. Well, that's nice. I hope you overheard what Sophie said. She is such a lovely woman, and you have been so rude to her."

"Rude? That's a bit strong. I am busy. Do you expect me to entertain all our guests?"

"Jane, it's not too strong. You have been rude, and that's not like you. You would never let me behave that way. Why don't you like her?"

"I never said I didn't like her. Why are you saying that?" I asked.

"*I* like her *so* much," Lucie said. "She would be a wonderful friend for you. I am sure you are lonely sometimes, even though you won't admit it."

"Well, thank you for looking out for my social life," I said, more sharply than I intended.

"Don't be like that," she said.

"I'm sorry," I said, anxious to change the subject. "All that aside, I am very concerned about the things she told you about Gertrude. I worried about her at first, but then she seemed so certain. I can sit down with her and ask about all of it, but I'm not sure how I'll get her to talk about her doubts."

Lucie put the glass down. "Françoise would tell you what to do."

I anticipated her next suggestion. "Don't even say it. The habit. I'm still uncomfortable about pretending to be someone I am not in order to manipulate a woman's feelings."

"But Jane—look what it did for Anne-Marie. I wouldn't have believed it myself if I hadn't seen it. She needed to hear from Our Lady of Perpetual

Grace. Where else can Gertrude experience grace? Not from herself—that's for sure. Not from the priest who is living in her head." Lucie was visibly agitated.

"I'll consider it."

Lucie got up and said, "Goodnight, 'Our Lady.'" She kissed me on top of my head. "See you in the morning." She blew me another kiss as she left the room.

Cheeky child, I said to myself. But as I finished my wine, I found that it wasn't Lucie or Gertrude on my mind. It was Sophie. For most of my life, I accepted the fact that I would be alone. I knew the word 'spinster' before I was eleven. I was too tall—too opinionated—too independent, too strange. Not, in other words, wife material. Fortunately, I enjoy my own company, and getting lost in books never seemed like a privation. I had one very painful exception to the rule that ended in disaster. Betty. After her, I gave up on love.

Yet, there I sat with Sophie on my mind.

CHAPTER 18

OUT OF THE HABIT

In my dream, I walked along a well-worn path at dawn. As I came over a hill, a pasture of long grass dotted with daisies appeared. There was a gathering—a circle of women holding hands and singing. As I approached, they parted to make a place for me. I clasped the hands of the women on either side and began to scan the circle. The women were different sizes and heights with skins of many hues in a variety of garb of all colors. I was surprised to see Françoise as the nineteen-year-old girl I met when Dr. Levy did her abortion. She wore a pinafore and frilly white gloves, her long blond hair held back with a band. I had forgotten how young she was. She smiled back at me. Next to Françoise was Kikuyo, a geisha I met in Kyoto. Next to her stood Catalina, a Mexican migrant worker from the Naval clinic in California. We nodded in recognition. Then Charlotte, Alicia, and Mimi. One by one I recognized women from Paris, from Alameda, and from Kyoto. All women I had helped with abortions. And finally, at my right hand was Lucie, who also belonged in this group of wise women.

I woke with a start, knowing exactly what to do. I dressed quickly and took the habit from the closet. By the time I reached the kitchen where Lucie and Françoise were drinking coffee, my plan was hatched.

"Good morning," I nearly sang, aware I was different from my usual only partly awake morning self.

Françoise looked suspicious. "Good morning, yourself. And where have you put our dear friend Jane?"

Lucie batted her arm. "Don't be mean, Françoise. Jane can be sunny in the morning if she wants to." Then she turned to me and wrinkled her brow. "She is right, Jane. What is going on?"

I took a seat at the table.

"I had a dream that made me realize something."

"What?" Lucie said.

"It's about you. You are ready."

"What is she ready for?" Françoise asked. "You are talking riddles."

"Lucie is ready to work with women. *She* should talk with Gertrude."

Lucie's eyes widened. "I have never done it before. I've only watched you."

"You have watched me and spent hours practicing. You are ready."

"But Jane," Françoise began.

"I understand. This is your friend. You must trust me. Lucie can do it."

Françoise stood up. "We'll need to go to the cupboard and see if there is a habit that fits her."

"No." Lucie put her hand out to stop her. "I want to wear the habit Jane wore."

I put the pile of slightly musty black serge on the table and pushed it toward Lucie.

And we soon discovered that Lucie was born to be a counselor.

It was such a splendid morning that we did our work with Gertrude in the garden, where the white roses bloomed. I placed my chair next to Sophie's. Françoise guided Gertrude to a seat. After a moment, a stately nun in a habit that was just a bit too long came gliding into the garden and took the chair across from Gertrude.

"Good morning," she began. "I am sent by Our Lady of Perpetual Grace to talk with you about anything that is troubling you."

Gertrude seemed hypnotized. "I have heard stories of you, My Lady. I prayed that you would come to me," she said.

Our Lady continued, looking deeply into Gertrude's eyes. "I am aware that you are grieving, my daughter," she said. At first I thought it couldn't be Lucie. I glanced down at Our Lady's feet. Sure enough, she was wearing Lucie's red shoes.

"I am grieving for so many things," Gertrude said. "My mother died not long ago. My husband is under a terrible strain to provide for our four children. There is not always enough food. The older children save their bread to share with the younger ones, and I often go without."

I looked at Sophie and saw the distress on her face. I don't think she realized how difficult times had been for her sister.

Gertrude continued, "I try my best to be a good mother. I love my children, but they need everything. They *take* everything from me. I wonder what my mother would say about what I have come here to do?"

Our Lady leaned forward and spoke quietly. "What do you think she would say?"

Gertrude was silent for several moments.

"I am not certain. She sacrificed for us, especially after our father died." She turned and looked at Sophie. "Mama was so good. Do you think she would understand?"

Our Lady gently summoned Gertrude back to the conversation. "This is an answer you must find for yourself."

"I don't know," she answered.

Our Lady waited a moment—allowing silence to sit between them.

Gertrude spoke. "Perhaps... I think she would want me to do what is best for my children, and my husband, and for me—even what is best for this new life—to send it back to the angels?" she said in a timid voice.

"Ah, my dear," Our Lady said, "You are speaking with the voice of a little girl. I wonder if there is a grown woman somewhere inside you?"

Gertrude sat up straighter, and said in a deeper, louder, more confident voice, "My mother would be proud that I have the courage to do what is best for my family. I am proud that I have that courage."

Our Lady spoke again. "Will your mother be with you as you carry out your decision?"

Gertrude smiled. "I think she will. I miss her so much. Yes, she will be by my side."

Lucie continued, "And what about God, my child?"

I worried that Lucie wasn't very familiar with the Catholic God, but held my breath.

"Does He look upon you? Does He love you and forgive you?"

"They say He has His eye upon me, just as He has His eye upon the sparrow. But why would He send this test to me if He loves me? And how am I supposed to pass this test? Is it a punishment for some sin? If I bring this baby into the world, I will fail my husband and my children. And myself. If I kill this child, will I fail God? What does He want me to do? There is no good thing to do. I prayed that He will take this baby from me—that He will make her an angel. But she continues to grow within me. How can I know what God wants me to do?"

Our Lady breathed slowly to give the frantic Gertrude a chance to calm down. "Could you ask Him?"

"I am afraid."

Our Lady whispered, "It is all right to be afraid."

Gertrude was quiet for a moment. Then she said, "Dear God, what do you want me to do? How can I be a good mother to my children and a good wife to my husband and still have another baby? I want to be good. Please tell me how?"

That elusive goodness I had also sought for so long.

They were quiet for a long time. Gertrude hunched her shoulders, and her body became rigid. Finally, she relaxed and let out an audible sigh.

"What is God telling you, my child?" Lucie asked.

Gertrude's voice was steady. "He tells me He loves me and my family and that He wants me to do what is best for us. He tells me that there is no sin, so there is no need for forgiveness." She began to cry.

"And the baby…? Is there anything you want to say to the baby?"

From Françoise's expression, I saw that she was afraid that Lucie was going too far. I signaled Françoise as if to say, 'Don't worry.'

"Speak to the baby?" Gertrude asked tentatively.

"Yes, dear one."

"I am sorry with all my heart that I cannot meet you and learn your story."

"Do you need to ask if this baby will forgive you?"

Gertrude was silent for a moment. Then she spoke. "Yes. I need to ask her."

She put her hand over her heart. "Dearest daughter, I am sure you are a girl. I have named you Eloise, after my mother." Next to me, Sophie let out a quiet sob. "You… you live close to my heart, so you know all my hopes and my fears. You know I love you. Too much to give birth to you when I cannot feed you or clothe you. I can't welcome you without harming others. I need to send you—to give you back to God. You are in my heart and will always be there. Will you… can you forgive me?"

The silence was palpable. None of us was breathing. Lucie shifted slightly in her chair. Something inside me was galvanized by Lucie's courage to ask these impossible questions.

Finally, Gertrude smiled a private smile. Then she spoke, "She says she came to be within me as a gift for a short time to bring me back my song and to remind me that I am strong and that I am loved. She understands and forgives me." Gertrude released her shoulders again. She said, "Our Lady, you have helped me release a weight I was afraid would kill me."

"What heals one of us heals us all," said Our Lady. After a beat, she continued. "And, my child, I bring blessings to you—blessings, forgiveness, and grace."

I could see Gertrude's shoulders release again.

"Blessings?" she said. "Blessings for me? Grace for me?" she asked.

Our Lady reached out and clasped Gertrude's hands in hers. "Yes, my love. For you. You have made a decision out of love and kindness."

Sophie looked at me and whispered, "How did you teach her to do that?"

I must have had my mouth open. Françoise looked equally amazed.

I shrugged my shoulders and whispered back, "I assure you, I did not. That was all Lucie."

CHAPTER 19

MON DIEU!

The sacred conversation was done. Françoise, Sophie, and I sat still and Our Lady escorted Gertrude back to her bedroom. None of us moved. Françoise broke the silence.

"*Mon Dieu*, Jane."

Sophie turned to me with tears in her eyes. "Thank you," she said. "Thank you."

"You'll need to thank Lucie," I whispered.

Lucie changed into her own clothes. *Our Lady of Perpetual Grace* was folded and put back into the cupboard. We allowed Gertrude to sleep for a couple of hours. Sophie checked in on her a few times. "She is sleeping so deeply," Sophie said, smiling. "Last night she tossed and turned. This has been a miracle." Gertrude slept through our light lunch.

Levy returned from Paris, and we all talked over each other to bring him up to date about the extraordinary conversation we had witnessed.

"What you are telling me is exceptional," Levy said. "I have been present many times when Our Lady provided a healing balm, but I have never heard anything like this."

"How did you know how to do that?" I asked Lucie. "How did you think of what to say?"

"I didn't have any idea what I was going to say before I started," she answered. "I just allowed myself to be Our Lady. I tried to become her and say what I wish someone had told me before my abortion. I didn't need forgiveness, but I needed more comfort than Oliver was able to give me. Then I gave Our Lady my voice. I don't even remember all of it. It was almost as though I was in a trance."

"You put us all in a trance," Sophie said. "Including Gertrude. And you got her to open up in a way I never could have. I was amazed."

After lunch, I asked Sophie to wake her sister. The two women came into the kitchen. It is a cliché, but I have to say that I almost didn't recognize Gertrude. She was not the poor haggard woman I first interviewed, and she was not the entranced woman I watched pour her heart out to Our Lady. In those early days of our work, I didn't know what to make of Gertrude's transformation. As I understand it now, I would say that she was 'present' for the first time since I had met her.

She sat down at the table and drank a glass of water. Then she looked around at us and said, "I can never find a way to thank you. When I came here, I accepted what I had to do, but it was a terrible burden—an obligation—one more sacrifice I had to make for my family. But now I see it is a gift that I will give to my family and myself. I had lost all sense of joy, but with Eloise in my heart, I can sing again. I am ready to do this."

I'd never heard a woman talk about an abortion like that. The entire morning had been a revelation. Looking back, I realize we all felt that Gertrude stood as a kind of model for the approach we developed—a North Star to guide us. But I still had a concern that I wanted Lucie to address. I wrote my question on a pad and showed it to her. She nodded and asked, "Gertrude, you have talked about how much you love your husband. How will it be keeping this abortion a secret from him?"

Gertrude shook her head slowly. "My husband is a blacksmith. There is not much demand for his services these days. He doesn't say so, but he is ashamed that he cannot provide for our family. He was in the Resistance, and they captured him and held him in prison. It changed him. The only thing that kept him alive was his Catholic faith. I cannot do anything that goes against the Church. He has never talked about what happened to him all those months in the camp, and he never will. He keeps that secret to protect me. I will keep this secret to protect him."

I sighed deeply. "Gertrude, thank you for talking about these difficult things. I have deep respect for you," I said. "If you are ready, we can proceed."

"Yes. Yes, I am ready."

"Next, we will explain the procedure. I want to be sure that you understand and are comfortable with the steps." Dr. Levy nodded approvingly. He had taught me the importance of explaining each part of the procedure to the patients.

I explained the next steps—including getting on the examining table with its custom-designed knee rests. By Gertrude's expression, I realized that she, like many women, had never had a formal gynecological examination. A midwife attended all her deliveries, so she was very confused when I tried to describe our modern equipment. It was stupid to try to explain things instead of showing her, so we all trooped down the hall to the examining room that had been painstakingly set up according to Levy's instructions. Lucie, Levy, Françoise, and Sophie huddled in the corner, and I resolved to be brief with my explanation. Gertrude's eyes widened at the sight of the table. Even though it was designed for comfort and ease, I had to admit that the leg rests sticking up at the end of the table looked a bit like a medieval torture device. If you have never seen one of these set-ups, you probably can't even picture it. I tried to reassure Gertrude that it would be relatively comfortable, and that this was the best and safest way for us to do the abortion. Then I picked up Dr. Nick's Uterine Suction Apparatus and showed her the tubing and explained the concept. This is the part that Lucie and Levy wanted to hear because they were not familiar with the device. Gertrude seemed to understand my explanation, but there was concern on her face.

"Is it going to hurt?" she asked, looking embarrassed.

"That is a good question," I answered, trying to put her at ease. "It will probably be uncomfortable, like some tugging inside. As your uterus empties out, it will close down like a balloon emptying of air. Since your uterus is a muscle, it will probably cramp a little, like it might when you have a period."

"But it won't be like having a baby?"

"Not at all," I answered.

She looked a bit relieved, but there was still something on her mind.

"Please—if you have any other worries or questions, you can ask me," I said.

She was silent for a moment, as if weighing a risk. Finally, she spoke in a halting voice.

"Is this baby inside me alive?" she asked.

In the hundreds of abortions I had done, no woman had ever asked me that, but I imagine some were wondering. I reviewed what I knew about biology and the progression of a pregnancy.

"Yes," I said. "But it has not developed. It is about the size of a…" I had struggled for a long time about how to describe an embryo. Giving the size of various innocuous fruits and vegetables was something I had tried before, but it never seemed quite honest. I considered an anchovy and dismissed the idea. Finally, I found a piece of paper and a pen on the table and drew the shape and size of what I thought Gertrude's pregnancy would look like. About an inch long, and a slender shape.

"Is it aware of what is happening?" she asked next.

I had read various Catholic treatises about ensoulment from the 5th century—forty days for a male embryo and eighty days for a female embryo. Rubbish. I pictured the many pregnancies that I had seen. And I gave my best answer.

"No. I don't think so," I said. "Awareness, as you and I understand it, is a function of the brain. At this stage, the brain is not developed enough for there to be any kind of consciousness."

"I just don't want to hurt her."

In any other setting, hearing a woman say that she didn't want to hurt what she was about to kill would have seemed a laughable contradiction. But I understood completely.

"I don't want to hurt her, either. At this early stage of development, there is not enough brain to have receptors for pain," I said. Then I remembered my conversation with Kikuyo.

"A lovely woman in Japan told me that they call the ones who are not yet born 'water babies.' That is how they describe a life that isn't quite developed. In Japan, women also have a way of keeping a memory of those babies. They knit hats of red wool that they put on little stone statues that resemble—well, gnomes."

Gertrude looked surprised. "Gnome? *Un lutin?*" she asked.

"Well—yes… It's a bit hard to explain. It's like a little statue of a god— and they put the hats on to send good wishes to the tiny spirits they are sending on."

"I like that," Gertrude said. "I can send good wishes to the tiny spirit I am sending on." She smiled. "All right. I am ready," she sighed.

Lucie took her to the bathroom to change into a cotton gown. They had thought of everything. Levy and I agreed that he would stand at the head of the table to watch for any problems, and Lucie would monitor Gertrude's blood pressure. Françoise and Sophie would stand beside the bed and Sophie would hold Gertrude's hand.

Gertrude came back into the room, an expression of resolve on her face. Since he was the only man in the room, Dr. Levy hung back to give her a sense of privacy. Françoise and I helped Gertrude onto the table and scootched her down—women understand this—so that we could lift her knees over the rests. When Françoise realized the purpose of the knee-rests, she insisted on knitting little cozies to make them more comfortable. We put a pillow under Gertrude's head.

"Are you comfortable?" I asked. "Considering this ridiculous position, that is." I smiled at her. Gertrude smiled back wanly. I could tell that something else was bothering her. "What is it, my dear?" I asked.

"I am so sorry to want something more—you must think me a terrible pest," she said. "But I was just wondering… it would mean so much… could Our Lady be here with me?" I could see that Gertrude both knew and did not know that it was Lucie in the habit. She knew, but it didn't matter. The power of her wish for the blessing was stronger than reality.

Lucie glanced at me and it was clear she wanted to do it.

"Go ahead," I said.

"I can take her blood pressure," Sophie piped up. "I did it all the time for my mother."

"All right," I said, and Lucie scurried out of the room.

I washed my hands thoroughly and put on sterile gloves. Then I returned to my perch on the stool at the foot of the table.

"We'll wait to begin until Our Lady is with us," I said to Levy, who nodded in agreement. In a moment, the figure in black joined us. Our Lady held Gertrude's left hand, while Sophie and Françoise stood at the right. Levy was at the head of the table, behind Gertrude, and I sat on my stool at the foot. It was surely the largest crew I had ever worked with.

Our Lady spoke softly to Gertrude. "I am here now. Are you ready to begin?"

"Yes, I am ready," Gertrude said. In days to come, asking that question became one of the hallmarks of our work—"Are you ready?" Such a simple question, yet one that creates a partnership to which most medicine doesn't even aspire.

As I began to work, Lucie whispered softly to Gertrude, "Hail, holy Queen, Mother of understanding—Our Lady of Perpetual Grace—Honor our courage and our goodness. Show unto us thy comfort and thy love."

I nodded at Lucie to note my approval of the changes she had made in the prayer. Levy was worried about whether the procedure could be done without gas or sedation. I had explained that the suction was very different from what he was used to. In California, we found that the new local anesthetics gave us adequate pain relief as long as the patient was emotionally resolved. Thank goodness Dr. Nick sent along a large supply of syringes and the miracle drug lidocaine, which worked rapidly and had none of the after-effects of the laudanum that Levy had relied on all those years ago in Paris. Levy was not convinced. His brow was furrowed.

Sophie instructed Gertrude to take deep breaths, which I had suggested as a very simple and effective mechanism for creating relaxation. I stood to perform a pelvic examination, realizing that all our work would be in vain if the pregnancy had progressed too far. Fortunately, I palpated a uterus that suggested a pregnancy of seven to eight weeks. Then I sat down on my stool and inserted the speculum that allowed me to visualize the opening to the uterus. I used cotton balls bathed in an iodine solution to clean the vaginal walls and then injected the local anesthetic into her cervix. I waited a few minutes for the anesthetic to take effect, then slid the slender instrument into the uterine canal to determine the size of the uterus and the direction of the opening. I proceeded to dilate the cervix, inserting a series of progressively larger metal rods with rounded ends. Gertrude moaned gently, which signaled the normal discomfort associated with the procedure. Then I inserted the metal tube—the cannula—attached to the clear plastic tubing and used the syringe to start the siphon process. By moving the cannula gently inside the uterus, I could determine that the blood, embryonic tissue, and decidua (loose lining of the uterus) were being removed, and I saw the products of conception entering the clear glass jar. As usual, Dr. Nick's invention worked like a charm. Quickly, I felt the uterus begin to contract around the tube—the balloon emptying of air—and I was done. I gently pulled the tube from the uterus and wiped it on a cloth. I glanced up to see a look of alarm on Levy's face as I pulled off my gloves and dropped them into the basin on the floor that held the iodine-infused cotton balls.

"Why are you stopping so quickly? What's wrong?" he mouthed—trying to make sure that Sophie was not able to see him.

"Nothing," I mouthed back silently. Then, aloud, I said, "We are finished. What's her blood pressure?"

Sophie looked at me as if I had hung the moon. Then she turned to the sphygmomanometer. "It's 117," she practically sang. I had to remember that translated into 110/70, which made me want to sing as well.

We removed Gertrude's legs from the rests, moved her to the head of the table, put a cotton pad in between her legs to absorb the light bleeding, and covered her with a blanket. I liked to allow the patient to fall asleep after the procedure, and that's what Gertrude did. Levy still looked worried when we discussed who would stay with Gertrude.

"I'd like to," Sophie said, "but it would be important to her to see you when she wakes up," she said to Lucie.

"I agree. I will be happy to sit with her," Lucie said.

"I'll stay, too," Françoise said. I wasn't surprised she might not be quite ready to see the pregnancy tissue.

Levy picked up the basin, and I took the glass bottle and tubing. Levy, Sophie, and I quietly filed out of the room and into the lab. Sophie glanced back at her sister and sighed.

"Men go to war—but women have their own battles to fight," she said ruefully.

I recognized that Levy was anxious to talk. The moment we closed the door, he started asking questions, unmindful of Sophie's presence.

"How could it be done that fast? Are you sure you got everything?"

I held up my hand to stop him from talking and looked at Sophie.

"We need to have this conversation," I said. "But you don't have to be here for it."

Sophie surprised me by answering, "I would love to stay. I am fascinated by this as well."

"How are you feeling about this? Weren't you raised Catholic?" I asked her.

"I was. But during the war, I lost any respect I ever had for the Church and its teachings."

"I understand," I said. "I am not religious, but I have been angry at many of the Church doctrines that keep women small and make them think they are intrinsically sinful."

Levy and Sophie sat on the stools in the clean white lab. I took the glass bottle and tubing to the sink, emptied the contents of the bottle into a tea strainer, and tapped it into a clear glass bowl. I added a little water to the bowl, and we all looked intently at its contents. Most of the blood was strained out. I explained to Sophie that what we were seeing was dark mottled decidual tissue that is the loose lining of the uterus. The white fuzzy tissue that looked like tiny roots was the placental tissue, and the translucent embryonic tissue was suspended in the water. As I had told Gertrude, the pale gray embryo was less than an inch long. You could see the start of arm and leg "buds," but it looked more like a shrimp than anything else.

"I can't believe it. It looks complete," Levy said. He looked worried.

"I assure you it *is* complete. The siphon is amazing, isn't it?" I replied. Little did I know that within a few years, we would receive the gift of a magical abortion technique that far surpassed even Dr. Nick's Uterine Siphon Apparatus.

CHAPTER 20

A MAGNET FOR MEN

In an hour, Lucie, in her regular clothes, and Gertrude, looking a bit tired but happy, joined us.

"How are you doing?" Levy asked her.

"I am quite well," she answered. "A bit sore and some mild cramps."

"That's to be expected," I said. "As a matter of fact, some discomfort is welcome. It signals that your uterus is returning to its normal size."

"So the pain is a good sign?" Sophie asked. "That seems so strange."

"Mild cramping is normal, and so is light bleeding or spotting for the next week or ten days. But if the cramping becomes severe, or the bleeding is more than your monthly flow, then get word to us or come back."

For the hundredth time, I wished we owned a telephone. It was all we needed to be in modern times, but 'they' told me we'd have to wait until some other amorphous 'they' brought the lines *à la campagne*—way out into the country. So wait we did.

Claude joined us for dinner, trying out the large trestle table that he built for the upcoming wedding. Thankfully, the refectory was built large enough to seat the twenty-five or so cloistered sisters who'd probably lived there in the convent's heyday. We would easily be able to accommodate the seventeen people who would be at the dinner the night before the wedding.

Exhausted after an emotional day, we all retired early.

"Thanks for being nice to Sophie today," Lucie said, as she kissed me goodnight.

"I am always nice," I answered.

The following morning, Françoise and Claude brought croissants from the bakery. After a quick breakfast, Sophie and Gertrude packed up and prepared to leave in Sophie's shiny black car. Levy whispered to me, "That beauty is a 1938 Peugeot Cabriolet Mettalique Decouvrable." He said it as though it were the Holy Grail.

Sophie noticed his expression.

"Isn't it elegant?" she said, caressing the front hood. "It was our father's pride and joy. He died before he had the opportunity to drive it, and it was in a garage throughout the war. Wait until you see how the top goes down."

She got in and fired up the engine. Moments later, the back of the car opened, and the top flipped up and slid down inside. We were all amazed.

"Do you want to drive it?" she asked Levy.

He was almost salivating, but he declined. "Thank you, no. Maybe another time. We still have so much work to do for the wedding."

"Go on," I said. And he almost ran to the car as Sophie slid out of the driver's seat.

"Just a quick drive," he said. "Claude—come here—you've got to feel how this rides." Claude almost skipped over to the shiny monster, and two little boys sped off. Sophie, Françoise, Lucie, Gertrude, and I laughed.

"That car is like a magnet for men," I said. "That must be a valuable accessory."

Sophie looked at me seriously. "I don't care about that," she said. There was an awkward moment.

Gertrude broke the silence. "My husband had the same reaction. He asked me to take a photograph of him in front of the car, as if it were some kind of hunting trophy! Watch out, here they come. Be careful they don't run us over!" Sure enough, Levy swept back into the driveway with a look of glee on his face.

"It's like riding on a cloud," he exulted. "I could have driven it all day. Thank you, Sophie." Claude was also beaming, and this made all of us women laugh again. If a shiny machine could delight our men, who were we to complain about a little dust and oil?

We helped Gertrude and Sophie load their bags into the car and waved them goodbye. I was sorry to see them go.

CHAPTER 21

YOU *DID* KNOW I WAS INVITED?

Our Lady, July 3, 1951

The days flew by. The afternoon before the wedding, as Françoise and I finished our preparations, I confessed my fears about the Hanovers' casual, and perhaps unconscious, anti-Semitism.

"I'm not concerned about Levy. He doesn't care about them. But the Goldfarbs are such lovely people. They deserve better."

"I will take them under my wing and do what I can to provide a buffer. And if Oliver's parents start to say something they shouldn't, I'll drop a plate and that will stop them in their tracks."

We laughed, and I put my arm around her. "Françoise, you are the best."

After a frenzy of work, we finally completed our tasks. We had prepared the bedrooms with fancy linens and fresh flowers. Two enormous legs of lamb roasted in the oven, sending out a heavenly scent of lamb and rosemary. We dressed, if not in our finest, at least in frocks that wouldn't lead our guests to confuse us with the scullery maids. We completed our tasks just in time because our visitors were scheduled to arrive shortly before dinner.

Françoise said she had one last detail to attend and strode down the hall toward the bedrooms. To celebrate the completion of our tasks, I went into the kitchen to pour some wine. I pulled down a bottle of red and opened it. She touched my shoulder. I turned to see what she wanted and was surprised to see… Gertrude's sister Sophie.

"It smells wonderful in here," she said. "How can I help?"

I sputtered for a moment. "Sophie…?" I said, as if she didn't know her own name.

"Well, yes, it's me. I'm sorry, I didn't mean to surprise you. Françoise met me at the front door. She insisted on taking my bags to the room. She said I should go into the kitchen, that you were having wine." Sophie hesitated. "You *did* know I was invited, didn't you?" she asked, looking concerned.

"Of course," I stammered. I was going to kill Lucie. "I didn't know exactly when you were coming." I felt like a fool, but I always seemed to feel like a fool around the lovely Sophie.

"Um, dinner is pretty well under control," I said. "The table is set; the potatoes are peeled and cut, and they won't go into the oven for another hour. The haricot verts are ready to be steamed at the last minute. The only thing left to prepare is the caprese salad, and I don't want to slice the tomatoes too soon." I bustled around the kitchen as though I had something to do, and finally motioned to Sophie to sit down.

"Would you like a glass of wine?" I asked, pointing to the Merlot I had opened.

"I would love some," she said. I got three glasses and poured the wine.

I was sitting at the kitchen table across from Sophie when Françoise scurried into the room.

"Jane... look who is here... Sophie!" she said, as if I weren't already sitting at the table with her. "Isn't this a grand surprise?"

I glared at her. Françoise sat down at the table and raised a glass to 'preparations completed.' We toasted. As Françoise and Sophie entered into a spirited conversation about Lucie and her guest list, I took the opportunity to look at Sophie. She was breathtaking.

She wore her blonde hair in a sophisticated chignon. A pale pink silk dress set off the flush in her cheeks. I decided that she reminded me of Botticelli's Venus, and that was embarrassing because Venus appeared on the shell *en déshabillée*, as the French put it. I didn't say much as we drank our wine. All too soon, the noise from the front driveway alerted us that our guests had arrived. Sophie sent us to meet the guests, insisting on preparing the caprese salad of mozzarella cheese and fresh tomatoes and basil from our garden. "It's one of my specialties," she insisted. Françoise and I ventured out to welcome our guests.

Levy had arranged for two cars to meet our visitors in Paris. He drove his car, and Claude and Oliver each drove one of the hired cars, so it was quite the caravan. Oliver sprang from the driver's seat of the first car. His elegantly dressed parents stepped out of the large station wagon that held multiple bags stacked on a luggage carrier at the back of the vehicle. In the car were an elderly gentleman I presumed to be Oliver's uncle, and a ruddy-faced, middle-aged man with a clerical collar—Dr. Lucas Kinkaid, the Episcopal priest. Oliver solicitously ushered them into the house. Claude drove the second vehicle, an enormous black Peugeot, which carried Lucie, Socorro, Paulette, and their luggage. Levy drove his own car and from it emerged my mother, the Goldfarbs, and Rabbi Mordecai Karmi.

I must admit, I was relieved when Oliver escorted his passengers to their rooms, promising to make introductions later. "I'll bring your bags," we heard him say from down the hall. My mother and the Goldfarbs ran to embrace me. Mother exclaimed she had no idea that the cloister would be so magnificent, and how she wished my father could have seen it. She stepped back to introduce the rabbi, who said he was very pleased to meet me.

After giving me enormous hugs and squealing with delight at our reunion after all these years, Socorro, Paulette, and Lucie disappeared into her room.

Claude came in carrying the girls' bags, and Françoise pointed him to their rooms. Levy came in laden with bags and dropped them in the front hall. Françoise put her arm around my mother and showed her to a room. When Françoise returned, I asked where she had placed everyone.

"Your mother is on one side of you and Sophie on the other," she said. I didn't make a comment. I returned to the foyer and led the Goldfarbs and the rabbi to their rooms. I was concerned we had left Sophie in the kitchen completing the preparations, but I also thought that it might be a relief.

It was an unusually cool evening for July, so we made a fire in the huge refectory fireplace. We gathered in that comfortable room for introductions and cheese and crackers. Until I introduced her as "Lucie's friend, Sophie," the Hanovers had assumed that Sophie was the hired help because she was passing the appetizers. Mrs. Hanover was mortified to have asked her for "another napkin, dear." Sophie didn't mind—in fact, she winked at me as she assembled the requested items... and later she laughingly reminded me of that moment many times.

Once the introductions were made and everyone had drinks and appetizers, we finally sat down to dinner. I noticed that Mrs. Hanover steered her husband, brother-in-law, and the minister to seats together at the end of the table. So much for the families getting to know one another. With Sophie's help, Françoise and I served the fresh salad to many oohs and aahs. Before we brought in the main course, Oliver's father, the venerable Oliver Butterfield Hanover II, stood up to make a toast. He cleared his throat loudly to get everyone's attention and then raised his glass.

"I would like to toast Dr. Bernard Levy for inviting us to this magnificent — well... place... on this magnificent occasion." The younger Oliver leaned over to his father and hissed an interruption, "Pop, this place belongs to Jane. To Miss Smith."

Dr. Hanover raised his eyebrows, as if to say it was highly unlikely that a woman could own anything, let alone a building of such splendor. Françoise closed her eyes and shook her head, almost imperceptibly.

"Be that as it may," he continued, "Maisie and I thank you for your kind welcome and for welcoming our boy Ollie into your family." All of Oliver's friends and family called him Ollie—but Lucie insisted that it was not an appropriate name for a grown man. So Lucie called him Oliver, and we did too.

When we brought in the lamb, Dr. Hanover insisted on carving and said something about how it only made sense because he was a surgeon, an unfortunate reference. He carved happily as we passed around the roasted potatoes and green beans. Once the plates were full, the minister and then the rabbi blessed the food and the company, thankfully quickly enough that everything didn't get too cold. Everyone seemed to love the dinner.

"Oh, ladies, this is so delicious," Maisie Hanover said. "I should have thought of lamb when you told me I shouldn't serve pork that time, remember, Jane?"

I looked everywhere for Françoise, who was in the kitchen. Before the conversation about dietary laws went any further, Sophie saved the day.

She stood up and said, "I'd like to make a toast to all of you for allowing me to be part of such a wonderful celebration." Everyone raised their glasses and Maisie's comment was obscured by huzzah's and here-here's. It appeared the Goldfarbs didn't notice. I thanked Sophie, and she nodded understandingly.

Disaster averted. I smiled as we watched everyone eating happily. We had decided not to assign seats because we wanted everyone to be comfortable. Since birds of a feather flock together, Oliver sat near his parents, his uncle, and the minister. They discussed politics and the economy of France and the United States. The Hanovers barely acknowledged the Goldfarbs, which was a blessing. Lucie, Socorro, and Paulette were still talking a mile a minute as if they hadn't seen each other in a decade, which they hadn't. Levy and Claude argued about the placement of the chuppah for the next afternoon's wedding. Hymie, Sadie, and the rabbi were in an animated discussion about the differences between their temple in Connecticut and his in Tours. My mother was trying out her high-school French on Françoise, who was a delighted teacher. That left me to talk with Sophie. I apologized for any awkwardness.

"Don't be silly, Jane," she said. "I was quite aware when Lucie invited me that I wouldn't be acquainted with the other guests. I didn't care. I wanted another chance to see you."

"You did?" I asked. And I had thought I couldn't feel any dumber.

"Yes. When I came with Gertrude, I asked Lucie some questions about how all this—Our Lady—came about, and she told me that it was your story, so I should ask you. Here I am, asking."

It wasn't the first time someone had asked about the cloister. Françoise had made it clear to me that I was free to tell *her* part of the story as long as the questioner was friendly. "If my experience can help another girl, please tell it," she had said. "I have nothing to be ashamed of." In many ways, it was Françoise's story, but Sophie was asking me. Even though everyone else was busy in conversation, I didn't want to delve into it during dinner, so I said,

"I'll be happy to tell you when it is more private. But for now, I wonder how Gertrude is?"

"It's hard to imagine we were here hardly a week ago. A lot has happened. We sold our father's car, which gave us each a bit of money. I am ashamed to say I had no idea her family was in such dire straits. The money made things much better for her and her family. But she was still restless and unhappy with her life, so she told her husband that he was such a wonderful father that she wanted him to take charge of the children and that she was going to get a job. She convinced him that not every man could be the kind of father he was. She boosted him up so much that his masculine pride didn't seem to be wounded. So she has been singing again. She is like a different person, and she attributes it all to you and Our Lady."

When everyone was almost done eating, Françoise, Sophie, and I slipped into the kitchen to get the very special dessert. I had tasted it many years before at a French restaurant with Dr. Nick, but neither Françoise nor I had ever made it. Fortunately, Sophie was an expert. Earlier in the day when I told her our plan, Sophie had said, "My mother loved this and made it often. You can make most of it ahead of time. Then you'll just need to ask your guests to be patient for a few minutes for the finishing touches." I thanked her profusely, chastising myself for wanting to impress Oliver's parents at dinner without having the first idea of how to do it.

We took the pancakes out of the oven and poured on the Grand Marnier and Cognac sauce that Sophie had prepared. Then Françoise carried the whole concoction into the dining room. I cleared my throat to get everyone's attention and said, "This special dessert is in honor of Lucie and Oliver, and we want to give Lucie the opportunity to bring it to life." We set the platter in front of Lucie, and Sophie proffered a long match. Lucie clapped her hands in excitement, struck the match and—whoosh—our Crêpes Suzette was lit. Oliver's uncle, who had proclaimed himself the best amateur photographer in the room, insisted on capturing the moment as we ate dessert.

"Just a few more pictures of the lass and her, ahem, her... the ones who took care of her," he said cryptically. He was remarkably spry for a man his age. He came to life as he climbed on chairs and had us tilt our heads up or down. He popped out flash bulbs and let them scatter on the floor like bullet casings because they were too hot to handle. He was obviously a man who presumed a woman would clean up after whatever mess he made.

After we had eaten the sumptuous dessert, Dr. H proclaimed for the entire group, "We are full and happy, and we are going off to bed so that we can arise in time for the wedding!" Françoise and I assured them that there would be plenty of coffee, breakfast, or lunch depending upon what time they happened to come to the kitchen. Lucie's friends were spending the night in her bedroom, and I didn't expect any of them to get any sleep. As Lucie started to leave the room with Socorro and Paulette, I asked for a moment with her. She gestured to them that she'd be right there, and turned to me with a mischievous smile.

"Yes, Mam'selle?" she said.

"Lucie—you invited Sophie to come, and you didn't tell me?"

"You and Françoise made it clear to us that you didn't care who was coming as long as we told you the number of rooms needed, which we did. Oh, come on, Jane. She is so nice, and you need someone. You can ignore her if you want to, but she likes you. Don't be so crusty." She gave me a playful hug. "But there is something I want to talk with you about," Lucie said.

"Before you ask, I have another question for you. Why does Oliver's uncle keep calling you 'lass?'"

Even in the dim light, I could see her face go pale.

"Oh Jane, it's just... I hate to even explain it. Because I have red hair, the Hanovers told him I am a Scottish orphan on whom the Goldfarbs took pity. Like a dog who raises a stray kitten."

"They told him *what?*"

"I know. I know. They are terrible. But they had to explain the rabbi and the chuppah, and they were afraid he wouldn't give us a wedding present if he realized I am Jewish."

"Lucie, what kind of family are you marrying into?"

"They are no worse than my friends' parents at school. Most of them thought Jews were either dirty beggars or greedy jewelers, determined to bankrupt the rest of the world. Oliver is not like them. Honestly. Thank goodness his parents are leaving right after the wedding. If we can just get through these two days, you'll never have to see any of them again. Please, Jane. If this is the fairy tale they have to tell themselves in order to be civil, let's not insist on the truth."

I shook my head as if I could unhear what I had just heard, then shrugged my shoulders. "I am not going to ruin your wedding by confronting them. But you mustn't keep secrets like this from me." I sighed an annoyed and disappointed sigh.

Lucie had the good grace to look slightly embarrassed. "I'm sorry, Mam'selle."

As usual, I couldn't stay mad at her. "Now, what did you want to talk about?"

She smiled. "Well, I obviously don't need to have the birds and the bees conversation with you, but I do want to ask you about something else. You'll say I should have already figured this out. But I haven't. Oliver just told me that since we'll be respectably married, he wants children. But I am not sure if *I* do. Not just now—I may not even want to have children. Is that wrong?"

"I can't believe you haven't told Oliver your feelings long before this. But my thoughts are a bit beside the point. You are asking a woman who is not likely ever to have children. But, of course, I don't think it is wrong. All these years of working with women and pregnancy have taught me one essential thing: it doesn't work to have a baby for someone else, and it doesn't work to have an abortion for someone else. When it comes right down to it, it is almost always the woman who is going to take care of and be responsible for children. Even women who *want* to have children can have a hard time with the amount of responsibility and selflessness it takes. I hope you won't have a baby until and unless you are certain about it."

Lucie embraced me and said, "Mam'selle, you can't imagine how much I love you." Then she turned and ran down the hall to join her friends.

CHAPTER 22

MAN AND WIFE

The wedding day was glorious. Françoise, Sophie, and I sat in the kitchen with our coffee, looking at our list. Even though we had been preparing for a long time, there was still a lot to do.

Oliver and his medical school friends from Paris had already celebrated. I laughed when I heard what the French called a bachelor party—'*L'enterrement de vie de garçon*'—literally 'burial of the life of the boy.' Unfortunately, most of the men I have met, married or not, have never bothered to bury the life of the boy!

By noon, our work was done, and the quiche with spinach was in the oven. We made a huge salad of lettuce, carrots, cucumbers, and tomatoes from our garden, and put baguettes with sweet butter on the kitchen table.

As we put away our checked-off list, my mother appeared.

"I am so sorry," she said. "I fully intended to be here first thing in order to help. It's these confusing time zones!"

"What is the difference in the time, Madame Smith?" Sophie asked.

"Oh, my dear, please call me Sylvia," Mother said. "Connecticut is six hours earlier, so I had a terrible time getting to sleep, even after all the wine I drank with dinner. When I woke up with the sun, as I usually do, my body registered two thirty a.m. Naturally, I fell right back to sleep. Now that you are getting ready to serve lunch, I am almost ready for breakfast."

"Mom, we have café au lait and wonderful croissants. Would you like that instead of quiche?"

"Oh, my no! Not if that is the quiche I smell. I swear I am gaining weight just inhaling!"

My mother cornered me before she got her food. "Darling, I am so delighted to see the renovation of the convent. I hope you like it."

"I love it. I meant to say thank you. It was more than I could ever have imagined. It's made me want to stay here. But I don't want you to feel abandoned. Are you all right?"

"I was having a difficult time when you left, but I am very well now, thank you. I've started singing in my church choir. That's why I have to leave so quickly. We have a big concert scheduled that I couldn't miss. But I want to come back when I have more time. I want to visit and see the wonderful work Lucie has told me you'll be doing here."

"Lucie told you...?" My life flashed before my eyes.

"Providing sanctuary for women in need. It's just like you, Jane, to want to help others."

I gulped. I couldn't speak. "Yes, yes, you'll have to visit."

Mom kissed me on the cheek and went to get her coffee.

My knees were weak. I sat down and took a breath. I didn't want to have these thoughts, but I couldn't wait for my mother and all the nosy parents to leave.

Early that morning, Françoise brought croissants, baguettes, and the wedding cake from the village bakery. We put the splendid two-tiered cake in the wine room, the coolest place we could find. A few minutes after my mother arrived, Oliver's parents and his uncle glided in on the scent of the quiche. Dr. H said a hearty, "Good morning," and his wife said, "It's already afternoon, dear."

"Well, morning or afternoon, it certainly smells good in here. Is there coffee?"

Oliver's uncle had his camera out. "I was hoping to get a few shots of the lass and her friends before the service."

I winced at the word *lass*. "Good luck with that. I doubt we'll see any of them before the music starts!" I said.

He laughed.

It wasn't his fault, but I wanted to be angry he'd believed that Lucie was Scottish. A stray kitten, indeed.

Sadie and Hymie Goldfarb followed the Hanovers into the kitchen. I scurried around, seated everyone at the kitchen table in their safe, separate groups, poured coffee, and offered a choice of croissants or the soon-to-be-ready quiche. A lovely Pinot Blanc was in a carafe in case anyone wanted to drink. I sent Françoise outside to gather the rest of our guests. The rabbi and the minister had arisen early and took a croissant and a cup of café au lait outside to their respective spots to think their respective theological thoughts. Lucie, Paulette, and Socorro were still in Lucie's room, likely discussing how much or how little makeup she should wear and whether her hair should be up or down. Claude and Levy were putting the finishing touches on the chuppah. It looked spectacular.

One night over dinner, Lucie explained that the chuppah symbolizes God's presence in their new home. She said breaking the glass symbolizes the unbreakability of the marriage vows. Initially, Oliver resisted the idea of stepping on the glass, but he finally came around when Lucie said, "Please, Oliver... in honor of my father?" Since her father had been killed by the Nazis, that was a hard argument to fight. He practiced wrapping a glass in a hand-kerchief and stomping on it with his right foot, with no luck.

Should that have been a warning to us all?

We finally found a very thin glass and set it aside for the occasion.

Oliver spent the night with Claude and Françoise at the farm. This was both a nod to tradition and an attempt at propriety for the sake of all the parents.

Lunch seemed to fly by, and soon it was time for us to get ready for the ceremony.

Françoise wore bright yellow and looked like a happy sunflower. My mother was in sapphire blue with silver piping, matching silver shoes, and a silver hat. Oliver's mother sported a pale blue empire waist dress with a little jacket, and a tiny fascinator hat with feathers perched on the side of her head that someone in New York told her was de rigueur for a European wedding. My dress was a tea-length, watery gray silk that swirled when I moved. It was very elegant, and, wearing it, I felt almost beautiful. I bought the dress at the Tall Gal's shop in New York before we left home. My mother helped pick it out. Well, she picked it out, and I tried it on.

Sophie looked stunning in a violet dress embroidered with tiny pink flowers with a fitted bodice and flared skirt. She wore her long blonde hair loose around her shoulders. I wondered if it was fair to upstage the bride. I still have a photograph of Sophie that Oliver's uncle took that day. It's tucked into the corner of the mirror in my bedroom.

All the men wore tuxedos except for Claude, who wore his best jacket. Lucie asked Dr. Levy and Dr. Goldfarb to walk her down the aisle, one on either side. They both looked elegant, each with a pink tea rose boutonniere.

Oliver's uncle continued his quest to photograph everyone. It was good that we were outdoors because he didn't need those infernal flash bulbs! Almost the moment we sat down, our little local band of fiddler and accordionist began to play music. One of Françoise's grandnieces, darling little Lulu, served as the flower girl. We all turned to see Lulu's mother coaxing her out into the aisle with her little basket of rose petals. Lulu tottered a few steps, hurled a handful of petals onto the ground, then tottered a few more steps. Then she decided she was supposed to go back and pick up the petals she had dropped, so that put a bit of a pause in the bridal procession. Socorro and Paulette followed Lulu in their long pale pink dresses, and Paulette shepherded the little girl back to her mother so they could proceed.

Once the bridesmaids arrived at the chuppah, the music paused for a moment. The musicians began a commendable job of the *Wedding March*, which Oliver insisted upon. We all stood. As I looked back, I saw Lucie flanked by the dashing Dr. Levy and the distinguished Dr. Goldfarb. They stood there for a moment and allowed us all to be astonished.

How can I describe my Lucie? My heart was bursting with pride. She had let her dark red hair down in gentle curls. The lace on her veil set off her pale skin and dark eyes, and there was a bloom in her complexion and a happiness that I had never seen before. When I glanced up the aisle at Oliver standing there in his tuxedo, I saw a boy whose every wish had been granted and a man watching his future walk toward him. For at least that moment, I was not afraid for them. Lucie's two fathers walked her down the aisle and delivered her to the hands of her future husband. Levy sat down next to me and squeezed my hand.

The minister began with the familiar, "Dearly Beloved, we are gathered here in the sight of God…" For his part of the service, Dr. Kincaid elected to include passages about love from Corinthians.

"Love is patient and kind; love does not envy or boast; it is not arrogant or rude. It does not insist on its own way; it is not irritable or resentful; it does not rejoice at wrongdoing, but rejoices with the truth. Love bears all things, believes all things, hopes all things, endures all things."

It was as if he had overheard some of Lucie and Oliver's heated 'discussions,' and wanted to fix them. Before I had a chance to think more about that, the minister said, "Lucie has asked her friend Sophie to read a poem as part of the wedding service."

Sophie walked to the front and took a moment to compose herself. I held my breath as she recited. Her voice was a strong, silken cord.

"He Wishes for the Cloths of Heaven," by William Butler Yeats

"Had I the heavens' embroidered cloths,
Enwrought with golden and silver light,
The blue and the dim and the dark cloths
Of night and light and the half-light,
I would spread the cloths under your feet:
But I, being poor, have only my dreams;
I have spread my dreams under your feet;
Tread softly because you tread on my dreams."

She recited the poem again in French, and there was a murmur of appreciation from the audience.

Kincaid turned to the vows, which were not part of a Jewish ceremony. He intoned, "Do you, Lucie Fortier Goldfarb, take this man…"

After Lucie repeated her vows (minus the agreement to obey, which never had a chance) and Oliver had done the same, the rabbi came forward. Most of our guests only spoke French, had only been to Catholic religious services, and had never even imagined a ceremony that represented two religious traditions. But no one seemed to be the slightest bit perturbed by the turn of events.

"Thank you, Dr. Kinkaid. Good afternoon, I am Rabbi Mordecai Karmi." It intrigued me that the Jewish portion of the service seemed more like a family conversation than a lecture.

"Today, you will see a braiding together of customs. We are here standing under the chuppah—a sanctuary—as the Temple of Jerusalem was a sanctuary, and yet open on the sides, as this marriage will be open to friends and relatives. A marriage requires love and support from friends, family, and community. Will those who have given their pledge to support this couple please stand?"

All of us parents, quasi-parents, and childhood friends stood.

"Thank you for loving this young couple and know that they will depend upon each of you in times ahead. My son and my daughter, we break the glass to symbolize the destruction of the temple, and the indestructibility of the promises you have made to each other today."

Oliver stepped back on his left foot and with a huge stomp successfully broke the glass with his right foot—to cries of *mazel tov* from the few Jewish people in the audience. The two holy men stepped forward and in unison intoned the magic words: "We now pronounce you husband and wife. You may kiss the bride." Dr. Kinkaid and Rabbi Karmi smiled at each other, looking proud that they had pulled off something new. Oliver and Lucie embraced and kissed sweetly.

Our little musical ensemble played something jolly as the bride and groom walked hand in hand back down the aisle. As they passed me, Lucie blew me a kiss. My heart melted.

We gave the newlyweds some moments of privacy while the rest of us set about opening champagne. When Lucie and Oliver came back outside, it was to a great huzzah. They prepared to cut the cake. Lucie had made it very clear that there would be no smashing of wedding cake into anyone's mouth, so they fed each other pieces very politely. Then they made their way to the head table. As we drank champagne and ate wedding cake, the toasts began. Dr. Goldfarb spoke first. He waxed on about how wonderful Lucie was and how lucky he and Sadie were to have her as their daughter. Then, as if an afterthought, said they were also glad to have Oliver as their son-in-law. Not to be outdone, Dr. Hanover stood and extolled his son at length—almost making Oliver blush. As he listed one accomplishment and award after another, it occurred to me that his toast was more like a resumé for a job application than the usual celebratory wedding fare. Following suit, Dr. Hanover mentioned Lucie as if she were a bonus added on to their purchase. Most of the guests couldn't understand a word either one of them was saying, and didn't lower their voices or pause in their merrymaking. It created a jolly cacophony. Then

Socorro and Paulette stood up and made a very giggly toast that they repeated in English, French, Spanish, and Italian. That caught everyone's attention because they all understood at least one version of it, and the crowd applauded wildly. I think the girls tittered out of nervousness. I had heard them the night before, whispering to each other that they couldn't even imagine wanting to be *married* to anyone. Then Dr. Levy made a brief toast, only in French, directly to Lucie.

"Lucie, my heart, in a world that became insane, in a world in which so many that we loved were lost, you are my treasure," he said, raising his glass to her. "I am honored to stand in for your father and mother. They would be so proud to see you today. I wish for you a most wonderful future."

Everyone was quiet, many of us thinking of the people and things that had been lost. I was glad Françoise had insisted on giving me one of her pale blue handkerchiefs.

When the cake was all eaten, except the small piece we had put aside to keep for their first anniversary, and everyone had danced until they had to take their shoes off, Lucie and Oliver got up from the table to change into their traveling clothes. At that moment, I realized that the wedding was almost over. After all the weeks of planning, it seemed impossible that the event had gone by so quickly. I wanted to block the door and not let her emerge as Mrs. Lucie Fortier Goldfarb Hanover III. But she did emerge in a stunning hot pink Chanel suit that set off her dark auburn hair.

Lucie called for all the single girls to stand behind her. I stood to the side with Sophie and Françoise. With her back to us, Lucie climbed up on a chair, raised the flowers, turned, and threw the bouquet right into my arms. A cheer went up, everyone laughing and telling me that I was going to be the next bride. I was still blushing when the couple gathered themselves up and left in the car with 'Just Married' scrawled in soap on the windows and the obligatory tin cans trailing from behind. We threw the rice that Claude had divvied up, and cheered. They waved, and then they were gone. Even when they got back from their honeymoon and we were all living together at the convent, it would not be the same.

Lucie was gone.

CHAPTER 23

TREAD SOFTLY

When I started to clean up, Françoise motioned me to sit back down. "There is no hurry," she said. "Just sit. You've done enough for the moment." She, of all people, realized what an emotional time this was for me, even though I tried my best not to show it. Sophie sat at the table with a bottle of champagne and an empty glass. I had already drunk a little, and I had that glow from the inside that I always get with champagne, so I smiled when she poured it.

She smiled back at me. I still clutched the bouquet Lucie had thrown.

"Lovely flowers," she said. She said it in a kind way, not a mocking way. I looked at the roses and nodded in agreement.

"Don't you want to be the next one to find a sweetheart?" Sophie asked.

"That is not in the cards for me. I love my friends. Nothing is missing from my life."

"So, you don't want a love of your own?"

Quite a forward thing to say. My first, but not last, challenge with Sophie's forthright manner. She said it in such a sweet and quiet voice that it almost didn't register. I nearly gasped at the pang in my chest, like the one I had as I watched Lucie and Oliver drive away.

I sat down across from her, but not too near. "*C'est ça*," I answered. "That's the way it is for me."

She spoke again in a normal voice. "Now that the festivities are over, will you tell me the story of how you came to be here and how you came to help women?"

I was relieved to be back on solid ground. "It's a long story," I warned her.

She said, "I'm not going anywhere."

And so I began the tale with the night that Levy asked for my help with Françoise's abortion.

By the time I finished the story and Sophie had asked a million questions, Claude, Levy, and Françoise had moved chairs and stacked dishes in the kitchen. We had already agreed that I would do the dishes. Sophie insisted on helping.

Everyone was heading to Paris. My mother apologized a dozen times for having such a short stay. The girls planned to spend time in town, promising to be back within a week. Levy was visiting with old friends in the Marais district. Oliver's parents and his uncle were ready to drive back to their hotel on the West Bank. We all agreed it had been a "very satisfactory ceremony," as Dr. Hanover called it, and we wished each other safe travels. Once they had driven off, Françoise and Claude bid us goodnight and returned home in their little horse-drawn carriage.

Left alone, Sophie and I went into the kitchen to face our chore. There was a kitchen full of dishes. We filled the sink with hot soapy water and agreed that I would wash and she would dry. At first we were quiet. There was something about Sophie that made it easy to be with her.

After a few moments, she said, "Jane, there's something I need to tell you about myself. I don't want you to think I came here to trick you."

"What do you mean?" I asked, plunging my hands deeper into the water.

"Remember when you said my car was a magnet for men, and I said I didn't care?" she asked. "It's because I… I am not interested in men in that way."

My mouth got very dry, and I realized I had already suspected that. My brain flooded with memories of Betty that I tried to repress.

She continued. "When I studied at the *Ecole Normale* for college, I fell in love with a wonderful girl. Claire was smart and funny and too brave for her own good. Lucie reminds me of her. When you told me the story of taking Lucie to America, I felt so many things. If only Claire had been rescued. She was part of the Resistance, but she took too many risks. She insisted on wearing a yellow star even though she wasn't Jewish. She and a small group of students organized a protest against the arrest of one of our teachers. Hundreds of others protested, including me. But the police found the ringleaders and executed them."

"Oh my goodness, Sophie! They killed her? Just a student? I had no idea! I can't imagine. So many terrible things happened in those years." I stopped washing and started to dry my hands on a towel.

"No, don't stop washing. I can't tell you about this if you are looking at me," she said. So I swished the plates around and pulled one out for her to rinse and dry.

"We were all so young. Remember I told you that I had lost respect for the Church? We petitioned the Archbishop to intercede, and he refused, saying it was a civil matter. The government wanted to demonstrate its power. Jane, the Gestapo didn't kill her. It was the French—the Milice—my own government."

A clean fork dropped back into the sink. We both reached to get it. The touch of her hand was electric. She entwined her fingers in mine.

The memory of Betty's betrayal squeezed my heart like a vise. I had resolved never again to make myself vulnerable to that kind of pain.

"Sophie, I tried love, and I failed. I am scared."

"You are the bravest woman I know," she said.

"I am too old for you."

"I am not a child. I know what I want."

"I don't even know your last name."

"It is St. Martin. You are just stalling," she said.

"I've nothing to give you," I whispered.

She looked at me with those cool blue eyes and said, "I, being poor, have only my dreams. I have spread my dreams under your feet. Tread softly because you tread on my dreams."

I bent down and kissed her, first softly, and then passionately. When we finally pulled apart, my face flushed, and I was trembling. I apologized for being so forward.

Sophie looked disappointed. She said, "Jane, there is nothing to apologize for. There is a lot I'd like to share with you. I hope you'll tell me if you want it, too, someday."

It was hard to let her go. To say goodnight. I did want more. I wanted her, but I couldn't take the risk.

Lying alone in my single bed, I was painfully aware of Sophie in the next room. I wondered if she was asleep or if she was thinking about me. I wondered… if I could have a different life. If Sophie could love me.

CHAPTER 24

FAISEUSES D'ANGES (ANGEL-MAKERS)

The next morning, Sophie woke before I did. The smell of coffee was like a siren's call. In the kitchen, I sat across the table from her. She smiled, and I sensed a kindness and ease about her that I had never experienced in my years with Betty. I smiled back, but she looked serious as she poured me a cup of coffee.

"Is everything all right?" I asked.

"Everything is wonderful, but I am afraid I may have acted prematurely."

"It's all right. I understand. I shouldn't expect you to want to be with me."

"You *don't* understand at all. It was impetuous of me to respond to your kiss, although I wanted to with all my heart. I want to be with you, Jane. I want to be here. But that 'failed love' you mentioned, it was with a woman, wasn't it?"

"Yes. It is a humiliating story, but I'll tell you if you want. It seems like I can tell you anything."

"Your family, your friends—have you told them about it?"

"Goodness, no. That relationship got me kicked out of the Navy on morals charges. I can never tell them."

"Then how do you imagine we could be together here? Do you think they wouldn't notice?"

I turned my attention to buttering a croissant.

Sophie waited for me to answer.

"I don't know. Even the possibility of this is so unexpected. I was with Betty in Japan. It was so far away from home. How could it hurt to keep a secret?"

"I lived like that. Sneaking around. Hoping no one would see. Lying to my mother and the people I worked with. Feeling ashamed. It killed my spirit." Sophie held my eyes with her gaze. "When I finally told my mother and my sister, the weight of the world was lifted. They weren't happy. They were afraid I would be judged, but the people I care about accepted me. They still loved me."

"Of course they did. You are perfect." I felt like a fool even as I uttered the words.

"There is nothing *perfect* about me. But I helped them see I was the same sister and daughter they loved before they knew. There hasn't been anyone in my life since Claire. When we were here for Gertrude's abortion, I told her I hoped you and I could make something special together. What I am trying to get at is that I can't go back to keeping this fundamental part of myself a secret. If I were to come here to be with you and be part of this amazing life, you would need to tell the people you love."

Panic rose in me at the very idea of telling my friends.

"I can't, Sophie. I just can't."

"Because the price of shame is too high? Are you familiar with the old poem, 'The love that dare not speak its name?'"

"No, but it's not hard to imagine what it refers to," I said.

"When they executed Claire, I vowed that I would no longer hide behind shame. That I would speak the name of my love."

Sophie stood up, her small valise packed and at her side.

"I'm going to go now." There were tears in her eyes. "I hope you will want me to come back. I can see that I may be asking too much. I will be heartbroken if you can't do this, but I will understand." She kissed me on both cheeks. I noticed her sweet, understated perfume.

I didn't follow her to the door. I paced back and forth in the kitchen, cursing. I was angry, but did I even have a right to be angry? In my only other relationship, it was Betty who had kept the secret of her dual life until her other girlfriend unexpectedly and unwittingly appeared at our apartment in Japan. It was Betty who kept a secret from Sandi and me—Betty who lied. And here was Sophie who only wanted me to tell the truth. How could I be angry about that? Or was it really fear? I paced some more and finally figured out the person I needed to talk to. By late morning, Nick would be finished with his work day. I drove to the dairy, promising Claude that I would pay them the ridiculous amount it would cost to call Japan. Claude left me alone in the kitchen. I knew the number by heart. Nick's live-in boyfriend, Bai, answered the phone, and I asked how he was and then asked to speak with Nick.

Nick sounded like he had won the lottery. "Janie! How wonderful to hear from you! Did your phone finally get installed?"

"Hi Nick. No, I'm calling you from the neighbors' phone. Is this a good time for you to talk?"

This signaled a serious conversation.

"What's wrong?"

I had written to him about meeting Sophie and thinking it was too danger-ous even to consider getting into another relationship. In the strange time-warp of letters back and forth from long distances, there wasn't time for a reply. So I filled him in about Sophie coming to the wedding and about our kiss. I told him about Sophie insisting that our relationship not be secret. He interrupted with the appropriate exclamations and clarifications.

"There haven't been many places I have been accepted," I said plaintively. "Here in France, with these people, I am. But they are not aware of this part of my life. I can't risk losing them, Nick. I just can't."

"You don't have to, Janie. But isn't it also a risk to spend the rest of your life without love?"

"Would you tell your family if Bai asked you to?"

"Not a chance. I live thousands of miles away from my family for a reason. You saw how my father sent his friends to our engagement party in California to spy on me and make sure I was on the straight and narrow. My father would disown me and my mother would cry."

"It is the crying part I am worried about. What if Lucie and Levy and Françoise are disgusted and hate me?"

"I'm not sure what to say. Perhaps I am not the right person to be talking to about honesty. Especially long-distance."

I pictured that jaunty Nick smile, one side of his mouth higher than the other, creases at the corners of his eyes.

"I'm afraid you are on your own with this, Janie. But you know your friends. You know how much they love you. Trust them."

I had found an old wishing well at the edge of the property and wore a path around it, muttering to myself. *I must have lost my mind to even consider this. Am I going to risk everything I have worked so hard for, just to have this woman in my life and then have my heart broken again? How can I tell if she is any different from Betty? If I tell the truth about who I am and lose everything, it won't be worth the risk. It's private. Why do I have to talk about it? Sophie is wonderful, but she is asking too much of me. She is asking too much.*

That afternoon, Paulette and Socorro returned from their time in Paris. They wanted to talk to me, so I pulled myself together and we sat at the kitchen table.

The girls looked nervous.

Finally Paulette said, "Is everything all right?"

I shrugged my shoulders. "Sure." Why stop lying now? "What do you want to talk about?"

"Jane, we'd like to talk with you about… about Our Lady. Lucie has told us everything and we want to do it too."

I was more surprised than angry. "When did Lucie tell you? *What* did she tell you?" I demanded.

Socorro answered this time. "Mam'selle—don't be angry. We are best friends. She has been writing to us about all of this since you first came back to France. Lucie wrote that she has found her work here—has found who she was meant to—to *be*. We want to learn to do it too."

"I can't believe she told you. Girls, you don't understand what you are talking about." I was so upset. "Nothing has been decided about the future here. Lucie took the reins as she always does and made assumptions about what I wanted. I should never have let her be part of it. It can be very dangerous. Do you realize that just a few years ago, a woman was guillotined for doing abortions?"

"We read about some of the *'faiseuses d'anges'* the 'angel-makers,'" Paulette said. "But those penalties were because of the Nazis. The laws are different now."

"Maybe the punishment is not as drastic anymore, but abortion is still not legal. What are the penalties in your countries?" I asked them. I was not surprised that they had no idea.

"I am not afraid," Socorro said, boldly. At that moment, she reminded me so much of Lucie.

"I'm not either," Paulette said, a bit more timidly.

"In any case, this discussion is premature. You'll need to finish your studies before you decide what you want to do."

"But what should we study if we *do* want to do this?" Paulette asked.

I thought for a moment.

"Despite what Lucie has told you, I am not certain we are going to do this. Perhaps we will just open a school. But if we decide to help women, well, I must warn you, it's a lot. Studying something to do with medicine would be helpful, although if you get any kind of license, it would be put at risk if you work illegally. You should learn something about psychology and religion. And politics and law. And a bit about history. And something about business organization—and something about how to run a hotel. That about sums up this work. And that is all I am going to say about it. Talk to me again when you have finished your studies. *If* we do what Lucie wants us to do, and you are still interested, I will teach you. Meanwhile, when Lucie gets back from her honeymoon, she is going to hear about this!"

I realized I didn't sound angry. I was worried about getting these girls into something so complex and dangerous, but I was very proud that Lucie had told them she had found who she was meant to be. I thought about how extraordinary she was with Gertrude.

The girls stayed another few days, then we kissed goodbye and Levy drove them to the airport.

As so often in life, I never could imagine how my past would become my future.

CHAPTER 25

TELLING SECRETS

Summer, 1951

It took me a week to get up the nerve, but when I finally did, telling my friends about Sophie was surprisingly anticlimactic.

"I want to tell you all that I love Sophie, and I'm going to ask her to come here and live with us."

Lucie took credit for the whole thing, and she asked when Sophie was going to move in so that we could enjoy the benefits of living with someone who loved to cook. Levy was just glad I would have someone. Françoise didn't get it at first. She asked a series of increasingly embarrassing questions until Lucie said, "Françoise, it's like you and Claude," whereupon Françoise said, "Oh. *Oh.* Oh!" and finally declared herself delighted. I asked Françoise if I should tell Claude. She assured me that he was significantly more open-minded than she, and that I had nothing to fear. Lucie didn't offer any such assurances about Oliver, but said she would tell him. I happened to be standing in the next room when she did.

He said, "That's disgusting. I should have known. It's obvious she hates men."

"She does not hate men. She just loves Sophie."

"That girl who read the poem at our wedding? She's certainly easy on the eyes, but it's not normal. I don't want anything to do with it."

"No one is asking you to, darling. You don't have to like it, but I *insist* you treat them with respect."

One more thing Oliver didn't want anything to do with. Fine with me.

I called Sophie from the dairy and asked her to come over for lunch. I told the others I needed some private time with her, so they all found something to do. I made my best cream of mushroom soup and a small salad, set a pretty table, poured some white wine, and opened the door with a little hug and a hopeful look on my face. Once we were sitting at the kitchen table, I had to tell her right away. Lunch would have to wait.

"I told them. I still can't believe I did it. They were wonderful—all except Oliver, and I don't care about his opinion. They only want me to be happy, and they think you are splendid. Lucie wanted to take credit because she invited you to the wedding."

"That's wonderful. How did your mother respond?"

"My *mother*? She lives thousands of miles away. Why would I tell her?"

"Isn't she the most important person to you?"

"Yes, but…"

"Then you can't keep this a secret from her," Sophie insisted. "What I would give for my mother to be here to meet you."

"It's not the same with my mother. I have stopped hoping for her approval, but I can't risk her disapproval."

"It's not about approval. It's about keeping the most significant part of your life a secret from her."

"I have done that all my life! Don't worry. My friends will keep this a secret. No one is going to tell my mother. I write to her every week and I am a master of knowing what to leave out. She will never even suspect."

Sophie put her arm around me. "I was so scared my mother wouldn't love me if she were aware that I loved Claire. My father was dead. Besides Gertrude, my mother was all I had. I wanted to tell her what they did to Claire, but I just couldn't. Mother and I lived together, but we were like strangers—polite strangers. But when I finally risked telling her, she was wonderful."

My shoulders slumped. "I'm glad. But you don't understand. I am already quite clear about what my mother thinks."

"How? How are you so sure?"

I closed my eyes, reliving a painful memory from years ago.

"As a teenager, my mother made me go to these dances—cotillions and summer dances. When I was fifteen, our community center held a Labor Day dance. I had been to ballroom dancing class, and I always had to lead because boys didn't like to come to those classes, and I was the tallest one. Somehow, Mother convinced me that this dance would be fun. The community center was down the road from our house, so I walked, singing to myself. But it wasn't the kind of dance I was used to. I had never met any of the other kids. At first I stood in the back. But one of the boys asked me to dance. He was as tall as I am, and I was embarrassed to say no. We danced to "Happy Days Are Here Again," but then the music slowed and the girls were just sort of hanging onto the guys. I didn't even know this boy. And it was as though he was hugging me. I felt scared and ashamed and burst into tears and ran out. I cried all the way home. My mother was surprised to see me—then worried—then annoyed. I attempted to explain what had happened, and she shook me by the shoulders and said, 'What is wrong with you?'"

Tears streamed down my face.

"I am so sorry, my love. That is a terrible story. I can see why you are afraid to tell her." She used her napkin to wipe my eyes. I took her hand.

Sophie continued, "But it doesn't change my need for honesty. I don't mean to sound sharp about this," Sophie said, sounding very sharp to me, "but you don't understand. You have your own life to live—I am not in charge of the choices you make. I'm not unreasonable. I am not saying you should tell the baker. Or the boy who milks Françoise's cows. Or the police inspector. But I cannot—*will* not—live in a situation where the fact that I love you is kept from your mother. I don't mean to sound righteous. It's only that I am afraid of a secret that is so important. I don't want to lose you, but I can't lose myself again. I hope you understand, *Cherié.*"

Sophie got up, kissed me on the cheek, and left without a goodbye. Stunned, I folded my arms across my chest. I had lost all appetite for lunch. I threw everything into the garbage. There was only one person I wanted to talk to about my dilemma.

I looked for Lucie. I didn't find her in her bedroom or the wine cellar. I finally found her in the back yard attempting to prune the sweet white roses that had begun to bloom.

She turned as I approached her. "Oh, dear. What is wrong?"

"I didn't say anything is wrong."

"You didn't need to. Sit down over here. Drink some of my lemonade." Lucie handed me her glass, wet and cold. I took a long swallow and sat next to her.

"You know me too well."

"Jane, you are transparent. You imagine you are good at keeping secrets, but you'd better not play poker."

I laughed, a tinny, nervous laugh.

"It's about Sophie," I finally said.

"How did your lunch go? Is she coming to stay? I can't wait until she is here," Lucie said.

"You and me both. But there is one small obstacle."

"Don't worry about Oliver. He'll behave. And he's not here often enough to make things uncomfortable."

"I wish it were Oliver. Sophie is taking this honesty thing too far. She wants me to tell my mother."

"Oh."

"You remember how she was about your abortion? She is going to be just as bad about this. I never realized my mother was so conservative. She is a Unitarian, for heaven's sake! I can't risk telling her."

"Could you be underestimating your mother? Nana Sylvia loves you so much. I know she wants you to be happy. Besides, didn't you tell me once that there is always more than one choice—that you simply have to be still and let it come to you?"

"Lucie, what I *don't* need is for you to quote my own supposed wisdom back to me. I'm talking to you because I don't know what to do."

"I can see how scared you are. Before the wedding I felt scared, too. But I think you have to take a chance on love. It might sound like a cliché, but you have to be willing to risk. This might be a time when telling the truth gets you something you want. Oliver is not perfect, but I love him so much. It means everything to have this connection. I recognize there are some things worth lying about. Aren't there some things that are worth telling the truth about?"

I was silent and unconvinced.

"So—what, you are going to let Sophie go? You are going to give up on love?"

"I think that is my only option."

"Let's cut some roses to take inside—I have an extra pair of gloves and another set of clippers on the table," Lucie said.

As we cut, the heady scent of the roses took me back to my childhood. My parents weren't terribly social, but there were dinners and events at my father's bank that they had to attend, and Mother let me come into their bedroom and watch her dress. She'd ask my opinion about which earrings or necklace to wear with her outfit, and what color lipstick would be best. She let me choose her perfume. She had four or five different bottles on her nightstand. I'd always squirt a little of each on the inside of my wrist, and I always chose the one called *White Rose*. My mother always nodded in approval, as if there were any chance I'd select *L'Air du Temps* or *Chanel No. 5*. Then she'd kiss me on the top of the head and say, "You always choose the perfect one." I lived for those rare kisses—for those intimate moments with her. Could it be? Was it possible she would think I could choose the perfect person to love?

I poured a glass of wine and took a hot bath.

CHAPTER 26

TROUSERS

Once again at loose ends and missing Sophie, I decided to spend some time exploring Paris. Even with the rebuilding funded by the Marshall Plan, six years after Germany's surrender, I saw signs of the war everywhere. Next to a new hotel were barricades left over from the Occupation. Yet Paris was still a magnificent city. I passed a charcuterie and bought a summer sausage. Then I spent a franc on a bouquet of daisies at an outdoor florist whose buckets were overflowing with tulips and enormous sunflowers. I juggled my purchases with the obligatory purse because my dress had no pockets. I wore one of the half dozen nondescript shirtwaist dresses my mother bought for me at the Tall Gal's Shop. I thought of clothes as an unfortunate necessity. When my mother found something that fit, she bought it in several colors and that comprised my wardrobe. I hate going shopping because I always feel gangly and—well, just wrong. The only time I can remember standing up tall was when I wore the habit, my teacher's uniform, in Paris in 1939. Otherwise, I wore anything that allowed me to blend in as much as a six-foot-tall woman can blend in. So I was surprised to be drawn to the window of a clothing shop which featured photographs of women who did not blend in at all. They were in rooms that looked as though they had been staged—a table here, a lamp there. Many of the women were as tall as I am. They leaned nonchalantly against each other. They wore trousers like Katharine Hepburn. Some had long cigarette holders. Some wore hats—bérets or fedoras. Their clothes were made of camel hair and tweed—fabrics I associated with menswear. As I looked more closely, I saw that not only their clothing was different. They seemed completely at ease. At ease in the clothes. At ease with each other. They were not like any women I had seen before. I had a funny feeling in my stomach—as if this was something that should be familiar. As if these were rooms I could walk into and be known.

As I stood gawking, a woman even taller than I am approached the shop and unlocked the door. Her hair was Scandinavian blond and her black béret set off her scarlet lipstick. She did anything but blend in.

"Are you coming in, then?" she asked with a British accent.

I stammered something about just looking, but she swept me in with her as if she had been expecting me. She looked me up and down and smiled. "I see you are in disguise as a schoolmarm. I'd say you're a size 12 or 14 tall," she said, moving behind a big old-fashioned cash register. "That corner." She pointed across the shop. In a trance, I made my way to the rack of clothes. Hanging there in all fabrics and colors were trousers like the ones in the photographs.

"The changing rooms are right behind me if you would like to try anything."

I wanted to. I really did. But I could not imagine taking my clothes off anywhere in the vicinity of this woman. I gulped and grabbed a pair of khaki slacks in a size 12 long—what I usually wore at the Tall Gal's Shop.

"I'll take these." I thrust them toward her as if they would bite.

"Sure you don't want to try them?" She smiled that 'easy in her body' look. I wondered if she were one of the women in the photographs. I shook my head, no. As she slid the pants into a bag, she turned to a shelf behind her and said, "I think you'll find this blouse is the perfect match. Crêpe de Chine in cocoa. And on sale!"

I must have nodded my head because the blouse went into the bag too. She gave me a price that should have made me change my mind. Instead, I handed her a large wad of francs and received a very small handful of change.

The woman looked at me and paused before she handed me the bag.

"She'll still love you."

"What?" I gasped. "Who?"

"Your mum." I looked at her in disbelief.

"Your mum will still love you whether you are wearing trousers or…" she made a face like she'd eaten something that had spoiled… "That lot," she gestured toward my perfectly respectable dress. She raised her hands in surrender. "I'm not clairvoyant. It's just I've been where you are now… well, close enough."

I couldn't breathe as I turned and ran out of the store.

CHAPTER 27

TELLING MORE SECRETS

As I moped around the convent that summer, Lucie wasn't shy about her advice.

"Trust your mother, Jane. She loves you, and besides, you'll survive no matter what her reaction. But you aren't fine pining for Sophie. Don't be stupid and lose her. She won't wait forever, even for you."

That, added to the unsolicited advice of the fortune teller at the clothing shop, helped me to realize I was acting like a child. I was ready to grow up. There was still no telephone at Our Lady, despite many entreaties, and I couldn't picture myself standing in the village phone booth, dropping centimes into the slot and trying to hear anything over the usual transatlantic static. So I decided to send a letter. I told Sophie what I was doing, and she wanted to add a letter of her own.

Dear Mother,

This is a hard letter to write. My mouth is dry; my palms are moist; and my heart is racing. I love you so much and I trust that you love me. But I have never been confident of your approval, even though you told me you were proud of me so many times. Now I understand that I will be all right whether you approve of me or not. And that you will love me whether you approve of me or not.

In all these years, I appreciate that you rarely asked if I was seeing anyone. Yet you often said you wished I had love in my life. I have yearned for that too. Now there is a wonderful person who loves me and whom I love. It is a woman. Her name is Sophie. You met her at Lucie's wedding.

I don't think it can come as much of a surprise to you that I was never interested in men. I remember all those terrible nights after those terrible dances. Do you recall that you asked me one time, "What is wrong with you?" That is how I thought of myself for a long time. That I was broken or even sick. When Lucie got in trouble for writing that school report about a woman who loves another woman in The Children's Hour, *I got a pretty good sense of how you and Lucie's mother, Sadie, thought about it. That was part of why I kept this secret for so long. But, at the age of thirty-seven, it is time for me to grow up.*

I am very happy, and I believe this relationship will last a life-time.

I hope we can visit soon so that you and Sophie can get to know each other.

I realize this news may be unwelcome. Please take your time to write back. Lucie and Levy know. I won't tell anyone else until I hear from you. Thank you for always being my champion.

All my love,

Jane

P.S. Sophie has asked that I enclose a letter to you from her.

Dear Madame Smith,

Although we met briefly at Lucie's wedding, so much was going on that we didn't get a chance to talk. I was just getting to know Jane then, as well.

Your daughter is the bravest, most openhearted person I have ever known, and I love her dearly. You are very, very important to her, and it would be devastating to her if our relationship came between the two of you.

Just to tell you a bit about myself. I was born and raised in France. Until my mother became ill, I was a professor of English literature at the Sorbonne. I cared for Maman for almost a year until she died of cancer. I miss her very much.

Although there have been other people in my life, Jane is the first to whom I have pledged my heart and soul.

I realize you may be hurt that Jane has kept this from you. And you may be scared that her life will not be normal. Those were both reactions my mother had. I want to assure you that the life she has created is outside the lines of the typical, but it is much richer and more real than any ordinary life. Jane credits you for teaching her about justice and about making a difference in the world, so thank you. I hope you can keep an open mind and accept that this aspect of Jane's life is not an aberration. It was meant to be.

Respectfully,

Sophie St. Martin

I was on tenterhooks for days after I posted the letters. Airmail to the states often took a week or more, so I would need to wait two weeks to get a letter in reply. But one afternoon, Claude appeared at our back door and told me to hurry to the dairy. He said Françoise had answered a call from my mother, who left the message, "Tell her I love her and to call me right back." I dropped what I was doing and jumped into the carriage with him. It only took ten minutes to get to their house, but I kept telling Claude to please hurry up. Françoise and Claude left the kitchen to give me privacy. I dialed the operator, my voice shaking. "I'd like to place a long-distance call to the United States. Yes. To Stamford, Connecticut. The number is Davis 2-4210. Thank you."

I waited a minute, pacing back and forth as far as the short cord would let me go. The operator said, "I have your party."

My mother said, "Is that you, darling?"

"Yes, it's me."

"I didn't want you to wait for a letter. I am so glad you are happy. Sophie seemed like a lovely person. Please don't worry about anything."

"Oh, Mom…"

"Jane, I am mortified that you felt afraid I might not accept your choice. I never meant to be like that—like my mother. Please let me apologize."

"There is nothing to apologize for. This was about my own childish fear. Thank you for calling. Thank you for loving me."

"My darling, how could I not? Let's plan a visit soon."

"Yes, I want to. Write to me. I love you."

"I love you, too."

When we hung up, I called Françoise and Claude into the kitchen. I told them what had happened, and they cheered me. I felt so lucky my friends cared for me more than they cared about the rules of society. Françoise drove me back to the convent, patting my hand as I wept in relief.

I went right to my room and opened the bag I had hidden beneath my habit. I took off my dress and tossed it onto the bed. My new trousers and blouse fit like they were tailored for me. Under my breath, I blessed the seer, or witch, or figment of my imagination who had so informed my life. I put my hands deep into the pockets of the high-waisted pants and turned to see as much of myself as I could in the small wall mirror. I cursed for the thousandth time that we didn't have a phone. I took the car, praying that I would find Sophie at home. Even before I got out, I saw Sophie at the door. She looked at me and raised her eyebrow. I nodded. Seeing her set my heart on fire. Sophie smiled like a sunbeam, ran down the steps, took me in her arms, and waltzed me down the sidewalk. As we danced, she whispered in my ear, "You look dashing."

I was born anew.

CHAPTER 28

CHASTAIN'S DAUGHTER

Shortly after, Sophie moved her belongings into my room. She fit right in with our little crew. As Levy said, having someone who loved to cook and was so good at it changed our lives.

The following week, a sunny morning found Levy, Sophie, Lucie, and me in the kitchen. Oliver was in Paris. Lucie made a big pitcher of lemonade.

As she poured, we talked about what to plan for lunch. Before Sophie finished proposing tuna fish salad with capers, Françoise came into the kitchen, looking serious.

"Something has come up." She turned to me. "Jane, don't be angry with me."

"Why would I be angry?" I was in too good a mood to see the quicksand right in front of me.

She looked at all of us. "I have been contacted by a friend who is in desperate need of our help."

I noted that there was all of a sudden "*our* help."

I couldn't believe it. "Not another one of your friends. Françoise, we have discussed creating a clinic, but I have not made a decision. I shall indeed be very angry if you tell me you are sharing our very illegal secret."

"Not precisely sharing. I grew up with Florent and his wife, Elodie. Their daughter, Corinne, is very special, and it is a terrible story."

"Everyone's daughter is special, and everyone has a terrible story, Françoise. We can talk about this and decide tomorrow."

Françoise stood up straighter. Since I was sitting, it was the only way to tower over me. "They are here now, Jane. Out in the carriage."

"Absolutely not!" I said, trying not to sound unhinged.

Levy reached over to take my hand. He was always good at calming me down. "Jane. Look at me. We have everything we need. It went so well with Gertrude. We can do it again, just this one time. Won't you consider it?"

"We talked about this. We could get in serious trouble with the law," I said.

"Not this time," Françoise insisted. "Florent Chastain is the head of the Garde Champêtre—he's the local police captain."

Lucie barged in. "Jane, this is just what you want! If we do this for the police captain, he'll leave us alone and we can set up a clinic. This will take care of that little 'going to jail' problem. It's perfect!"

"At least let Florent come in. Let him explain the situation," Françoise implored.

I glanced at Sophie and she nodded her head. Lucie and Levy chimed in that I should hear the man out.

"All right! Let him come." I gave in. Why did I always give in?

Françoise brought the inspector and his daughter into the kitchen. His young daughter, Corinne, was holding his hand and looked up at him with perfect trust.

Françoise said, "Corinne and I are going to go into the garden to count the flowers."

Chastain took a seat at the table and shook his head at the offer of coffee.

"Thank you for hearing me out. My darling Corinne is fourteen years old, but her mind is like a little child's. My only job as a father is to keep her safe, and I failed. The man who had his way with her has been imprisoned. He will not harm another. But…"

From a decade of providing abortion care, I recognized the look in his eyes and the falter in his voice.

"She is pregnant."

He looked away and nodded, as if saying the word would make it more true.

"I am so sorry, Inspector."

"Corinne doesn't understand what is happening to her. My wife is desperate. How can we force an innocent to bear the child of a monster?" He looked at me and cleared his throat. "Our dear Françoise has told us that you… that you know how to help."

Drat that Françoise! As hard as I work to keep secrets, she throws them to the wind like scattering seeds.

"What you are asking about is illegal."

"I am well aware of that. But this is my daughter. My only child."

"I don't know if… "

"She is very obedient," Chastain interjected. "If she needs to be still or quiet, she can do that."

"Do you have any idea when her pregnancy began?" Levy asked, afraid she might be too far.

"When I arrested the scoundrel, he admitted he had interfered with my Corinne when I was in Paris. That was two and a half months ago."

Levy turned to me. "That would be ten weeks. We should be fine. If… If you want to do this."

I turned to my team. Lucie's eyes were glistening. She nodded that she wanted me to do the abortion. Levy and Sophie did the same. It was obvious what Françoise wanted. So they were leaving it up to me. I sighed and nodded.

"All right, Inspector. We will help Corinne. But you must agree never to speak of this."

Lucie chimed in. "And will you protect us from arrest?"

The inspector looked solemn. "I give you my word to keep this secret. Only my wife will be aware of this. And I will do everything in my power to keep you safe." He turned to me.

"This would be a great deal easier if you were, indeed, a convent. Then I'd bring the men in my department over and convince them not to interfere with your holy affairs. I think they have to see you with their own eyes to follow my orders. Is that possible?"

Lucie looked at me with a mischievous smile, as if this had been her plan all along.

"We'll see," I said, having no idea of the adventures this answer might take us on.

And so, taking a little extra time to keep her calm, and with a few extra hugs, we did Corinne's abortion. She stayed very still. Françoise held the girl's hand; Sophie monitored blood pressure; and Dr. Levy and I ended a pregnancy that should never have begun.

Corinne rested for an hour. We let Inspector Chastain take her home because they lived close by and her bleeding was very light. We gave him instructions about possible complications which became part of our standard practice.

Back in the kitchen, we sat around the table drinking sparkling water while Sophie prepared lunch.

I wanted to talk about Corinne's procedure, but they were busy planning a clinic I had not agreed to.

"We'll need to write down some policies and procedures so we are all following the same plan," Levy began.

"Policies? We never had that in Paris!" I said.

"In Paris, I was the only one giving care. The procedures were all in my head."

Sophie said, "What about what Chastain said? That it would be easier to protect us if we appeared to be an actual convent?"

"I am never entirely comfortable impersonating a nun, even if it is what a woman needs," I said.

"Françoise, you are Catholic. Does it offend you for us to wear habits and pretend to be nuns?" Lucie asked.

Françoise gave a hollow laugh. "I am Catholic because my parents were Catholic. Because everyone in my village is Catholic. But I am under no illusions about the Church."

"What do you mean?" I asked, shelling peas into a bowl.

She paused. "Besides permitting the horrors of the Second War, my church betrayed women long ago. Look at the stories they tell. From Eve to Mary Magdalene, they blame women as the original sinners. All the evils of the world are our fault. And we are only vessels to bring forth baby after baby until we die of exhaustion. If wearing a habit lets us do our work, it is fine with me."

Lucie looked up from the potatoes she was peeling.

"Françoise, I have never heard you so angry."

Françoise shook her head. "Not so much angry as desolate. This is how the Church treats us, yet it is all we have."

I pulled the leaves from a head of lettuce that had been freshly picked from the garden and dropped them in a bowl to wash.

"I'm thinking about the women I've helped. Sometimes I wore the uniform of a nun. Sometimes of a Navy nurse. They were dressed as shopgirls, geishas, farm-workers, and students. What we wore separated us and defined our roles, yet only on the surface. Underneath we were all the same."

"But isn't the habit supposed to be sacred?" Lucie asked.

Françoise answered. "The habit itself is just a piece of cloth. It is what we do when we wear it that conveys meaning. If we can use the accoutrements of the Church to help women feel whole, it is only fitting that we do it. Now let's get this salad on the table and call Levy for lunch." It was a relief to see Françoise back to her normal, cheerful self. But her words stayed with me.

After we ate, it was time to make a momentous decision. Would we follow Inspector Chastain's suggestion and establish Our Lady as a convent where coming for a religious retreat might mean seeking an abortion? Could we get away with it?

Sophie was the most neutral of us, not having been involved in previous discussions.

"Jane, I am the new person here, so I don't want to overstep, but as I hear it, everything needed for a wonderful clinic is already here, and this morning's experience with Chastain provides a protection we didn't have before. Is that right?"

I nodded, reluctantly. I hated feeling pressured by anyone, even the lovely Sophie.

"And isn't this what you have always wanted? To provide this care without interference?" Clearly Lucie had bent her ear.

I nodded again. "But even if the police don't come after us, how do you suppose we'll get away with pretending to be a convent? The Catholic Church has at least as much power as the police—perhaps more."

Françoise put her hand on my arm. "You are right about that, Jane. But what you may not know is that there are congregations that have broken away from Rome. France's Catholicism may be called 'the eldest daughter of the church,' but our law allows the right to establish independent religious communities."

"So we'd be the independent community that provides abortions? Come on, Françoise. You know that won't work."

A cacophony of voices argued that we could make it work.

"Hold on. One at a time. Maybe we could get away with it. But this idea puts all of you at risk, not just me. I can't ask you to do something that might put you in prison or have the Church rise up against you so that I can follow my dream," I said.

Lucie spread her hands open in a gesture of surprise. "You don't have to ask us. I think we are all asking *you*." She looked around. "Can't it be our dream, too? Is there anyone who doesn't want to do this?"

I looked at the open faces of my friends.

"It appears," Levy said, taking the last of the crisp, lemony sugar cookies Françoise brought for dessert, "we are in agreement."

Later that week, Chastain came by and asked if we would wear habits that afternoon so that he could honor his promise and bring his men over. As if we were getting ready for a Halloween party, we rooted through the cabinet where Françoise found the old habits. I already had one, and we found one for Françoise and one that fit Lucie. One was a bit too wide for Sophie, but it would do. We agreed that I would do the talking, and they would just be nice nuns sitting in the background praying. The knock came at the door and I opened it. My heart clanged like church bells.

Chastain came in, flanked by four young officers who all took off their hats. Chastain introduced himself as if we had never met. I invited them into the drawing room and told them I was the Mother Superior. If they wanted more of a name, they didn't ask. Sophie was knitting, Françoise was reading a Bible she had brought from the dairy, and Lucie was piously writing in her journal. Levy listened from the next room.

Chastain stood tall and spoke with authority.

"*Mes officiers, attention.* This is a convent. There will be no cause to come here after today. We do not interfere with these sisters, their special retreats for women, or their prayers. We ignore any rumors that may come from envy of the sisters' holy mission."

The young men looked scared, as if we might whack their hands with rulers.

"These are ladies' affairs. It's none of our business what they do here, and you shouldn't be asking, understood?" our protector exclaimed, putting his hat firmly back on his head.

All four men nodded soberly. Chastain clicked his heels and led them out the front door, turning to give me a wink. And so, with no more guarantee than a wink, we began to plan the abortion clinic hitherto known as "Our Lady of Perpetual Grace."

CHAPTER 29

WHAT DO WE THINK WE ARE DOING HERE?

Back in the kitchen, we started in earnest to design a clinic. "Now that we are a team," I said, grinning, "let's plan our policies and protocols. After all, we are doing this in a convent. The least we can do is provide a sacred service."

Françoise began. "The whole plan is genius. No one cares about women and their religious retreats. Even when my father was very sick, my mother went on a three to four-day religious retreat every year without fail. No one ever questioned it. Women are invisible in this world. They are just someone's mother. Someone's wife. Someone's daughter. No one wonders what they would create if they could. But here, they are real. We see them. We see their dreams and pain. No woman leaves here the same as she came."

"Agreed. Here's another thing we have to address. As a team, we won't always see things the same way," I said. "Can we disagree and still be friends?"

"We'd better!" Françoise said. "We are all each other has."

Levy said, "I'm concerned that we need to keep notes." And so the conversation began in earnest.

First, we tried to agree on our mission. Providing abortions was obvious. Caring about women was too vague. Levy wanted something about education, but we vetoed that as too boring.

"Isn't the main thing the love? The love we have for our patients, and the love they bring for themselves and their families?" Sophie said.

"*C'est ça!* Care with love." The smiling faces around me told me we had our North Star.

We agreed on a three-day process. The first day would be dedicated to providing each woman with information, learning how the woman was feeling, and helping to resolve any issues or concerns. The second day would be for the procedure. The third day would be for recovery. Sophie volunteered to research what buses came close enough for patients to walk to the convent. Lucie started a budget to determine the lowest possible fee that would cover our basic costs, including food and supplies. Françoise offered to keep a list of supplies and groceries we needed and bring them from the village on her way each morning. Levy volunteered to make a basic script to edit for each patient as needed, covering an explanation of the procedure and what to expect afterwards. I offered to write information about the Uterine Suction Apparatus so that we would each be able to explain the procedure the same way. And Lucie and I worked together on training Sophie and Françoise about the consultation to tailor our services to the needs of each woman.

"Are we still planning on wearing habits?" Sophie asked. "If so, I'm going to need a new one." We had all laughed when Françoise used clothespins to clip the back of Sophie's musty old habit.

"We will all need new ones," Françoise said. "I will talk with Elodie Chastain. Fortunately for us, she is the best seamstress in the village, and the only one we can trust to keep our secret."

Sophie said, "I don't mind wearing a habit when it helps. But what will happen when a woman who trusts us figures out she was not forgiven by a real nun?"

No one had an answer.

"Won't they understand we are showing them the mercy they should have gotten from the Church?" Françoise asked.

"Perhaps. But when they leave us, they are going back to their churches and their priests, and we'd better prepare them so they are not shocked or disappointed. Or just angry. That could undo all the work they have done with us," I said.

"When would we tell them?" Sophie asked.

"Maybe not before. Because we *are* listening to them and intervening with our best approximation of the love of the Virgin," Françoise said.

"I don't think we can say that—or not exactly that. When they come to us, they are confused and in crisis. What I mean by that is the same word as crossroads, like the shape of a cross. They are facing a crucible—choosing a pathway for their lives. We must meet them at that crossroad with open hearts and minds—inviting them to open *their* hearts and minds. Once the work is done, they will know the Church they grew up in doesn't allow the kind of exploration, forgiveness, and healing on which our work is anchored," I said.

"We could assume that. But I think we need to agree on a way to be honest. Each of us has had the experience of wearing the habit. I'm sorry, Levy. I didn't mean to exclude you. We have been fortunate enough to see transformation when a woman trusts us that way. We have to agree on a way to be honest about this," Sophie said.

That conversation led to a statement we worked and re-worked until we agreed it was the best we could do.

I think you know that I am not a nun in the Roman Catholic Church.

The woman will either nod or look surprised.

We are women who care more about your true soul than we do about the rules of the Church. Those rules were not written by us or for us. They were written by men to address their comfort and power..

By then, we imagined every woman would be nodding her head.

So when you go home, your priest and the nuns in your church will not have this same conversation with you. They have not been at this crossroad. They only know about sin. They use that word to mean something that makes you less—that puts you outside your own heart, and outside the heart and blessings of God. But an ancient translation of the word sin is "missing the mark"—an acceptance of the reality of being human. Our work is about the harsh reality of being female, and with it, a new possibility of experiencing yourself as good and whole.

Françoise said, "What if they can't remember how they felt when they were with us?"

Sophie said, "Let's tell them they can come back and talk with us if they need to remember their own goodness. And remind them they can take us with them in their heart."

"How will anyone find out about our services?" Sophie asked.

"I will never understand just how it works, but women who need us are going to learn about us," Levy said confidently. "That's what happened in Paris. My wife and I never told anyone what we were doing. Women who trusted us told other women who needed us."

I was holding back a blunt truth that I needed to share. I was afraid of what my always-honest Sophie's reaction would be.

"One last thing before we finish. I want to tell all of you that I am *not* going to tell my mother about our work. As far as she is concerned, we run a hostel for women who need a place to retreat from life's difficult situations."

"I think that describes us very nicely," Françoise said.

Sophie glared at Françoise. "But why, Jane? Why won't you tell your mother?"

"You didn't see her reaction after Lucie's abortion," Levy said. "She was a madwoman. Sylvia made us all promise never to utter the word."

"Where did that come from? Was she raised Catholic?" Sophie asked.

"She was, but she is a Unitarian now. She always said she wanted to get away from the idea of sin and punishment. But I guess hearing that abortion is an abomination never wore off. I had to travel more than 3,000 miles away from home to do the work I love. I have to impersonate a nun and befriend the police chief to do it. This work is sacred to me. I'm not going to jeopardize it on the off chance that my mother would have me arrested for murder." I folded my arms. "This is something I won't compromise on, Sophie. Leave if you have to, but this is a secret I am going to keep, for all our sakes."

Sophie didn't leave. But every time my mother wrote asking to come for a visit and I had to put her off, the secret haunted me.

CHAPTER 30

CLOISTER DOG

As we attended to our usual daily tasks, our first cloister dog appeared—part German Shepherd, part who knows what? She sauntered into the kitchen one morning through the open door while we ate breakfast. The dog found a corner she liked, circled around a few times, and plopped down. Lucie claimed her immediately.

"I'm naming her Gracie for Our Lady of Perpetual Grace," Lucie declared, sitting cross-legged on the floor next to the dog and scratching the thick fur under her chin.

Françoise made the appropriate inquiries in the village for a missing dog, with no result. So we welcomed her as ours.

In those days, only hunting dogs were trained. Or dogs that herded goats or sheep. Otherwise, dogs just did whatever dogs did. But Gracie astonished us. She took on two jobs. On weekday afternoons, she escorted the women leaving the convent, walking the half hour with them to the crossroads where the bus stopped. Then she met the women who got off the bus to guide them to Our Lady. She became so dependable that we simply told patients to follow the German Shepherd. Her second job was to take care of Lucie. To no one's surprise, it turned out that Oliver didn't much like dogs. He thought it unsanitary to have them in the house, much less on the mattress. On the many nights Oliver stayed in Paris, Gracie slept on Lucie's bed, so Lucie had one bedspread for the nights Oliver came home, and a different one when Gracie slept on the bed next to her. She spent a considerable amount of time cleaning dog hair off anything Oliver might see, but she never complained. On the increasingly rare nights that Oliver stayed at the cloister, Gracie slept with Sophie and me, curled up on a rug at the foot of our bed.

That summer, we were busy and happy. We celebrated Lucie's birthday, took care of the honeybees, ate salads with fresh lettuce and tomatoes from Sophie's garden, and performed abortions for our patients. But by fall, it became obvious that Oliver was getting impatient dwelling with the "in-laws."

One day, a tearful Lucie sought me out at my quiet place by the wishing well. "Oh Jane, he is not happy. Is it my duty as his wife to keep him happy?" she asked.

"I have never been a wife," I answered, trying to stay calm. I hated that Lucie was distressed. "Besides, didn't it used to be Oliver's job to keep *you* happy?"

"Yes. But now we are married, and it seems that there are new rules. He says I am not acting like a good wife!" she wailed.

In my head, I said, *Thank the Lord for small favors that I am not a wife.* But aloud, I said, "Françoise and Claude seem to be content. Why not talk with her about this?" I felt a little guilty about pawning off Lucie's misery, but I still didn't like Oliver. I had never liked him. And I didn't even want to imagine trying to help my zany, independent Lucie become subservient to the likes of him.

About a week later, Françoise came into the kitchen where I was peeling potatoes and gave me a look.

"I had a talk with our young Lucie," she said. "She wanted to know what Claude and I do when we argue." Françoise sat at the kitchen table. "I told her that when Claude and I disagree, we do it politely, and we seek a compromise. Lucie said she doesn't have any idea how to argue politely. Oliver wants to move to Paris, and Lucie doesn't. She doesn't want to leave us—and Gracie. She was almost crying when she said that. But I had an idea. Remember that empty cottage on the farm? I suggested that if we all pitched in (all except Oliver, of course, because he is far too important), we might freshen it up and make it suitable for them. She wouldn't be living here under your nose, but she'd come to the convent with me every day. She said she would ask him."

It made me sick to think of me and Oliver vying for Lucie's affection.

A surly Oliver agreed to move into the cottage on the farm, on the condition that Gracie could not come with them. We overheard several terrible arguments about it with many entreaties, but he wouldn't relent. After a whirlwind of painting and cleaning and buying new furniture, they moved in September.

"I'll come back every day," she said to me. "This is so important to Oliver." Lucie sat on the floor and buried her face in Gracie's fur. Then she took the dog's muzzle in her hands and spoke very low. "Gracie, I love you so much. Thank you for being my best friend. How will I handle life without you? I promise to come back to see you every day, and you will be safe with Jane and Sophie." I hardly understood the last part because she was sniffling and crying so hard. This was my Lucie—twenty, going on thirty, going on seven.

At first, Lucie did come back every day. She came when we had women on retreats, and even when we didn't. But Oliver was still not happy. At

Christmas, they came for dinner—one of the few times we'd seen him. Standing in the kitchen, he began complaining to Levy, who was barely listening.

"I hate commuting. When I stay out here, it takes me two hours and sometimes there is no place to sit on the train. I'm forced to wake up so early to get to work that it is ruining my sleep. And if I need to be in Paris for a social event, I must sleep on a couch in some terrible apartment. To get promoted, it is necessary to present the image of a stable family man—with my beautiful wife on my arm. You know what I mean, Levy—as a fellow physician?"

Levy looked up at Oliver as if he had just noticed he was there.

"Surely you realize that I am not that kind of physician, Oliver. I am a Jewish refugee who performs illegal abortions on women who are pretending they are on a Catholic retreat," he said. No love was lost between Levy and Oliver, but I had never heard Levy be so caustic. My heart sank. Even Levy thought Oliver was a pompous ass. I hated to think of Lucie with him.

After a few months of living in the cottage, Oliver put his foot down and demanded they move into Paris.

"I have leased an apartment close to the Sorbonne," he declared during a rare family meal. "Lucie can go back to school as she has always wanted."

Lucie looked at me sheepishly. It was I who had constantly nagged her to finish her education.

"If I must move to Paris, I might as well get something out of it," she said peevishly. Whatever kind of compromise they had made did not look like a partnership—at least from my perspective. "I am going to study psychology," she said. "It's because of my work here at Our Lady. I want to understand human emotions." Under the table, she was feeding small bites of salmon to Gracie, who was glued to her side.

"We will miss having you here," I said. "I will miss you."

"I will too," Sophie and Levy each said, nearly in unison.

Oliver cornered me in the cupboard. "Lucie *wants* to move to Paris. You heard her. As long as she is attached to you, she'll never *really* be my wife. You'll always come first. I need her. She's all I have." I had never imagined that I would see Oliver in tears, his fists clenched at his sides. After the tears came the threats. "If you do anything to get in the way of our moving, mark my words, I won't hesitate to contact the authorities about your little enterprise. You and your dyke friends. Your illegal medicine. You can tell my parents anything you want. Do you think they would believe you? I know you don't care about yourself, but it would be a shame to see your pals locked up because you couldn't keep your nose out of our lives. And not one word of this to Lucie."

Yes, that was the Oliver I knew. I had not imagined he would go that far, but I saw he was serious, so I held my tongue. This was everything I had feared—not just for myself, but for Françoise and Levy. Surely Oliver wouldn't implicate Lucie in anything that could get her arrested? I had counted on Oliver's need to be certain his family never learned he had almost killed Lucie with his ignorance. Any leverage I had with him was gone. I hated it that my Lucie was with this horrid man.

When the day came, the furniture was loaded into a rented truck, and they made the pilgrimage to Paris. Lucie cried as she said goodbye, but I'm not sure how many of the tears were for us and how many for her beloved canine companion.

Once again, Lucie was gone.

I couldn't get used to not seeing her every day. She wrote to me every week, just as she had for all the years I was in California and Japan. Her letters from Paris were full of excitement about her studies. She loved her professors; she loved her fellow students; and she loved Paris. I was very happy for her and recalled those heady days during my nursing school in Alameda when there was so much to learn.

But I worried about what Oliver could do to all of us, and what was in store for my darling Lucie living under his sway.

CHAPTER 31

DON'T MOLLYCODDLE ME

I woke disoriented, breathing hard. By then Sophie anticipated my night-mares and they no longer alarmed her. She simply held me and helped me slow my breathing.

"Do you want to tell me about it?"

"No." My breathing was almost back to normal, but my head was still spinning, and I was still afraid.

"Did you dream about that same woman?"

"Yes. I'm sorry I woke you. Let's go back to sleep."

"Jane, this will keep happening if you don't talk about it."

"How would that help? Don't mollycoddle me. I just need to get over it."

"I have no idea what you said."

"Sorry. It's something my mother used to say. I guess it means you shouldn't treat me like a child."

"Being kind is not treating you like a child. It is loving you. This woman disturbs your dreams too often. Your silence gives her power over you. Please. Humor me. What is the story of this person who causes you such distress?"

By then, we sat up, both awake. "This story requires some hot chocolate," I said. Sophie put on her robe and went into the kitchen. As I waited for her to return, I wondered where to start the story of my nemesis, Brigitte.

Sophie returned with a tray. Steaming mugs of hot chocolate with a little pile of Madeleines brightened my mood. I took a couple of sips and finished a cookie, and with a deep sigh, began the story.

"I have had nightmares for as long as I can remember. As a little girl, I would wake from a bad dream and cry and wail until my father came. When I finally heard his footsteps, I also heard my mother call after him, 'Don't mollycoddle her. She'll be all right in a few minutes. Just let her cry. She'll have to learn to get over this.'

"My father would sit on my bedside and sing 'Speed Bonnie Boat' and 'There is a Tavern in the Town.'

"Adieu, adieu, kind friends adieu, yes adieu
I can no longer stay with you, stay with you
I will hang my heart on a weeping willow tree
And never, never think of thee.

"By the time I was six or seven, he didn't come anymore. After all, he'd sung 'I can no longer stay with thee,' so often that it was just a matter of time. I'd lie in bed panting, my heart drumming, sweat running down my back, my eyes wild, trying to breathe. Finally, as my mother predicted, I would be all right. But the nightmares never stopped. I learned I'd have to overcome them by myself.

"My parents alternated putting me to bed. My father read from books he had loved as a child. *The Secret Garden, The Wonderful Wizard of Oz, Peter Pan in Kensington Gardens, Robinson Crusoe.* On her nights, my mother invented fanciful stories about fairies, leprechauns, and witches.

"I knew she loved me. But I also realized I was a deep disappointment. There were so many ways in which I didn't quite measure up. My nightmares were the least of it. I grew to be too tall for a girl. Though she tried to hide her dismay, it wasn't hard to discern. She constantly complimented my smaller friends. Which meant all my friends. I recall one of our conversations.

"'Darling, didn't Cynthia look sweet in that wool coat? I wonder if she would ever lend it to you?'

"'Yes, Mother, Cynthia looked wonderful in her new coat. And she is very generous. But she is seven inches shorter than I am.'

"'Is she really? I never would have thought.'"

"That explains a lot. Your mother is not always kind," Sophie said.

I laughed, closed my eyes, and shook my head in agreement. "No. She's not. But I still need to tell you the story of the terrible Brigitte. In 1939, I traveled to France to be a teacher at my aunt's school in Paris."

"Your Aunt Mathilde, your father's sister, right?"

"Yes. I had finished college and all my friends were getting married. When my aunt wrote asking if I would come, it seemed like a good opportunity. I had never been a teacher, but my mother persuaded me it wouldn't be hard to teach seven-year-olds, and I wanted to see Paris. You might have thought my parents would be worried about the impending war, but everyone pretended it could never happen. So I sailed. When I got to the school, Aunt Mathilde was cordial enough, but very preoccupied. She sort of pawned me off on the cook, Danielle, the groundskeeper, Marcel, and the maid, Brigitte. From the very start, Brigitte didn't like me. She had been a good friend of the former teacher who died. Brigitte didn't consider me fit to take Madame Rochand's place. And Brigitte was mean. So I tried to keep to myself and not make trouble. When we feared the Nazi invasion, Brigitte loudly expressed her delight.

She said they would get rid of undesirables and put the country right. It turned out that my aunt planned to smuggle little girls out of Paris through her school during the Occupation, so she had to fire Brigitte lest she turn us in."

"Thank goodness Brigitte wasn't there to torment you anymore."

I took another sip of my now-too-cold chocolate. "That's not the end of the story. As you know, I fell in love with my ten seven-year-olds. Especially Lucie. My students had wealthy parents. As war appeared more and more inevitable, their parents sent for them. Except Lucie, whose scientist father had been killed. Every day, girls in danger were brought to the school. No matter how many came, we found a uniform to pin on them, food, and a warm cot. When she could, Mathilde obtained forged documents authentic enough to get the girls through the Nazi checkpoints. But when she couldn't get documents, the girls piled up in our dormitory. One day, I took twenty girls to the park. Maybe I shouldn't have, but it had been raining for a week and we were all stir crazy. Brigitte was there and she could see that the girls I had with me were not Aunt Mathilde's students. She threatened to turn us in."

"*Cherié!* You must have been terrified."

"Petrified. I tried to bribe her by giving her the money in my purse, meant to pay for groceries. And I gave her my ring."

"This ring?" she asked, touching my hand. She knew how I valued my topaz ring. It was a gift from my parents all those long years ago when I had first sailed to Paris.

"Yes. I'll explain how I got it back. But first I'm going to warm up my chocolate. Would you like more?"

"*Merci.*"

I put my robe on, took both cups into the kitchen, and returned with two full cups. For a few minutes, we just blew on the hot drinks.

"When I learned that Lucie was Jewish and realized both her parents were dead, I was determined to take her to America, where she would be safe during the war. So Levy and I sailed with her, pretending to be her parents. Then I joined the Navy. To save myself, to have an independent life, I left her."

CHAPTER 32

DANGER IN THE CLINIC

Sophie was always kind about my nightmares. Telling her those hard stories about my time in Paris made her even more understanding.

"*Mon tésor*, leaving home to live a life on your own terms is not a sin. You did not abandon Lucie. You made sure she was safe with a loving family."

Sometimes I was able to believe her. The women who came to us sharing their hopes and dreams and fears took my mind off my own demons.

At Our Lady, we prided ourselves on our safety record. But biology has a way of overcoming the best of intentions.

We were working with a patient named Amélie. She had three children, and didn't want more. She told her husband she was at a religious retreat. The abortion went as expected. Only afterwards, I recognized the problem. When I examined the contents of the glass bottle, there was no pregnancy tissue in her uterus.

I called to Sophie, "Quick. Get Levy. He'll need to drive her to the hospital in Paris. Quick!"

I turned to explain to the patient what was happening. She was lying half asleep on the procedure table, covered by a blanket.

"Amélie, I'm sorry to wake you, but you need to get dressed right now. We are afraid your pregnancy is developing in the fallopian tube instead of your uterus. This can be dangerous. We'll take you to the hospital and you'll need a simple surgery. Have you felt pain or cramping on one side?"

"A little on my right side. But I thought it was just normal." Amélie got off the table and began to dress. "How will I tell my husband where I am?"

I made a mental note to tell Dr. Levy it might be the right tube, and to ask Françoise to call from the dairy. Drat not having a telephone. "I'll get a call to him. The surgery you need is perfectly legal and you don't need to keep it secret. Dr. Levy will check you into the hospital. There is some risk, as with any surgery, but I hope this will go well and you'll be safe."

"Am I going to die?"

"No, *Chérie*, you should be safe. We have found this problem very early. It's dangerous when the slender tube is ruptured—broken by the developing pregnancy. We don't want that to happen, which is why Dr. Levy is driving you to the hospital right away."

"Will I still be pregnant?"

"No," I assured her. "They will remove the pregnancy when they remove the tube."

Amélie nodded her head. Levy drove up with the car. Sophie and I bundled Amélie into the car and Levy sped off. Françoise took the wagon to the dairy to call Amélie's husband.

We were not used to emergencies. I was accustomed to doing abortions in a hospital. But we were not in a hospital. I realized we would have to face the possibility of complications and make a plan for how to handle the various emergencies that might emerge.

I ticked them off in my mind:

- Ectopic pregnancy
- Allergy to medications
- Infection after the abortion
- Pregnancy more advanced than we expected
- Too much bleeding—including the dreaded Disseminated Intravascular Coagulopathy (DIC) when a woman's clotting factor is impaired and bleeding cannot be stopped.

I had a couple of experiences with that one, and I hoped never to have another.

Amélie was fine. The surgeon removed her right fallopian tube and congratulated Levy for his skillful medical intuition.

For several days after Amélie's visit, I was haunted by visions of Mimi who died in Paris in 1940. Mimi, who came to me and Levy too late, who was already septic after someone else attempted to end her pregnancy. Mimi, who took her last breath with my body leaning over hers. That last breath was lodged in my bones, like fear made manifest. I had been through other emergencies. In California, I'd seen a patient who had a DIC. She was saved by my old colleague, Dr. Nick. Françoise's niece, Anne-Marie, could have had that same emergency. DIC was difficult to manage even in a hospital where a transfusion was possible. Almost impossible where it was not. As I considered those frightening experiences, I wondered if it was hubris to imagine we could do abortions safely at the convent. Women came to us for help—trusting us—perhaps not understanding they might have a complication, or even die. As I realized this, I felt ashamed. Sophie and I talked about it one night in bed after we had turned off the light.

"Sophie. Are you still awake?"

"Yes, love." I was sure I had woken her.

"I can't sleep. I can't stop thinking about Amélie and what might have happened. Are we being fair? We ask these women to be honest with us. To tell us everything. But we don't tell them they could have a medical complication—or could die. Is that fair?"

Sophie reached out to turn on the light, but I put my hand on her arm. "I can talk about this better in the dark." I don't know why, but I didn't want her to see me crying.

"I'm not sure what to say, dear one. It scares me, too," she whispered.

"You think we should at least tell them, don't you? Tell women what could go wrong," I said.

"I don't want to make them more scared than they already are. They are waiting to be struck down by the Church. How can we talk about this without them expecting punishment?"

"I don't know. Years ago, Dr. Levy impressed on me the importance of telling the woman what to expect with the abortion procedure. My old colleague, Dr. Nick, was very impatient about it. He said women don't want to know all that, and I should just get on with it. How can a woman make a true decision if she is not aware of the possible implications of her choices?"

"*Cherié*, this is so important. I want to talk about this when I am awake. Can we delay this discussion until we can have a meeting to talk about it?"

"Of course. I'm going outside for a little while. Don't worry about me. I'll come back to bed soon."

Sophie was used to my nightmares and my venturing outdoors. I put on my robe, found my slippers, and slid quietly down the hall to the front door. The moment I tiptoed out and closed the large wooden door behind me, I saw the glow of a cigarette. I welcomed it, knowing that behind the cigarette was my dear friend Levy.

Levy scooted over and made room for me on the wooden bench. His cigarette smelled good—not as good as my father's pipe—but the tobacco gave a kind of welcome. We sat next to each other quietly for a few minutes.

He broke the silence. "Couldn't sleep?"

I laughed softly at the banality—the obviousness of the question. Levy knew how to read me and how to approach carefully.

"Mimi is never far from my thoughts," I said.

"Mine, either. But Jane, Amélie isn't Mimi. She is safe. If we hadn't done our procedure, she might never have known she had a tubal pregnancy. Many of the women who have this die. We saved her."

"You're right. I didn't see it that way. Thanks. We saved her, so why can't I stop obsessing about the one we didn't save?"

"Remember what also happened to you around that terrible time? You in the alley with those German soldiers. The fear and shame, and the secret you kept about it. What happened to Mimi is all mixed up with what happened to you. Have you told Sophie?"

"*No*. No. I can't, Bernard." I never called him Bernard.

"Jane, it will help you to talk about it. Sophie is strong. She can handle it. When you leave it a secret, it comes between you. You aren't allowing her to know you."

"Why would I want anyone to hear what happened to me?"

"As terrible as it was, it is part of your reality. Part of what has shaped you. Part of what makes all of this with Amélie so much worse. Let Sophie in, Jane."

I began to weep again. I leaned against him as I considered what it would mean to tell the woman I loved about a day I was a victim—something I never wanted to be. Would she pity me? Would she be repulsed? Would she ever think of me the same way? I calmed myself by synchronizing my breathing with his.

We sat, breathing together, until the sun rose. The myriad colors in the sky were almost enough to make me believe in God.

I was startled by the door opening. The scents of breakfast acted like smelling salts.

"Coffee's on," Sophie said in her most motherly tone.

That afternoon, I started to write an outline for what we ought to tell women about the risks of abortion. How we might tell them without frightening them. But as I wrote, something Levy said kept intruding into my thoughts. *Let Sophie in.* It was a beautiful day—mild and sunny. I considered a picnic, but realized I wouldn't be able to eat. So I settled for asking Sophie to share a bottle of wine. It had been a long time since I'd used alcohol for "liquid courage." The last time was when I confronted my old love, Betty, about her infidelity. This time it was to help me tell a story that I wanted to forget. I carried the wine and two glasses. Sophie carried a blanket. We walked down the stone path to the wishing well where I had always found a measure of serenity.

She didn't pressure me. We lay on the blanket, the bottle of wine forgotten. Finally, I began the story. A five-year-old whose parents had been killed by the Nazis. Me wearing my habit, bringing the little girl to my Aunt Mathilde where we would put her in a school uniform and care for her until we arranged safe passage. Three German soldiers—one of them just a boy. The alley. The cuts and bruises from two soldiers pushing me up against the stone wall and taking what they wanted because I was "pretty enough." My relief that they left the child with the young soldier so she didn't have to watch. My descent into fury in the aftermath—unable to recognize myself for weeks. The kindness of my aunt, the cook, and the children. And dear Dr. Levy, who cared for me, although it broke his heart.

Sophie listened intently. She didn't ask any questions, and I didn't stop until it was all out. Partway through, she lay her hand on my heart, and started crying, softly. Her body grew rigid next to mine, and she was radiating heat. After I was done and had been silent for a few moments, Sophie sat up very straight. She was trembling.

"I want to kill them. Not shoot them—that would be too kind. I want to eviscerate them—like in the Middle Ages. And then burn them alive—what is it? Draw and quarter them?"

I had never seen Sophie so angry. Murderous. To my astonishment, I laughed out loud. She glared at me.

"Oh, *Cherié*. I am not laughing at you. I am so grateful for your reaction. I was afraid—afraid you would judge me. I am just relieved." I took her in my arms and in a moment we were both laughing.

We lay back on the blanket, her head on my chest. She whispered, "Thank you."

That night, I poured myself a glass of wine and took a hot bath.

CHAPTER 33

SECRET RECIPES

I had a nightmare that I had lost a little girl in a pinafore—Lucie. The dream was so familiar, like a cranky relative who says mean things, yet keeps getting invited to dinner. The punishment for losing her was the worst thing imaginable—I was cast out.

I have wanted to be included all my life. I had a sense of belonging at my Aunt Mathilde's school in Paris. And with those great gals in my Navy nursing class. Even after four years, I never had that sense with Betty—almost as though I should have expected her betrayal. I feel that comfort here at the convent with Françoise and Claude and Lucie and Levy. And Sophie. As though my whole life has been leading up to this. It scares me. Thank goodness for Oliver's obvious disdain, which lets me know my happiness is not a fairy tale.

As I promised Sophie, at one of our morning meetings, I brought up the need to tell our patients what might go wrong with their abortions. I shared the list of possible complications I had made.

"They come to us and put their trust in us. We must be honest with them," I said.

Sophie said, "I agree. But I'm not sure how to do that without scaring them or making them think we are talking about a punishment that they are already anticipating."

"I have been doing this for years with very few problems, Jane. Think about the alternatives they face in Paris. No one there cares about leaving a bleeding woman alone on the side of the road to die. They certainly don't worry about telling her it might happen. Women already realize they are taking their lives into their hands. That tells us how desperate they are not to be pregnant," Levy said.

"I don't have the experience you have," Françoise interjected, "but why tell them all these terrible things and then say they probably won't happen?"

"Look at Amélie. She had an ectopic pregnancy, and she had never even heard of it. This is their life, Françoise. Don't they have a right to know this, just as they know about the procedure we are going to do? That's different, too, Levy. No hospital does that, but you taught me it was important. Isn't this also part of giving excellent care?"

Levy's shoulders sank. "You're right. These are grown women and they should be trusted to take these risks, or not. If knowing they could die or never be pregnant again makes them decide to have a baby, they should be able to make that decision. The thing that is nagging at me is that they are far more likely to die from having a baby and no one tells them that."

"Why don't we tell them both things?" Sophie asked. "That way they would understand there is a risk in whatever they chose and they could do what they felt was right for them?"

Françoise said, "That makes sense. Jane, will you write this all down so we can each tell them the same way?"

As the weeks went by, we continued to care for women who came for our special retreats. We added the information about risks, and we did our best to adhere to strict standards of quality in our care. In my nursing training, I was told over and over, "If it isn't documented, it didn't happen." But in this situation, documentation could spell our downfall. I wasn't sure that not writing things down would protect us in case of an investigation. It was not an easy decision.

Levy said, "I agree with Jane. We must keep records."

Françoise and Sophie were worried about having anything in writing if we were ever investigated.

Lucie, with us from Paris for one of her infrequent visits, said, "Records are exactly what would give us away if anyone were ever looking at what we do. I say we continue the way we always have. Write what we need on a piece of paper, and burn it when the case is complete."

For several months, that is what we did.

One morning, Françoise swooped in with a bag of fresh croissants. "I've got the answer!" she exclaimed.

I looked up from the book I was reading. "The answer to what?" I asked.

"The answer to keeping records. It came to me in a dream. Jane, you know how you always say that we are hiding in plain sight? And that no one cares about women's spiritual well-being, so no one is watching a convent?"

"Yes. I remember saying that."

"Jane says something like that about once a week," Levy added.

I glared at him and swatted his arm with my newspaper. Sophie smiled.

Françoise ignored us and charged ahead. "Well, my dream was about something else that no one cares about. Women's recipes."

"You've lost me," I said.

"It is not exactly figured out, but what if we asked every woman who comes to us to bring us a hand-written recipe? We put her name on the top of the page, and we file the recipe alphabetically by her first name with her last initial. We include the date, and every recipe is placed in a loose-leaf note-book—like an informal cookbook. We add our notes to the back of the page. We'd make a code, but the recipe could say something like 'Serves a family of two children aged three and nine and two parents'. Even if a police officer came to do an investigation, I doubt that he would ever bother to look closely at women's recipe books, especially if the recipes were written by hand."

I stood up from the table and paced around the way I did when an idea was gelling. "Françoise, you are a genius. This is brilliant and we can make it work. What do you think, Levy, Sophie?" I asked, turning toward them.

"I agree," Levy said seriously. "We simply need to establish a consistent way to notate basic information about the woman, the time we start and the time we end, and her blood pressure and bleeding during the procedure. These parameters will allow us to evaluate and compare the quality and consistency of our work."

"It is a marvelous idea," Sophie added. "Every woman has recipes. Maybe it will make this seem less frightening to them."

We discussed what information we would document for each woman. We had pens in several different colors, hoping this would be less obvious if anyone were to inspect the pages. Each recipe would be unique because it would be written in the hand of the individual woman, which was part of the brilliance of the plan. Later that morning when Lucie arrived for a weekend visit, breathless with stories about the hypnosis class she was taking, we filled her in. She was delighted at the cleverness of the scheme.

"You realize," I said to all of them, "even with Chastain's protection, we are taking quite a risk here. If we were arrested, we wouldn't likely be guillotined these days," I watched as Lucie flinched, "but we would still be put in prison. We are not protected."

"But who would turn us in?" Lucie asked. "Every one of the women will have had an abortion. If they informed on us, wouldn't they be putting themselves at risk of prosecution as well?"

"I'm not sure," I answered. "At the very least, we need to get each of them to agree not to talk about us except with other women who need help. Then we'll hope that's enough to keep us safe. We have a lot of knowledge and wisdom in this group, but we still need a lawyer."

"I am working on that," Sophie said with a mysterious smile.

A new chapter was the long-awaited installation of the telephone. We benefitted from a government program to assist the farms that still dotted the countryside outside of Paris. Although our patients still found us by word of mouth, it was wonderful to be able to set up actual appointments, make sure they had the times of the buses, and prepare them to stay with us.

Naively, I thought sharing information would help us avoid any misunder-
standings. But human beings are human beings, and the test of our system
came sooner than we expected.

CHAPTER 34

CONSECRATED GROUND

Françoise's 'recipe' record keeping seemed to be working very well. Our latest patient, Solange, gave us a recipe for croque monsieur to serve eight people, and we added the additional information according to plan. Lucie was with us for another visit and had involved herself, as usual, in the lives of *our women* as we had come to call them. She counseled Solange and coddled her a bit more than I would have. The abortion procedure was successful, but we had one sticking point. Solange wanted to take the 'baby,' as she put it, home with her to bury in her own churchyard. We couldn't agree whether we should permit women to take the small pinkish-gray tissue wrapped in a cloth to bury.

"The tissue should be disposed of right here, in our churchyard. It is consecrated ground. We can baptize them—or the woman herself can, if she wants to. That's within the dogma of the Church. That should be good enough for anybody," Françoise argued.

"And one of the most important things is there will be nothing to find here, even if someone should investigate," I added. "These embryos are not ossified—there are no bones to discover. They will return to the earth quickly. The most anyone would find would be some decomposing handkerchiefs."

"It is highly irregular in medical practice not to handle the disposal of tissue ourselves. It is a mistake for us not to," Levy had said. We were sitting at the kitchen table, and he was scratching Gracie behind her ears. "I am concerned that this girl—Solange, is it?—may be immature. We should not let her leave with the tissue."

"But she lives in Lyon. She said she doesn't want to be so far away from her baby. She wants to bury it herself," Lucie protested. "Isn't that her right? She'd probably just put it in her yard. No one will ever know."

"That in itself makes me worry," I said. "If she is so attached to it, is she all right to leave? Do we need to do a little more talking with her?"

Sophie said, "Solange can't stay any longer. Her mother depends on her to help care for the family's six younger kids. It was a miracle they even let her come on retreat. But she is so pious and such a good girl that they let her come."

"Six!" Levy said. "No wonder she didn't want to add a new one to the brood."

"Levy, don't be insensitive. All right, if she can't stay any longer..." I was pacing again. "Lucie, are you sure this is a good idea?"

"I'm positive. I will talk to her again before she leaves. But this is very important to her, and I'm confident it will help in her healing."

So, with some trepidation, I wrapped the almost translucent tissue of the tiny seven-week embryo in a lavender-scented handkerchief and watched Lucie press it into Solange's hand as she left in the hired *fiacre*.

We were busy the following few weeks, and I didn't think about Solange again until our old friend, Florent, knocked at our door.

"Bonjour, Inspector Chastain," I said. "Come in. How are Corinne and your lovely wife?" It always seemed wise to ask about his family.

"They are fine, thank you," he said, looking pained. "I am here on a difficult matter outside my jurisdiction. I need to inform you that the Garde Champêtre in Lyon has contacted me. It seems a local priest discovered one of his parishioners, a young woman, weeping in the church cemetery. When he asked her why she was there, at first she refused to tell him. Finally, she said she had buried a baby that had been removed from her body here at Our Lady of Perpetual Grace. The priest wasn't able to find anything, but he contacted his local *gendarmes*, so we may be visited even as soon as today. This would be a good time for all the 'sisters' to be available."

My stomach clenched. I thanked the inspector profusely and showed him out, assuring him we would be ready.

We gathered in the kitchen.

"We can't save ourselves by lying about the women who have come to us!" I exclaimed. "That goes against everything we do here—all our values!"

It was Françoise who convinced me. "Jane, if we have to do this to help other women, we will do it."

Later in the afternoon, there was a knock on our huge front door. I answered it, this time in my habit, and found the inspector standing next to a young police officer. Inspector Chastain introduced himself as though we had never met and then introduced the other officer as a *gendarme* from Lyon. Since I was a nun for the moment, I didn't shake their hands, but invited them in, shooing the dog outside to avoid any problems with the low growl I was hearing.

I introduced myself and Sisters Françoise and Sophie, who were attired in their matching habits, and sitting in chairs near the fire, knitting.

"May I offer you some tea?" I asked the two policemen.

"No, thank you. We are here on a rather delicate matter," the inspector said.

"Please sit down," I gestured to the small rickety rattan sofa. I thought it might help if they were a bit uncomfortable. Levy was listening from the other room, which gave me more confidence.

"How can we be of help to you?" I asked sweetly, as if they had come seeking spiritual solace.

The inspector cleared his throat. "As I mentioned, this is a delicate matter," he said, looking as though he might shatter us with news that was too harsh.

"We live in a healing cloister," I said. "We minister to women who have been harried by the world, so we are accustomed to hearing about delicate matters. Please go on."

The inspector turned to the young officer, who was blushing bright red. Whether he had never been in a room full of nuns or whether he had never before discussed 'women's matters,' I don't know, but it wasn't just our sofa making him uncomfortable. It was heartless of some police superior to send this babe-in-the-woods to investigate something so intimate. Still, I was afraid. Earlier in the day, we had talked about the various possible scenarios. So I had rehearsed, but of course, I only knew what *my* lines would be.

"Um… I am here from Lyon." Stating a fact he was sure of seemed to give the young man a bit more confidence. "Our parish priest, Father Foucault, contacted my department because he heard from a woman parishioner that she had… that she had a baby removed from her here at this establishment."

The last part of his sentence came out in a garble, but unfortunately, I understood it all too well.

As we had practiced, all of us took in a gasp of horror, and we looked both stricken and concerned. It was a look Françoise had to practice several times. She kept looking as though she had seen a ghost.

"I am so sorry you have had to come here on this mission," I said. I figured there was no one more sorry about it than he. "Might this young woman's name be Solange, by chance?"

The officer looked hopeful. "Yes, that is her name." He looked at a little pad he was holding. "Solange Dumont."

"Ah," I said. And the other sisters all repeated, "Ah," as if he'd stumbled upon the answer to the entire mystery.

"You know her?" he asked.

"Yes. Dear Solange came here on retreat a few weeks ago. She was a lovely girl, but a bit confused."

The officer looked confused himself. "What do you mean?"

We had decided Sophie would play the role of the sister who had been with Solange, since our dear, persuasive Lucie was back in Paris.

"Oh, Officer, it was very sad. I'm afraid Solange was in the family way, but she was losing the baby when she came to us. Perhaps she hoped we'd make a miracle for her. This happens quite frequently."

So far, all of that is true.

"So you're telling me the pregn—that it ended while she was here with you?"

"Sadly, yes. We called a doctor to check her afterwards, and he said she was fine. Even though we offered to bury the baby here in consecrated ground, she desperately wanted to bury it closer to her, so we wrapped it up for her. We had no idea she would try to bury it herself in the churchyard. Please give our apologies to the Father," Sophie said, looking pious. She was so lovely I imagined the policeman would believe anything she said.

Chastain put his hat back on, as a signal the conversation was over. He looked at the younger man sternly, and the officer put his hat back on, too.

"Thank you, Sisters. This issue is resolved. We are sorry to have interrupted your prayers."

I guess in his world, knitting and praying were pretty much the same thing.

"Yes," the younger man said, "Thank you. I will make this report to my superior and they will inform the priest."

"Bless you both and bless young Solange," Sophie said, making the officer blush again.

I didn't realize I had been holding my breath until they walked out the door and closed it behind them, Chastain giving me a knowing wink.

Levy came back into the room and we embraced. He went to the door and, now that there was no one to growl at, let Gracie back in.

"Well, that was too close for comfort," he said.

Françoise frowned. "*Way* too close. Lucie will think this is her fault. But even *I* was so sorry for Solange that I wanted to give her the tissue. She was so pitiful."

"Fault isn't helpful here. Any one of us might have made the same mistake. But this situation could teach us some very important things," I said.

"Like what?" Sophie asked.

"Well, for one thing, until we can find a way to protect our ability to provide services, we bury the embryos here, no exceptions." I said. Everyone reluctantly nodded in agreement.

"And for another, if women are pitiful, we can't help them. We can talk with them about their lives, but if they remain pitiful after all our efforts, we *must* not do an abortion. We can tell them they have been misinformed about what we do in our Special Retreats. Pitiful women are dangerous to us and to themselves."

"What do you mean?" Françoise asked. "Obviously, the women we see are pitiful. They are in terrible situations they can't get out of. How can they be *but* pitiful?"

"I'm afraid it is that damned picture I keep hanging at eye level." My friends looked totally lost. "I'm sorry. It is a metaphor, meaning I have only seen something from my own perspective. I mean, we can't *leave* them being pitiful. We have only been doing this one way—not seeing there are women who need something else. We must find a way of helping women stand on their own feet and experience their power. It is as important as helping them know they are forgiven. Maybe not everyone needs grace. We need an additional lady."

"Our Lady of Perpetual… what? Backbone? Spirit? Bravura? Guts?" Sophie searched for the right word.

"All those are close," I said, "but not quite right." I found my thesaurus on the kitchen shelf next to our recipe books and an old dictionary.

"It has to express power from within," I said, leafing through the book. "In French, maybe something like *'fermeté'* or *'intrepidité*. Or wait—this is it! The root of the word *courage* is *coeur*—heart, in French. That is it. *'La Dame de La Courage Perpetuelle.'* It is perfect."

Levy looked serious. "Jane, you are determined our women will have forgiveness *and* courage? Aren't they showing their courage just by showing up here? You are asking a lot."

"I am asking that we give these women whatever they truly need—not only what makes us comfortable. If we can't help them achieve resolution, then we must not perform an abortion. And that is why we *must* figure this out," I insisted. No one ever accused me of setting the bar too low. "I want to get Lucie to come soon, so she can help us."

Levy said, "Jane, this is not what I taught you. You cannot judge what a woman needs. If she tells you she wants an abortion, you must do it. I think you are making a big mistake."

"But how will she live with herself if she has not come to peace with her decision?" I asked.

"These women don't have peace in any other part of their lives. Why should they expect to have peace about this?" Françoise asked.

"It's not what they expect. It is what *we* should expect. Levy, you said yourself that doing this work is a huge responsibility. How can we do it knowing women might lose all faith in their own goodness?" I was on to something important. "And if a woman comes to us asking for something so consequential, I want to be sure she is confident—that she is at peace with what she is asking."

"And that she is not weeping uncontrollably and at the same time telling us she is fine," Sophie said.

"Or acting like a porcupine, all angry and prickly," Françoise said.

"Or being so numb she won't talk at all," Sophie added.

"Or saying one thing, but showing us another," Françoise said.

We were each remembering a different woman who challenged us.

"What they are telling us is from their head—their logical part. And what they are showing us is their feelings—their heart. If their head and their heart are saying different things, they are caught in a bind," I said.

"I'm afraid they will think I am accusing them of lying if I say their head and their heart don't match," Françoise said.

"In a way, they *are* lying—as much to themselves as to us. Don't you think they feel it? What if we asked them if they were having a sense of disconnection instead of telling them?" Sophie asked.

"Most of our patients have never made a major decision before. Everything in their lives has been determined for them, first by their fathers, then their husbands. We can be gentle about this, but we have to be firm. Otherwise, when they remember this experience, it will seem as though we made their decision, not them," Sophie said.

Levy shook his head. "If the woman tells you she wants an abortion, you simply must *do* it. All this speculation about how she might be feeling is just that, speculation. I can't support the idea that you would say no. You would be driving women into the hands of unscrupulous practitioners. They are everywhere. Jane, after Mimi died in your arms, I can't believe you are even considering this. I've got to go. I have a meeting." Levy collected his notebook and coat and was out the door before I could think of anything to say.

"In all the years I have known him, we have never had a disagreement like this," I said.

Françoise said, "Oh, don't mind him, Jane. He is just cranky."

I looked to Sophie for corroboration. She said, "I'm sure Françoise is right. He loves and respects you. He'll come around. Let it go."

I nodded my head. I tried to let it go, but a familiar sense of shame lingered. What if he was right?

"We need to focus our attention on the priest in Lyon," Sophie said, sensing the tension and changing the subject. "Won't the Church realize we are not a real convent?"

"If they investigate, we'll tell them we are an order that broke from the Church. Rome will have no authority over us," Françoise insisted. "But beyond all that, Solange is teaching us we need a better way to commemorate these babies that will not be born."

"Solange wanted a way to honor the baby she was not able to have," Sophie said. "She wanted to keep its spirit close to her. If we bury the embryos in consecrated ground, will that be enough? The Jews put stones on top of headstones when they visit the graves of those they love. Unlike flowers, the stones last forever."

I recalled the women I had worked with in Japan, and I remembered the carefully made-up face of the geisha, Kikuyo, and the brightly clad Jizo statues used to watch over the souls of the babies they couldn't keep.

"The stones!" I said. "What if every woman whose baby is buried in this consecrated ground chose a stone—one of those polished river rocks lining the cemetery—to take with her in memory?"

"I love that idea," Sophie said. "No one would ever know what it stands for—a woman could keep it in their pocket, or put it in her garden, or even in the cemetery at her own church, and no one would be the wiser."

A new ritual was born at Our Lady.

CHAPTER 35

MADAME CHEVALIER MAKES A SCENE

Our Lady, Winter 1952

Just after Christmas, shortly after the near-disaster with Solange, we lost Levy, but in a happy way. He had been traveling back and forth to Paris on mysterious 'business' for some time, and he finally confessed that he had met someone he wanted to marry.

"She is a lovely woman with two teenage sons." Levy was grinning. I had never seen him so happy.

"But how can you want to marry someone we haven't even met?" Françoise asked in her usual direct way.

"I wanted to be certain. After all, it's not just her I am marrying. We will be a family. There are things to be considered. And you are quite a bit to take all at once. I hoped I might ease into it."

"He means he hasn't told her about us. About what we do," Sophie said, gently.

"Oh," I said.

Françoise added, "And he isn't going to tell her."

"My dear friends, I am sure you can understand. Rachel is a widow who has been raising two boys on her own. They will depend on me. I can't be involved in anything outside the law." Levy's voice was pleading.

"What will you do?" Françoise asked.

"I met some of Lucie's professors at the Sorbonne. They offered me a position in the School of Midwifery," he said. "I'll be on staff at the La Pitié-Salpêtrière Hospital."

"Oh, Bernard, that is wonderful," I said, and you know I never called him Bernard. "Congratulations. I am so glad you found someone. This explains the good mood you have been in." I put my arms around him and hugged him as if I were never going to see him again. I didn't know how I would stand to be without him.

"The wedding will be on a Sunday at her temple. I hope you will all come."

That night, as Sophie and I snuggled in bed, she asked me how I was doing. "What do you mean?"

"Jane. We are past pretending. I have known you long enough to guess what Levy's moving to Paris—to a whole new life—means to you."

I started crying in spite of my best intentions. "He is my oldest friend. He taught me—he taught me everything. I can't imagine doing this work without him."

"I understand. I'm sorry, darling."

"Things haven't been quite right between us since that silly argument about feelings. I know he didn't mean what he said. He has supported every step of this work."

"I'm sure it was just a misunderstanding. And he's been preoccupied. That's the only reason you two haven't worked things out. I'm sure you will."

When Levy left the next morning with his suitcases packed, he promised he would stay in touch and said I should call him anytime for a consultation.

"But you don't need me, Jane. You know more about this than I do now. It's a new chapter for both of us. The student has become the teacher."

I wanted him to be happy. I did. I really did. But when he left, I went to my wishing well and cried the tears of someone who has lost her best friend.

A few days after Levy's wedding, Sophie came to me with a letter. "I was hoping to receive this sooner, but it will be an answer to our prayers," she said, smiling. As I read it, she said, "It's from my uncle. He is high up in the government and if we ever get into real trouble, we can call on him for help."

The letterhead said *Matthieu Neuville, Under Minister of Justice*. The letter was very cordial, and also very non-committal.

"Sophie, you didn't… did you *write* to him about what we are doing?"

"Of course not, *Chérie*," she answered, tucking her hair behind her ear. "I visited him in Paris when I was there two weeks ago. I did *tell* him—I had to in order to ask for his help, but not before I felt him out about it. He was very sympathetic, and he agrees with what we are doing. I am certain he will be discreet. He didn't get where he is without knowing how to thread the political needle."

Matthieu Neuville, Under Minister of Justice, would come to our rescue sooner than we imagined.

One afternoon, a woman who introduced herself as Madame Chevalier came to the convent with her daughter Colette. Colette—called Coco—was seventeen. In counseling, Coco told Sophie that Madame Chevalier was her *boyfriend's* mother, not hers. The older woman had dragged Coco to us without asking her what she wanted

"What *do* you want, Coco?" Sophie asked.

"I don't want a baby. After I told Luc I was pregnant, he turned into a sniveling little boy. And I definitely don't want *her* as my mother-in-law. I want my mother here with me, but Madame Chevalier didn't even give me a chance."

"Would you like to talk with your mother and come back?" Sophie asked.

The girl burst into tears. "Yes. My mother will be disappointed in me, but she wouldn't want me forced into marriage. But I'm afraid Madame Chevalier will be furious."

Sophie and Colette brought Mrs. Chevalier into the room. When Sophie began to explain what Coco wanted, Madame Chevalier started screaming.

"My husband is wealthy. I insist you do an abortion on this *salope*—this *whore*—immediately. She will ruin my son's life. She'll give birth to a baby just to force him to marry her. Luc has infinite potential! He has an impressive rock collection and is an excellent speller. He will be an important man one day. My husband is a lawyer." She wouldn't stop ranting.

Sophie and I escorted her to her car as she struggled against us, screaming insults. Once in her car, Madame Chevalier peeled out of the driveway, throwing gravel into our faces. We looked at each other, not knowing whether to laugh or cry.

Our schedule was so full that there was no one to take the girl home. Françoise called Claude, who drove Coco to her house and waited in the truck. In half an hour, Coco and her mother emerged, their arms around each other, smiling, though their faces were streaked with tears. Claude brought the two women back to Our Lady, where we made sure Coco was at peace with her choice, then we performed Coco's abortion.

Three days later, Sophie answered the door to find Inspector Chastain, in his uniform, standing on the steps, looking uncomfortable.

"I must speak with Mademoiselle Jane," he said formally.

I came to the door, wiping my hands on a dish towel. Because I'd heard it was Chastain, I hadn't bothered changing into a habit.

"Mademoiselle," he said, "I regret to inform you that a charge has been leveled against the convent." He pulled a sheet of paper from his satchel and read, "Our Lady of Perpetual Grace is charged with refusing to provide solace to a young woman."

"What are you talking about? Who has brought this charge?" I asked.

He looked down at the complaint. "It has been brought by Mâitre Edouard Chevalier."

"That is Coco's *boyfriend's* father." It was shocking and ridiculous. I was overcome with nervous laughter. Sophie and Françoise were standing behind me.

"This is nothing to laugh about," Sophie insisted.

Françoise reached out and grabbed the paper from Chastain's hand.

"Jane, it says you are to appear before the magistrate in Paris a week from today, and that you must be accompanied by your *avocat*. Your attorney. Do we even *have* an attorney?"

Chastain took the paper back. "Madame Duchamps, please," he said. "As Mademoiselle Sophie says, this is serious. I am sorry to bring this bad news."

He handed me the document, clicked his heels together, and left.

We returned to the kitchen. Françoise and Sophie sat at the table. I paced around the room until Sophie suggested that I might as well finish washing the dishes, since I was not able to sit still.

Francoise asked again. "Well, *do* we have an attorney?"

"My uncle is the Under Minister for Justice." Sophie said.

"He says he will help us if we get in a bind," I said, placing a clean dish on the rack to dry.

"I'd say this is a bind! The charge is that we refused to pray with a young woman who came to us on retreat." Françoise said, reading the document. "That can't be a crime, can it?"

"And it came from that horrible Madame Chevalier." I said, splashing dish soap as I gestured wildly. "This is ridiculous," I said, raising my voice. "She is just trying to scare us—imagining she would coerce us to do an abortion on Colette—an abortion that, ironically, is already done."

"Can't we just tell her that?" Françoise asked.

"Absolutely not!" I insisted. "We are going to protect our patient's privacy!" I exclaimed, pounding the edge of the sink and soaking the front of my apron.

"Calm down, dearest," Sophie said. "We will not tell anyone about Coco's abortion," she continued. "I'll call my uncle."

Sophie reached Matthieu on the phone and explained the unusual circumstances.

"What is the attorney's name? Edouard Chevalier?" Matthieu's laugh was so loud that we heard him through the phone. "I know him. He is a buffoon, a third-rate lawyer, and a laughingstock controlled by his wife. And that charge is completely specious. Let me make a few calls. You don't need to worry."

We thanked him, all of us worrying in spite of what he said.

Miraculously, Matthieu made the whole thing go away. A few days later, he called to say, "It was ridiculous. In the first place, they fabricated the charges. But, Mesdemoiselles, you may not always be so fortunate. I will do what I can to protect you, but you must find a better way to keep your secrets. It is terrible this is not legal. I wish there was something I could do. I am so sorry."

For that moment, we breathed a sigh of relief.

"That was a mess," Sophie said, almost in tears.

I put my arm around her and said, "It's going to be all right, *Chérie*. Thank goodness for your uncle."

Françoise said, "When patients call, we must tell them they are not guaranteed to have their problem solved. They must understand that for us, this is not about money—it is about each woman coming to peace with her choice. That choice is not always an abortion."

"I agree. Madame Chevalier was angry because we *didn't do* an abortion. What about the times we say 'no' because it's so obvious that a woman isn't sure? Many women are already confident, but if the women who are struggling don't want to talk it through, they should not come to us. We don't want any woman to think she has been tricked. But if we are not confident that a woman wants an abortion, we shouldn't do it," I said.

"Our Lady is not like anything else they have encountered," Sophie mused. "People won't believe we are doing this, not to get rich, but because it is what our hearts tell us is right."

"They may not believe us, but we must try."

That evening I strode past the gardens to the edge of the property and sat alone beside the wishing well. The moon was just a sliver, and the stars crowded the sky. I cried, realizing my dream of helping women without the interference of men wasn't as easy as I had hoped. Despite our best efforts, my dream might get us all put in jail.

That night, I poured myself a glass of wine and took a hot bath.

CHAPTER 36

WELCOME, HENRI

September, 1953

The woman's voice blasted shrill and demanding over the phone. She spoke so quickly and without pause that I didn't get to ask my usual questions.

"It's for my daughter. She is seventeen and just barely pregnant. You must take care of this. My friend's girl came to your convent and said there was nothing to it. We must come right away. I am very wealthy. My husband is an important financier. This must be a secret. It would kill him. He will be fine with our going on retreat, but we must come right away." She finally stopped to take a breath.

"I am Jane Smith, and with whom am I speaking?" I asked in my calmest voice. I tried to avoid people like her altogether—arrogant, entitled—so often mean.

"I am sorry. Where are my manners? My name is Madame—well, you don't need my husband's name, do you? Let's just say I am 'Madame Marcel.'"

"*Ah bon.* Madame *Marcel*," I said, pronouncing the name, as she did, like a small piece of fiction. "May I speak with your daughter?"

"That is impossible. She is in boarding school. I will go pick her up."

"*Ah, bon,*" I said again. It seemed like the best policy to maintain that everything was just fine. "Can you tell me how you are certain that she is pregnant? And how far along?"

"She has told me her symptoms, but claimed it's the flu. But that's exactly what I experienced during pregnancy. Thank goodness she didn't go to the school nurse, so the secret is safe. When I asked about boyfriends, she told me that she only met this boy a few weeks ago."

"And are you certain that your daughter wants an abortion?"

"Must you use that ugly word?" Mrs. 'Marcel,' said in disgust. "Of *course* she does not want a baby. She is only seventeen, and this winter will be her *debut* into society. What young girl would want to ruin her life over a careless moment? Besides, she might have been forced. She wouldn't talk to me, so I have no idea."

I decided to try out some of the language we had agreed upon after the Coco debacle. "Here at Our Lady of Perpetual Grace, we take the time to talk with every woman, and to assist her in coming to a decision that she is confident about," I said in my most professional voice.

"Have no fear," she said in an icy tone. "She will agree this is the right thing to do."

"Madame Marcel, we will not provide this service for a girl who is being pressured. This must be her choice."

"You are not listening to me. It will be her choice without a doubt," the woman said.

Her response worried me, but I didn't know what more to say. I looked at our schedule.

"We will have a room open tomorrow afternoon," I said. "Is it workable for you and your daughter to share a bedroom?" It seemed prudent to ask ahead of time.

"Share?...Well, if that is all you have."

"We won't have a second room open until next week."

"Then we shall share."

"I'll make the reservation," I said. "What is your daughter's name?"

"Her name is Chloe. Chloe Dan... Chloe Marcel."

And so, in the midst of other patients coming and going, Mrs. Marcel and young Chloe arrived, carrying one large and one very small suitcase.

Chloe was a skinny, pimply girl with long wavy brown hair and a sallow complexion, bundled up in enough layers of coats and sweaters to be in the Arctic. Her mother appeared to be in her early forties, very chic with a tweed coat and matching skirt, and what I assumed were genuine alligator pumps.

"Here she is," Mrs. Marcel said. "She is not feeling well. She didn't say a word to me the entire drive, though that's not unusual. I passed a vending stand with fresh apples along the way, and I'm just going to leave her with you and pop back down the road to buy some fruit. I'm sure she is in good hands."

Before I could say anything, the woman was out the door. I had the impression that she couldn't bear to be in her daughter's presence. I wondered if that's how my mother felt when she was so critical of me. I was too tall. I mustn't slouch. I hadn't curled my hair properly. I wasn't nice enough to the boys at the cotillion.

I was familiar with the fruit stand. It was the end of the season, so there couldn't be much to buy, and it was more than an hour away, so I didn't think we should expect Mrs. Marcel back any time soon. If she returned at all.

Françoise was standing next to me and took pity on the girl. She gathered Chloe up, and they shuffled down the hall to the bedroom. In a moment, Françoise cried out for me to come quickly. When I got into the room, I saw Chloe lying on the bed. Françoise was standing behind the bed holding Chloe's shoulders. The layers of clothes had been shed, revealing what must have taken a lot of energy to hide—

"This girl is in labor!" Françoise exclaimed. "She started moaning the moment we got into the room."

I went to the foot of the bed and gently pushed Chloe's legs open.

"My God, she is crowning," I said. I ran to the door and cried out for Sophie, who was in the kitchen. By the time I was back at the bed, Sophie was in the room. In an instant, she understood the situation.

"What do you need?" she asked, breathless.

"Clean towels, gloves, clamps, a suture set, a plastic suction bulb, hot water, the plastic sheet—and some olive oil."

Sophie was a champ and never bothered to ask why I was asking for anything, although I imagine she wondered if I was planning to make a salad. She set off to get the items I requested. So, I had before me a never-before pregnant teenager who had had no prenatal care and was probably in denial about the pregnancy for months. I had heard of women who gave birth claiming they had no idea of what was happening, but I never quite accepted that it was true.

I attempted to recall the things I learned about childbirth from Dr. Nick. I had attended dozens of births, but there was always a doctor in the next room in case of an emergency. Nick was adamant about helping women to labor without tearing the perineum, but that involved weeks of preparation that we didn't have.

"See if you can help her slow her breathing," I said to Françoise. "Try using her name and speaking softly into her ear. Let her hear you breathe."

Those suggestions might not have been any help at all, since this young girl looked like she was in shock. In moments, Sophie came back into the room. Together, we lifted Chloe's hips and spread the sheet under her. I washed my hands in the laboratory sink before donning gloves. Back in front of Chloe, I poured some of the olive oil onto a cloth and daubed it around the tight pink flesh of the perineum that already strained against the baby's head. I hoped to help soften the tissue to avoid tearing when it stretched. I realized that the birth would resemble the only one I had seen done under general anesthetic. The wife of one of the Naval officers had insisted she wanted to be asleep, no matter how much Dr. Nick argued in favor of a spinal anesthesia. The woman's body labored, with the help of some Pitocin, which induced contractions, but she wasn't part of it at all. Dr. Nick's voice rang in my head. "It's all right. Her body will do the work." I tried to believe that even without medication, this young girl's body knew what it was doing—because Chloe was simply not there.

In a moment, the head was born. I prayed that the girl would dilate enough to free the baby's shoulders without tearing the perineum. By a miracle, I was able to rotate the tiny slippery body just enough to free both shoulders, and the rest of the little creature slid out into my hands. Sophie handed me a soft towel, and I wrapped the infant in it. I didn't even have to suction for mucus—the crying started right away. It was a most welcomed sound and hearing it allowed me to start breathing again. As I glanced up, I saw that the glassy stare on Chloe's face had been replaced by a look of terror.

"Françoise—talk to her. She is scared now." Françoise bent down and whispered words of encouragement in the girl's ear.

Sophie had opened the suture set and handed it to me for the scissors and clamp I needed to cut the umbilical cord.

Françoise spoke softly from her position at Chloe's shoulders. "Is it a boy or a girl? Is everything all right?"

I clamped and cut the cord and answered, "It is a boy. He appears very healthy and you can tell his lungs are working well," I said over the lusty cries. "He appears to be full term."

Sophie brought a moist cloth to wipe his face, and said, "He is perfect."

Mrs. Marcel finally returned with a dozen apples and nearly fainted when I told her that Chloe had given birth. She left without even talking to her daughter. Chloe stayed with us for three days, all the time insisting that she didn't want a baby. She refused to even see him. We were able to find infant formula and the medications needed to stop Chloe's milk. Sophie helped bind her breasts, though the girl hardly seemed to register the pain we knew she was having.

"Are you sure you don't want to see him?" Sophie asked, very gently. Chloe just shook her head.

The girl's parents couldn't wait to sign adoption papers. And that is the story—or at least the most important part—of how Françoise's niece, Anne-Marie, finally got the baby she had yearned for. I am proud to tell you that, in gratitude to me, Anne-Marie and Thomas named him *Henri Smith* Duchamps after my father.

CHAPTER 37

BROTHER TIMOTHY

Our Lady, October 1953

Françoise looked at the morning's appointments and said to me, "Suzanne DeMille is here. She was referred by Dr. Levy. She said he gave her all the information. Will you talk with her?"

"Sure." I took the recipe card and found Suzanne sitting in our waiting area. She was in her mid-thirties, flawlessly made up, wearing an elegant tweed suit. I introduced myself and she followed me into a counseling room.

"I will be so glad to get this over with so I can stop worrying about it," she said.

"That's a very good way to begin. What are you worrying about?"

"What do you mean?" she said. "I just told you. I want this over and out of the way so that I never again in my life have to think about it. This is not the kind of thing that is supposed to happen to women like me."

"What is it that isn't supposed to happen to women like you?"

"You are going around in circles. I don't want to talk about this. I just want to do it. Are you not hearing me?"

"I don't mean to be difficult, Mrs. DeMille. I want to get an idea about how you are feeling about this situation."

"Well, excuse me, but I don't think that is any of your concern."

My stomach was in knots. "I'm afraid Dr. Levy left out a bit of the information you needed. At Our Lady we attend to emotional needs as well as physical needs."

"I don't have emotional needs. At least I won't once you get this thing out of me. It's a bit inconsiderate having this take place in a convent. Where every corner reminds you that what you are about to do excommunicates your soul, even if no priest ever hears of it."

"How is that for you, believing your soul would be cut off from the Church?"

"How do you think it is? Miserable. In case you missed it the first ten times, that is why I want to get this over with. I am going to pretend it never happened and go back to my normal life."

"It doesn't quite work that way. May I call you Suzanne?" She rolled her eyes and nodded. "We have found that when a woman has strong beliefs against abortion," she winced at the word, "she may experience a very hard time afterwards. That's why we want to talk about it, before you do something you can't take back, to be sure this is in line with your values."

"How could murdering a baby be in line with my values? Are you nuts?"

I felt like I had walked into a trap. But Levy would never use a patient to make a point, so it must have been an innocent decision to send her to us without quite giving her all the information.

"Suzanne, those are very strong words. If you honestly believed abortion is the same as murdering a baby, I doubt very much you would be here."

"Whatever your doubts, I can see I am in the wrong place. Dr. Levy told me he didn't have an appointment until next week, and I didn't want to wait. But I can see I am not going to get what I need from you. If you'll just show me out."

Mrs. DeMille threw the door open and strode out of the counseling room. By then, several other women were there, and they all looked worried as I tried to keep up with her. She stopped long enough to say, "I will be telling Dr. Levy about your inappropriate demands. It will be a month of Sundays before he sends another unsuspecting woman here."

If the door hadn't been so heavy, it would have slammed.

The other patients needed our attention, so it wasn't until the end of the day that I got to sit down with Françoise and Sophie.

"Oh, Jane. That was terrible. I can only imagine the conversation you had. Thank goodness I wasn't talking to her. She would have made me cry," Françoise said.

Sophie nodded as she poured us wine. "Me, too. I hate those angry ones. But you are usually really good with them. What happened?" she asked.

"What happened is that when Levy gave her all the information, he conveniently left out that we would be exploring her feelings. I caught her by surprise. You can guess this is not a woman who wants to talk about her feelings. But she told me so much, just by the things she did say—like assuming she would be excommunicated even if a priest wasn't aware she'd had an abortion."

"I've had patients who started out saying that, but pretty quickly, they said they were responsible for their own relationship with the Virgin. In truth, we've got a bunch of Protestants here, but they don't even recognize the difference." Sophie tried a smile, but it wasn't enough to ease my fears.

I said, "I don't see how that woman will be able to forgive herself for having an abortion. But we didn't have any real conversation. I guess I'll call Levy and try to head Suzanne off at the pass." Dr. Levy wasn't in his office that day or the next. By then, I was so worried he would be angry. When the phone rang, Françoise looked apologetic as she said, "Yes," and held the receiver out to me. I was waiting for my comeuppance, but it was a sad Levy on the other end of the line.

"I'm sorry. I didn't realize. I've never seen anything like this. I'm afraid she will hurt herself. Can you help her?"

"Levy, what happened?"

"I was upset when you didn't do an abortion for Suzanne. She has been my patient for years. I know she can be demanding. I have always found the best policy is to do what she wants. I imagined it would be simple enough that I could do an abortion with your USA suction machine without an assistant. It started out fine—Suzanne talked on and on about how relieved she would be to get it over with. Then, a few minutes into the procedure, she started wailing that I was killing her baby. I was afraid someone in my department would hear. It was too late to stop. There was nothing to do but complete the procedure. When I came back into the room after examining the tissue, she had curled up in a ball on the table, weeping. She can't tell her husband what happened because the pregnancy was from an affair. I can't take her back to my house because how would I explain to my wife? Can I bring her to you?"

"Oh, Levy. I am so sorry. Of course you can bring her here. I don't know if we can help her, but we will do what we can. At least she will be in a safe place. I don't have any desire to say I told you so. I didn't want to be right about this—I just wanted to help this woman."

Suzanne stayed with us for a week. She wasn't all right when she came, and she wasn't all right when she left. She kept saying, "I needed help, but I couldn't talk about it. I was so ashamed. I'll never get over this. I could not have done this. There had to be another way."

My mother kept writing that she wanted to visit. I kept putting her off. There was a reason I had to travel more than 3,000 miles to do the work I was born to do.

Other threats were out of my control.

One morning we had a visitor who alarmed us at least as much as the *gendarmes*. The knocker on the front door banged, and Sophie went to answer it. There was a small black Ford in the driveway, and a short, round, balding middle-aged man in a black cassock with a pointed black hat standing in front of her.

"*Bonjour, mademoiselle. Je m'appelle Frére Timothée. Comment ça va?*" he said. "I would like to visit with the prioress of your abbey."

We had no patients that day, so Sophie wore corduroy pants, garden clogs, and an oversized Greek fisherman's sweater. It was only the two of us because Françoise was working at the dairy farm.

"Please come in, Father," she said, bowing awkwardly and pointing to a chair in the entryway where he sat down. "I will fetch her."

She ran out to the garden where I knelt up to my elbows in manure, fertilizing potatoes.

"I'm afraid it has finally happened, Jane," she said breathlessly. "The Church has sent someone to check up on us."

I wiped my hands off on an old towel and sat back on my haunches.

"Well, we have talked about this enough times," I said. "Here goes nothing. Can you keep him busy long enough for me to get changed?"

"I'll do my best," she said, running back into the convent.

The cleric stood up as she came into the room. Sophie motioned for him to sit, and he did.

"May I offer you some coffee, Father? Or tea?"

"I am a Jesuit, but not ordained, so it is Brother. Thank you. Tea would be very welcome. I have had a long drive," he answered.

Sophie left him alone only long enough to put the pot on. She ran back to sit with him while it boiled, then ran back into the kitchen, put the tea in the pot to steep, pulled cups and saucers, a small pitcher of milk, and a tin of biscuits from the cupboard, placed it all on a tray, and returned before he had a chance to blink.

Gracie was lying on the floor next to Brother Timothée, and Sophie started to shoo her out, but Timothée made a motion that the dog should stay. Sophie poured his tea and offered milk and sugar, which he declined, though he did accept several of the crumbly shortbread biscuits that Françoise had brought from the bakery the day before.

He took a sip of tea, tilted his head to the side a bit, and looked at Sophie. "And you are...?" he asked.

"Oh, please forgive me. I am Sophie St. Martin," Sophie said, wondering if she should curtsy. "I help around the... I help around Our Lady—keeping things cleaned and taking care of our women."

"Your... women?" he asked, giving Gracie a scratch behind the ears.

"I mean—the women who come here on retreat. They are often coming because of some troubles in their lives, and we care for them as kindly as we would our own family."

He put the teacup on the saucer with a little clink. "Yes, Miss St. Martin, I have been told some interesting things about your... special retreats."

"I hope they told you good things," Sophie said, a bit too defiantly for the situation. She was very proud of the care we gave women who came to Our Lady.

Just then, I entered the room. Sophie glanced at me nervously.

"Reverend Mother, this is Brother Timothée," she said, stepping aside. Sophie seemed impressed at how commanding I looked in my tailored habit, but a second later she glanced nervously at my gardening clogs. I hoped that the brother would accept the idea that nuns in the countryside were a bit more relaxed than the severe and decidedly unrelaxed nuns he knew.

The priest stood and bowed his head to me, and we both sat.

Sophie hovered and said, "Mother, may I pour you a cup of tea?"

"Thank you, my child," I answered, trying not to reveal the fraud I was. As Sophie poured, I turned to the man sitting across from me.

"Welcome, Brother," I said, as Sophie handed me a cup and saucer. "To what do we owe the pleasure of your visit?" In other words, why the hell are you here?

The brother smiled, and I had the feeling that he was a kind man.

"Please just call me *Timothy*," he said, since it was obvious I was not French. "Monsignor has sent me to learn more about your order. We have had two women who came to you for a retreat. Although they returned much healed in spirit, they wouldn't tell us much about you, except that you cared for them... how did they put it...? 'like angels.'"

I bowed my head with humility befitting the Mother Superior I was clearly born to be. "I am so glad to hear that. We are nurses in a small order affiliated with the Old Catholic Mission."

"Is your work concerned with any specific aspect of health? Is pregnancy involved?" he asked.

My heart missed a beat, but I took a breath and said, "Our work is to provide healing for women in body and spirit. Sometimes that involves helping women whose pregnancies cannot continue." I hoped I was explaining it in a way that was both truthful and vague enough to keep us safe. "What else can I tell you?"

"You are not affiliated with the Church of Rome, then?" he asked, looking a bit skeptical.

"That's right. The Order of Our Lady of Perpetual Grace split from Rome in the late 1800s," I answered, just as we had practiced. Thank goodness Françoise had an encyclopedia that I hoped gave us all the correct answers we needed in situations just like this.

"We will still consider you our sisters," Brother Timothy said. "And I can see that the work you do is important to the women in our parish."

In my mind, I said, *More than you'll ever know.* What I said aloud was, "We welcome them, Brother. Let me show you around. Would you like to see our gardens?"

"I would love that," he said.

We walked outside, and he was properly complimentary about our roses and peonies, wishing he could see them in the glory of their blooms. Surprisingly, he could cite the Latin names of many of the medicinal herbs that Sophie had planted.

"My mother was a healer," he said. "She was not accepted by the men who were busy establishing themselves as doctors. And she was shunned by the Church because she helped women who didn't want to become pregnant. The Church fathers insisted that pregnancy was always a gift from God that had to be welcomed, whether the mother was thirteen or thirty—whether she had no children or ten. Mother used to tell me that celibate men had no business telling women when to have babies."

"That is a strong stand to take against a powerful church," I noted.

"It didn't make us popular. Life was sometimes a struggle. She never made much money, but she cared for many people. She used to take me with her to births and deaths and to minister to all the sundry illnesses that afflict every community, particularly the poor rural community where we lived. I know she was disappointed in me when I decided that the best way to help people was to become a priest. Maybe she feared I was giving in to the very convention that she had battled against all her life."

"But you care for women, in your own way. I'm certain she would be proud of you."

"Perhaps. I hope so. I am a Jesuit," Brother Timothy continued, "so I have learned a bit about independence. As you may be aware, my order has often been viewed with suspicion by both the government and the Holy See. In addition to attending to my parish, I am priest to a community of Algerians. During the war, they were brought to France to work. Now they practically live as indentured servants."

"That is like the Bracero program that brought people from Mexico to do agricultural work in the United States," I said. "I was a nurse in a clinic that served some of the very poor. It is painful to see people used like that—for the interests of businesses. But ironically, it sometimes gives them more resources than they would have if they had stayed in their own countries."

"It gives them more money—but they lose so much—their homes, their extended families, their communities, their language, their history," Brother Timothy said, shaking his head sadly.

I answered, "I can't imagine the courage it requires to take a risk like that. Many of the people I worked with saved everything they could to send money home."

"That is the same with these people. There is some government funding to help them with housing and social services, but they are very isolated—and, in some cases, deeply resented. I have found myself acting as an interpreter, a bodyguard, a teacher, and a babysitter—almost anything you can imagine.

And a spiritual figure in their lives. Many of them are Muslim, but they accept me as the closest thing they have to an imam, their religious leader. I am often sorry to be a poor imitation of what they need. But I can't complain. I am grateful to be of help."

I winced at the words 'poor imitation,' then looked at him and took a risk. "Brother, won't you stay for lunch? We are having cassoulet and a salad fresh from our garden. Sophie is an excellent cook," I said.

"I would be delighted," he answered. "But first, would you be so kind as to direct me to a washroom?"

I pointed down the hallway and explained that the bathroom was the second door on the left. Sophie was scowling at me.

"Jane, what are you thinking?" she said breathlessly. "We may have gotten away with it up 'til now, but what are we going to talk about with him? It's one thing to be a nun when a troubled woman needs you—it is quite another to succeed in the masquerade with an actual cleric!" she said, clearly very worried.

"I can't explain why I asked him to stay. I just have a feeling about this man—that in some way, despite his being a brother—-he can understand the work we are doing," I said thoughtfully. "You heard him. He as much as said that his mother used herbs to provide birth control when he was growing up. That is quite an admission for a brother to make."

"You're not going to *tell* him, are you?"

"No. Not in so many words. But I think he knows a little more about what we are doing here than he lets on. He understands poverty and isolation. I think he could become our friend. I understand you think I am crazy, but I want him to eat with us. Besides," I said playfully, "Your cassoulet could convince anyone of anything."

"We'd better serve a large bottle of wine with it!" she said. Then she rolled her eyes and went into the kitchen to set the table.

And so, half an hour later, we were all sitting in awkward silence at the rough-hewn wooden kitchen table. In front of us were a large bowl of salad dressed with Sophie's amazing vinaigrette, a tureen of bubbling hot cassoulet, and a large bottle of Burgundy. Brother Timothy saw that he hadn't quite won Sophie over, so he began by praising her food.

"I can smell the fresh thyme and the pancetta," he said. "It is amazing. This was one of my mother's specialties."

"I hope it is as good as hers," Sophie said, spooning the hot casserole onto our dishes and motioning us to help ourselves to salad.

"I am certain it will be wonderful," Timothy said. Then he asked, "Shall I pour the wine?" in what I saw as another bid for friendliness.

"That would be lovely," I answered. I wasn't doing anything, so I heaped my salad plate with the fresh romaine and arugula that Sophie had picked from the garden. She had shaved a carrot on top of it, and the colors were vivid. I broke off a piece of baguette that Sophie had placed in a woven reed basket, and passed the rest to Brother Timothy, who had just finished filling my wine glass. I almost made a toast when I remembered that I was the Mother Superior of a convent, and instead bowed my head in prayer and said solemnly, "Bless us, O Lord, and these, thy gifts, which we are about to receive in thy name. Through Christ, our Lord, Amen." Then I made what I sincerely hoped was a properly executed sign of the cross.

Sophie and Brother Timothy joined in the amen, and we began to eat.

The food was so rich that none of us said a word for several minutes. Finally, Brother Timothy said, "Mademoiselle St. Martin, I think you have my poor mother beaten with this cassoulet. It is magnificent."

Sophie couldn't help but smile. "I think it is because so many of the ingredients are fresh from our garden."

"I have a suspicion that you are the one who tends the medicinal herbs?" Timothy asked her.

"Yes. It's something I love. Ja—Reverend Mother tells me that your mother was an herbalist?" she said.

"She was. And a witch if you heard some of our neighbors speak of her. She was wise about many things—what needed to be planted under the full moon—whether the roots or the bark of Angelica should be used for purification, how to use rue to help bring on a woman's menses."

Sophie and I both stopped eating when he said this. We knew that rue was historically used as an abortifacient, but did he know?

He held his hands up as if in surrender. "*Desolé*—I'm sorry—I didn't mean to pry. When I came out of the bathroom, I took a wrong turn and ended up in one of your medical rooms. I saw some instruments laid out. I know what those instruments are used for."

When the blood drained from Sophie's face, I knew what I looked like. It crossed my mind to fabricate an excuse, but I couldn't think of anything to say.

Sophie burst into tears.

So much for my brilliant plan.

CHAPTER 38

AN UNLIKELY ALLIANCE

Timothy spoke slowly and quietly, as if approaching a doe in the woods.

"Please don't cry, Mademoiselle St. Martin," he began. "I would like to be your friend. When my parishioner, Madame Toussaint, returned from her retreat, it was as if the weight of the world had been lifted from her shoulders. I raised the funds to send her to you because I feared for her sanity when she told me she was pregnant again. Her husband is a nice enough man when he is sober, but he is drunk too often to depend on. I had already begun searching for clothing and blankets. When she came home, she told me she had been mistaken, and she wasn't pregnant after all. I suspected that wasn't true, although I couldn't think why she wouldn't tell me honestly if she had lost the baby. Then when Mademoiselle Laurence came back and thanked me over and over for suggesting that she come to you, I realized something was afoot."

"What are you going to do?" I asked in a shaky voice.

"What do you mean? I'm not going to *do* anything," he answered. "I recognize that my vows don't entitle me to determine how other people should live their lives. I will always argue in favor of continuing life, as I believe I must. And I will humbly step aside when another choice is made. I know what my church says. And I know what my heart says. I wasn't recruited to visit you—I volunteered because I thought you might need protection. My obligation to my mother is older than my obligation to my church."

"But... what will you say to your monsignor?" Sophie asked, her voice trembling.

"I'll tell him the truth—that I have ascertained that you are not affiliated with the Church in Rome, and that you offer very special retreats for women in need," he said. And then, because he could tell that Sophie was about to burst into tears again, he said, "Mademoiselle, I promise I do not wish to make any trouble for you."

I gave Sophie a reassuring smile and turned to him. "Thank you, Brother Timothy. We welcome your friendship."

He stuck out his hand to me and said, "Let's begin again. I'm Tim."

I shook his hand and, pulling the wimple off my head, said, "I'm Jane."

Sophie shook his hand, too. "I'm still Sophie," she said, laughing haltingly instead of crying. "I suggest we get busy finishing this bottle of wine because I've made an apple tart for dessert."

We ate the wonderful tart, commenting on the perfect juxtaposition of the sweetness of the custard filling, the tartness of the apple, and the crunchiness of the pastry. Then we talked more about the work of Our Lady.

"I hope it is fair to presume that you are skilled at what you are doing... I mean, in terms of your special service?" Timothy asked, wiping custard off his chin.

"More than fair, and so glad you asked about that," I answered. "We have been well trained by more than one physician who cares deeply about women, and we use specially designed instruments that make the service safer and simpler than ever."

Sophie added, "We don't depend on rue anymore."

"I sent those two women here because they needed some time in quiet contemplation. Are there women who come to you just for that?"

"Yes, a few, and we are glad to welcome them," I said. "As for those who are pregnant, we have learned many things about how to care for the hearts of women as well as care for their bodies. We explore their feelings with them so that they have a sense of peace about ending their pregnancies—or else about continuing them. We don't have any preconceived idea of what they are going to do."

"The decision must be theirs," Sophie said.

"And why in a convent? With a habit?" the brother asked. As Sophie lit a fire to warm against the afternoon's cool, I told the long story of Our Lady to our newest, and most unlikely, friend, Brother Tim.

CHAPTER 39

THE LAP OF THE VIRGIN

Our Lady, 1953

Girls and women are unique. Even more importantly, their situations are unique. After these many years, I understand that it is the circumstances, as much as the individuals, that determine whether a pregnancy is sought, welcomed, warmed to, tolerated, accepted, become numb to, or actively opposed. Each of these responses is part of a spectrum, and a woman may experience many of these during a pregnancy in no particular order.

One could argue that if a woman is having sex with a man, she had better be ready to become pregnant, but that is ridiculous. No matter what some churches say, sex and procreation are not linked in most people's minds. You may be aware that some animals only experience sex when the females are fertile. For those creatures, sex and procreation are inevitably part of the same experience. But human beings seek sex for so many reasons—for comfort, for passionate release, or for love and acceptance. Too often, sex is taken by men through violence, or by the command that it is a woman's wifely duty.

Churches don't explain why their god would create humans to want sex when there is no chance of pregnancy. If their claim is correct, that sex is only for the creation of children, humans would only want sex when women are fertile. When women use birth control to seek some degree of authority over when and whether to get pregnant, they are faced with the reality that birth control is often withheld by governments, and it doesn't always work.

Because the pregnancy is located within the woman's body, men have a lot less at stake in preventing it, even when it is not welcome. And because they don't experience changes in their bodies, pregnancy may be more theoretical than actual. Some men actively oppose women using birth control. In the politics of relationships, it is a rare woman who can stand up for herself, withhold sex, or even leave such a relationship. We all want to be loved, and for many women on this planet, especially those who are already mothers, the economic support of a man is still essential to survival.

Over the years, and through much discussion, we at Our Lady learned to tailor our conversations to the needs of the patient. We even developed a shorthand with each other about which aspect of Our Lady we would represent, depending on what kind of support the woman seemed to need. We had Our Lady of Grace, Our Lady of Courage, and Our Lady of Peace. Even so, there was so much more to learn. We don't mean to be arrogant, supposing we know more than the patient does about what she needs. But we listen carefully to everything she says.

Our kitchen shelves groaned under the weight of recipe books—the unlikely archives of our work. Occasionally I sat at the table and leafed through them, as if to surround myself with the women who came to us in so much pain—and left us, if we had done our work well, with a sense of confidence and peace.

I remember Jeanette. She was early in her pregnancy when she came to us with a baby on her hip. As you can imagine, the abortion process is limited by the biological timetable of pregnancy. We never have as much time as we need or want, so we do the best we can. Like so many of our patients, she was Roman Catholic. That, or being brought up in any other fundamentalist religion, often presents the first hurdle for a woman who is attempting to find her own answers. Jeanette was a tiny woman. At first, she seemed to be just a girl, but she told me that she was 28 years old. She was married and had two children, a six-year-old named Pasquale, being cared for by a neighbor, and a two-year-old—a darling mite named Martin, who had spina bifida. His head was abnormally large, and he had no control over his legs, so she carried him everywhere, including to Our Lady. Her husband abandoned her when it became clear that there was something wrong with their youngest child. So she was on her own, attempting to survive as a seamstress, with a six-year-old and a very needy little one. She tried to get her husband to come back by preparing a romantic dinner. The result was a pregnancy, but still no husband. She seemed at her wits' end.

"I can't eat. I can't sleep. Even the smell of food makes me feel sick. I can hardly work. There are two children I need to take care of. What am I to do?"

"Jeanette, how can we help you?" I asked.

"Don't ask me to kill a baby, Sister. I can't do that. I won't."

My heart ached for her. "I'm not asking you to do anything. What were you hoping for when you came to us?"

"Hoping for a miracle. Every day I prayed to the Virgin for a miscarriage, but it has not come."

"How would it be different if you had the miscarriage that you prayed for, or if you had an abortion?"

Jeanette was quiet. She sighed. "It wouldn't be... it wouldn't be my fault."

"It is very hard, isn't it, to be the one responsible? Yet, as a mother, you are painfully aware of that, aren't you? Doesn't it seem that being a good mother often means saying no?"

"I seem to be saying 'no' to my older son all the time. Already I have no energy to take care of him or give him the attention he needs. How can I be a good mother to him and to the little one who needs me so much if I give birth to another one?"

"What do you call what is inside your body?"

"A baby, of course."

"Of course. And what would happen to the baby if you had a miscarriage?" I asked.

"She would go to Heaven, and the Virgin and my grandmother would take care of her," she answered softly.

"So, this baby would be a girl?"

"Yes, I am certain of it."

"What would happen to her—to her spirit—if you have an abortion?"

"I am afraid that she would be punished for my sins," she answered, crying.

"What are your sins?" I asked.

She was silent. Then she sighed. "The sin of wanting too much? Of wanting my children to be safe and to have enough to eat?"

We both laughed.

"Ah," I said. "The sins of good women." I asked, "Jeanette, is God real to you?"

"Yes, naturally. And He is very angry."

"Who does He remind you of?"

"He is like my father when he has drunk too much. And like my husband when dinner is late."

"So, for you, God is a disgruntled man who doesn't get His way?"

"Well," she squirmed in her seat, "That's not exactly right. When I was small, there were two nice ones—the Virgin and Jesus. And the mean one who was called God. My own version of the Trinity."

"Do the Virgin and Jesus have as much authority as the one you call God?"

"Oh, yes. They are the ones who take care of us every day. They are the ones who attend to us and help us."

"Okay. What if we call upon the Virgin and Jesus to help you now?"

"Only the Virgin. She will understand. My little one is different. She had a baby who was different, too."

"Does the Virgin know what is in your heart?"

"She knows everything about me. She knows every minute of my life."

"And does she love you without condition? Does she know you are doing your best every day? Can she forgive you?"

"She does love me. And she forgives me. And she knows how hard I work for my children every day. She understands that I cannot have this baby."

"Jeanette, perhaps there is someone else who would need to forgive you if you decide to end this life."

"Who? My husband? He doesn't even care. My father? I would never tell him about this. Who else would I ask to forgive me?" she asked.

"Look inside," I suggested.

"Oh. Yes, I see. It is me. The one who can't forgive myself for not being perfect."

"Jeanette, did God create you to be perfect?" I asked.

"No. He created me in sin."

"Is that another way to say that you are only human? That you are created imperfect?"

"Only human... yes. Imperfect... but I am supposed to make myself perfect."

"Ah, I see, Jeanette. You know better than God."

We both laughed again.

"It takes courage and love to forgive yourself. You have love and courage for your children and for other people. I wonder if you are brave enough to find it for yourself. How would you begin to look for self-forgiveness if you wanted it?"

"I would climb into the lap of the Virgin and allow her love to flow through me. She was only a woman, too, and she made sacrifices for her child."

"What a wonderful idea. I'd like you to picture that in your mind. Take your time. Imagine yourself in her lap. Breathe slowly. Can you sense her love? Can you sense yourself being filled with her love?"

Jeanette closed her eyes. "It is like sunshine. Her love is bright like sunshine. She is whispering to me that I can forgive myself."

I stayed silent for a moment to let that sunshine sink in.

"What about the spirit of that little girl? If you have an abortion, do you want to release that spirit to go to Heaven, or do you want to keep it in your heart close to you?" I asked.

"*Can* I keep her close?" she asked in a whisper.

"That is up to you. As a good mother, it is up to you to make these hard choices, but you don't need to be alone. You can keep her with you."

"I can talk to her?"

"If you want. And you could choose a stone from our churchyard to remember her by so that you can keep her with you always. When you need comfort, you can look inside and speak to this spirit, and you can ask the Virgin for help. Jeanette, after you've fed your sons and put them to bed, why not spend a little time talking with the Virgin and this baby's spirit and ask for guidance and forgiveness? Then perhaps you'll be ready to decide."

"I am already certain. I am going to have an abortion."

"All right. But I want you to sit with that and see if it is right in your soul."

CHAPTER 40

A TINY SPACE OF LIGHT

After a few days, Jeanette came back. As so often happens, she was no longer the needy woman who first came to us. She had found a neighbor to take care of her children. "I had to come on my own. To stand strong. This choice is as much for me as it is for my children. I am going to ask for more help so I can give my six-year-old the attention he needs. And my cousin offered to give me the wheelchair her son used. I have tried to do this alone, but I can't. When this is done, my life will change for the better. I'll be the one to change it."

Jeanette's abortion went easily. Sophie, wearing the habit of Our Lady of Perpetual Grace, stood beside her and held her hand.

People who are against abortion seem to be concerned that there are so many. I have thought a lot about why so many women need abortions. Sometimes a young girl is so isolated that there is no one to notice that she is at risk of 'falling pregnant,' as they say in England. A woman who is in survival mode may be too overwhelmed to make intentional choices.

I know the story of a French girl who was in love, but was obliged to marry a German officer. The travails of a Jewish mother in the ghetto who could not feed the children she had, much less make room for another. I know about a teenager who was too ashamed to share that she was pregnant, even with people who loved her unconditionally.

I never planned to be an abortion counselor. I had tried on other identities—teacher, attorney, perhaps a school principal? But I chanced into abortion, and, as happened with those ten little girls in Paris, I fell in love. I am well aware that the word "love" and the word "abortion" don't often appear in the same sentence. But I am resolved to tell you the truth—and the truth is, that for me, abortion counseling is a love story. We created something very special at Our Lady. Something that didn't exist anywhere else in the world. 'Refuge' was the best word I had for it, but it wasn't quite right.

Part of the work of an abortion counselor is to open a tiny space—a gap in which a woman is able to stand outside her desperation and panic and make an actual choice. It means that she has the opportunity to own the decision she makes, even when she has no viable options. It is the owning of it that so often determines whether she sees herself as a victim or someone who is accountable for her life. If she isn't able to do that—and if there is no one who can help her see beyond victimhood and mere survival—there is a chance that she will emerge from an abortion physically whole, but emotionally wounded. Survival is essential, but it is not enough. We all deserve more. As an abortion counselor, you have a chance to encourage her to experience herself as the author of her life, or at the very least, author of her interpretations. It's not always easy.

Manon was an extreme example. When she first called, I had the most ridiculous notion that it was Betty calling to play a trick on me. It was the same husky, commanding voice.

"You've got to help me," she demanded. Not, "Allo my name is Manon," or, "Is this Our Lady of Perpetual Grace?" or even simply, "*Bonjour.*"

I evicted Betty from my mind. "*Bonjour*, I am Jane Smith at Our Lady of Perpetual Grace. How can we help you?" I said, using my customary phone-answering manners.

"He will hurt me if he finds out I am knocked up. And if I don't get rid of it. There's no choice. I will be there tomorrow. Is there a bus?"

She spoke so quickly that it all ran together, and I had to ask her to repeat herself more slowly, which she did.

"And what is your name, age, and how many weeks pregnant are you?"

"I am Manon Lefebvre, twenty-four years old. Maybe two months," she said. "Could be more." She sounded both furious and terrified. I was trying to imagine what could be bad enough to scare this woman.

Sophie, Françoise, Lucie, and I had agreed that it wasn't a good idea to do abortions on women who seemed committed to being victims. But I recognized that this woman *was* a victim, and I wanted to help her. Lucie had shown us that with an effective process, it was usually possible to help even the most helpless woman find a sense of resolution about what she wanted to do. I hesitated a moment because it was a big commitment with no certain outcome, and I looked at our schedule.

"*Bon*. We have a room tomorrow. The #47 bus comes within a quarter mile of us. You just continue down the tree-lined road. Can you walk that distance?"

"*Bien sûr*," she answered, and I saw she was trying to get off the phone.

"*Attends!*" I said. "A few more minutes."

"I cannot stay on the phone. He will be angry," she whispered.

"I need to know what you want us to do," I said, quickly. It was essential that the woman ask for herself.

"Get rid of this thing inside me," she barked, and hung up the phone.

I dreaded Manon's arrival. For one thing, she had hung up on me before I had a chance to give her better directions to the clinic. On the evening of her call, Françoise and Claude were with us for dinner and I spoke about my concerns.

"I guess I can handle it, but she sounded so hostile and so panicked. I guess I feel a bit insecure."

"What? Our Lady? Insecure?" Françoise gave a gentle laugh.

"I'm not even sure whether to wear the habit," I said.

"It is hard to predict someone's reaction," Sophie interjected, "but when it works, it is awfully effective. Which Lady would this be?"

"I'm not sure," I said. "Perhaps she would need Our Lady of Courage?"

"It sounds to me like she has a bit too much courage already," Françoise chuckled.

Sophie rolled her eyes. "Françoise, don't be like that. This woman is obviously in trouble." She turned to me. "I'm sure you will figure out what to say. But it will probably be easier if you are wearing the habit."

She was right. I had so often seen miracles occur when a woman had the freedom to talk with an icon rather than with just another person. So I considered it. That night I dreamed about Gertrude's abortion and watching Lucie function so skillfully as Our Lady.

At breakfast the following morning, I told Sophie about my dream.

"Did it change your mind about how to work with Manon?" she asked.

"I think it did," I answered. "If she actually comes, I will be greeting her as Our Lady, though perhaps not as one I've ever been before. The bus gets to the intersection at three p.m., so I'll be ready."

It was almost 5:00 when Manon finally showed up on our doorstep. She was cursing as she hauled her suitcase up the front steps and banged the iron doorknocker. When I opened the door, I saw a striking, bedraggled, frustrated young woman who looked up at me with undisguised contempt. Gracie stood behind her, ears down and tail between her legs.

"Perfect," she said. "First, I get lost and walk for half an hour the wrong way with this mangy dog nipping at my ankles. Then I finally change direction, and the heel on my shoe falls off while I am hiking to this horrible place. And finally, the door is opened by a nun who is as likely to condemn me to hell as anything else. I'm already in hell, Sister, so you can't send me there for my sins."

You could hardly blame me for not telling her to follow Gracie since she had hung up the phone so abruptly, but I was dismayed that the dog, arguably the most intuitive member of our team, was already feeling like a failure with the formidable Manon. Gracie slid past her and ran into the kitchen, as if anxious to be done with this angry woman.

Manon was tall with dark hair swept into a chignon, tendrils hanging loose after her long walk. Her eyes were heavily made up, and her dark red lipstick was peeling. Her fake leopard-skin coat was hanging off one shoulder. She carried her suitcase in one hand, and her handbag and shoes in the other. Her stockings were torn and dirty from walking without shoes. The offending broken heel dangled from a pump. The heel was much higher than I would ever wear, and certainly not for a trip to the country.

Françoise helped get Manon's bags into the bedchamber, and we gave her time to change clothes. She emerged from the room looking like a model. Her makeup was skillfully repaired, and her beautiful complexion and bright red lipstick reminded me of Disney's Snow White. She was wearing a slim black skirt with a scarlet red cardigan sweater set, and another pair of ill-suited high heels. I invited her into one of our counseling rooms. There were two comfortable overstuffed wing chairs upholstered in pale pink and green chintz, a little round wooden table with a small vase of flowers, and a window that looked out onto the gardens. Manon sat down abruptly in one of the chairs, and I could see that the elegance of the room was quite lost on her.

"Sister, or whatever you are, I just want to get this over with. I have done it before, so I know it hurts like hell and I'll be lucky if I don't die from an infection. I know everything I need to know, and I am already a criminal, so I won't turn you in," she said with a sneer. Even that horrible expression wasn't enough to ruin her beauty, though it was painful to imagine how lovely she could have been without it.

I had no idea where to start with this angry young woman, so I said, "How are you already a criminal?"

"Isn't it obvious? I am a prostitute. The man who owns me sends me out every day to bring back the money—on my back, as it were."

Jane, you are in over your head with this one. I thought about my sweet Lucie stuck in a relationship I could never fathom. Lucie, whose studies in psychology were so helpful to others, yet seemingly useless to her. What would Lucie suggest?

One of Lucie's admonitions was to get out of our own way—and that we should be honest when we feel self-conscious. I had found that Lucie was annoyingly and invariably correct, so although I was scared to show my vulnerability to this hostile woman, I decided to take a risk.

"Manon, my name is Jane. I am so sorry we didn't talk on the phone long enough for me to explain that we are a little different here."

"A *little* different?" she snorted. "I'll say. There were no nuns at the last place. Has the Church changed its mind about abortion, then? About sex? Are they now endorsing my line of work?" she laughed loudly, then furrowed her brow. "Don't try any tricky religious stuff on me. I'm onto you folk."

"I am here to support you," I said. "And I am not sure about the best way to do that."

"I already said it—just get this over with. I told my man I was getting the infection treatment, so I can be gone a couple of days, but no more. Can't have your girls spreading the pox when they are meant to be for fun, now, can you? I hate that I have to do this again, but at least I will be able to stop heaving my breakfast by the time I get back to Paris. Just tell me where to go and I'll spread my legs to get this thing out."

At that moment, I must have channeled Lucie, because the anger and fear in the woman's voice made me burst into tears.

"What the... Sister? What is wrong with you?" Manon sputtered.

I just let myself experience her despair. I allowed the pain into my heart, and I cried freely. After a few minutes, I wiped my eyes with the handkerchief I kept in the pocket of my robes.

"I am crying because I can see that someone—probably many people— have hurt you so deeply."

Manon looked at me in disbelief. She opened her mouth to say something, and then shook her head and closed it. We sat together in silence until she doubled over. Manon sobbed loudly for what seemed like forever. Then she wept. Then she made sounds like the whimpers of an animal caught in a trap for so long that it has lost all hope. After a while, I put my hand on her shoulder—just lightly. I gave her a clean handkerchief. She blew her nose, but kept her head down. I learned from my own experience that the shame that had exploded within her would not allow her to look me in the eye. I wasn't in any hurry. I was surprised to hear a scratching at the door. Gracie had never before interrupted a counseling session, but when I cracked the door open, there she was. I wanted to give Gracie a chance to redeem her sense of importance, so I turned to Manon and asked, "Do you mind if the dog comes in?"

Manon gave a muffled answer that sounded like 'I don't care,' so I opened the door. Gracie came in and went straight to Manon's side as if she had known her forever. Then she did something that I had never seen that dog do. She put her head in Manon's lap and sat still until she got a scratch behind the ears.

"Manon," I said. "I have some paperwork to do. I apologize, but I'm going to be busy for a few minutes. If you want to, you can tell me about yourself while I am working." I turned my back to her and began to shuffle through a pile of papers on the table. After a ragged sigh, Manon began in a very soft voice, while Gracie leaned against her.

CHAPTER 41

COLLABORATION HORIZONTALE

"We lived in Brittany. From the age of eight, my father interfered with me. Then he died in a German prisoner of war camp. I suppose I'm supposed to feel bad about that, but I don't. I hated him. During the war my mother got food for me and my brothers through what our neighbors called '*collaboration horizontale*,' in other words, fucking German soldiers. As if the whole country didn't collaborate, anyway. That supposed war hero, Pétain, allowed the Nazis to waltz right in and take over. In my mother's case, it wasn't just one German officer—a parade of them came in and out of our house at all hours. But we had plenty to eat. I was old enough to understand what was happening and also old enough to be humiliated. I took care of my two little brothers as well as I could. I loved them so much. The neighbors made horrible noises behind our backs when we shopped at the market.

"At the end of the war, when the allies came, those same neighbors rounded up women accused of collaboration, including my mother. Jeering and screaming, those self-righteous citizens shaved the women's heads for entertainment. They painted my mother with a swastika. These '*tondeurs*' put my mother in a wagon and drove her through the village. Boys ran behind them, hurling stones. People came to watch as if it was a carnival. A man who had been a collaborator himself dragged my mother out of the wagon and the people in the crowd killed her. For trying to feed her children. I hate them. They were no better than the Nazis.

"I had nowhere to go. At first, a neighbor took us in, but the good people of my village hounded her until she made me leave. I am just grateful that she kept my brothers. So I took a bus to Paris where everyone was a stranger. But there were no jobs, except the one that's always available for those with a female body. Valentin, the man who keeps me, is a bastard, but he protects me from the other bastards who are as bad or worse. One of the other girls told me what to do to stop a baby, but it obviously doesn't work. This is the second time for me. I don't have any choice. There is no choice for a girl like me."

"Oh, *petite*," I said, turning to look at her. She turned her face away from me but continued talking.

"My mother told me she named me after a woman in an opera. I was so proud that I told everyone. It wasn't until I got to Paris that Valentin informed me that Manon Lescaut, the woman in Puccini's opera, was notorious for becoming a prostitute. Ironic, isn't it?" she said sadly.

I murmured a non-committal response.

"Sister, may I have a drink of water?" she asked, as politely as any twelve-year-old.

"*Bien sûr,*" I answered. Then I smiled. "What if we sat in the kitchen in front of the fire while you told me the rest of your story?"

Her tear-stained face was suddenly so hopeful that it was as though I was looking at a different girl. Manon nodded her head, and I took her by the hand and led her toward the kitchen, where a warm fire blazed. Gracie followed at Manon's heels.

"Would you like water or hot chocolate?" I asked.

She looked at me as if she couldn't believe her good fortune. "*Chocolat, s'il vous plaît,*" she answered, as if hoping the offer wouldn't be revoked. The two of us and Gracie walked into the kitchen, and I motioned to the comfy chair next to the fireplace where Sophie did her knitting. Manon curled up in the chair, and Gracie curled up at her feet.

By the time I had heated the milk and made the cocoa, Manon had fallen asleep. When Françoise came into the room, I put my finger to my lips.

"Jane, who is this tame creature, and what have you done with the horrible beast who came here?" she whispered, smiling at me. "I overheard how she was talking to you, and I must admit, I didn't even have the courage to ask if you needed help."

"It's that magic of Lucie's," I answered.

"Non, Jane. This time, I think the magic is all yours."

We let Manon sleep for an hour, then woke her to take her to the bedroom and tucked her in. It was as though she hadn't had any true rest for years. At suppertime, I asked Sophie to get her. I had no idea what to expect, but the sweet version of Manon was still with us through dinner. Lucie had warned us that transformations were unpredictable, so I took Manon to the side after we had finished eating and spoke with her for a few minutes.

"I realize you were angry when you got here—and you have every reason to be. Anger is a powerful and important emotion. It is good to learn to use your anger effectively—to direct it where it should go. I'm not your enemy. If you give me a chance, I would like to try to help you use your feelings to care for yourself."

"I don't know what you mean, Sister," Manon said, warily.

"I can explain it better tomorrow. And if you must protect yourself from me or from any of us, I understand that too. But I hope you'll give us a chance. Please don't go before we can talk again."

She looked surprised that I had guessed her plans.

"Please?" I asked again.

"Maybe. Maybe I'll stay," she said.

"And I have one more thing to ask, if you can do it."

"I can do anything I want," she said, a bit of the old metal in her voice.

"Of course you can," I said. "Will you just consider what your heart wants?"

She snorted. "What's the point of that?" she asked.

"Only that since you can do anything you want, why not imagine it?" I said, gently.

Manon rolled her eyes. "If it makes you happy, Sister, I will do it. But if I am going to stay, we will need to get this thing over with soon. It's all very well to make me blubber and tell you my life story, but it doesn't change the reality of my situation."

"*Bon, Chérie*. We have an agreement. You will allow your heart to tell you what it wants—and if you do that—really risk doing that, then we will help you," I said. I considered kissing her on the cheeks, but she had suddenly become so prickly that I didn't think it was safe. "If you need anything tonight, you may knock on my door—it's this one," I gestured. I had never told any patient that before, and I can't tell you what made me do it that night.

At about 2:00 a.m., Sophie and I were roused by a gentle knock and a small voice calling, "Sister, Sister." Asleep on the rug at the foot of our bed, Gracie gave a low growl. Sophie turned on the light and opened the door. Manon stood there, looking as pale as a spirit.

"I am so sorry—so sorry to wake you. I had a very upsetting dream."

Sophie brought Manon over to our bed, and the two of them perched on the edge.

I shook my head to wake up and sat up against the pillows. "Tell us about the dream," I said, stifling a yawn.

"My mother came to me. In the dream, her hair was long and black. It was before—before everything that happened. She told me that she was sorry she had not protected me from my father, and that she had tried to find another way to take care of us when the Germans came, but she couldn't. She said she never meant to humiliate me or abandon me with the responsibility of taking care of my brothers—and that she loved us all very much. And she asked me to forgive her for choosing a name that would embarrass me. She said she had never learned the story of the opera, only thought it was a beautiful name." Manon's eyes were wide. "Then she fell down on her knees in front of me and asked me to… to forgive her." Manon was talking through her tears. "She told me that she was so happy that I was going to have a baby." Manon looked at me, then Sophie, then me again. "How could my mother know that?" she asked. I was still a bit asleep, so I didn't even try to make sense of the question.

"Then my mother put her arms around me and told me that everything would be all right. I am aware that is a ridiculous thing to say. But I believed her, just then, and I could smell the perfume she always wore—*Muguet des Bois*." Manon put her hands to her face. "Lily of the Valley—I can still smell it. Now I am afraid to go back to sleep."

Sophie moved one of her pillows and patted the mattress as if inviting Gracie to jump up. Manon climbed in bed between us. The dog followed Manon to the edge of the bed ready to join her, but Sophie sent Gracie back to sleep on the rug.

"You'll be safe here with us," Sophie said, pulling the covers over the young woman. "We'll talk about this in the morning." I wondered, as I had many times, how I deserved to be loved by a woman as tender as Sophie St. Martin.

At breakfast, the three of us acted like schoolgirls after a sleepover.

Manon asked for more coffee and addressed me as Sister, even though I was still wearing my nightclothes.

"Now that we have slept together, perhaps you'd better call me Jane," I said, which made us all laugh again. Françoise arrived as we were talking, and she tentatively joined in on the fun.

"Well," she said to Manon, "It appears things are better for you today."

Manon snorted. "That is an understatement, Madame Françoise," she said.

I was relieved to see a more moderate version of Manon that morning— not the extremely tough woman whom I had first met, nor the vulnerable child we had seen the night before. She had let her hair down, dressed in softer colors, and applied a bit less makeup—although she still looked like a woman out of a fashion magazine. Manon was still strong, but it was like the metal without the blade. Even Gracie seemed to have noticed the difference. She entrusted Manon to us and went outdoors to do her usual doggy things.

I turned to Manon and said, "I am glad we can laugh, but we also need to be serious. I want to give you more time to decide, but I don't want to send you back to Paris. If you find that you want an abortion, we will do it safely and simply, and we will help you figure out a way to explain your absence to Valentin."

"He only thinks about me when he wants money. Otherwise, I am invisible to him," she said, shaking her head.

"Invisible?" Françoise said.

"Yes. Women are invisible unless a man wants them for something. You couldn't do what you do if anyone noticed us. No one cares about silly women and their silly religious retreats."

"Were you afraid of coming to us?" Sophie asked.

"I have been afraid almost all of my life. But once I got here, I wasn't."

"Why not?"

"You have created a safe place here—a sanctuary, *n'est-ce pas*? This is the first time I felt it wasn't a sin to be a woman."

I realized that was the word I had been searching for. Sanctuary. A sacred place free from the laws of men.

"Will you stay with us until you are certain?" Françoise asked.

"I will. But how can I turn what I want into what is possible?" she said, looking at me. "Even *you* don't have a magic wand."

But I thought I might have something like it.

CHAPTER 42

I NAMED HER LUCIE

That afternoon, Manon and I sat together in the garden, inhaling the intoxicating scent of roses. We talked more about feelings—about how feelings might help us rather than sabotage us. She nodded soberly as I talked. I couldn't tell how much of it she was absorbing, but it seemed important to try to give her some tools. She gave a great sigh, as if to say she had had enough of the lessons.

"Now that you have heard everything about me," she said, her nose pressed into a huge white bloom, "it seems only fair that you should tell me your story."

By that time, Manon was already more intimate with us than most guests, so I didn't see why not. I launched into the story, starting with Lucie and, interestingly, ending with Lucie.

"So, our conversations—the ways you helped me—happened because of this, Lucie?" she asked.

I nodded, yes.

Manon stayed with us long enough for us to get word to Brother Tim, who arrived in his little Ford. He came with good news. One of his parishioners, a widower, had two boys and was in need of a nanny. The brother assured Manon that she could have her baby and take care of the children if she wanted the job.

"Pierre is a good man, and he is desperate for help," Brother Tim said.

Manon beamed at him. "I took care of my little brothers all the time. I can do that very well."

"Pierre has had a hard time since his wife died. He warned me that the boys are little hellions," Brother Timothy said.

"I know a bit about Hell, don't I, Jane?" she asked, smiling. It was extraordinary to see her smiling. "Besides," she added, "I am no Mary Poppins myself. I hope you told him about my own hard times?"

Brother Tim assured Manon that he'd shared everything and that Pierre was all right with it. But I still wasn't certain that Manon had made a decision.

I asked Brother Tim to excuse us and took Manon into a counseling room.

"Manon," I began gently, "I understand you don't want to pretend things are other than they are. If you go to work for Pierre, you'll still be a mother with no husband, and that can be difficult no matter what story you fabricate. You won't have any money or property, and you will be reliant on the good graces of a stranger. The future is uncertain if you decide to have this baby. Of course, the future is always uncertain."

"Sister, do you think I can be a good mother?" she asked, looking me straight in the eye.

I waited for what must have felt like an eternity.

"Do you?" I finally asked.

Brother Timothy offered to take Manon back to Paris to collect her things, but she assured him that there was nothing there she wanted. They drove off to her new life in Brother Tim's Ford, Manon waving until they were out of sight.

The following week, Lucie was visiting from Paris, and we sat in the kitchen talking about our experience with Manon.

"Which Our Lady did she need?" Lucie asked.

I answered thoughtfully. "I had imagined she might need Our Lady of Peace because she was so distraught, but when I listened to her story, I was overwhelmed. I lost any idea of a plan, and just reacted honestly."

"So, Our Lady of Honesty?" Sophie suggested.

"Honesty—yes," Lucie said, "But I think the important thing is that your honest response intruded on her typical hostile, angry state. What do you think of Our Lady of Intrusion?"

That made us laugh.

Françoise said, "I guess I would go with that, but must the intrusion be *perpétuelle*?"

The mail brought an interesting letter that day from Sophie's uncle, who agreed to provide legal help if we got into trouble.

October, 1951

My Dear Miss Smith,

I hope we can meet soon in Paris to discuss the steps necessary to change the legal status of your work in France. As you can imagine, other practitioners of your craft are quite unsavory and would not serve to forward an effort toward legalization. You would be the perfect person to advance this cause. Please let me know when we can meet

Your humble servant,

Matthieu Neuville, Under Minister of Justice

Right, Monsieur Neuville. That's all I need. My name and face in the *Paris Herald Tribune*. My mother would clip the articles and share them with her friends. And visit me in prison! There had to be another way that didn't involve me. Sophie and Françoise wondered if decriminalizing abortion was even possible, but they knew enough not to push me.

Brother Tim kept us apprised of Manon's life. She had the baby and apparently managed the two little boys and the baby very well. Over a year later, she came back for a visit. I almost didn't recognize the woman who got out of Timothy's car holding an infant wrapped in a brightly colored quilt. This Manon was beautiful in a different way—she radiated love and happiness. Gracie recognized her instantly and followed her from the car, tail wagging.

Manon patted Gracie, then kissed me on the cheeks and said, "Do you want to hold the baby?"

"Please!" I said. Manon placed the baby in my arms while Sophie stood close behind me.

"Oh, Manon, she is the prettiest baby!" Sophie exclaimed. And she really was. She had thick, dark hair, pale skin, blue eyes like her mother, and a perfect rosebud of a mouth.

"I named her Lucie," Manon said shyly.

"Brother Tim told us. Welcome to Our Lady, little Lucie," I said. And we all smiled to have a Lucie within our walls again. After the baby fell asleep, we had a glass of wine.

"Pierre is a very kind man, and he has been good to me. His housekeeper is a midwife, so I had the baby at home. We have had some rough patches. Brother Timothy didn't exaggerate when he said the boys were hellions. I was angry at first—I tried to make them behave by being strict. But that just made it worse. Then I realized that my anger was just fear—like you told me, Jane, remember? You said, 'If anger were a blanket, and you peeked under it, what would be there? Fear!' So I could lighten up a little and even admit that I was scared. When I finally saw their hurt—just the way you saw mine—everything changed for the better. Pierre and I respect each other. There are still difficult moments with the boys, but we are the best of friends and we are like a family. After the war, I could never track down my brothers, but with these two, it is almost like I have them back."

Lucie was absolutely delighted to learn that she had a namesake. She and Manon were about the same age, and I thought they would be great friends. Lucie insisted that we send her pictures, so we asked Tim to take some of us, all circled around the baby. Today, one of those pictures on the table next to me.

CHAPTER 43

VERY PLEASED

Our Lady, 1956

My mother remained determined to visit. Her letter said, "I want to see how you are using the convent. I am so proud of you for helping women." I was pretty sure that *proud* would not be the word she chose if she understood our actual work. I put her off by saying we had terrible, rainy weather in the spring, and we should plan a visit for another time. For me, 'at another time' might as well have been on another planet. Just thinking about facing my mother made me shudder. We experienced a steady demand for our services, so I couldn't imagine closing our doors to allow a visit from my mother, even for a few days.

The Goldfarbs made an unexpected move from Connecticut to California when Sadie accepted a job as the head librarian at the University of California in Berkeley—near Alameda, where I attended nursing school in the Navy.

Lucie's studies in Paris occupied her time and attention. After some months, her letters became shorter and more guarded. She finally surprised us with a visit and told me in private that Oliver was again pressuring her to have a baby.

"Now that it will no longer be a disgrace to his family, he wants an heir! And the worst thing is that he is adamant this next Hanover must be born in the United States. His father wants him to move to New York and join the practice. I want to stay in France. What should I do?"

I wasn't surprised that Oliver would give so little consideration to what Lucie wanted. On his rare visits back to Our Lady, he had come to resemble his autocratic father more and more. Oliver had also started to make disparaging remarks about the work of Our Lady. His supposed jokes about sending us all to jail made me distinctly uncomfortable. I didn't bother revisiting my original misgivings about freedom-loving Lucie, marrying rule-loving Oliver. Being right brought me no joy.

Lucie and I reprised the conversation we'd had on her wedding night.

"Lucie, it is a big decision to have a baby. Don't let him bully you," I said.

"He thinks I'm just scared. It's true the whole idea of being a mother terrifies me—perhaps because I never had a mother myself. He says I'll be missing out on the most important part of a woman's life if I don't. What if he is right?" she asked plaintively.

"I'm sure it is important for many women—maybe even most women. But surely not for all of us. You need to decide for yourself. We have met lots of great mothers who love their children, but remember Irene? She was like the walking dead. Remember, she told us what a burden her children were to her? How she never wanted any of them?"

Lucie shuddered. "Yes, I remember her. But I would never be like that, would I? I would never resent my own child."

"Of course you wouldn't," I answered, with perhaps a little less certainty than I would have liked.

"I still love Oliver, but it is not as easy as it used to be."

"Is he controlling you?

"No. Not really. But neither of us is happy. Oliver is convinced it is because we are not a 'real family' since we don't have children."

"Sophie and I are a real family."

Lucie ignored that.

"There is one more thing," she added. "I am afraid he is terrified I might not be able to get pregnant because of the complications after the abortion. Even though it turned out so badly, he did the best he could. He has gotten very teary about it a few times. Perhaps I should get pregnant so he doesn't feel guilty."

"I don't need to tell you that is a terrible reason to get pregnant."

Lucie looked miserable. "No, you don't need to tell me."

The announcement of Lucie's pregnancy arrived about three weeks later. The letter came from Oliver, as if it were his achievement. I never asked Lucie about her visit, but it wasn't hard to guess she was already pregnant. I have always wondered if she was considering her own Special Retreat. By May, they had moved back to the United States to a house near his parents. One more gift with strings attached.

Once again, Lucie was gone. And with her, a piece of my heart.

We had a busy spring and summer. Little Henri spent a lot of time with me and Sophie so his parents could tend to their duties at the dairy. We celebrated his third birthday in our garden enjoying homemade ice cream.

Lucie's letters got shorter. She reported being deathly ill, long after morning sickness abates for most women. I hoped Oliver was being kind. She didn't mention him in her sporadic letters.

In October, Oliver's telegram read:

Baby Girl: Mathilde Fortier Hanover born 10/16/1956, 2:30
am, 6 lbs. 4 ounces. Very pleased. Regards.

"Very pleased, regards"—the quintessential Oliver. Not a word about
Lucie. The formality of the telegram was probably the closest he would ever
come to acknowledging his disappointment in not having a son. Later I realized disappointment might be too mild a word. Determined to have an heir,
as he had put it to Lucie, Oliver insisted the nursery be painted blue. When
the bad news arrived in the form of a baby girl, he had workers rush in and
re-paint the room pink before Lucie and the baby—Tildy, as they called her—
came home.

I smiled to myself when I realized Lucie had finally gotten to honor
Mathilde by naming the baby after the woman she had once called her shero.
My beloved Aunt Mathilde owned the boarding school in Paris, where Lucie
and I first met. Her courage saved so many Jewish girls by smuggling them
out of Paris until she was killed by the Nazis. I hoped Lucie's daughter, Tildy,
would live up to the name. I wondered whether the naming had been a bone
of contention between Lucie and Oliver. If there was any disagreement about
it, Lucie never said so. When I heard the story of the blue room turning pink,
I was ashamed that adult humans need to use a color code to instruct baby
humans who they are expected to become.

After the baby was born, Lucie's letters became brief and then stopped
altogether. I worried about her, but I thought it was only natural that she was
too busy to write. Sophie, Levy, and I made plans to visit the new family after
they had a little time to get settled. My mother wrote that she had gone to see
the baby, and she was uneasy about Lucie's state of mind. The Goldfarbs visited from California, and Sadie wrote to me that she was worried about Lucie,
too. But we all knew that having a new baby was a big adjustment, so we
weren't too anxious. We were excited to meet the new baby ourselves.

Françoise and Claude offered to hold down the fort and feed our sweet
pup, Gracie, who had gotten rather old and stiff. Late November found Levy,
Sophie, and me dressed in our finest, following other excited passengers up
the gangway onto a shiny plane. It took about 24 hours from Paris to New
York. It was the first flight for both Sophie and Levy, so I got to be the old
hand and show them the ropes. The pretty, young stewardesses wore snappy
blue quasi-military outfits that reminded me of the picture of my old girlfriend
Betty on that naval recruitment poster. They wined us and dined us on a gru-
eling trip. There were none of those clever lying- down recliner seats they
have today, so the trip was almost as uncomfortable as our train ride through
the Pyrenees when Levy, Lucie, and I fled Occupied Paris. Truly, quite a jaunt,
but we wouldn't have missed meeting our little Tildy for the world.

CHAPTER 44

SHE *IS* THE BABY'S MOTHER

Connecticut, November 1956

It was colder in New York than I remembered, or perhaps the wind made it seem so. We bundled our coats around us as we cautiously made our way down the steep metal steps from the plane. Oliver's father sent his chauffeur, who held up a sign with 'Dr. Levy' written on it. We collected our baggage, and a porter wheeled it out to the waiting automobile, a huge black Bentley— very elegant—all wood and leather inside. It took a little less than two hours to get to Oliver and Lucie's house. The drive down the Parkway was as scenic as I remembered. It made me nostalgic for my childhood home.

The senior Hanovers' latest gift to Oliver was a house in New Canaan, Connecticut, one of the fancy suburbs of New York, about ten minutes from them. Oliver commuted into the city every day on the train, which surprised me, since I remembered how much he hated doing that in France. The huge circular driveway put me in mind of visiting a diplomat or some kind of roy- alty. The house (I thought of the word 'mansion') was an enormous two-story Colonial built of gray wood with a pitched roof and multi-paned windows. The many chimneys visible from the outside made me anticipate a fireplace in every room. When we scheduled our trip, I assumed that we would stay in a hotel, but Lucie insisted she had plenty of room at their house. We planned a short visit because Levy had limited time off from work. We'd stay with Lucie for a few days, then go to my mother's house about thirty minutes away.

Maisie Hanover met us at the door, all smiles and welcomes. At first, I wondered if we had been taken to the senior Hanovers' house by mistake. But Maisie said that Lucie and the baby were both having a nap, so I had to assume we were in the right place. The chauffeur carried our bags from the car, took them into our rooms, and then disappeared. Sophie and I were chagrined to find they had housed us in separate quarters, but it didn't seem worth a dis- cussion.

We left our coats in our respective bedrooms and went back down to the enormous living room, where a huge fire roared. I couldn't believe the size and opulence of the house. One part of me wondered if Oliver thought he had to compete with the convent to impress Lucie.

A young woman in a frilly white uniform brought a tray of hot chocolate and some crispy sugar cookies. Lucie had not mentioned having a maid, who Maisie introduced as Clara. I thought that perhaps the maid was temporary—a baby gift from Oliver's parents? I was correct that having Clara was a gift from Oliver's parents, but I learned that it was a permanent arrangement. Clara also seemed to function as a nursemaid for the baby. As it turned out, Oliver's mother had been staying with them since baby Tildy was born, and Maisie seemed to be ruling the roost.

"Maisie, this is lovely, but we need to see Lucie." I didn't mean to be pushy, but that's why we were there.

"Oh my dear Miss Smith, you shall. But you'll need to wait until tomorrow. She has finally gotten to sleep."

I started to protest, but I felt like an uncooperative child.

"Surely you don't want to harm her, do you? The doctor has insisted she be left alone to get the sleep she needs."

Levy looked at me and raised his eyebrow, so I put on a cardboard smile. The cocoa was comforting, and the sofa was so soft that I feared I would fall into a nap myself. The grandfather clock told me that it was after five p.m. It was six hours later in France, so it was already way past my bedtime. My compatriots also struggled to stay awake. Maisie finally noticed our distress.

"Oh my, I had forgotten the time difference," she said. "We'll need to get some dinner and then get you into bed. But I know you want to see the baby first," she beamed. It seemed that at least one person was thrilled with the baby, no matter her unfortunate gender. Maisie motioned us to follow her up the stairs. We tiptoed to the second floor to a very pink room with a crib topped with a ruffled lace canopy. We leaned over and marveled at the tiny baby sleeping soundly under a pink blanket. Tildy was truly enchanting—chubby, with pink cheeks and long eyelashes. After a few moments, we quietly filed out of the nursery and Maisie closed the door.

Maisie beamed and whispered, "Isn't she a doll?"

We all agreed.

"Are you sure you want to close the door?" Sophie asked. "Isn't the baby likely to stir?"

Maisie beamed again. "We have the most wonderful device called a Radio Nurse. One part of it is in the nursery on the nightstand, and the maid has the other part of it so she can hear the baby when she cries or wakes. It is quite extraordinary."

The three of us looked at each other with thoughts and questions that would remain unspoken for the time being. Maisie started back downstairs, and I realized that I had no interest in eating dinner.

"Maisie, I can't speak for these two, but I am exhausted. The hot chocolate and those yummy cookies have spoiled me for dinner. I am sorry if I am causing any inconvenience, but I need to go to bed," I said.

"Not at all, dear," Maisie said. "Lucie takes her meals in her room—the little that she eats—and I usually just have a bite in the nursery if I am not at one of my meetings. So it is no inconvenience." She turned toward Sophie and Levy. "Can I have Clara put anything at all together for either of you?" They shook their heads and suggested they also wanted to sleep more than they wanted to eat. Maisie nodded her understanding.

"I'll have Clara put this evening's chicken and vegetables into the Kelvinator, and we can have them for lunch," she said, as she began to herd us to our rooms.

"But I want to see Lucie before we go to bed," I said. "Just to let her know we are here."

"Oh, no dear," Maisie said, knowingly. "She is sleeping, and Dr. Burns has cautioned us against waking her once she has finally managed to fall asleep. You'll see her in the morning." I finally realized whose voice Maisie's reminded me of. It sounded like that saccharine-sweet, nasal lilt of Glinda the Good Witch from *The Wizard of Oz*, but without the 'Good.' There was no use objecting, and I felt awfully tired, so I acquiesced.

CHAPTER 45

LUCIE HAS *NEVER* BEEN FRAIL

As Maisie bid us goodnight, she said, "Ollie had to stay in town tonight, but I'm sure he and Dr. H will be with us for dinner tomorrow. Please come down whenever you want. I remember that the time difference makes everything so strange. I asked the maid to set out some breakfast whenever you awaken."

We thanked her, and she went back down the stairs. Sophie and I had already agreed that we would sleep together in the double bed in my room, so we nodded goodnight to Levy. We washed our faces and got into our nightclothes. We were both too sleepy to say any of the thousands of things we needed to say—too exhausted, even for a hot bath.

We woke up around nine a.m. to the loud growl of a garbage truck stopping at each house on our side of the street. We were in complete confusion since it was only two a.m. on our internal clocks. We recognized that it would have been wise to make a plan for how to acclimate to the new time zone. Levy must have been awakened by the same truck, and we met at the top of the stairs.

It appeared that Lucie was having her own time issues. When we trooped into the kitchen after nine-thirty, Maisie told us our friend was still asleep. She, herself, acted bright and cheerful and didn't seem surprised or alarmed at her daughter-in-law's somnolence.

I guess Clara heard us moving around upstairs because we each had a soft-boiled egg in one of those cute little egg holders, with bacon, toast, butter, fresh orange juice, and coffee. It was heavenly. Maisie joined us at the table. Then Clara came in carrying the baby, who was wide awake and smiling.

"Thank you for such a wonderful breakfast," Sophie said, as Levy and I agreed.

Clara nodded silently, being as invisible as 'good help' is supposed to be. Tildy seemed delighted to be passed around. The baby cooed, and we cooed and smiled back at her.

"What a darling," Sophie said, and we all agreed. Tildy was only a month and a half old, but we exclaimed we could tell how smart and beautiful she was going to be.

"But where is our Lucie?" Levy finally asked after the breakfast dishes had been cleared and Clara took the baby away to be changed.

"As I explained, the doctor said she needs to get as much sleep as possible, so I don't disturb her. She had a difficult time with the birth," Maisie answered hesitantly. "I think she was just exhausted by it. I tried to persuade her to postpone your visit until she was better, but she wouldn't hear of it. She was determined she wanted to see you."

That alarmed me. It wasn't like Lucie to miss anything, least of all so many of her baby's smiles.

"Do you think it would be all right for me to look in on her?" I asked. "Just to see if she might be awake and not realize we are here?"

"If you feel you must," Maisie answered, looking uneasy. "But only one at a time, so as not to overwhelm her."

I had the suspicion that they were drugging her, like in some terrible Victorian novel. Levy and Sophie nodded, encouraging me to go. Maisie took me upstairs to Lucie's room—which seemed to be across the hall from Oliver's. I hadn't expected them to have separate bedrooms, and I didn't know quite what to make of it.

I nodded to Maisie that she could leave, knocked softly on the door, and opened it. Lucie's room had heavy damask curtains blocking the light. In the darkness, I could just make out a four-poster bed. On the bedside table sat a framed photograph of ten impossibly young girls in two straight lines with an impossibly tall imposter-nun posing in front of the Eiffel Tower. My high school graduation gift to her. I tiptoed in.

"I am not asleep," she said hoarsely.

"Lucie, it's Jane," I said, perching on the edge of the bed.

She sat up and wrapped her arms around me.

"Mam'selle! Mam'selle!" she exclaimed. "Thank God you are here." I held on to her as long as she wanted, and looked her in the eye.

"Can I let some light in here?" I asked. "I can hardly see you."

"You don't want to see me. I am a mess," she said. "But you can open the curtains. I want to see you! I am so glad you are here!"

I opened the drapes just enough to illuminate the room softly and returned to perch on the bed. I was shocked. Lucie had dark circles under her eyes. She was thin, her skin was sallow, and her hair looked as though it hadn't been washed in weeks.

"My darling," I said, pushing her stringy hair back from her face, "Didn't you remember we were coming? I told you all of our travel plans in my letters."

"I have lost all track of time," she said. "The doctor has given me sedatives and I don't seem to have any energy. But at least I am finally able to sleep." Aha! My image of the Victorian novel reappeared.

"Sophie and Levy are downstairs. We have met your sweet daughter, and they are dying to see you and know that you are all right. Shall I help you get up and wash your hair and we can all eat lunch together?"

Lucie smiled wanly, as if she had forgotten how to do any of that. I got her to the bathroom, bathed her, and washed her hair the way I did when she was a child. She dressed in a simple pale blue shift with a kimono-like robe and slippers. We took the stairs slowly, one at a time, with Lucie leaning against me.

Levy saw her first. "Lucie!" he cried and rushed to her for an embrace. Sophie looked alarmed as she took in Lucie's weakness, and I answered with my own look of alarm. After kissing Levy on the cheek, Lucie turned to Sophie and embraced her as well, this time with a bit more energy. Lucie walked on her own into the dining room where Clara had set the table. Maisie seemed surprised she had come downstairs, but accepted a quick peck on the cheek. We sat down for a lunch of a fresh salad and the chicken from the night before.

While we ate, Lucie was quieter than I had ever seen her. As far as I could tell, she pushed the food around on her plate but didn't eat at all. She accepted our oohs and aahs about the baby with a shy smile, as if she had nothing whatsoever to do with the creation of a creature named Tildy. We talked with great animation about everything and nothing in order to fill in the strange void. Lucie continued to smile in an absent way, making the occasional bland comment. She was a shell of herself. After we finished eating, Lucie said she needed to excuse herself for a nap, and Levy and I helped her back up the stairs. When we returned, we confronted Maisie, who was knitting in front of the fire.

"What have you done to her?" Levy thundered.

Maisie looked defensive and terrified. "I don't know what you are talking about. She is much better now that she is under the doctor's care and able to sleep. She's just a bit frail, that's all."

"Lucie has *never* been frail," I said. "Can't you acknowledge there is something terribly wrong? She must be getting an overdose of whatever this sedative is. She is hardly here. She didn't even ask about the baby or hold her."

"She is under the care of Dr. Prescott Burns, one of the most prominent physicians in New York. He has diagnosed Nervous Tension, which apparently afflicts some women after childbirth. Surely you don't think you know better than he? The sedative is called Miltown. It is the very latest, and it is perfectly safe. Why, a dozen of my friends are on it. I assure you that she is much better now." She put her knitting down and glared at me. "I told Oliver you would make this more difficult. Ollie and I implored her to let us postpone your visit until she was stronger, but she simply refused."

Sophie chimed in more gently. "Maisie, is she even spending time with the baby? I noticed Clara giving Tildy a bottle, so it seems she's not nursing. Lucie told us she was planning to breastfeed because it helps the mother and child bond."

Maisie looked a bit squeamish. "Of course she sees Tildy—almost every day. Clara takes her into Lucie's bedroom, and they sometimes take their naps at the same time. It's all according to the doctor's orders for her not to be overstimulated. She did try that kind of feeding at first, but she was just too nervous, so it is much better for the baby to have the bottle."

Levy spoke again, "I'm sorry, Maisie," he said. "I didn't mean to shout, but I have known Lucie since she was a little girl, and I have never seen her this way. In her letters, she didn't write much detail about what was happening. How long has she been on these sedatives? Was it a difficult birth?"

Maisie looked annoyed. "The doctor put her on Miltown at about seven months into her pregnancy. For her anxiety. So she's only been taking it for a few months. And the medication has helped immeasurably, as I said. The doctor told us that the birth couldn't have gone smoother. I don't like to talk about these personal things, but she had a general anesthetic, so it wasn't even painful. I wish they had given me that when Ollie was born. She was in the hospital for about three days, just the standard. I don't understand what it is that has been so hard for her, but you don't need to worry. Lucie is in the best hands, and I'm sure she will be back to her old self soon. Thank goodness we have modern formula now. It was quickly very obvious that the baby would need a bottle."

"What do you mean? It was obvious that the baby would need a bottle?" Sophie asked.

"Well, at first Lucie wouldn't even look at the baby and didn't want to hold her, much less feed her. But it was no problem. They have chemicals for that now, so they were able to dry up the... you know. We had already hired Clara before Tildy was born—and I was here—so they had a lovely homecoming. Lucie was just able to stay in bed. She has everything she needs, and so does the baby."

"What does Oliver think about this?" I asked.

"Well, he wouldn't say so, but he was terribly disappointed not to have a son. I'm sure he didn't mean to blame Lucie, but after all..."

"After all, what? What do you mean?" I asked.

"Well, she *is* the baby's mother."

"I don't think the mother alone determines whether the baby is a boy or girl," Levy interjected.

"So you say," Maisie responded, looking smug. "Anyway, Ollie has been working so hard that he's scarcely been here since Tildy was born. He's coming for dinner tonight just because of your visit. This has all been hard on him."

"I'm sure it has," I said, sarcasm dripping from my voice. It seemed to go right over Mrs. Hanover's head.

"Oh, my, it's two thirty. My goodness," she said, putting her knitting away in a basket beside the chair, "I think I'll just have a bit of a lie down before dinner myself. I understand you all mean well, but this conversation has been very trying. There is leftover chicken in the Kelvinator if you want a snack. Dinner will be served at six p.m. sharp." She stood up and patted her face as if she were brushing off the unpleasantness, then headed up the stairs to her bedroom without a backward glance.

The three of us sat in stunned silence, none of us knowing where to begin.

CHAPTER 46

I COULDN'T GET HER AWAY FROM YOU QUICKLY ENOUGH

"Lucie didn't say anything about this in her letters," I began. "I had no idea she was in this condition. I am appalled. What can we do?"

"I am familiar with problems like this after childbirth, but I never imagined the solution was sedation. Surely Lucie needs support to learn what is troubling her?" Levy said. "I recently read a new book called *Counseling and Psychotherapy* by a professor in Chicago named Carl Rogers. He calls his work Person-Centered Therapy. This is who we need."

"But Lucie can hardly get out of bed. How could we get her to Chicago?" Sophie asked. It was true. I agreed we were limited to local resources.

"I have a good friend at the university there. Perhaps Rogers has trained people in New York, and my friend can make a referral. You would both love what Rogers writes."

"Shouldn't we ask Lucie what *she* wants?" Sophie said.

"Of course we would, in a normal situation," I said. "But I'm afraid she can't advocate for herself in this condition. If we can give her some options, it won't seem so overwhelming." I glanced at the clock—it was just before three p.m. "Try to get your friend on the phone right now and let's find out what's possible."

Levy retrieved his address book and made the call. He was successful in reaching his colleague and got the name of a therapist who practiced in Norwalk, only a town away. Melinda Jacobs, Ph.D. Even her name sounded nicer than Prescott Burns. I was delighted it was a woman. Lucie had had quite enough of men in authority in her life.

The three of us went upstairs to Lucie's room. I knocked softly, and we went in. This time Lucie seemed fast asleep, so I shook her shoulder gently and she stirred. When she saw it was us, she sat up dully and pulled a large pillow behind her back. She looked like a sad, lost princess whose sleep was disturbed by a wayward pea.

"Hey there, sleepyhead," I said, and smiled at her.

"Hey there, yourself," she answered. This time, her smile looked more like the one I had fallen in love with so many years ago.

"Did you survive being alone with my mother-in-law?" she asked.

"Barely. Lucie, you've got us worried," Sophie said. "Why didn't you write that you were having such a hard time?"

"I didn't want to alarm you," she said. "According to the doctor, it is simply a case of mother's nerves. He said I will get over it."

"But meanwhile, you are a wreck!" I said, not one to mince words with her.

"Yes, I'll admit, this has been the worst few months of my life. Oliver didn't want me to tell you because he said you would swoop in and take care of me."

"Well, he was certainly right about that!" I said, laughing. "And I wish I had. We wanted to give you a few weeks to get settled before we came. Obviously, that was a horrible mistake. Who is this alleged doctor that is treating you, and why does he suppose that keeping you in a coma is a good idea?"

Lucie laughed softly. "He is a psychiatrist. They think the world of him, but I swear he is so formal and rigid that he appears to be made of stone. I hate it when he comes. He doesn't want to listen to anything about how I feel. He takes my blood pressure and asks me how many hours I slept. I told Oliver I don't like him, but ever since I had Tildy, it seems the balance of power in our relationship has shifted completely. I'll never be able to make it up to him that I didn't give him the son he wanted."

"So, you think you let him down?" Sophie asked. "That you failed as a wife?"

"Failed as a wife—failed as a mother," Lucie said ruefully.

"Lucie, you are not a failure!" I exclaimed. "We are so sorry we weren't here before, but we are here now. You are in trouble, and we are going to get you another kind of help—not sedatives that make the real Lucie disappear—but therapy that will help you find yourself again. Dr. Levy knows of a wonderful psychotherapist who is based in Chicago, and we found someone who works near here and trained under him. It's called Person-Centered Therapy. It sounds like what I would want if I were in your situation. Levy thinks it would be perfect for you."

Lucie looked horrified. "Oh, no! Oliver will never agree to that kind of treatment. If it is not done by a medical doctor, he is convinced that it is quackery. It would bring even more shame on our family." She grabbed at my arm to emphasize what she was saying. "Please, please don't suggest anything like that to Oliver or his parents. They believe that stuff is for witches, and they would as soon see me drown for my unnatural thoughts as allow me to be treated by anyone like that. Please don't say anything!" she implored.

"Okay. Don't worry," I reassured her. Obviously Oliver and his parents were living in the stone age.

"But not talking about it with them doesn't mean we are not going to get that help for you," Levy said. "This therapist sounds nice, and she practices a few minutes from here. You don't have to ask for their permission to get the treatment you need. Lucie, you absolutely must have help."

Lucie looked distraught.

"What has happened that all of a sudden he has this power over you?" I asked. "Has he been beating you?"

Lucie answered in a small, blank voice. "Of course he is not beating me. He loves me. He tells me all the time that he still loves me, even though I didn't give him a son. But I can't even look at the baby——the evidence of my failure. Oliver will never forgive me." She looked at us and said, "I am wrung out. I recognize you want to help me, but I can't talk about this anymore. Can you forgive me? I need to sleep."

"Darling, Lucie, we don't need to talk about this now, but at least consider the therapist Levy has found, won't you?" I asked, kissing her on the forehead. Levy and Sophie each kissed her cheek, and we tiptoed out of her room and closed the door behind us.

Oliver didn't come for dinner as promised. Maisie said he had a business meeting and asked her to extend his apologies. Lucie didn't come down. The four of us had an extremely formal, extremely quiet, dinner of lamb chops with little white paper pantaloons on them so you could pick them up without getting your hands greasy. There were also lovely asparagus and boiled new potatoes. Fortunately, Clara was a good cook. There were finger bowls at each place setting. When my companions looked perplexed, I motioned to Sophie and Levy to follow Maisie's lead. Sophie still looked worried. After our main course, Maisie dipped her fingers daintily into the warm water and wiped them on the special finger bowl napkin, so we did the same. Clara collected our finger bowls and brought in warm peach cobbler with scoops of vanilla ice cream.

After dinner, Maisie put some classical music on the Motorola record player and we sat in front of the fire. She attended to her knitting, while Sophie, Levy, and I worked on a jigsaw puzzle of Monet's water lilies that was laid out on the card table. Maisie suggested that Levy pour some after-dinner drinks. I do not understand why women are supposed to do everything related to food, and men are supposed to do everything related to alcohol. But Levy found the bar and poured us each a glass of Cognac. We hadn't gotten very far with the puzzle when Maisie folded her knitting back into the bag and told us she was going to say goodnight. We didn't bother with kisses on the cheek. We just said a polite "Good evening, Maisie, and thank you for the lovely dinner," as if she had done anything other than order it to be cooked.

By some unspoken agreement, for the rest of the evening we didn't talk about Lucie, or Oliver, or the baby, or therapists—or anything—other than whether there were any more dark blue edge pieces. We refilled our glasses and worked on the puzzle until there was no more wood for the fire. None of us wanted to go outside for firewood, so we ambled up the stairs to bed. Sophie and I kissed Levy goodnight, and we barely had the energy to wash before we tumbled into bed.

I slept restlessly. At midnight, I was wide awake. Because of the time difference, my body thought it was six a.m., which is when I usually got up. I tried to go back to sleep, but I lay in bed worrying, listening to Sophie's breathing, and cursing myself for not taking the sleeping pill she had offered. Finally, just before dawn, I couldn't lie there anymore. I tried not to wake Sophie as I dressed and left a note on the pillow. As the sun was rising, I slipped out the front door to take a walk. I was startled to see that Levy was already outside, smoking a cigarette and brooding.

"I guessed you'd be here soon," he said, giving me a quick embrace. "I was not able to sleep either. Let's walk."

"Oh Levy, this is so much worse than what my mother wrote to me. They are all trying to cover up the terrible shape Lucie is in."

"It seems so. And from what she said last night, she is going along with it. She is in no condition to fight back. This is just not Lucie."

"I want to see what Oliver has to say about this. Did Maisie say when he would be back?"

"She said he would be here for dinner tonight, so we can use today to contact that therapist and make a plan."

We walked for about an hour, making a loop. By the time we returned to the house, all the lights were on, and a big black car was parked in front. Maisie met us at the front door with uncharacteristic enthusiasm.

"Good news—Ollie is here!" she almost sang, as if Christmas had come early. "I spoke with him last night and he came home. He's in the kitchen. We can all eat breakfast together. You two must be crazy going out in this cold," she said, taking our coats and hanging them in the closet. "Get your boots off and put on some slippers. There are extras right here," she pointed to a big pile of furry pull-ons that Levy and I happily traded for our frozen boots.

We looked at each other. We recognized that a moment of truth was coming, but perhaps we'd get to have a cup of coffee first. Oliver sat at the kitchen table, looking imperious. He had changed a lot since the days when he and Lucie were my abortion care students, and I didn't like the change. Even less hair and even more arrogance.

"Well, well," he said, half standing at the table to greet us.

Was it my imagination, or was he starting to sound British?

"Good morning, Oliver," I said, kissing him on the cheek. Levy extended his hand. We seated ourselves around the table, and moments later, Sophie came in.

"Good morning everyone. I'm sorry if I am late. Jane, were you ever going to wake me?" she asked, smiling. "Oh, hi Oliver. I didn't realize you were going to be here this morning." He nodded at her. I knew he could have been here from the start. Dermatologists are seldom called for emergencies.

I pulled out the chair next to me for Sophie and said, "You are not late. We just came in from having a walk. It's freezing out there," I said, rubbing my hands together. "Did you have a good sleep?" Sophie recognized that as an accusation rather than a loving question, but she wasn't taking the bait.

"Yes, thanks dear, I did. The sleeping pill did the trick. Will you pass the toast?"

The table was filled with yummy things—toast and butter and jam and honey, scrambled eggs and bacon, freshly squeezed orange juice, and a large carafe of coffee.

"It looks as though someone needs her coffee," Oliver said, filling my cup.

I forced a smile as we passed food around and filled our plates. It smelled wonderful, and I was hungry, though it seemed disloyal to eat with so much about Lucie unresolved.

"Is Lucie…?" I began. "Will Lucie be joining us for breakfast?" I asked, hopefully, though without much hope.

"I expect not," Oliver answered curtly. "But have you seen her? Have you seen our little miracle?"

It took me a second to realize he had changed the subject from Lucie to the baby. I was relieved to recognize he had apparently gone from stricken to delighted.

"Oh yes, Oliver. She is a beauty," Levy answered, giving me a look that said, *Jane, watch yourself.*

Sophie chimed in, "She is a delightful baby. And how wonderful that your mother can be here to help out for a little while." Then she decided to be brave.

"But Oliver, it doesn't seem that Lucie is doing well. Has she… will she be able to take care of Tildy when Maisie leaves?"

Oliver chewed his toast for a moment. "Of course she will, but no need. I have already hired a nanny—that was always the plan. She'll be here tomorrow. And I may as well tell you that Dr. Burns has suggested Lucie would benefit from a longer rest. She's going to be at the best facility on the East Coast." He looked at me directly. "She'll have everything she needs to get better, and in a month or so, she'll be back with us."

"A month or so?" I said, incredulous. "But what about the baby?"

"The baby will be well taken care of by the nanny. She will never even know about this. And I mean that. Tildy is *never* to be told that her mother had this... this little episode."

I mustered up my courage and realized I was about to break a promise. "Oliver, Levy has found a therapist who might be perfect for Lucie. We'd like to contact her. She has more of a personal style in the Rogerian mode, if you are familiar with that."

"Naturally, I am familiar with that... that... well, I'd have to call it *balderdash*. Lucie is under the care of the finest psychiatrist in New York. She will go to the facility he recommends, and she will be fine. The baby will be fine. We will all be fine as long as you don't meddle!" He dropped his knife loudly on his plate, and we all stopped eating and looked at him. The opening salvo had been fired.

I stood up. "There is no need to be unpleasant about this. We can agree that Lucie needs help, and it is perfectly appropriate for us, as her oldest friends, to be part of the conversation about what help she gets."

Out of the corner of my eye, I noticed that Maisie had started to come into the room, but backed away when she heard our raised voices.

Oliver stood to face me. "It is *not* appropriate. I am her husband, and her care is strictly within my purview." He raised his voice and pointed his finger at me. "It is time for you to understand, *Mademoiselle*, that you are *not* in control of Lucie. You are *not* her mother. You suppose that just because you rescued her," he waved his hand at me and Levy, "you have some kind of hold on her. But you don't. She is not the little girl you met in Paris." He turned to me and glowered. "Lucie told me the stories, Jane. I know all about the 'good days and bad days.' You acted like you owned all of those little girls, but did you realize what you were doing to them? What you were doing to Lucie? She spent those years with you in Paris *terrified*. You made them all participate in smuggling girls out of the country—trafficking in human beings. Did you ever stop to consider the danger? The risks to them? I couldn't get her away from you quickly enough.

"And all those women! You didn't think I was paying attention, but nothing gets by me. I read your so-called 'recipe books.' I remember the name and circumstances of every woman you preyed on. I don't need to tell you there is no statute of limitations on murder. I wouldn't hesitate for a moment to bring this information to the authorities in Paris. Your little police inspector won't be able to protect you now. I don't need your help to take care of her. I don't need your constant interference, and Lucie doesn't either. She doesn't want you sticking your nose in this. Go home, Jane. *Go home*."

Shame washed over me. While I was trying to come up with a retort, I also feared there was some truth to his accusation. Part of my brain realized that I *had* put Lucie at risk, although another part of my brain was arguing that it was the war that put her at risk.

Sophie noticed I was overwhelmed. She put a gentle hand on my shoulder and said in a steely voice, "Oliver, I know you want to protect Lucie, but you have spoken out of turn, and you have been cruel. You are well aware of how much Jane loves Lucie—and how much Lucie loves Jane—and Levy, too. This is a difficult situation, and we all want the best for Lucie. Blaming Jane won't help anyone. And what you are saying about remembering the women we cared for is just absurd. You haven't been to the convent in years. We are not going to be cowed by your ridiculous threats."

Oliver smirked. "I can see that your dear Mademoiselle Jane has failed to tell you I have an eidetic memory. I remember everything I have seen or read."

To be truthful, I had forgotten that. I felt sick to my stomach. I can't say whether I was happy or sad that Sophie's intervention saved me from telling Oliver that I had always considered him a pompous, arrogant, self-centered bastard who cared more for himself and his reputation than he did for Lucie. Not to mention that he nearly killed her because of his incompetence and self-ishness. I said all of that, and more, to Sophie and Levy after Oliver stood up, red-faced, and stormed out of the house, slamming the door behind him like a little boy. But, even as I tell this story all these years later, I can still feel the shame of his accusations.

I realized that my self-doubt wouldn't help Lucie, so I took a deep breath and tried to get over it. Once Oliver stomped out of the house, back to who-knows-where, Sophie asked if it was true what he said about his memory.

"I'm afraid so. It's just one more thing that makes him seem more like a machine than a human." Sophie and Levy looked as unsettled as I felt. None-theless, we called the therapist and left a message about what we needed. Levy nodded to me that he wanted to go outside for a smoke.

There was no sign of the maid, so Sophie said, "Go on, you two." She cleared the dishes off the table and filled the sink with water as Levy and I put our coats and boots back on.

Once we were outdoors, Levy lit a cigarette, and he began to talk carefully, as if approaching a wild animal. "Jane, I am afraid I have to agree that Lucie may need more than some visits to a therapist. If I were her doctor, I would also be looking for inpatient care." We walked shivering down the tree-lined boulevard in front of the house. Our breath came in white clouds in front of us, and I was glad I had brought my mittens.

"I can't disagree, but it scares me. I have read such terrible things about mental hospitals."

"The ones for the poor are, indeed, awful. But when you have money, eve-rything is different. There will be a place that will take good care of her with-out lowering her standard of living," Levy said, wryly.

I batted him on the arm. "I am not talking about luxury!" I said. "I just don't want her to be in one of those places that smells like urine, where they put you in a closet."

"You have been watching too many old movies," he said, dropping his cigarette to the ground and stubbing it out with his foot. He bent down to put the butt in his pocket, as I had taught him to do. We walked along in silence, arm in arm, remembering the little girl we rescued all those years ago.

CHAPTER 47

SKIP THE LEECHES

Levy and I came back inside and took off our coats and boots. We were happy to find that Sophie had made a fire and prepared more hot chocolate. It was welcomed since none of us had eaten much of our breakfast.

"Has the doctor called, by chance?" Levy asked, sipping his cocoa and creating a little mustache that I would have found amusing any other time.

Sophie handed him a napkin and motioned to his upper lip. "No. The house has been quiet. Maisie is upstairs with the baby. She is upset that her little Ollie isn't happy." I was a bit surprised. It took a lot to make Sophie sarcastic.

"Tell us," I encouraged her.

"After I finished the dishes, I went upstairs to find Maisie in the nursery rocking the baby and crying. She said, 'Oh, dear, oh, dear, I just can't abide it when Ollie is upset.' I did my best to be comforting. I sat next to her and told her I understood that he was as worried about Lucie as we were. Maisie said, 'Well yes, and that on top of the disappointment of not having a son. I must admit he is handling that splendidly. He is doting on this baby. Good thing, since her mother doesn't seem to be,' and she gave me a sour look. I kept trying to be diplomatic. I said, 'Maisie, I'm sure you realize that Lucie is not well. Otherwise she would be caring for Tildy. This happens to some women following childbirth. It's no one's fault.' She answered, 'Naturally you are on *her* side. Ollie said you would be—that you all would be. But what normal woman doesn't want to hold her own baby?' Maisie abruptly covered Tildy with a blanket and said, 'All that aside, I am sorry to have left you with the dishes. It is the maid's day off. I had to pay her extra to cook breakfast this morning. I was planning for us to go out to dinner tonight, but with all this unpleasantness and Lucie unwilling to even get out of bed, I don't know what to do.'

"I assured her I didn't mind doing the dishes and said the two of you would work this all out with Oliver. I suggested we might get Lucie to come down-stairs for lunch if she was willing to take care of Tildy. Her reply was, 'Who do you think has *been* taking care of her?' It almost made me regret having compassion for her. Then she said in a nasty voice, 'I'm happy to stay here with Tildy—I've brought a sandwich up, so don't fuss over me. I don't want to be in the middle of your mess. But, you'll see, Lucie won't come out of her room.' I sighed and came back downstairs."

"Oh, Soph. How unpleasant. I'm sorry we left her to you," I said.

"I don't mind. It was helpful for me to realize how much she has been in control."

"Sophie, Levy is thinking Lucie might need some kind of residential care. What do you think?" I asked, moving my chair closer to the fire and sticking my frozen toes as near as I could get them without scorching my wet socks.

"I have to agree. I can hardly imagine any place that would be worse for her than here in the bosom of her disapproving mother-in-law. I'm not an expert," Sophie said, musing—"but I don't think she is going to get any better living this way, with Oliver so unpleasant, Maisie looking over her shoulder, and some nanny taking care of the baby. Even if she has an appointment with a therapist every day, she'd still be coming home to this. If it's possible to find a good place—one that would help her heal, not drug her—I would agree."

We discussed whether we should go up to wake Lucie and decided we would wait a bit in case the doctor called back. We wanted to have something substantive to tell her. Within a few minutes, our patience was rewarded. When the phone rang, Sophie answered with the formality the maid had used.

"Hanover residence, this is Sophie. May I help you?"

"Yes, this is Dr. Melinda Jacobs. I am trying to reach Dr. Bernard Levy."

"He's right here," Sophie said, holding the receiver out.

Levy almost ran to the phone. "Dr. Levy here. Thank you so much for calling back, Dr. Jacobs. I am calling about a patient in New Canaan who is suffering from a nervous condition since the birth of her child about six weeks ago. You will be familiar with the symptoms—she has lost interest in everything, has no energy or appetite, and has no attachment to the baby. Even before the birth, she was prescribed a sedative. Since the baby was born, she has been bedridden. I am hoping to find an appropriate in-patient facility that will provide her with a place to rest and heal." Levy held the receiver out so that Sophie and I could listen to both sides of the conversation.

"Doctor Levy, I am so sorry about your patient. I have worked with women on an outpatient basis after that kind of depression, but only after they have begun to recover. I agree that inpatient is the right idea. If the family has means, there is an excellent facility in California."

"California?" I said, alarmed. Apparently, the doctor heard me.

"I understand it is quite a distance," she said, "but I am afraid it is the only residential treatment program I can recommend without reservation. A woman founded it, and it is groundbreaking. They only treat women, and do not resort to the heavy medication and shock treatments that are stock-in-trade for most residential facilities. I am familiar with several of the staff physicians. I took the liberty of calling to ask if they had an available bed. They do, but you'd need to call today or tomorrow. If you have a pen, I'll give you the information."

"Just a moment," Levy said, gesturing to me to find a pen and paper. "Okay," he said.

"The facility is called River Oaks. It is in Glendale, California." The doctor described more of the things that made the facility so special, and gave the address, phone number, and name of a contact person. "Please keep my information, Doctor Levy. I would be happy to see her on an outpatient basis once she has been released. Follow up is extremely important in these situations."

"Thank you so much, Dr. Jacobs," Levy said.

I almost clapped my hands. "This sounds like the perfect place for Lucie! And thankfully, this family would have the means to send her to Timbuktu if that's where the hospital was. What a relief!" We all sat back down on the couch in front of the fire.

Levy looked concerned. "Don't be relieved too soon, Jane. You heard Oliver this morning. Do you imagine he is actually going to agree to send Lucie to a facility on our say-so? This is as much a power play between you and him as it is a need to find help for Lucie."

I was deflated.

Sophie said, "But still, it is wonderful that we have this information. We just have to figure out the best way to present it and then accept that we are not in control of what happens." She turned to me. "Jane, we are *not* in control. Since Lucie isn't in any shape to help herself, this is Oliver's call. As he said so indelicately this morning, he is her husband. For better or worse."

"What if she *were* in a place to advocate for herself?" I asked. "Wouldn't that change the dynamics?"

"I can see a plot being hatched behind those steely eyes. What are you cooking up?" Sophie asked.

"Well, what if we could at least get her to dress and come downstairs for lunch? Couldn't that make her feel more like herself? We could explain the situation and she would see that River Oaks is where she should go. Then she could advocate for that with Oliver," I said, hopefully.

Levy shook his head. "You don't understand depression. It is not something that goes away because you get dressed and comb your hair. Scientifically, depression is both an issue of chemistry in the body and the nature of the life situation. The two seem to reinforce each other. Depression has been discussed in the medical literature for thousands of years. Sadly, there has never been a dependably successful treatment, though doctors have prescribed everything from cold baths to leeches."

"Ugh," I said. "I wouldn't mind the baths, but let's skip the leeches."

"But would it hurt to get her out of bed?" Sophie asked.

Levy laughed. "I can see that I am up against a formidable team. No, that would not hurt her."

"Then *you* go up, Jane. She is most likely to respond to you. Levy, will you put more wood on the fire? I'll make lunch," Sophie said. She was always happiest when there was a plan.

It wasn't easy to persuade Lucie to get dressed and come downstairs, but I did.

"Are you sure Maisie won't be there?" she asked tremulously. "Maisie hates me because I didn't have the boy her little Ollie wanted."

"I don't think she hates you, and I don't think she'll join us for lunch. It's just you and me and Sophie and Levy. We want to talk to you. We have some ideas about how you can get better."

Lucie looked at me skeptically, but she allowed me to hang up her robe and pick out a loose-fitting dress.

"Oliver has already made plans. Jane, please don't make trouble. I can't bear it," she whined.

I helped pull her nightgown off over her head and handed her some under-things, which she put on slowly, as if she were drunk or asleep.

"I'm sure Oliver will approve of this idea," I said, being sure of no such thing, but sensing that I was with a version of Lucie even younger than seven. "We don't want to make any trouble. Levy and Sophie and I just want you to get better. Don't you want that?"

She sat on a hassock, partly dressed, and sighed. "Sometimes it seems as though it would be easier for everyone if I weren't here at all."

I wanted to cry and shake her, but that wouldn't help, so I continued to speak to the lost little girl.

"Let's just go downstairs and see what Sophie has found for lunch. And we'll tell you about what we have learned." She allowed me to help her put on the dress and then leaned on me as we made our way down the stairs.

"Until yesterday, I hadn't been out of my room for a while," she said. "It is so big that I'm a little afraid. Isn't that silly? I am afraid of my own house."

"Not silly at all," I said, wanting to cry.

CHAPTER 48

YOU ARE NOT ALLOWED TO DO THIS HERE

Sophie had set a festive table in the dining room. She brought evergreen boughs from the backyard and added holly with bright red berries. Lucie accepted kisses and sat down at the table. Sophie and Levy looked at me for information. I shrugged and shook my head, as if to say I hadn't gotten anywhere.

"Lucie," I said. "Look at the lunch Sophie has made for us. There's tomato soup, bread, roast chicken, potatoes, and asparagus. A lunch fit for a queen."

It did look and smell irresistible.

Lucie said, "I am not very hungry."

"Just some soup then," I said. It was her favorite. "And a little bread and butter." Lucie didn't protest as I ladled soup into her bowl and put a pat of butter and a piece of French bread on the plate next to her. I felt encouraged as she buttered the bread and dipped it into the soup.

"You are not allowed to do this here," she said, dunking her bread into the creamy soup.

"Not allowed to do what?" I asked, buttering my own bread.

"It is not polite to dip your bread into your soup. We do not do such things in this household," she intoned, in a voice that I immediately recognized as Oliver's at his most pompous.

We all laughed, and Lucie managed a mischievous smile—the first I had seen of her old self. She continued to consume the soup—eating it any way she wanted—and ate a bit of chicken, but then the front door swung open, bringing the icy wind with it. It was Oliver, accompanied by another man, bundled up in overcoats and hats. Oliver strode into the dining room and glared at us while the other man closed the door.

"Where is my mother?" Oliver demanded, looking at me like he suspected I had sold her into slavery.

"She's upstairs with the baby," Sophie said.

"All right then," Oliver said, as if he had won an argument. He glanced over and noticed Lucie at the table.

"What are *you* doing here?" he asked, in a not-very-nice voice. "I thought we agreed that you would take your meals in your room until you were better."

Lucie sat up straighter in her chair. "I *am* better."

"Just as well that you are part of this conversation. Dr. Burns has come all this way to talk with us—to make it clear to all of you why you need a residential program. He is quite busy. You'll have to finish eating later."

Another meal ruined by Oliver. He strode back into the living room and took the doctor's coat and hat. Sophie, Levy, Lucie, and I looked at each other in dismay, but we left our half-eaten lunches and trudged into the living room. Oliver had laid the coats over the back of the couch—I wasn't certain he was even aware of where the closet was, since his mother always waited on him. Levy stoked the fire, and then we all sat down like children called to the principal's office. The two men towered above us.

Oliver looked directly at me. I assumed he would make introductions, but he didn't seem to find it necessary.

"Since I have had some difficulty conveying the seriousness of Lucie's condition to you, Dr. Burns has graciously agreed to explain."

I started to protest that we understood, but Sophie put her hand on my arm.

Prescott Burns was a tall, slender, elegant man with silver hair, and what used to be called a Van Dyke—a prissy sort of mustache and beard. He was wearing an expensive gray wool suit with a vest and a patterned ascot. He was quite imposing, and I imagined he might intimidate all but the most confident.

"Harrumph," was Dr. Burns' opener. I could hardly wait for what was coming next. "Ollie here tells me that you are friends with Mrs. Hanover. As such, I am sure you are disturbed about her present condition and want her to have the best of care, which is what I can offer her. A postpartum nervous syndrome of this kind requires intensive treatment—often medication and even electroshock therapy."

"Never!" I exclaimed, standing up. "You can't…"

"Now see here, Mrs. …"

"*Miss* Smith," I said, my jaw and fists clenched.

Sophie and Levy each took an arm and pulled me back to the sofa. Lucie just looked lost.

"*Miss Smith.* I will repeat myself. I am sure you understand that Mrs. Hanover has a serious nervous condition that requires the highest standard of medical care."

"I assure you, doctor, that I understand her condition is serious. I am close to her, and it is obvious that she is not herself. But I don't want her to be drugged, or shocked, or left in a corner to rot. I want her to get well." I was nearly shouting.

Dr. Prescott Burns looked exasperated. "I'm sure you do, but you are not an expert in modern psychiatric care for this kind of condition. You are not a physician, and you can't know what Linda…"

"*Lucie!*" I hissed.

"Yes, yes," he said in a patronizing tone. "Lucie. You can't know what Lucie needs in order to get better. The facility I have in mind is…"

I interrupted, "From what we have been told, River Oaks would be the perfect facility, and they have a bed available, and…"

"Did you say Ri-ver-Oaks?" Dr. Burns asked slowly, holding his hand up as if stopping traffic. "That is quite another matter altogether."

"Just because it was started by a woman doesn't mean it is bad," I protested, already anticipating his criticisms.

"Ri-ver-Oaks, hmm," he said, enunciating each syllable as if it were a separate word, ignoring me completely and stroking his beard as he paced around the room. "Ri-ver-Oaks." He pronounced the name as if it were some kind of magic incantation, akin to abracadabra. "Hmm," he said again. "If I am not mistaken, the young doctor who established that facility received an award from my alma mater. 'The Prescott Burns Award for Excellence in Women's Medicine.' Quite a feather in her cap, if I say so myself."

He suddenly stopped pacing, stood up straight, and said to Oliver, "Now that I think of it, River Oaks would be an excellent choice for Mrs. Hanover. Good work, Burns. Good, good, good. Ollie, your wife should do well there." He paused and nodded at Lucie, as if noticing for the first time that she sat right in front of him. "They have a sterling reputation for results. And you say there is a bed available? Wonderful. Now that we are all in agreement, I will instruct my girl to make arrangements straight away." With that, the good doctor took his hat and coat from the back of the sofa and walked purposefully out of the house, with a startled Oliver following closely on his heels.

The minute the front door closed behind them, I let out a whoop of nervous laughter and grabbed Lucie around the shoulders.

"It's going to be all right!" I said, giddily. "You're going to be all right."

Lucie was glassy-eyed.

Sophie said carefully, "It is good news that Lucie will be going to River Oaks, but it is still a bit scary, I'm sure. Lucie, how are you doing?"

We seemed to have lost her again, and she emitted some little squeaking noises.

Levy reached over and put his arm around her shoulders.

"We can tell you about the place. And when you come back, you could work with Dr. Jacobs, who told us about River Oaks."

Lucie pulled away from him. All of a sudden, she was filled with energy, and there was fire in her eyes. She said, "You may be celebrating, but Oliver is going to think you have bested him again, and it's going to make him furious." She turned to me. "I heard you arguing with him this morning. Jane, you mustn't upset him. He is under a lot of stress at work, and now he'll be all alone when I am gone. I am so glad you came to see me... and the baby... but I think... I think it would be best if you go to your mother's sooner than we had planned. I just can't be in the middle of you two. Can you go? Will you go—*now*? I'm sure Dr. H would be happy to have you use his car service."

I was speechless. Levy, Sophie, and I looked at each other. I wasn't sure if this was a request we should be granting or one we should ignore, but the look on Lucie's face made me say, "Of course, Lucie. I'll call my mother right now."

"And I'll call Oliver's father about the car," Levy said.

Sophie chimed in, "It won't take but a moment for us to pack."

Lucie sighed and looked relieved. "This is for the best," she said, looking at me apologetically. "It really is."

When I called my mother, she was surprised but said she'd be happy to see us sooner than we'd planned. Sophie insisted on re-heating our soup and chicken, so after we were packed, we spent a few minutes in the dining room finishing our lunch. As usual, Lucie said she wasn't hungry, but I noticed that she devoured the rest of her chicken and her soup, so clearly something had changed. We ate mostly in silence, none of us knowing what to say. The chauffeur came to the door and took our bags out to the car.

And so it was that we found ourselves saying a stiff goodbye to Maisie and kissing the baby—the baby we had come so far to see, who was in the middle of such turmoil. At the door, Lucie embraced me with a fierceness that almost knocked me down. She was crying that scary, silent kind of tears that just come in a stream.

"Jane, thank you for coming to rescue me again," she whispered in my ear. "Thank you for knowing that I needed you. I'm going to be all right."

I embraced her and whispered, "I hope so, *Chérie*."

Lucie hugged and kissed Levy and Sophie. "Give my love to your mother," she said, as we bundled up in our coats and hats and bustled down the stairs. Just before I got into the car, I looked back at her standing in the doorway. Lucie could tell that I was questioning whether it was right to leave. She nodded at me and closed the door.

"What just happened?" Sophie asked, shaking her head as we drove away.

"It was strange, indeed," Levy said, nodding toward the driver to remind us that we were not alone. "I, for one, need a cigarette."

Sophie and I laughed since we didn't smoke, and he was obviously the only 'for one.' As he lit up, I said, "I'd have one of those myself if I thought it would make me feel any better."

Sophie leaned against me. She said, "Lucie is strong and resilient. She'll find her way back to herself. The one I am worried about…"

I held her close and finished her sentence. "I know. The one you are worried about is Tildy."

We spent a lovely week visiting with my mother. She and Sophie got along, as I hoped they would. My darling Soph went with her to church and to volunteer at the soup kitchen. I was too preoccupied to be good company.

We had resolved not to contact Lucie unless she called us, which she finally did on the day we were scheduled to fly back to Paris. Lucie sounded a bit more like herself, though strangely formal. I held the phone receiver out so that Mom, Sophie, and Levy could listen to her side of the conversation.

"I am so sorry I was such a terrible hostess," she said, laughing. "What a mess. I wanted to tell you that I am scheduled to leave for California tomorrow. I was hoping it would be today so that we could all be at the airport together, but apparently that wouldn't suit. Oliver is all right with everything. We have made peace. The nanny came, and she is a nice young woman named Natalie. Tildy and Oliver will be in good hands while I am gone. Maisie can be here as much as she likes, but she won't have to miss her bridge luncheons, which, for her, was one of the worst parts of my… my disarrangement."

"Lucie, you sound better already," I said. "Please don't think twice about us. We were so glad to be of help—that is, if we were—and so glad to see your enchanting baby."

"Oh, you were of help, I assure you. It may have seemed that I was in outer space, but I overheard everything that happened. I know, I absolutely *know* that without your intervention, I would have been sent to one of those places where I would have been—how did you put it? 'Drugged, shocked, or left in a corner to rot.'"

We all laughed in relief at our beloved Lucie being herself.

Sophie took the phone. "Lucie, travel safely. You must write to us all about California. They'll probably make juice for you at the hospital just by going outside and picking oranges right off the tree!"

Levy added, "But don't go to Hollywood for a sandwich, or someone will discover you and put you in the movies, and we'll never see you again!"

Lucie laughed on the other end of the line.

"Thanks, Levy," she giggled, "but I think my starlet days are over. Jane, I'll write to you."

"I know, my darling, every day."

We were reassured enough about Lucie's welfare to make the trip home. I did get letters, delayed by a week when all patients were prohibited from making contact with anyone in the outside world. I could tell that she was getting stronger and getting back on her own feet. I had a feeling that Oliver was going to welcome home a very different Lucie.

CHAPTER 49

ENCORE BRIGITTE

Our Lady, 1958

During the two years after our tumultuous visit to Lucie, she wrote to me sporadically. As I had predicted, the Lucie who came back from River Oaks was not the pitiful victim we had seen. Her letters were full of energy and dreams for the future, but they included few details about Tildy, Oliver, or any of the daily matters that I expected would engage a new mother.

I read Lucie's letters and my replies aloud to Sophie and Françoise.

May, 1957
Dear Jane,

    Yale accepted all my credits from the Sorbonne, so I am officially enrolled in the Psychology Graduate Program. My therapist has encouraged me to go for a doctorate. That will be some years off, but I am so happy. I keep thinking about that day I sat with Gertrude in the rose garden wearing the habit. Do you remember? That was the best day. That's what I want to do. To help people that way. Without the habit, of course.

June, 1957
Dear Lucie,

    Congratulations. You will be a wonderful counselor. It's great to hear you so energized. How are things going with Tildy? How are you and Oliver doing?

July, 1957
Dear Jane,

    Oliver hates it that I am in school. In fact, I'm paying for it with the money my father left me—one less argument. He does enjoy bragging at cocktail parties that his wife is getting an advanced degree from Yale. But the University isn't what I had hoped. The Psych Department is focused on changing behavior through conditioning. My therapist warned me about this, but I was so excited to go to an Ivy League school, I didn't listen. I think I need to transfer. The heads of my department dismiss everything Rogers wrote—everything I have learned from my own therapy about how to listen to your patient. I want to work with people, not rats!

August, 1957
Dear Lucie,

I only know a bit about behaviorism, but it seems like a very male approach to human beings—as if we were machines. I hope you can find a place that teaches what you want to learn. But how is Tildy? You haven't mentioned anything about her.

September, 1957
Dear Jane,

I'm going to the University of Connecticut! Not nearly as prestigious as Yale for poor Oliver. They have an external campus in Hartford, so it's not a bad drive. One of my classmates has an extra bedroom, so I stay with her when I have early morning classes. This is just what I was hoping for. I'm planning to use my maiden name professionally. Enough of this hoity-toity Hanover. I keep imagining a day when Dr. Preston Burns can be introduced to Dr. Lucie Fortier Goldfarb. He'd never recognize the mousey Lucie Hanover married to his pal Ollie.

October, 1957
Dear Lucie,

I can't believe Tildy is a year old. Is she walking? Is she talking? Will you send pictures? We are so sorry to be missing her precious baby years. Anne-Marie and Thomas's son, Henri, is almost exactly a year older than Tildy. Since they are managing the dairy farm, Françoise brings Henri over with her almost every day. Henri is an enchanting child with a dimpled smile and curly brown hair. He loves me and he adores Sophie. Most of the guests

*enjoy having him here and he thrives under the attention of so
many hugs, kisses, and cuddles.*

October, 1957
Dear Jane,

*Thanks to you and Sophie for the colorful rattle. I'm sure Tildy
enjoys playing with it. My second-floor study overlooks the back
yard, so when I am there I can see her falling down and getting up
a hundred times, and racing around like a squirrel. She is so fast
that Nanny has a hard time keeping up with her. And yes, she prat-
tles on about whatever is in her little mind. When I leave the house,
I always kiss her on the head and say, "Mummy loves you," as
Oliver insists I should. To be honest, I find her exhausting, but I
spend at least an hour with her on Sundays when the nanny is off.
Almost every Sunday.*

November, 1957
Dear Lucie,

*I am sorry you aren't enjoying being with Tildy. I understand
that caring for a little one can be tiring, but isn't that what the
nanny is for? So you can be with her without all the drudgery of
diapers and bottles?*

February, 1958
Dear Jane,

*I'm sorry I've taken so long to reply. I am so busy with my
studies, but loving every minute. Your mother has called a few
times and I keep putting her off. I just don't have time to eat lunch
at Bloomingdale's or go to a museum. Will you please thank her
for me and explain?*

March, 1958
Dear Lucie,

*My mother is writing to me that she is worried about you. She
thinks you may be too caught up in school. I'm not there, so I can't
say. I don't want to tell you what to do, but you will never have
this time with Tildy again.*

June, 1958
Dear Jane,

I realize you are only watching out for me. You always have. But you can't imagine what it is like. Oliver has always been a bully—you tried to tell me that so many years ago. But my life is so much easier now that he has a daughter to mold to his will. He takes Tildy everywhere with him, and she is delighted. She is a smaller version of him, like Athena, born from Zeus's head. She is as demanding and critical of me as he is. You are going to say she is only a baby and can't be those things, but you don't know her. I'm sorry. I'm having a bad day. I should throw this away and start again tomorrow, but then you'll think I am never going to answer. So this goes in the mail today.

July, 1958
Dear Lucie,

I take no pleasure in saying I told you so about Oliver. I'm just sorry. We all are. When we have a glass of wine at the end of the day, I read your letters to Sophie and Françoise, so they are up-to-date with your life. We are all sending you love. I know you are doing the best you can. I don't pretend to have any simple answers. Take care of yourself.

October, 1958
Dear Jane, Sophie, and Françoise,

I'm glad you are all hearing my letters. I have felt so guilty about being out of touch with you, my dear friends.

It is impossible that Tildy is two. Even more impossible is Oliver. He has bought her a pony. Not that she can ride it alone, but he takes her to the stables and they spend every weekend there. The enclosed photograph shows them in their matching English riding outfits, complete with helmets. I don't know how Maisie found someone to tailor those tiny jodhpurs, but it is a great relief to me because I can study without being berated for my selfishness. Surprisingly, it turns out that Maisie was quite the horse-woman in her youth. She has an enormous glass case of ribbons and medals hanging in their library. So Oliver is busy turning his daughter into his mother. I don't even know what kind of complex Freud would assign to that behavior.

We laughed so hard at the photograph, grateful that Lucie hadn't lost her sense of humor. Françoise gathered her things to go home. Almost out the door, she turned and said, "Jane. I forgot to tell you. I ran into Chastain in the market. He said we should be careful because he will be away for several weeks for training. And they are putting a woman on the police force. He doesn't know who or when, and I must say he didn't seem very enthusiastic about it. But I think it is high time, don't you?"

In the weeks to come, Françoise's enthusiasm turned to dread. We were about to face an existential threat to Our Lady of Perpetual Grace.

Sophie's uncle, Matthieu Neuville, had become an important member of parliament. He wrote to me again, and explained that to help him challenge the illegality of abortion, I would have to be arrested—just as a symbolic act—and I would be asked to testify as to the benefits to society of changing the law. He *guaranteed* me he had the votes to make the change, and *guaranteed* me that he would keep publicity to a minimum. I had seen guarantees before, and I wasn't having any of it. But it was a shame that I wasn't able to help. Every week, there was news of a woman in Paris found dead or injured from an experience the newspapers didn't even deign to name.

Brother Timothy heard questions and rumors about Our Lady, and he came to us with his worries.

"Jane, you must appear in public in some way. Right now, the convent is too much of a mystery. You don't want that attention."

"I don't mind being a mystery," I gave a little chuckle, "but I agree we don't want any attention. What are you suggesting?"

"There is a committee being set up to coordinate services for women and children. If you'd go, wearing the habit, and talk about the special retreats you offer that really *are* retreats, perhaps all this talk will stop."

"But I don't want to do anything that requires being with people."

"Jane, you must be with people. It's the only way to stop them from speculating."

I sighed. "All right, Brother Tim, but only because it is *you* asking. And only if Sophie will go with me."

Sophie smiled at me. "Of course I'll go."

Tim gave us the details of the meeting, which was scheduled for a couple of weeks away in the village next to ours. We shifted our schedule so that we would be available on that day, put on our spiffiest habits, and drove an hour to the village hall where the meeting would be held.

I was grumpy that morning during breakfast, as I often am when I have to deal with people who are not patients. "This is silly. Who cares if people are speculating about us?"

Françoise sat in the kitchen, cutting recipe cards for the following week. We had a variety of colors, but we found that it made storage much easier when all the cards were a uniform size.

"*I* care. And you should too!" she said, brandishing her scissors in a menacing way. "Do you want Chastain on our doorstep again, this time with a legitimate complaint? I am too old to be worrying about going to jail! Every time I remember poor Marie-Louise Giraud going to the guillotine, I shudder."

Sophie, always the peacemaker, said, "Now, Françoise, no one has said anything about going to jail, let alone losing our heads! That's why we have Monsieur Neuville."

"Well, you two have entirely too much faith in him. And in our luck. It is just a matter of time before one of our patients decides she isn't happy and turns the militia onto us." Françoise was clearly not mollified.

"Militia? Hardly," I laughed. "Let's not exaggerate. Chastain is far from the militia. And since when are you so worried? He is our friend."

Françoise put the cards she had cut on the table and looked at me seriously. "He is *my* friend, Jane. And he is a good man. I don't want to put him in a position where he can't do his job. And I have been worried since forever. Someone has to worry. This community thing is an excellent idea, and you had better be nice."

"I'm always nice!" I said, and we all had a good laugh.

It was a bright winter day. Sophie and I enjoyed the countryside as we made our way in our trusty Peugeot to the village office. The parking lot was almost full, and I squeezed in beside a white truck.

The meeting room was large, with tables formed in a circle and a few dozen people milling about.

"Save me a seat, *Chérie*. I'm going to the ladies' room," I said. Sophie went in and I turned to follow the sign to the restroom.

After I flushed the toilet, I heard a voice that made me put my hands over my face. I tried to catch my breath, to listen again, but the sound of my heartbeat pounded in my ears. It couldn't be. It couldn't possibly be. There were two women. One voice was unfamiliar. I recognized the other voice from my nightmares. It was Brigitte.

Brigitte, the Nazi-loving housemaid whom my aunt Mathilde fired.

Brigitte, who wanted to rid France of the undesirables.

Brigitte, who was supposed to be in the South of France.

Brigitte, who so disliked me.

I had hoped never to see her again. And here she was—a full seventeen years later. I couldn't imagine how this had happened. I considered sneaking out of the building, but I couldn't leave Sophie. I considered fainting there in the ladies' toilet, but I realized that wouldn't save me. So, instead, I followed behind the two women into the meeting room.

Sophie stood up and smiled at me, her crisp black habit a stark contrast to the pink flowered dress of the woman sitting beside her. She patted the empty chair on the other side, as if I might not notice it. I walked around to her back and sat down, being careful not to make eye contact with any of the twenty or so women seated around the table. In a moment, the only man in the room introduced himself as Blaise Alarie, Minister of Social Services. He welcomed us to the first meeting of the Committee for the Welfare of Women and Children, or CWWC, as he called it. I stared down at the table. It was obvious that something was wrong with me. Sophie nudged me in the side with her elbow, but I couldn't look at her. I was sure we were done for. When Monsieur Alarie asked representatives from the various agencies to stand and talk a bit about their services, I stayed glued to my seat, and left it to Sophie to talk about our beautiful convent and the quiet retreats we offered to women. When Brigitte stood up to share, I was utterly shocked to hear not just her voice, but *my name*!

"I am Brigitte Delacroix. Before I tell you about my organization, there is someone here I must thank for my mission in life. Mademoiselle Jane Smith. Sister Jane, I am so glad to see you again so I can tell you how you changed my life. You may not recall, but you asked me to promise to speak for someone who has no voice, and I have done it. My organization is called *La Voix de Ceux qui ne Sont Pas Nés*. I speak for those without a voice. I work as a matron in the women's prison. Through my parish, I minister to pregnant women to be sure they have proper nutrition and safety to bring their children into the world, and I report on anyone who might be interfering with the natural completion of pregnancy." She sat down with a satisfied look on her face.

As I translated the title of her organization into English—"the voice of those not born"—I remembered with horror that I had, indeed, asked Brigitte to promise she would do exactly that, speak up for someone who did not have a voice. I never imagined how my innocent hope for good could spawn a danger to Our Lady that was like none other we had faced before.

My mind reeled as the other women continued their introductions. A hot coal sat in the pit of my stomach. After the meeting, Sophie nudged me again to ask what was the matter. I whispered that she should meet people and say hello, and I would deal with my problem and explain it later. Sophie looked concerned, but she made the rounds, chatting with the other participants. I motioned for Brigitte to meet me outside. We sat on the stone wall in a little patch of sun next to the parking lot to 'catch up,' as she said. Brigitte and I were two wary alley cats, taking each other's measure. That she had reappeared in my life was some impossible version of karma. That she was crediting me for inspiring her anti-abortion organization was more than I could bear. What did I do to deserve her re-entry into my life?

Finally, she began. "How is your dear aunt—Mademoiselle Smith?"

I saw no point in anything but raw candor. "She is dead. Murdered by the Nazis not long after I left Paris."

"Such a shame. She was a very strong woman."

And as for Brigitte? There was not a shadow of shame about her collaboration.

Then it was my move. "I didn't realize you became so involved with the Church."

"For several years, I lived in my family home in the South of France. I was too traumatized by my encounter with the German army to do anything but lie low. That turned out to be advantageous for me because, as you are aware, the Germans lost the war. My neighbors collaborated with the Germans because they were certain the Nazis would be victorious. They had an awful time of it. Since I had kept to myself, I suffered no repercussions.

"After my brother died, I moved back to Paris to take care of my niece. I got a terribly boring job as a clerk in the tax office. When I went to work as a prison matron, I became more involved with the Church and found a community of sorts there. One of the parishioners told me she'd had an abortion. I was familiar with it, of course. I celebrated with the rest of the country when they executed Marie-Louise Giraud—killed, just like she killed those babies. I knew that women in my church—right in Paris—were still having abortions. Then I understood what you meant when you told me to advocate for those without a voice."

What was I thinking? I said to myself, shaking my head.

Brigitte continued. "I remember the day so clearly. I had been arrested because I fell in love with a Communist. I smelled like a wet dog—I hadn't showered or changed my clothes in a week. We ate croissants. You saved me from a labor camp."

I huffed. "I also remember that day very clearly. I evened the score between us so that you would not inform on Mathilde for getting Jewish girls out of Paris through her school. But what…?"

"You inspired my life's work that day…"

I started to interrupt her.

She raised her hand to stop me. "You asked me to promise to become an advocate for someone without a voice. And I did. But soon I will begin a new job. I am to be the first female member of the Garde Champêtre."

I could hardly swallow. Chastain's department. This was the woman he had told Françoise about.

"I must tell you that there are rumors about the true nature of your *retreats*."

I shook my head slowly. "No. I can't believe this…"

"You'd best believe it, Mademoiselle. I am afraid we have come to a chapter that will not end well for you."

If we had been two men, I would have punched her. I almost did.

I'd like to tell you about the rest of the conversation. But that is where both my mind and my journal are blank. Somehow, we finished our 'catching up' conversation without fisticuffs.

I asked Sophie to drive us home. Despite her attempts to get me to talk, I rode in silence, stewing about how to tell her and Françoise that we would need to stop doing our work. When we got home, we made cocoa, and I reminded Sophie of the story I told her after my nightmare—of Nazi-loving Brigitte taking the school's grocery money and my ring in exchange for her silence about twenty little girls in danger in Occupied Paris. And the story of my taking on the mantle of my formidable Aunt Mathilde and saving that same wretched Brigitte from a work camp, or worse. And the promises I extracted from Brigitte as we parted ways forever. Sophie instantly understood what Brigitte had made of her promise—and what I had made of Brigitte's… I can't call it a confession… of her proclamation of duty.

"Jane, no matter what she says, you couldn't have anticipated this—"

"My darling, you don't need to try to make it all right. There's nothing that can make this all right."

"But Jane, surely…"

I took her in my arms. "I know you don't want me to feel guilty, and I love you for that. But I'm afraid I need to sit with this. To sit with the knowledge that, not two hours away from us, lives a woman who would destroy everything we created. And she expects a benediction, and thanks me for being her inspiration. All the obstacles we have encountered—the *gendarmes*, the angry mothers, the threat of a church inquisition—pale in comparison with Brigitte."

In the ensuing days, Sophie, Françoise and I were a bunch of nerves. I decided that, for the foreseeable future, we shouldn't schedule any abortions. I was frustrated that it was as if we were letting Brigitte make decisions for women, but I didn't know what else to do. My mother telephoned and said she was coming for Christmas and had already purchased a plane ticket, so it seemed as good a time as any to give in. With no patients on the horizon, I could enjoy our visit without worrying she would find out my secret. I imagined we needed to lock a few doors. But Sophie and Françoise were worried.

"Jane, even if we don't have patients, this is not a good idea. What are you going to tell your mother when she asks what we do here?" Sophie asked.

"We've given her enough of an idea. We take care of women. She won't ask any questions."

Francoise said, "I'm afraid Sophie is right. You might not recall that she financed the renovation of this building. She wanted us to write her about every detail. When she came for Lucie's wedding, she said she wished she could stay long enough to help us set up for our work."

Sophie folded her arms across her chest. "I'd better go to my sister's while your mother is here. You can't ask me to lie to her. I won't do it." I was more than familiar with that stance.

"No, no. Don't even consider leaving. I want you to spend time with her. Françoise and I will answer her questions, won't we?"

Françoise looked askance. I put on my most pleading expression and she acquiesced.

I knew it would be a night with a glass of wine and a hot bath.

CHAPTER 50

MOTHER MAKES A VISIT

I drove into Paris and picked Mother up at the Orly airport while Françoise and Sophie finished tidying the convent and locking up our procedure rooms and medical equipment. Françoise even insisted on locking away our Secret Recipe patient records.

"It would be just like a woman to look at the recipes, Jane. We can't take the chance."

We worried that Brigitte might snoop around, so we kept the front door locked, explaining to Mother that we had been having trouble with the latch. One evening, Levy and his family came for dinner. My mother loved meeting his wife and her two boys. Sophie and my mother cooked together, and encouraged by Sophie's endless patience, Mother practiced her high school French. I'm pretty sure that Mother liked Sophie better than she liked me. Five-year-old Henri was a hit—another substitute grandchild. She squeezed him like a melon.

"Lucie says she is better, but she is still not her old self," my mother said. "I hate to say it, but that child, Tildy, is an exact replica of Oliver. I'm only thirty minutes away, but I don't like to visit. Speaking of visiting, it is so lovely to finally be here. If I didn't know better, I'd have thought you didn't want me to come." It wasn't exactly a question, so I laughed weakly. I saw panic flash across Sophie's face and my stomach clenched.

We all worried about making a good impression on my mother. Worried that something would slip. Worried about the women who had to find abortion care somewhere else, or had to make do with no care at all, having babies they didn't want or couldn't care for. Worried about Brigitte. Sophie told me that a woman named Charlotte, who didn't come for her scheduled appointment the week before, had called several times and begged to come despite being informed we weren't seeing patients.

We tried to conceal our nervousness from my mother.

"We played all the card games in my repertoire. What else can we do to entertain her?" I asked.

"Jane, there is a bigger problem." Sophie sounded as though she had seen a ghost.

"What?"

"I just saw your mother talking to someone in the front yard."

"Who?" I looked out the window and my mother was sitting on the bench, embracing a young woman.

"I'll bet it's that Charlotte. She wouldn't accept no as an answer," Sophie said.

"But how would she know where to find us?" Now I sounded like I'd seen a ghost.

"She had an appointment last week, so she would have gotten all the information about the bus. I didn't even think about keeping Gracie in, so I'm afraid that our beloved hound trotted off to meet patients at the bus stop and escort them back here, just like she always does," Françoise said.

Sophie continued. "I'm afraid she may have told Sylvia what she is here for."

I threw up my hands. "Really? This is how my mother is going to find out my deepest secret? By accident?"

"Maybe not," Sophie said, without any hope in her voice.

I sighed. "There is nothing to do but face whatever there is to face. I'm going out there."

My knees were weak, but I mustered up my courage and strode to the front door, pulling my heavy coat from the peg on the wall. Sophie and Françoise trailed behind. My mother's back was to me. She stood up as I approached, shivering from the cold. She turned, her eyes not fiery with anger as I had anticipated, but red-rimmed with tears. She smiled at me, then turned to the other woman and said, "Charlotte, this is my wonderful daughter, Jane."

CHAPTER 51

I AM SO SORRY TO DISAPPOINT YOU

I put my arm around her shoulders and said, "Mom, come inside. Come inside, both of you. It is freezing out here."

She let me lead her back into the house, into the dining room where the fire blazed. I only half-heard Sophie say, "I'll get chocolate." And Francoise say, "I'll take care of Charlotte." I had never seen my mother so compliant. Like a child coming in from the cold. She pulled a seat close to the fire and stretched her hands out. I put a sweater around her shoulders and a blanket on her lap. For an eternity, we watched the flames lick up around the logs and the embers dance.

Finally, I began.

"I should have told you long ago. I have been providing abortion care to women for nearly twenty years. I am so sorry to disappoint you. That's what we do here. There is no way I can explain that, for me, this work is the essence of love and morality, so I won't try. I am ashamed that you paid for the renovations of the convent that made my work possible, but Lucie and Bernard didn't know how strongly you are against abortion. They wanted to give me something I cared about so much. I assume you'll want to pack and get out of here as soon as you can."

Sophie came in with the mugs of hot chocolate that smelled like comfort and safety. She stood to the side, not wanting to interrupt the confession I had waited so many years to make.

"I hope you can find a way to still love me and believe how much I love you." I didn't want to look at her, but I had to. Her face crumpled into tears. Then Sophie and I started crying, too. I found some tissues in my pocket and handed them around. My mother couldn't look at me, I assumed, because of her disgust. She bowed her head and began to talk haltingly.

"It is I who should… who must apologize."

My mouth opened, but nothing came out.

"For over half a century, my mother's voice has thundered in my head. Shame. Sin. I put that on Lucie when I had no right to. Yes, Charlotte told me why she came to you. She asked me if she would go to hell for having an abortion. Can you imagine? She asked *me*. Naturally I said 'no.' Although *I* have been in hell about it."

"Mother…"

"No. Let me finish. I wasted so much time on this. I lost you because of it. I realized there were things you weren't telling me. When you told me about Sophie coming into your life, I hoped the secrets between us had ended. But why would I expect you to share your secrets when I had not shared mine? That girl who wants your help? I was in the same situation."

"Whatever it is, you don't have to…"

"I want to." Mother looked up at Sophie. "Will you both sit by me? And can we drink that before I begin?" She gestured to the mugs Sophie carried. We drew our chairs near hers and Sophie handed her a mug. She took a sip.

"It's so good," she said.

For the first time, I saw the little girl she had been. The teenager, chafing under the rule of a tyrannical mother. The young woman who married and had a baby—who sought out a new church and a new way of being. I had only seen her as my mother—the rule maker—the standard setter. This vulnerable mother was new to me.

She began in a very quiet voice. "I am going to tell you something I never told a living soul—even your father. At seventeen, I met a boy. We spent hours in the basement of the church rectory. I was so starved for love that I did whatever he wanted. Your granny paid attention to my monthlies, so she realized I was pregnant before I did." She paused and put her head in her hands. "When Mama figured out what had happened, she slapped me. Then she stopped talking to me. Abortion was illegal, but you could find a practitioner if you knew where to look. I can't imagine what it cost my fiercely Catholic mother emotionally, but she found a place. We took the train to Pittsburgh in total silence. We walked from the train station, Mama marching ahead, following directions she had written on a piece of paper, with me trailing behind. I had no idea of our destination, though I suspected something terrible was going to happen to me. It was a nice day—isn't that a strange thing to recall? The rest of it is a blur. We traveled home on the train, again in silence."

"Oh, Mom. I am so sorry."

"I need to finish, dear. I need to finish. Unbeknownst to my fellow travelers, I had a rubber tube sticking out of me and a hot water bottle taped to my stomach. When it was all over—the bleeding, the agonizing pain, and the nasty clots—my mother told me that I must never utter a word about what had happened. She said that I was ruined—that no man would ever love me or marry me—that I would never bear children because I didn't deserve them, and that I would go straight to hell for my sins. I spent most of my life trying to forget about it. When Lucie got pregnant and nearly died, it was like experiencing that slap over and over. But I am mortified that I reacted just like my mother. I didn't want to be like her—to treat you the way she treated me. I didn't, did I?"

"Oh, Mom. Of course you didn't. The worst thing you ever said to me was, 'Don't slouch, darling.' We can both agree that was pretty benign."

Thank goodness we were still able to laugh, if weakly.

I said, "So much is making sense now. Your reaction to Lucie's abortion shocked us all. I imagined it was the remains of your Catholic girlhood."

"I love that girl as if she were my own child. Mama's words nagged at me—I feared no one would ever love her." She paused. "Jane, I wanted to be different from my mother, but all these years, you thought you had to keep your work a secret."

I answered, "I felt guilty because they spent your money to renovate the convent. Even though I believe so deeply in this work, I hated to betray you."

"Come here." My mother stood up and reached out and I fell into her arms. We just stood there, laughing and crying—the strangest mix of feelings. I was so glad Sophie was there to see it because I never could have explained what it was like for me.

"Mom, my fears about telling you didn't just come from your reaction to Lucie's abortion."

"I wondered about that. I'm afraid this might have something to do with my mother."

"You're right. Do you remember that summer when I was eleven and you and Daddy flew to Europe and I stayed with Granny?"

"Yes. But what does that have to do with…?"

I put my hand up to stop her.

"Just let me tell you. At first, I liked being at Granny's apartment. She made hamburgers, and we listened to her soap shows and mysteries on the radio."

"Mama and her soaps. She listened to those until the day she died."

"Sometimes she acted nice. But sometimes she got mad and yelled. She called the neighbors bad names and then laughed about it and told me not to tell you."

Mother rolled her eyes.

"One day it was too hot to be indoors, so we ate lunch on the fire escape. I sat on a step above her, reading the paper and balancing my plate on my knees, trying to keep my tuna sandwich from falling off. Granny liked the *New York Journal* because they ran crime stories. There was a front-page story about a man arrested for having surgical instruments and dead babies on his farm. When I read the article, I didn't understand, so I asked her what abortion was. She slapped me across the face. My plate flew three flights down and shattered on the ground, and I nearly followed it. She said, 'If you ever utter that dirty word again, your mother will put you out like a piece of trash. It'd kill her. Never, never, never say it again. Do you hear me? And if you say anything about this when your parents return, you will be sorry you were ever born.' So I didn't. I didn't tell you what had happened, and I didn't think about it again for many years. From the way you reacted to Lucie's abortion, I realized Granny was right."

"That terrible, terrible woman!" my mother said, her voice hoarse and steely. "I am so sorry. I never should have left you with her. I thought she loved you and that she would never harm you the way she harmed me."

"You and I have more in common," I said, reaching for her hand. I told her about Paris. About the German soldiers and the alley—my face pushed against the bricks—my black robes shoved up. Emotionally leaving my body as they took what they wanted. My relief that they let me go and didn't harm the five-year-old child in my care.

I glanced at Sophie, and she smiled at me and nodded her encouragement.

"And I got pregnant. Only Levy was aware of what happened. He saved me by doing an abortion. I didn't tell anyone, even Mathilde. I was overcome with humiliation, as if I had done something wrong. That experience changed me. I was hurt, and also, like a piece of metal, forged."

My mother took both my hands in hers. "Oh, darling. I can't bear it that you experienced that horror and never told me." She was crying.

"I was so ashamed, even though I knew it wasn't my fault. It was as though I took on the shame they didn't bother with." I was crying, too. "This secret cemented my dedication to women—not a dedication to abortion—a dedication to women's wholeness, to their unguarded spirits, to the courage they had to love something they couldn't keep. Mother, if you knew the stories—if you were able to imagine what it means to midwife a woman through the process of finding her own choice, her own soul — you would see that doing this work has blessed me beyond measure."

I searched my mother's face for a sign that she accepted what I was telling her. Her face softened.

"Mom, this is the work I was born to do. To provide abortions. But so much more than that. To guide women into the underworld of their beliefs and hopes and fears. To work with them to find their strength and power. To challenge them to choose their most essential selves. The humiliation we are talking about is what we have been trying to heal here—that shame and self-blame that are heaped on women from both the outside and the inside." I reached out and took my mother's hand. I held it until she sighed and her breathing slowed down.

"I should have known you were doing something like this. You have always been a crusader, wanting to help people."

"Not people. I am helping *women*. It seems to me they start so far behind in this world," I said. "And I'm telling their stories. It was you, with your magical bedtime tales, who taught me how to be a storyteller."

"I wonder how my life would have been—what *I* would have been like—if I had known someone like you back in those dark times." My mother wrapped her arms around herself. "This has been quite an afternoon," she said, moving back from the fire.

"Sylvia, would you like something to eat?" Sophie asked.

"Thank you, dear one, no. I'm not hungry. But I am going to have a long, hot bath, then take a nap. My mind is reeling—I wonder if you have anything stronger than wine? I don't think I can sleep without a little help."

"Absolutely." Sophie went to the kitchen and brought back a bottle of Scotch that had hardly been touched.

"I'm going to have some too," I said.

"Get three glasses, will you?" Sophie said, smiling. It was unusual for either of us to drink hard liquor, but there are times when nothing else will do. I got glasses from the sideboard and Sophie gave each a generous pour.

"Mom, I hate to ask, but is it all right if we tell Françoise your story?"

"Of course, dear. And Levy, too, if you want. I can only imagine you have all been trembling with the weight of your secret."

Mother kissed us each on the cheek and started to carry her glass of liquid amber down the hallway.

She stopped and turned. "I always thought I would die with that secret. Thank you, girls." She continued down the hall.

As the door to Mom's bedroom clicked closed, the side door burst open. Françoise bustled into the room. She was wearing a heavy coat with her woolen hat pulled down over her ears—her face red with cold. She pulled off her mittens and threw them on the floor, holding her hands over the fire.

"*Merde*, it is cold out there," she said.

"Françoise! Where have you been? Where is Charlotte?"

"That's the question, isn't it? Where *is* Charlotte? I took her to a counseling room because I knew something big was going down here…"

"Thank you so much for that," I said.

She waved her hand to show it was nothing. "I started by getting to know her situation and trying to help her feel safe. But she wouldn't answer any questions and looked like a scared rabbit the whole time. Finally, she asked me to explain how an abortion is done. I wouldn't normally start out that way, but at least it was some kind of communication. I did my best to explain it in ways that weren't too frightening. Then she asked for a drink of water, so I went to the kitchen to bring back a glass and a small pitcher, and when I got back to the room, she was gone."

"What do you mean, gone?" I asked.

Françoise gave me one of those Françoise looks, as if I were a moron. "I mean, she wasn't there, Jane. I looked in the other counseling rooms and in the bathroom, and she wasn't there either. I wasn't sure what to do, so I decided to go after her. I put on my coat and ran as fast as I could to the bus stop." Françoise glanced at her watch. "She got to the stop before I could catch up, and I think she caught the bus. Gracie was sitting at the bus stop wagging her tail. If only that dog could talk. Gracie and I got back here as fast as we could. I was so worried about you."

Here she glanced around. "Where is your mother?" she asked, almost in a whisper.

Sophie answered, "You don't need to whisper. She's taking a nap."

"What happened between you two?" she asked, still whispering.

I answered, "If Sophie will make you a cup of cocoa, we'll fortify it with a bit of single malt, and we'll tell you everything." Françoise warmed up and shed her layers of coats and scarves. She listened as we revealed two lifetimes of secrets. As I shared the stories, for the first time, I felt like my mother's daughter.

Suddenly, the heavy knocker on our front door clanged like a metronome.

"Sophie, look out the window and tell me who it is."

Sophie ran to the side window. "It's Brigitte! Oh no, Jane. Is she here to arrest you? All of us?"

"I don't know. But she can't arrest us if we don't open the door."

"But we can't just let her keep banging. She's going to wake your mother."

"We're just going to have to hold on and depend on my mother's sleeping deeply enough not to hear," I said.

The banging continued for what seemed like forever. Finally, it stopped. Sophie peeked out the side window again. "She's gone." We started breathing again. My mother didn't come out of her room, so I thought we were safe.

"This life is too exciting for me, Jane," Françoise laughed as she put her coat, scarf, and mittens back on. "I'm going back to the dairy to ask Claude to tell me some frightening stories about the war to calm me down."

"Very funny," I said, pushing her out the door.

Sophie and I sat at the kitchen table. I leaned against her and closed my eyes. What I had feared most, what I had done everything to prevent, had happened. And telling my mother about my work had transformed from disaster into healing.

CHAPTER 52

MOTHER MEETS A SQUIRREL

Charlotte didn't call the next day or the day after, so we chalked her up to being one of those women who can't decide what they want. Relieved of her secret, my mother was like another person—playful and silly. Perhaps I was, too. Claude, Françoise, Anne-Marie, Thomas, and little Henri came for dinner and a rousing game of charades. My mother played very well, despite her limited French. Henri insisted on playing, so Sophie whispered various animals for him to portray. He did an admirable job of acting out a cat, a cow, and a dog, all to thunderous applause.

I hardly gave another thought to Charlotte until Sophie answered the phone the next morning. She put her hand over the receiver. "It's Charlotte. She apologized for running away and says she wants to come again. She insists on talking with Françoise."

"It's all right with me. Françoise already planned to be here this afternoon, so tell Charlotte to get the bus that arrives at one. She obviously knows how to get here, but we'll send Gracie."

"You're sure?"

I nodded my head. "Maybe we'll learn what's going on with her."

Sophie gave the instructions, and we resumed eating our breakfast. My mother couldn't help but speculate about the young woman who had been the tremor that precipitated the avalanche in our lives.

"She was so afraid of going to hell. It was like sitting with my mother. I tried to comfort her, but she is carrying a weight that she wouldn't reveal."

Françoise arrived just after noon and we brought her up to date.

"She wants to talk with me? I can't imagine why. I failed utterly to learn anything about her."

I laughed. "Françoise, you can't see it as a failure. People are enigmas."

Charlotte got to the convent at about 1:30, flanked by Gracie, who deposited her precious cargo, trotted into the kitchen, and noisily drank from her water bowl. Françoise welcomed Charlotte, and they went into the counseling room they had used before. Françoise came out and poked her head into the kitchen. "Sylvia, she wants to know if you will come in."

"Oh, no. I couldn't. This is so private," my mother said.

"She is asking for you."

"I... okay. If that's what she wants."

After half an hour, Françoise left my mother and Charlotte and came into the kitchen, looking thoroughly defeated.

"She is still so closed down," Françoise said. "I can't get anything out of her, except that she *has* to do this. She needs you, Jane. Will you talk with her?"

"Of course, *Chérie*," I answered. "I'll do my best. Come back in with me and let's see what we can do."

We returned to the counseling room, and I perched on a chair. My mother looked worried. She mouthed, "Do you want me to leave?"

I mouthed back, "No. It's all right." What was all right? A bit of hubris. Charlotte's head was bowed.

Françoise said, "Charlotte, I'm hoping Jane can help us out. Is that all right with you?"

Charlotte nodded her head dully.

I had just read one of Lucie's letters about Rogerian therapy, so I began with a statement in an attempt to mirror Charlotte's feelings.

"It seems that it is very hard for you to be here."

Charlotte gave a great sigh but said nothing.

I took a different tack. "You came to us twice and then left. Can you tell me about that?"

Charlotte shrugged her shoulders.

I realized it was time to depart from the usual conversation.

"Charlotte, if you were an animal right now, what kind of animal would you be?"

The question prompted a tiny smile. The young woman thought for a moment and said, "I would be a dead squirrel."

I clapped my hands together. "Well, that explains a lot," I said, looking at Charlotte as if she had just discovered the secret of the Rosetta Stone. "A dead squirrel can't make any important decisions—or any decisions at all. How brilliant."

Charlotte looked perplexed.

"What is making you feel like a dead squirrel?" I asked next.

She considered the question, and for the first time, began to talk.

"My parents mean everything to me, but they don't know I am here. They never liked my boyfriend—and in that they were so right. He turned out to be a cheater. I am embarrassed that I was ever with him. But now I am afraid they will hate me and be so disappointed. My grandmother lives with us, and my mother takes care of her. I don't see how I can have a baby, but I don't see how I can have an abortion and keep such a secret from them."

"So keeping that kind of secret from your parents would be very painful for you?" I asked.

"It would be unbearable," Charlotte said, crying softly.

"Then it sounds as though you've got some work to do," I said. "What would it take from you to tell them?"

"What do you mean?" Charlotte asked, sniffling.

"Well, what characteristics would you need to muster? Like courage or honesty…"

"Both of those, for sure. Courage. Honesty. Love, I guess. Trust that they would understand. Humility to accept that I am only human and I don't need to keep pretending I am perfect." Charlotte pulled a tissue out of the box and blew her nose.

I was taking notes as Charlotte was talking. I started reading back, "So, courage, honesty, love, trust, humility—what else?" I asked.

Charlotte closed her eyes for a moment. "Strength. The strength to do the right thing for myself, even if they don't agree."

I added strength to the list. "Anything else?" I asked.

Charlotte laughed. "Isn't that enough?"

I handed her the list. "We are going to send you back home to take care of this essential business. We will be glad to see you on another day if you find that this is what you truly want. Is there anything else we need to talk about?" I asked.

"Françoise did a great job of explaining things," she said, turning to her. "I'm sorry that I couldn't answer any of your questions."

Françoise smiled. "It's all right. That was before we realized there was a dead squirrel in the room!"

We all laughed, and I called Claude to see if he would drive Charlotte back to the bus station. I didn't know whether we would hear from her again.

After they left, we sat at the kitchen table.

"How did you think of asking her that question?" my mother asked.

"It was something Lucie wrote to us—to turn ourselves into receivers and tune into the frequency that the patient needs in order to express herself. That's not always easy to do. There are some patients who drive Sophie crazy. The very pitiful ones are hard for me. Frankly, they scare me."

Sophie said, "I don't like working with the ones who are angry, so Jane or Françoise works with them."

I continued. "I'm not sure how the animal question came to my mind, but she had an interesting answer, didn't she?"

Mother reached out and took my hand. "I was touched by how important her parents are to her. I hope they will be understanding."

"I hope so too."

My mother continued, "She would hardly look at me when Françoise left the room. I wanted to tell her that it would be all right, but that didn't seem honest. Do you think she will come back?"

"I think so, but it is never wise to predict," I answered. "Human beings are complicated creatures." I shrugged my shoulders. "It's time for a glass of wine."

Back in the kitchen, I poured each of us a glass of my mother's favorite, Châteauneuf-du-Pape Blanc. The scent of the *garrigue*—the rosemary, lavender, and juniper that grow abundantly on the hills surrounding the vineyard—will forever remind me of her. Mother sliced apples as I cut pieces of the baguette Françoise had brought over. We slathered the bread with Brie, and a more sumptuous lunch was never known.

Lunch was interrupted by a pounding on the door. A familiar voice barked, "Open up!"

"Who is that?" my mother asked. "Who has been banging on your door?"

"No one. Just ignore her and she'll go away. I hope she'll go away."

"Jane, let's not have any more secrets."

"We have a... I don't even know how to explain it. There is a woman in the gendarmerie who has been my enemy since she worked at Aunt Mathilde's school in 1939. Her name is Brigitte. Mathilde fired her from the school because she sided with the Nazis. She just moved to a village near us, and has become the first female on the police force. She is Catholic and detests abortion. She wants to close us down."

"How have you gotten away with this for the past eight years? Why haven't the police gotten word of what you are doing?"

"The local police officials have looked the other way because we have done abortions for many of their wives and daughters. And they don't want any scandals in their jurisdiction. We have had a couple of close calls, but I'm afraid we can't get out of this one. I'm taking all the blame. I can't have Sophie or Françoise implicated. Our attorney, Sophie's Uncle Matthieu, has talked with people in the government who agree that abortion should be legal. He thinks the best way to begin the lawsuit would be for me to be arrested. He says it's just symbolic. We have been providing care for so long that there are people who might come forward to testify—to help with legalization."

"He wants you to be *arrested*?"

"He told me I wouldn't go to jail. That I'd be released immediately if a lawsuit were filed. I'll do it if that's what it takes."

Brigitte pounded on the door again.

"I'm not ready for this. Ignore her and she'll go away."

It was frightening to have Brigitte banging on the door and shouting that I had to come out, but I swallowed the fear and did not budge. After half an hour, she left.

CHAPTER 53

MOTHER MEETS A LIONESS

A few mornings later, Sophie answered the phone while we were drinking coffee. She spoke for a moment, then put her hand over the receiver.

"It's Charlotte. She has told her parents. She wants to come back today, and her father is going to bring her. Can I tell her to come now?"

We all agreed, and in less than an hour, she arrived, and her father introduced himself very formally to each of us.

"Bonjour. I am Maurice Dupont, Charlotte's father. My wife sends her apologies that she could not leave her mother to be here." When he got to my mother, she said, "Bonjour, I am Sylvia Smith, Jane's mother."

His face broke into a smile. "Ah, Madame Smith. You must be so proud of your daughter. Such a rare combination of skill and compassion."

Mother's eyes welled up. "I am. Indeed, I am."

We suggested that Mr. Dupont wait in the kitchen. My mother indicated she wasn't interested in seeing the medical part of our work, but Charlotte said, "Madame Smith, will you just accompany me to the room? You don't have to stay, but it would be like having my own mother there."

My mother was not one to say no to such a request. So Charlotte kissed her father on both cheeks, "Papa, thank you for being here," and we proceeded down the long stone hallway.

"Charlotte, I know you are scared," Mother said. "That's only natural."

Charlotte reached out for my mother's hand. When we got to the procedure room, Charlotte sat on the examining table and listened to the instructions.

I said, "Before you undress, I have to ask you. What kind of animal are you today?"

Charlotte raised her face and smiled at me. "Today I am a lioness."

My mother squeezed Charlotte's hand and asked, "Do you need me to stay?" I was touched by what it took for her to make the offer.

"*Merci*, Madame," Charlotte answered, shaking her head. "I am in safe hands."

Mother kissed her on the forehead and said, "I'll be in the kitchen with your papa."

Within an hour, Charlotte was well enough to leave. As she was saying her goodbyes, she stopped and said, "Oh, I forgot." With her father already in the car, she ran out and breathlessly came back, panting. "This is for you," she said, with her hand out. She was holding a tiny porcelain animal. "It may not mean anything to you, but my father sent this to me when he was in the war and I kept it near my bed. I want you to have it to remember me."

I turned the tiny white lioness over in my hands. It was lovely.

"Thank you. I promise I will never forget you, my lioness."

That gift is on my bedside table.

As we waved them off, my mother said, "Jane, this is magic you do here."

We were in the kitchen preparing lunch when the pounding began again. Françoise, Sophie, Mother, and I looked at each other.

"She's not going to leave us alone. She probably got a warrant yesterday," Françoise said.

"Sophie, once she has taken me away, call Matthieu and tell him. Remember, I am the only one responsible. Mom, I'm sorry you had to be here for this." My heart was pounding as loudly as Brigitte's pummeling on the door. I was afraid of what would come next, but I had no regrets. Sophie came to my side and together we opened the door.

As I expected, Brigitte stood there in her police uniform. Next to her was a dark-haired woman in her twenties. I put my hands out for the cuffs. To my surprise, Brigitte said, "Fool, I'm not here to arrest you. This is my niece, Lydia. She isn't like those other girls—she is special. And she needs your help."

EPILOGUE

ABBIE WILDER

Albuquerque, New Mexico, 2025

I answered the phone early on Sunday morning — it was only one of a dozen calls that weekend, but this woman grabbed my attention right away. She was crying so hard that I had to ask her to start over twice. Her name was Tami. She told me it was spelled with one m and an i. The perfect name for a twenty-two-year-old living in Frisco, a small town outside of Dallas. She was married, with a six-month-old. Her sister had assured her she couldn't get pregnant if she was breastfeeding. But pregnant she was.

"We just can't do it. My son has colic and my husband and I haven't slept in months. I smell like baby poop, and I look like hell. My husband is a mechanic for the power company, but there is never enough money. I know it is wrong, but we can't do it. I can't do it. Is it illegal? Can you help me?" She dissolved into tears.

"Tami. Tami, take a breath, all right? Breathe in deep and hold for the count of four—good—now breathe out slowly, counting to five. Good. Now do that again. You can breathe like that any time you get overwhelmed. Okay. My name is Abbie. The first thing I need you to tell me is what you want."

"What do you mean?"

"What help are you calling for?"

"I already told you. I'm pregnant and I can't take it. Didn't you listen to me?" Ah, so Tami has a temper.

"I heard you, but you need to tell me what you want."

"A damned abortion, *obviously.*"

I had been told that it was essential the caller ask directly for an abortion. Unbelievably, some people have nothing better to do than to try to entrap us volunteers. Even when the patient is direct, there is no guarantee they are not setting us up. But I felt pretty sure this woman was genuinely desperate.

"Okay. How far are you in the pregnancy?"

"I saw my OB. In between obnoxious congratulations, they told me I am eight weeks. I tried to explain my situation, but he wouldn't even talk to me about abortion. His nurse sneaked me a piece of paper with this number."

I made a note to ask the name of her OB so we would be sure the nurse was in our network. "With that $10,000 bounty on anyone who helps with an abortion, the Texas law has everyone scared. That's what it was meant to do."

"So what do I do now?"

"You are early enough in the pregnancy that we should be able to help you get here for an abortion."

"What do you mean *here*?"

"To New Mexico. Abortion is legal here, but you can't get one in Texas."

"But you can just send me the pills, right?"

"I'm sorry. It is too dangerous for us to help you with an abortion in Texas. You will need to travel to one of the clinics here in New Mexico."

"That's impossible. How am I going to get there? Who will take care of the baby? I... I have never been out of Texas."

"I looked this up. The drive from Frisco to Albuquerque is only nine-and-a-half hours."

"We don't have a car. My husband can't take his work truck that far." She started crying again.

"Tami, you need to breathe again." I counted for her. I had a variety of resources to call on—money for the procedure and hotels. But childcare was a constant challenge. People don't realize that most women who have abortions are already mothers.

"Let me see if there is a volunteer near you who could drive and one who could take care of the baby."

"Strangers?"

"Strangers who are willing to take big risks to help you. Tami, you are in a very hard situation. Texas, along with half the states in this country, has let you down—has let every woman down. I'm going to do my best to help you get an abortion, if that is what you want. But it is going to take some courage from you."

"That damned governor. If I had voted, I was going to vote for him, and he screwed me."

It took everything I had not to react.

I asked for more information from her, said goodbye, and got to work. I was relieved to find a volunteer in nearby Plano who would drive her, and one who would do child care. They were both in the organization called Grannies for Justice, which fought for legal abortion in their twenties and were appalled when it was stolen away. I recognized that Tami needed to go to Jane's convent, even though it added more than two hours to the drive. That meant speaking more with the prickly Tami about what to expect.

"I am sending you to an unusual clinic," I began, hesitantly. "They aren't just going to do an abortion. They are also going to help you sort out your feelings about it so you can have peace after this whole thing is over."

"What are you talking about? I don't want to talk about it. I just want to get it over with and never think about it again."

"I know it sounds impossible, but will you give it a chance? The woman who is driving you has taken others to this clinic, and she can tell you about it. But you must be willing to talk with them about your feelings. Will you?"

Tami made a sort of growling noise. "My mother always told me that 'beggars can't be choosers,' so I guess I am the beggar here. I'll deal with whatever I need to." I wished her well.

I worked six other cases in the next week and a half, always with Tami at the back of my mind. With the hotels, meals, and gas, her abortion cost our fund more than $500. What should have been paid by health insurance, whether private or public, was made up from donations. Sometimes we ran out of funds before the month was over. That was nothing compared to the cost for a woman who was later in her pregnancy.

I didn't hear back from many patients, but Tami called me one afternoon a few weeks after her abortion.

"Abbie, I want to thank you. I will never forget what you did for me. It was hard, but it was worth it. All those feelings I never knew I was having. If there is a girl who needs help, I want to help. I don't have any money, but if someone is scared, I can tell her how kind everyone was. I am not the same woman you sent to that clinic. Not a beggar anymore. My new life starts now. And they gave me an IUD. Nothing is 100%, but it is very reliable, and it lasts for ten years! I won't be afraid of getting pregnant again unless I want to."

"I am so glad. I thought it would be the right place for you. I will put you down on our volunteer list to talk with women. But I want you to understand that was a very special place. Most of the clinics don't ask you about how you are feeling."

"Why not? That's what made the difference. It was as important as getting the abortion."

"Most clinics don't have the staff, or the time, or the knowledge. And, frankly, they don't understand how important it is."

"So if I talk to someone who I think needs that kind of help, can they go to the convent?"

"You can tell me. I'll give you my direct number. It's… it's just not as important to most of the volunteers as it is to me, and they don't want women to have to spend two extra hours on the road. It's much easier just to send people to Albuquerque."

"Abbie, I still can't believe they have taken away women's choices."

"I can't, either. Jane Smith, the woman who started that clinic, was a dear friend of mine. She died in 2016 shortly before the election, so thank goodness she didn't see Trump become president. To learn he won over two such eminently qualified women as Hillary Clinton and then Kamala Harris, surely would have killed her!"

Tami said, "I saw a picture of Jane at the convent. She was so tall. You really knew her?"

"She was one of my grandmother's dearest friends. She was the bravest person I have ever met. I am writing a trilogy of books about her life. She first worked in abortion in Paris before the Nazi occupation. She gave her life to learning how to help women resolve their feelings about their pregnancies."

"I want to read those books!"

Jane died October 23, 2016. She left this earth still eagerly anticipating the election of the first woman president. I miss her every day. I miss the way she always saw the bigger picture—a game of chess, not the whack-a-mole we are playing. I'm barely keeping up with the calls I'm getting, let alone devising a strategy to guarantee reproductive freedom to everyone. Not to mention Reproductive Justice, which addresses the range of circumstances that need to be in place in order even to want to continue a pregnancy—like safe housing, good educational opportunities, childcare, gender equality in salaries, affordable, accessible healthcare—things that some people take for granted.

Jane was right about the threats to freedom. Today we are facing a political regime dedicated to dismantling democracy, privacy, and individual choice, and to vilifying people whose race, heritage, or sexuality leaves them outside the sphere of the white, heterosexual, patriarchal elite in power. All kinds of people are being deported by force, regardless of their citizenship status. Strides our country has made in women's rights, civil rights, gay rights, and ecology are treated as unpatriotic. None of this was forced upon us. Americans elected Trump a second time, knowing who he was and what he wanted to do to our democracy and our society. Many Americans decided that educated liberals were against them and Trump was their savior. They put their trust in him and his billionaire minions. The Trump-Pets revel in their cruelty. They do not care who is harmed in their little-boy process of building the biggest sand-castles, and blowing up government programs and agencies that have served people for generations. Trump himself is entirely without values, except winning, lining his own pocket, and exacting revenge on anyone who opposes him. Even the Republicans, who recognize how dangerous he is, kowtow to him. One day, there will be a reckoning, like the Nuremberg Trials, for those who knew how many people they were harming, nationally and internationally.

This administration will re-activate the 1873 Comstock Act, which considers anything pertaining to birth control or abortion pornographic and prohibits sending such materials, medications, or devices through the mail. We'll once again see homes for unwed mothers and orphanages where children grow up without families. The president's erratic and incompetent approach to the economy will lead us into a worldwide depression. His cabinet choices leave us vulnerable to pandemics and diseases we thought were eradicated generations ago. Attacks on the press threaten the most basic tenets of a free society. People could lose every right they take for granted. A glimpse of women in the Middle East shows you that women who once dressed as they chose are now encased from head to toe in burqas—women who had attained the status of citizens are once again property. I recently re-read George Orwell's dystopian novel, 1984. I was chilled to the bone.

"War is peace
Slavery is freedom
Ignorance is strength"

Despite many challenges, Jane never gave up. She stood tall—providing abortion care without permission, without authority, and without apology, outside the laws of men. We must each decide what we will risk for justice.

*I hope you'll continue the journey with Jane, Sophie, Françoise, and Lucie, and Lucie's childhood friends, Socorro and Paulette. In **Without Apology**, the last book of the trilogy, they visit a land of magic. A bit of magic is a welcome antidote to despair.*

Abbie Wilder

AUTHOR'S NOTE

Like Jane and Abbie, I began writing this book in 2016, filled with hope and anticipation for the inauguration of the first woman president, Hillary Clinton. For years, Republican state legislators had been passing extreme laws designed to make it nearly impossible for clinics to provide abortions. I wanted to write a story that imagined abortion care as it *should* be—free from politically motivated restrictions, and grounded in respect for the emotional and spiritual wholeness of the patient.

By the time I was ready to publish, the Supreme Court had overturned Roe v. Wade. There has never been a more urgent time to tell our stories about abortion.

Without Authority is a work of fiction inspired by real events. While much is drawn from life, some parts are purely imagined. A few historical notes:

* Dr. Nick's early invention of a suction device in the novel predates the real-life Del-Em, a DIY menstrual extraction tool created in the 1970s by Lorraine Rothman, using a glass jar, tubing, and a stopper.
* The vacuum aspiration machine that became standard for abortion care worldwide was developed by Dr. Harvey Karman and Dr. P. G. Sathe in the 1970s.
* A lecture by Carl Djerassi in Dallas in the 1980s gave me the idea that the U.S. Navy may have had a responsibility to provide abortions in post-war Japan. I haven't found evidence that it actually occurred, but it inspired a fictional element in the book.
* The idea of helping a woman connect her head and heart in making a pregnancy decision began, as far as I know, in the 1980s at the Dallas clinic I ran. That work continues today through my website: http://beforeandafterabortion.com.

A word about language: In today's world, people identify in many ways—male, female, non-binary, trans, gender-neutral, or otherwise. People who don't identify as women may still need abortions. Jane's world is binary, so I use the word "woman" in this book. But if you stay with the trilogy, you'll see Jane assist a trans man with an abortion in Book Three.

At the time of this writing, abortion is practically inaccessible in half the states in the U.S. If you or someone you love needs an abortion, http://ineedana.com is a trusted resource. If you want to donate, volunteer, or stay informed, search "abortion advocacy and activism" online to find groups doing this work. Most of them need your time and support.

Please vote—especially in states where abortion rights are on the ballot. And don't be afraid to start the conversation. You might say, "I don't know where you stand on abortion, but I believe that parenthood should be a personal decision, not a government mandate." You'll find that most people agree. If we don't speak up and fight for our rights, we can't be surprised when those more determined than us take them away.

For decades, I've worked with women who struggled to decide whether to have an abortion—or who carried unresolved feelings afterward. I wrote these books for you, too. If you're one of those people, I invite you to visit my website: http://beforeandafterabortion.com.

I wrote this trilogy to share stories shaped by my work and to leave a legacy that affirms the emotional and spiritual dimensions of reproductive decision-making. If *Without Authority* resonated with you, please leave a review on Amazon, share it with your friends, or post about it on social media. Most independently published books reach about 200 people—the friends and family of the author. Since Roe, over 70 million abortions have been provided in the U.S. I know there are many people who would find connection, comfort, and meaning in Jane's story. Please help me reach them.

DISCUSSION QUESTIONS

For Book Clubs, Women's Groups, or Personal Journaling

Charlotte would be delighted to Zoom into your book club conversation if she is available. E-mail her at hello@charlottetaft.com.

1) There is a saying, *"If it's to be, it's up to me."* Girls and women are often conditioned to obey authority. What is your experience with being a follower versus taking charge? When have you challenged authority in your own life?

2) How are the times Jane lives in—1950s—similar to our current era in terms of women's rights, reproductive justice, and LGBTQ+ issues? How are they different?

3) Sophie refuses to keep a secret of her love, and requires Jane be honest with her friends and family if she wants to be in a relationship. Why is that so hard for Jane? What happens when Jane meets the woman who sells her the trousers? Have you ever kept a secret, like Jane, because you feared you would be rejected or condemned by someone important to you? What prices did you pay?

4) Lucie is a character who is connected to Jane—sometimes literally, sometimes metaphorically. What do you think Lucie represents to Jane? How did you feel about Lucie's presence throughout the story?

5) When Jane, Sophie, and Levy visit Lucie and her new baby, they find her in the depths of post-partum depression, a condition not formally named until 1994. Have you experienced or known someone who has experienced this? Do you see this as connected with self-doubt and hopelessness?

6) Which scenes or characters from *Without Authority* have stayed with you the most? Why? Were there any moments that surprised or moved you?

7) In the 1950s, Jane believes her homosexuality is wrong. How have social attitudes changed since then? Are there ways in which we still struggle with acceptance of LGBTQ+ identities? Could we go backward?

8) In the convent, Jane and the others sometimes wear a habit so Catholic patients will feel comforted—as if they are being forgiven by a nun. As time goes by, they realize comfort is not the only thing women need to feel whole. They discuss different versions of "Our Lady" depending on how the patient presents herself, including Our Lady of Courage, and Our Lady of Peace.

   In Chapter 33. *Consecrated Ground*, Jane says, "We can't *leave* them feeling pitiful…We must find a way of helping women stand on their own feet and experience their power just as much as we are helping them believe they are forgiven… I am asking that we give these women what they truly need—not just what makes us comfortable. If they can't, then we must not perform an abortion… how will she live with herself if she has not come to peace with that decision?"

How do you respond to Jane's conviction that peace and wholeness are as important as the abortion itself?

9) What does the overturning of Roe v. Wade mean to you personally? What do you think it means historically—for women, families, and society?

10) Why does Abbie send Tami to Jane's clinic instead of the closer clinic in Albuquerque? Have you or someone you know carried unresolved feelings about an abortion? Please see http://beforeandafterabortion.com.

11) These books are intended to be inspirational. What have you done or said since you read these books that took courage?

12) Now that you've read *Without Authority,* are you interested in reading the final book in the trilogy, *Without Apology*? What are you hoping to discover in the last book of the trilogy?

ACKNOWLEDGMENTS

On May 1, 2024—just a month before the paperback launch of *Without Permission*, the first book in the Jane Smith Trilogy—I was diagnosed with invasive breast cancer. The year I had envisioned for readings, podcasts, book clubs, and other kinds of promotion became a year of chemotherapy, multiple surgeries, and radiation.

I am unspeakably fortunate. I had unwavering support from my partner, Shelley, and an outpouring of love from friends and family. Unlike so many others, I had excellent, affordable medical care (thank you, Medicare and Dr. Schulze and Dr. LoRusso at Nexus Health), and the time, means, and good fortune to make it to the other side of treatment with most of my body, my energy, and my sense of humor intact.

I want to acknowledge the millions who have joined the breast cancer club no one wants to be part of. Most have done so quietly, without fanfare. Some—dear friends among them—have lost their lives. I had so many misconceptions; there was so much I didn't know.

As of this writing, about 1 in 8 women will develop breast cancer. It's estimated that 1 in 4 women will have an abortion. These are two experiences, lived mostly—but not exclusively—by women. Two secrets. And as is so often the case, our secrets are killing us. **No more secrets.**

My deepest gratitude goes to my partner, Shelley Oram, a writer to envy, who read and re-read the manuscript with care, offering sharp edits and wise counsel I usually took. For years, she has been my fiercest champion.

Milles baisers to my faithful writing group—Annie Lewis and Phyllis Leavitt—for their constant and unwavering support. And to the many champions and cheerleaders of these books—you know who you are—your support means everything.

My parents are both gone now, but I thank them for listening to my earliest stories and for instilling in me a belief in justice.

My love to the staff of the Routh Street Women's Clinic in Dallas, where I gave my best, made many mistakes, learned even more, and invested my heart.

Thanks to the members of November Gang, who helped sharpen my skills and inspired countless ideas to improve abortion care.

Endless appreciation to my extraordinary beta readers—Annie Baker, Emily Cruse, Phyllis Leavitt, Shelley Oram, Arlena Ryan, Karen Thurston, and Alfreda Wright—who lovingly supported this book. They helped me cut 100,000 commas, researched and corrected countless details, and insisted the book must be published immediately. I hope the final version honors their enthusiasm and generosity.

To my long-time writing teacher, Anya Achtenberg: you were the one who gently broke it to me that my original manuscript was too long to publish—and voilà, a trilogy was born. Your insight and encouragement have been central to my writing journey. And to my fellow classmates over the years—across time zones and geographies—thank you for helping shape *Without Permission*, *Without Authority*, and *Without Apology* into books I'm proud of.

Thanks to Melody Ermachild Chavis for permission to use the quote in the epigraph. It expresses the heart of the work I do.

Diane Zinna, developmental editor and author of *The All-Night Sun*, gave me early feedback that propelled me forward: "I don't think you know how good your book is." Every writer deserves to be read as closely and generously as Diane has read my work.

Jennifer Leigh Selig of Empress Publications has been a wise and skillful midwife for these books. I'm deeply grateful for her guidance and experience.

Thanks to 100 Covers for helping me create an image of Jane welcoming a woman to Our Lady of Perpetual Grace.

Edgard Rivera at Stepbridge Studios in Santa Fe helped me bring the audiobook versions to life.

I am also deeply thankful to the many generous souls who've shared encouragement and advice on independent publishing. Your guidance helped make all of this possible.

Finally, I carry in my heart the thousands of women who entrusted me with their most intimate stories over the past half-century. I hope the effort to meet your emotional and spiritual needs made a difference. I carry your stories with me always. Some of them, disguised, are retold in these books. I hope you see yourselves in these pages.

For those who carry unresolved feelings about abortion, I wrote these books for you. In these books, I offer a roadmap—to forgive yourself, to heal, and to reclaim the knowledge of your own goodness. I hope you'll go to http://beforeandafterabortion.com.

ABOUT THE AUTHOR

Charlotte Taft has worked in abortion care for more than half a century. Though most women do well with the experience of abortion, there are some who struggle. Charlotte developed tools to identify and assist the women who need deeper emotional exploration to find peace and confidence with whatever decision they make.

After earning a bachelor's degree from Brown University and a master's degree in feminist studies from Goddard College, Charlotte served as the director of an abortion clinic in Dallas, Texas, for seventeen years. During this time, she worked with her staff to pioneer a unique style of abortion counseling tailored to meet the emotional and spiritual needs of each patient, sometimes called Head and Heart Counseling.

In Dallas, Charlotte served as the media's go-to person on the topic of abortion. Charlotte was interviewed by national publications such as *The New York Times*, as well as appearing on dozens of local and national television programs including *The Today Show*. Her non-fiction publications are available at Rewire.com.

Charlotte is featured on the 2020 FX documentary *AKA Jane Roe.*

With her partner Shelley Oram, Charlotte created *Imagine* to provide experiential workshops and retreats to deepen abortion providers' understandings of themselves and their work. Charlotte served as the director of the national non-profit organization Abortion Care Network for six years, where she was at the helm of supporting independent abortion providers and fostering open conversations around abortion.

Today, Charlotte lives in rural New Mexico with Shelley, her partner of thirty-six years. She continues to work with women who need help looking deeper in order to make a decision and resolve difficult feelings after an abortion. Her website http://beforeandafterabortion.com offers insightful videos designed to further assist women in finding peace before and after an abortion. Visit her author website, http://charlottetaft.com, to learn more about *Without Permission*, *Without Authority,* and *Without Apology*.